Heart of Evergreen

Heart of Evergreen

(Heart of Evergreen Book 3)

By
Mary L. Schmidt

Heart of Evergreen
Mary L. Schmidt
Copyright © 2024

by Mary Schmidt (M. Schmidt Productions)

All rights reserved.

Book and cover painting and design by Mary L. Schmidt

This book is a work of fiction drawing upon the locals and inspiration of the area in which the author lives and works. Names of towns, places, facilities, and people have been changed. Any resemblance to persons living or dead is purely coincidental in nature and places where events take place are fake to the author's knowledge. No portion of this book may be reproduced, stored in a retrieval system, or transmitted in any form or by any means-electronic, mechanical, photocopy, recording, scanning, or other-except for brief quotations in critical reviews or articles, without the prior written permission of the author(s). No part of this book may be adapted into a work in any other medium such as film, video, or audio without permission of the publisher. The author wants to thank all the physicians, nurses, and trusted family and friends who stood by her in authoring this story.

BISAC Subject Headings:
Fiction / Christian / Romance / Suspense
Fiction / Crime
Fiction / Thrillers / Psychological

Library of Congress
ISBN- Paperback 979-8-9903262-2-4
ISBN-13: Ebook 979-8-9903262-3-1

CHRYSLER, DODGE, JEEP®, RAM, MOPAR®, SRT
copyright FCA US LLC (FCA)

Land Rover® Tata Motors (India)

Nothing in this book was written with artificial intelligence. The characters are the from the author's own, real-life memoir, Her Heart, and others Christmas in Evergreen, both written by Mary L. Schmidt, and the rest in the author's imagination. Scenes used are either real-life or make-believe. Certain medical issues are from the author's own real-life experiences; thus, I wrote them as my reality.

First edition published December 12, 2024
Blog (https://www.whenangelsfly.net)
Facebook (https://www.facebook.com/MMSchmidtAuthorGDDonley)
Twitter (https://twitter.com/MaryLSchmidt)
Deviant Art (http://mschmidtartwork.deviantart.com/)

Table of Contents

Prologue ix

PART ONE 1

    Chapter One: Characters and Back Story 3

PART TWO 13

    Chapter Two 15

    Chapter Three 25

    Chapter Four 39

    Chapter Five 51

    Chapter Six 59

    Chapter Seven 63

    Chapter Eight 71

    Chapter Nine 77

    Chapter Ten 81

    Chapter Eleven 85

    Chapter Twelve 93

    Chapter Thirteen 101

    Chapter Fourteen 109

Chapter Fifteen 117

Chapter Sixteen 123

Chapter Seventeen. 129

Chapter Eighteen 135

Epilogue 139

Biography 141

Memoirs 143

Children's Books 145

Dedication

Aways to my faithful readers and followers, I would not be where I am without you,

Always to Shane, and Sammy, who taught us so much about life, bravery, and that a baby and a five-year-old can be wiser beyond their brief time on Earth,

Always to Gene, our son, who we cherish so much, and has been wise beyond his years, and has turned into a kind man,

Always to Michael, my beloved husband, partner, and best friend in the entire world,

Always to Mary, my beloved wife, partner, and best friend in the entire world.

Prologue

Dmitry wasn't sure what to do…his handler stateside was dead…no intelligence… even worse was the fact that the Russian agent who'd infiltrated Scotland Yard had news…Olga Pasternak had been caught placing a chipped frame onto a painting in London at the art gallery…that intelligence was unsettling to put it mildly… he needed that chip! He needed Olga Pasternak doing her part…now he was fully alone…Olga Pasternack was kept locked up somewhere…and she could break…the complications maddened him…he must stay calm…be the Russian you were born to be…the one heavily trained in special tactics and more…the expert…keep that persona inside and remain the nice, rich, oligarch from Russia…that he could do with aplomb…until the oligarch above him stopped sending intelligence to him…and that would mean only one thing…he would then be on that Russians' hit list…best not think about that overly much…

He had become a liability and Dmitry had to protect himself. He would not take his own life like the general who'd infiltrated Washington, DC. Yes, he was heavily trained in special tactics, and yes, his own oligarch money sat nicely in a Swiss bank account under a holding company that was untouchable. Russia could do absolutely nothing about his Swiss bank account. Yet he WAS touchable!!! Even though he, himself had never once killed anyone, he had been complicit by his position between those who ordered hits and those who carried them out. Thus, he packed a bag and drove his luxurious SUV down to Denver, to the Federal Center, and asked at the gate for Director General James Tilson, that he, Dmitry Ivanov, had top-secret

information for him. One of the guards radioed inside and spoke with the director. General Tilson informed the guards that two members of his team would go to the gate and escort Dmitry Ivanov inside. Dmitry had to turn himself in if he wanted to live! His romance with Susan Davis, a gorgeous 25-year-old, green-eyed redhead who painted like an angel...in watercolor...he would never see her again...he'd come to love her...love...true love...now that part of his life was over...he wouldn't see any of the people he'd come to know during his time in Evergreen...Regrets. He had them in spades. He had them in tripe spades.

PART ONE

Chapter One

Characters and Back Story

In "*Her Heart*," a stand-alone book and true memoir, we meet Dr. Aaron and Sarah Leawood, and their children, Danny, and Lisa, Aaron's mother, Alice, and his housekeeper, Sadie.

Sarah has wavy blonde hair with blue eyes and is a registered nurse in the emergency department of a hospital in Lakewood, Colorado, and Dr. Aaron Leawood is a tall, dark-haired, and dark-eyed emergency room physician in the same ER as Sarah.

Sarah had been married to an abusive man, a man who brutally raped her repeatedly shortly after giving birth. He took what he wanted, leaving her bloody body to be filled with years of physical abuse and pain, emotional and mental scars that led her to believe she was worthless, a happy life was hopeless, and she had nowhere to go.

Sarah became pregnant and thought she'd finally have the best in life – a new baby – and she'd make her home filled to the brim with love.

Her life was shattered once again when her oldest son, John, died at birth.

Hope finally came when her next baby, her rainbow baby, a dark-haired and blue-eyed boy named Daniel, was born followed by a surprise baby, a towheaded blue-eyed baby boy named Simon.

Both boys knew they were loved by their mother, and it finally became intolerable one evening when Sarah arrived home after work to find him passed out drunk on the couch and the boys soaking wet and asleep on the carpet by the couch. They had played in a bathtub full of water and broken glass was scattered around on the bathroom tiles.

After turning the water off, Sarah grabbed towels and fresh pajamas for both boys. Working quickly, she dried each one, helped them redress into fresh pajamas, tucked them into their dry beds, and gave each one a kiss.

Sarah knew she had to act and act fast. This time his drinking put her two precious sons at risk. They could have drowned in the bathtub or cut themselves on the broken glass. Now she was afraid for her children.

She had to protect her little boys; despite the death threats she'd received from her husband if she tried to leave him. She packed some boxes and placed them inside her children's closet, before finally falling asleep exhausted in her own bed.

The next day, Sarah found a cheap apartment and later that evening he passed out once again on the sofa. Daniel, aged six, told his mom that his father had passed out and was sleeping on the sofa. At six, he knew what "passed out" meant, and he knew there were packed boxes in his closet.

Danny informed his mom that he would help her carry their things to her car. Once loaded, with both boys secured in their seats, Sarah never looked back as they were on the road to freedom.

They were happy for six months, Sarah, her middle son, Danny, had just started kindergarten, and Simon was in preschool. Sarah filed for divorce, then Simon became sick.

For four of those six months, Simon had a sinus infection every other week, lots of x-rays, scans, antibiotics, yet no true reason he was so sick.

While sick, Simon had received a positive Epstein Barr Virus (mononucleosis) test at age four years. The doctors were amazed. Sarah was not. She knew his little immune system was lowered with all the antibiotics he'd been on, and she also knew that saliva carried this virus. Only Simon had the virus.

Sarah and Danny did not have the virus so the only places possible for Simon to pick it up were tainted silverware in a restaurant, at the preschool (no one sick there), the metal or plastic parts of a grocery shopping cart, or in the doctor's office at appointments.

Sarah never expected what was found four months later. A soft tissue mass was found in Simon, a cancer of the upper throat (nasopharyngeal cancer). The main mass was the size of her fist with extensions through the cerebral fossa (skull) into his brain!

Simon endured a horrific cancer battle which culminated in his death at age five years. His cancer was Rhabdomyosarcoma. Simon's treatment had killed him as upon his death, his autopsy showed zero cancer cells in his little shell of a body.

You can read his story in two books, both by Mary L. Schmidt, "When Angels Fly" for adults, or "Sammy: Hero at Age Five" written from the point of view of a five-year-old boy and for children.

Determined to make it on their own, Sarah moved to Lakewood, Colorado, with her only living son, Daniel, and she slowly felt renewed strength in being far away from her ex. Sarah was determined that no one would ever hurt her or Danny again.

She was done with love, for she'd never known true love and she wanted to raise Danny with all her love focused on her son.

Danny had been diagnosed with attention deficit hyperactivity disorder (ADHD) and Sarah focused on helping him and shaping his bright future.

Note: The Epstein Barr virus can affect many parts of the body, including the nervous system, blood, and lungs. EBV may cause complications such as heart muscle swelling called myocarditis, and increased risk for cancers such as Burkitt's lymphoma, Hodgkin's and non-Hodgkin's lymphoma, and cancer of the upper throat (nasopharyngeal cancer – this was what Simon had).

Dr. Aaron Leawood had a daughter, Lisa, a curly blonde-headed, blue-eyed little girl. His ex left him right after Lisa was born (she didn't want to be a mother), and he was determined to focus on Lisa, and Alice, his grey-haired, blue-eyed mother, who had moved into a small cottage behind his own home in Lakewood.

Alice had lived with Aaron's sister in Colorado Springs until he found out about ongoing abuse in his sister's coffee shop the Thanksgiving before Sarah and Aaron had married.

From that very day, grey-haired yet sprite, Alice had her own small cottage behind Aaron's home, and she sees her grandchildren, Danny, and Lisa, as often as she likes. Keeping busy with her book club, grandchildren, plus a surprising new beau, her life is fulfilled and peaceful.

Sadie, a short grey-haired woman with green eyes is the Leawood family's housekeeper, and she, too, has her own small cottage behind The Leawood's mountain home, close to Alice.

Sadie helps with housekeeping and cooking, but not every day as Aaron and Sarah also love to cook. Sadie has become family to all the Leawood's, and both children called her "Grandma Sadie," which thrilled Sadie as she'd never married or had children of her own.

Slowly, with painful honesty and perseverance, Sarah overcomes her struggles, and Aaron shows her how a woman should be treated, spoken to, and their deep friendship turned into honest and true love... the kind of love...can't live without your love, generous love, and Aaron adopted Danny.

Honest love is never taken for granted. A few months after their marriage, Danny started calling Aaron "dad." Sarah was "mom" to Lisa. A real family of four with two special grandmas living behind them. Was life perfect? No, never. But with the right love and fullness of faith, anything gets better.

In the first book of the Heart of Evergreen trilogy, we read about Kim Daily in the thick of things in "Christmas in Evergreen." She's not alone in this mess of subterfuge and espionage, and what she'd once thought was the perfect marriage, was instead, a sinister death trap.

What would you do if you found out you were the next target on your husband's hit list? Steve intentionally left his laptop open for me to read. He simply can't be an assassin! I would know. Or would I? No! That's impossible! Steve has been the kindest husband for five years and he was a crack ass private investigator; not an assassin. Yet why was my name at the top of his hit list? Why did he even have a hit list? My mind reeling in shock, I had to do something to stay alive! Think, Kim, think! Get your best game on right now as time is running out!

It had been five years of blissful marriage for Kim, a beautiful woman with long wavy blonde hair and green eyes who lived in the world of art, at home and at her gallery in the Beacon Hill area of Boston.

That bliss changed in a single heartbeat, when the day came that Kim inadvertently came across a hit list on her husband›s laptop with her own name at the top! Her husband, Steve, was not a private investigator! He was a ruthless hired gun!! An assassin!!!

Upon realizing that Steve was an assassin, alongside their neighbor, Gary Moore, Kim makes a run for it. The incident leads to a series of events, including involvement with the CIA, FBI, Homeland Security, and a fatal motor vehicle accident.

Fortunately, Kim and her friend, Nancy Moore (Gary's wife), a beautiful short haired, pixie cut brunette with blue eyes, leave Boston behind them as they drove to arrive in the serene city of Lakewood, Colorado.

Kim's best friend, Sarah Leawood and her husband, Aaron, take both women into their home to recover and start a new life, free from the danger and turmoil of Boston. Kim and Nancy finally felt safe and secure.

Both women relocate up the canyon to the town of Evergreen, Colorado. There, they heal from old wounds, find new homes, make new friends, and Kim finds true love with a new man, Dr. Paul Smith, a tall, dark-haired, and dark-eyed man.

They had met at the Leawood's home one evening, and Kim decided to see him for a consultation on her spinal pain as spinal issues was his specialty. Paul helped Kim with her spinal pain issues by way of a spinal stimulation device, with two wires that blocked most nerve pain impulses from reaching her brain. Kim was ecstatic when her device gave her 70% less pain on average every day.

Kim purchases an art gallery, renamed it, The Gallery Loft of Evergreen, and Nancy works for her. Neither Kim nor Nancy realized they were on borrowed time, despite themes spanning love, betrayal, disappointment, healing, undeniable suspense, and new beginnings, the danger was lurking nearby, and no one knew it!

One reader wrote "Christmas in Evergreen" highlights the author's talent for creating a multifaceted story that blends mystery, thriller, suspense, and romantic elements. The authenticity and unpredictability never slow down.

Another wrote *"Christmas in Evergreen"* is a cozy romance tale with a tinge of suspense and intrigue and is an engaging read from beginning to end. Mary L. Schmidt doesn't take much time to put readers into the scheme of things and weaves a plot as unpredictable as it is entertaining. While the book's first half plays out like a thrilling mystery, the second half turns into a heartwarming slice-of-life story full of romance and drama. Each character brings something of their own to the narrative, and I especially enjoyed the friendship between Kim and Nancy, who stick together through thick and thin.

Zoe wrote her take on *"Christmas in Evergreen."* "Wow! Be prepared for the fast pace as you begin reading this novel. It takes off from the launch pad with rocket speed and doesn't stop until the very end. I was impressed with the author's medical knowledge and explanations. It was also obvious that Ms. Schmidt was familiar with elk and their habits in Evergreen and anywhere elk live. Excellent cautions and explanations were included in the dialogue. If only more people heeded them. And to top the storyline off, a nicely woven set of cozy love stories are introduced. Well worth five stars."

"*Romance in Evergreen*" is book two in the Heart of Evergreen trilogy. Just when things are looking up and life is running smoothly, a crisis comes, one after another, repeatedly. In book two, Kim Daily, now Smith, and Nancy Moore, both main protagonists in the trilogy, are shocked when Special Agent Thompson bursts into Kim's art gallery in Evergreen, Colorado.

"What did you just say? The senior officer (Special Agent Thompson) of the two men from Homeland Security, that both Nancy and Kim knew prior, repeated, 'Rob and Liza Caldwell were taken out as a hit' in Boston last night and we think their assassin is the agent handler extraordinaire, who put out the hit job on the President, and on you, Kim, last November. The hit man's name is Jeffrey Sanders, we don't know any alias, ethnicity, or if male or female. Security cameras were disabled before the actual hit. Rob and Liza were asleep when it happened early this morning. Unfortunately, a second hit happened to the couple who bought your house in the Beacon Hill area. A silencer was used, and neighbors heard their dog barking non-stop and became worried. The couple checked on them, found them dead in their bed, and called 911. The police detectives could tell it was a professional hit and called us. Special Agent Hughes and I flew directly here from Washington, DC. A note left at the scene read, 'four down, ten to go' and the ten, if not more, to go are both of you, the President, and people unidentified but close to you. Make no mistake. The hit man will take out anyone with you, when, NOT if, they find you."

Thus, Kim and Nancy, along with Nancy's new boyfriend, Richard Manse, a true tall mountain man with dark hair, beard, and blue eyes dropped his wood carving tool in the back room of the art gallery.

He joined the women going down the canyon in armored SUVs to the Denver Federal Center. Dr. Paul Smith had been out trout fishing and was instructed via cell phone to meet them at the Denver Federal Center, so he could be kept safe, too. Director General James Tilson, of Homeland Security in Denver, wanted everyone safe under the protection of Homeland Security.

Of the ten expected people, nine made it to the Denver Federal Center including all six from the Leawood home, Kim, Nancy, and Richard. Dr. Paul Smith was involved in a rollover accident that landed him in the hospital with a complex broken bone in his leg, in Lakewood, just west of the Denver Federal Center, with two armed guards keeping him safe.

One reader wrote, "Schmidt has woven a tale intertwined with romance, a wedding, a newborn baby, and a crazy assassin who attempts to kill the husband of the protagonist, Kim, the owner of an art gallery. Playing cat and mouse never ran so intensely. The assassin was caught but died while in custody, and a mysterious person appeared in Evergreen disguised as a Russian oligarch, Dmitry Ivanov. General Tilson and the Special Agents suspected that the assassin(s) were looking for a special computer chip when Kim's art gallery was broken into. Danger, worry, and suspense trail close to all those close to Kim, yet life goes on."

Another reader wrote "As far as sequels go, 'Romance in Evergreen' is a brilliant follow-up to 'Christmas in Evergreen.' Suspense, mystery, and romance color the pages of Mary L. Schmidt's captivating tale, which is devoid of any dull moments. Using a fast-paced plot full of surprises, Schmidt crafts a narrative that never lets your attention waver and is entertaining from beginning to end. One of the primary highlights of the book is the relationship dynamics between the characters. Both the couples, Kim, and Paul, as well as Nancy and Richard, display genuine feelings and emotions that make them feel like real people. I also enjoyed the characterization of Director General James Tilson. Overall, I thoroughly enjoyed this book and can't wait to finish the trilogy."

An editorial review includes, "in 'Romance in Evergreen,' a Russian spy is working undercover in close quarters trying to get his firsthand intelligence that is unknowingly in Kim's possession. Mary L Schmidt straightforwardly narrates the story, with vivid descriptions of settings, character thoughts, and emotions, and as a reader new to the series, I was soon engrossed in the plot. Even while the suspense part of the story progresses, the dynamic of the relationship between the main characters Nancy and Richard also develops. The focus is not just on one relationship but also on the relationships between Sarah and Aaron, Kim and Paul, and the blossoming relationship between James and Alice. The author ensures that this story has a resolution while leaving readers with a clear idea of who the next story in the series will focus on."

Alma Boucher for Readers' Favorite wrote, "Dmitry Ivanov, a tall man with dark hair, beard, and moustache, disguised as a rich Russian oligarch wearing business attire and sporting a gold watch with an emerald face and gold numerals under the crystal, surrounded by round white diamonds, gave Kim his business card, introduced himself, and said he was an art collector. After reviewing all the information about the assassination, Homeland Security Director General Tilson felt that he was still lacking a crucial piece of the puzzle. *"Romance in Evergreen"* by Mary L. Schmidt was a page-turner. It was fast-paced and packed with action, and I was hooked from the start. With all the twists and turns, I never knew what would happen next and was guessing until the end. It was an easy read, and the chapters flowed into each other. The suspense kept me on the edge of my seat, and it was difficult to put the book down. The characters were authentic and relatable, and my favorite was Kim. She felt responsible for all the deaths around her and would go out of her way to keep everyone close to her safe. The story was beautifully written, and I enjoyed reading it. It was much more than I expected and exceeded my expectations by far."

A second reviewer from Readers' Favorite wrote, "Romance in Evergreen" by Mary L. Schmidt is an engaging novel that weaves together elements of family drama and thriller into an intricate tapestry of secrets and suspense. Set against the quaint backdrop of Evergreen, the story unfolds during the Leawood family's Thanksgiving celebrations, which are abruptly disrupted by the threat of an unknown assassin. As the family contends with unexpected guests and buried secrets, they find themselves ensnared in a web of espionage that challenges their loyalties and threatens to alter their futures irreversibly. Schmidt skillfully manages multiple storylines, propelling the narrative with quick twists that maintain the reader's interest. The incorporation of espionage elements lends a thrilling edge to familial conflicts, creating a compelling blend of personal stakes and broader intrigue. The novel's pacing is effectively managed, with tension building steadily towards a climactic resolution. The story, grounded in rich premise, offers an ambitious narrative style. At times, the prose is intricately crafted with complex sentences and a brisk introduction of new characters, designed to challenge and engage readers more deeply. While this approach might distance some from the emotional core of the story, it adds layers of complexity. Additionally, the transitions between scenes, though occasionally abrupt, contribute to a dynamic and evolving plotline that keeps readers on their toes. The novel shines in its depiction of intimate family dynamics and tense espionage activities. The quieter moments of reflection interspersed throughout provide a welcome respite from the high stakes and help to pace the narrative thoughtfully. "Romance in Evergreen" offers a unique blend of suspense and drama that highlights Schmidt's versatility as a writer. This book will engage readers who enjoy stories where personal and secretive worlds collide."

Chapter Two

"*Dmitry was a liability!!! He WAS touchable!!! Dmitry turned himself in at the Denver Federal Center gate with top-secret information for Director General James Tilson.*"

Thus, Dmitry Ivanov packed a bag and drove his sleek SUV down the canyon to the Denver Federal Center, and asked at the gate for Director General James Tilson, that he, Dmitry Ivanov, had top-secret information for him. *It was the last Thursday in May, a lovely day in the mountains, and he wondered if he would ever see the mountains again…or daylight, for that matter…or Susan Davis…he'd come to love her…at age 30, his budding romance with Suz, a gorgeous 25-year-old, green-eyed redhead who was a perfect angel…his angel…she painted like an angel…in watercolor…he would never see her again…he'd come to love her…love…True Love…now that part of his life was over…again…he wouldn't see any of the people he'd come to know and truly care about during his time spent in Evergreen…so many regrets…he'd come to care deeply for the children as well…he was racked with grief for what was not to be…and for his numerous regrets…*

One of the guards radioed inside and spoke with the general, then two special agents came out and walked Dmitry Ivanov, minus the bag he'd packed, into the Denver Federal Center.

He was checked for weapons and anything that he could use as a weapon, after which, both agents escorted him inside a stark room with two chairs and one table for discussion and probable interrogation by General Tilson.

Agent Hughes directed Dmitry to a seat at the table, the general walked in behind them, and he sat in the opposite chair. Dmitry wasn't hand cuffed, but he was guarded by Agent Hughes from inside the door and Agent Thompson guarded from outside the door. The agents saluted the general and he did likewise.

General Tilson had made it clear to his top agents that they were the only ones to know what was going on and who was being interrogated – for now, due to the extreme high sensitivity of possible forthcoming intelligence.

General Tilson looked Dmitry in the eye and stared. He had come to know this man over the last year, but friends they were not, neither were they enemies, mutual acquaintances, yes.

They'd even dined as guests in the same home of mutual friends several times in the last year. He'd always known there was more to Dmitry than he'd let on. This should be interesting, to say the least.

Most spies and secret agents were detained and interrogated in Washington, DC. This move by the general was not normal by any means, but General Tilson had collected intelligence on Dmitry for most of the last year and he knew Dmitry better than anyone in DC.

Therefore, with his electronic recorder turned on 'record mode' (a green light that didn't record), and placed on the table, General Tilson began, "Why are you here, Mr. Ivanov?"

With a huge sigh, Dmitry stated in a calm and collected voice, "I'm the same man you already know. I'm a Russian oligarch, and I love and collect quality art of all kinds. Every single day, I enjoy the finer things life has to offer.

"I've come to know many people and I fought to not like them, but I failed. The Leawood family has taught me how a family should behave and be real, so loving, kind, and honest. The same for the Smith and Manse families. Even you, General Tilson.

"Yet, just as a coin has two sides, so do I. I'm willing and able to impart upon you and your team top-secret intelligence and plans in exchange for sanctuary in this facility.

"I've become a liability to my native Russia, and I want to live, not die, at the hands of one of my compatriots. I prefer the United States."

Dmitry suddenly stopped speaking as he measured the look on the general's face.

"How can you prove to me that you have actual intelligence worth knowing? How can you prove to me that your life is in danger?" The general pointedly asked.

General Tilson wanted proof that Dmitry knew intelligence, he wanted to know why Dmitry thought he was a target to take out, and he wanted the name(s), if possible, of the one who had marked him as a potential threat to Russia, a potential "hit" for another Russian to take him out, the names of known associates, and what and how he'd come to know so much about the United States.

"I have intelligence that will help you find the people you seek regarding the microchips that are planted inside wooden frames while paintings are on display in gallery showings in London." Dmitry watched for a reaction from the general. None was forthcoming. General Tilson was formidable by far, and that gave Dmitry comfort. He knew the general to be a fair and honest man.

He trusted no one in Russia...they were out for themselves and what they could gain...not a care for life...not a care for anything but lining their pockets...the atrocities he'd witnessed in the past were beyond horrific...what the elite in Russia wanted...only the billionaires dared to control this goal...and they could well afford it...Dmitry had billions himself...a true oligarch...yet he also had real human feelings... the biggest regret was not seeing Suz even one last time...he'd finally found true love...love he'd never thought was possible...she'd taught him true love...how caring and honest she was...and now he'd let her down big time...so many regrets... too many regrets to count...

"Please, do go on, Mr. Ivanov. I can't help you if you don't give me enough intelligence, so I know you do have knowledge. You are completely safe - for now. At this time, it remains unknown if you will be given protection until you give me more to work with." General Tilson checked the recording device, and it was still working as it should (a fake device), as was the electronic microphone in the overhead light.

The general liked those he interrogated to think he had the one recording device. The general made it look like it was all he used, and if a suspect became irate and busted it, thinking that nothing remained of the interrogation, to think the general had zero on the person, the better Tilson liked it. A bit old school, yes, but it'd proved useful more than once, and had garnered additional intelligence he might not have obtained, if he'd not used it.

"I know that Scotland Yard caught Olga Pasternack on a spy camera that was jointly set up by Scotland Yard, the United States, Canada, General Ness, and the Brigadier General at Ramstein Air Base in Germany.

"She was caught reframing a small landscape painting that already had a frame, with a new one that contained a microchip, just so a certain oligarch would buy said painting no matter the price. I do not know the name of this oligarch.

"Furthermore, I also know that on General Ness's order, via the commander-in-chief - your president, and the Brigadier General at Ramstein Air Base flew Olga Pasternack to Denver along with the frame that contained a microchip carefully sealed in a locked, shiny, silver Halliburton case.

"Additionally, I know that a Russian agent infiltrated Scotland Yard. The same agent who informed me via a coded email about Olga Pasternack, and the fact that she is now back in Russia. The same Russian agent with Scotland Yard was caught and is now in prison, I think.

"Those two were the only ones who sent me coded emails. Is that enough, General Tilson? You want to know what I know. I know for sure that I want to live and there could be a hit man already in Colorado."

This time Dmitry knew that General Tilson had heard enough and that he, Dmitry, was authentic, since no one in the United States outside of General Ness and his top men, General Tilson and his top men, the president, and the Brigadier General at Ramstein Air Base knew this intelligence.

General Tilson stood up and stated in a matter-of-fact voice, "I need to make a phone call, Mr. Ivanov. Please wait patiently until I get back to this room. You are safe right now. No one can get to you here." With that General Tilson left the room.

As it so happened, General Jack Ness was in Denver on another case, and he'd been invited by General Tilson to watch and listen to what Dmitry Ivanov said through the two-way glass mirror in the wall of the adjoining room. General Tilson need not say a word as General Ness said, "red phone" and both knew what that meant.

Thirty floors below the Federal Center's ground level, both generals sat together in a large room with quality lighting and full secrecy from anyone inside or outside of the facility. The room was rarely used except for the most serious needs, and General Tilson used the special red phone that dialed the president upon picking it up. General Ness turned it on speaker mode.

"Go Time," came the coded response that meant the president was on the line.

"Good morning, Mr. President. General Tilson here and General Ness is with me. As you now know, we have a red phone situation. A Russian man, Dmitry Ivanov, is here in an interrogation room and guarded by my top agents."

"Isn't that the man you have been monitoring, General?" The president asked.

"Yes, Sir, it is," replied General Tilson. "Mr. Ivanov has divulged enough intelligence for both of us to know that he is, indeed, an agent or spy of some sort, and he has more intelligence to give us. He's asking for safety, and to stay here at the Federal Center, for protection as he is sure that he has been compromised."

"Normally, this kind of thing is taken care of here, in DC. This case is special though, so I'm leaving it with both of you, as you are the ones who have worked on it since the beginning, you both know all the details, and are the most qualified to do so. You two know what to do, take the next steps per your judgement. Remember to maintain my plausible deniability. It's a busy day. Thank you for calling. Goodbye, gentlemen."

General's Tilson and Ness went back up the elevator and both walked into the interrogation room. It was time for a realistic accident.

"Mr. Ivanov, this is General Jack Ness. We are going to give you protection – for now. There's a good chance that your assassin has not made it to Colorado yet. With that in mind, we need you to have a realistic accident at your home. One that leaves no trace of your home, belongings, or you in the ash and rubble."

"What kind of accident? What's your plan?" implored Dmitry. "I'm honestly here to help, not only sanctuary."

"All right, but we'll move to a bigger room so plans can be made ASAP. Agents Hughes and Thompson will escort you down the hall to the room we will work in."

Dmitry sat in a comfortable chair in the middle of the rectangular hardwood table, drinking coffee, with Agents Hughes and Thompson on either side of him. The generals sat across from them. Agents Mason and Woods stood guard outside the closed door.

"Well men, first things first. In case no one is in Colorado yet, it is possible to destroy all evidence related to Mr. Ivanov. Do you understand what this means, Mr. Ivanov?" General Tilson stared at Dmitry, waiting to see how his face changed, if at all, and other clues he might reveal via his expression.

"General Tilson, all I have with me are my clothing and shoes. My keys are in the SUV near the gate with my packed bag. My beloved emerald faced gold watch was left at home. My art collection? At home. All personal items are inside my home. You must destroy everything, yes?" Dmitry knew he was right. All his things had to be destroyed.

His SUV, his beloved Bentley, priceless jewelry and beloved and treasured art collection, his home in Evergreen...everything that he had certainly had to go...I wonder if they would make it look real? Of course, they would...they had to make it real...it's not like things couldn't be replaced...he was an oligarch after all... he could simply buy more anytime he wished...depending on the outcome of turning himself in...life would never be the same again...not ever...but he was man enough to do the right thing...he owed the US for what they had done for him...he wasn't a Russian traitor, but he knew the rogue oligarchs were relentless...for power in any way they could obtain it...no matter the cost...money wise or if people were killed in their zest for increased power and control...

"That is correct," General Tilson replied. Then Tilson laid out the bare bones plan for the destruction to his men. General Ness had his parts to give, and the agents were quite adept at figuring out all that was required for "Operation Do."

"All right then, Agents Hughes and Thompson, I leave this in your hands. Keep me apprised."

"Yes, Sir. Understood," Agent Thompson responded as he and agent Hughes stood up, saluted the general, and left the room.

Agents Mason and Woods took over for Agents Hughes and Thompson at the Federal Center and Agent Mason called for two more agents to stand guard at the door, Agents Knight, and Woodson. All four agents had been involved with prior events with this case.

"For now, Mr. Ivanov, Agents Knight and Woodson will take you to a 'guest room' that has been prepared for you. You will receive fresh clothes, food, a comfortable sofa with ottoman, books, a single bed area, and a bathroom with toiletries.

"Your door will be locked and always guarded. Food will be brought to you and snacks are already in place. You also have a flat screen television so you can watch the news or a movie. No phones of any sort, a tablet or computer allowed." Looking at both Agents, the general remarked, "Agents, take Mr. Ivanov to his room."

"Yes, Sir," they replied in unison and gave him a salute.

General Tilson drummed his fingers on the top of his desk. He knew his agents would be as thorough as possible concerning Mr. Ivanov's home and possessions. He was waiting to hear back that "Operation Do" was successful, and his four agents were safe.

Working with explosive materials was always dangerous and his team were experts in explosive materials. Since the United States army makes all explosives for the military, this meant that each type was sealed up in the best way for transporting.

His team had driven Mr. Ivanov's SUV back to his home in Evergreen and parked it in the garage next to the Bentley.

Only one military SUV was parked near Mr. Ivanov's home, two blocks away and near the driveway of another home. Fortunately, Dmitry Ivanov's home had a large open space around the house.

The agents worked quickly in the strategic placement of TNT (Trinitrotoluene) - the benchmark for all other military explosives. TNT's insensitivity to shock and friction reduced the risk of accidental detonation.

With skill, careful placement of the C4, manufactured into the M183 "demolition charge assembly", which consists of 16 M112 block demolition charges and four priming assemblies packaged inside military Carrying Case M85, was deployed and in place.

Everything set up, the agents went back to their SUVs, and Agent Hughes phoned General Tilson, "All is good on this end, General."

"Good to know, Agent Hughes. It's a go." General Tilson heard the explosions when Agent Thompson hit the detonators for the charges. It was done. His men were safe.

Generals Tilson and Ness, along with Agents Hughes and Thompson, and including Dmitry Ivanov were seated at the hardwood table in the same conference room they had used for planning much earlier that day.

All eyes and ears were glued to the flat screen television and the news stations reporting on the multiple explosions in Evergreen. New's helicopters flew above the debris until the fire was out and photos of the smoldering ash remains were taken.

One agent wore firefighters clothing and took control of the scene. The Evergreen and Genesee fire departments knew this was a military maneuver of some sort, and no questions were asked.

The fire was slowly and safely put out in a manner that showed difficulty in fighting the blaze, so that reporters would report on that fact, and it meant more destruction of all things in the home. With the large open space surrounding the home, no pine trees caught on fire, and it was contained 100% as it was slowly put out.

No one was hurt in the process or suffered smoke inhalation. Dmitry Ivanov's name and photograph were used repeatedly in the reports, and questions remained that evening as to Mr. Ivanov's remains. He was assumed to have been killed in the fiery inferno that destroyed his home.

Absolutely nothing was salvageable, no body was found, nor was a body expected to be found, due to the complete destruction of the home.

Both military and local agents and officers inspected the remains and found nothing of any use, not one single clue to the cause of the explosions and subsequent fire.

It was widely reported that Mr. Dmitry Ivanov had been killed in the explosions and no remains would be found due to the extremely hot, heat intensity of the fire. Most everything was incinerated.

General Tilson made sure that the news was left that way – no cause, no part of a body, nothing remotely a piece of anything recognizable was all that was reported. *Russia would buy this as real...time would tell...and he was a patient man...he knew how to present incidences such as this to the media...his men knew what to do...*

Chapter Three

*N*o way!!! Dmitry dead? He was just in the art gallery yesterday…he bought that wonderful winter, mountain oil painting….No way!!! That house had belonged to Richard! Why couldn't he get out of the house in time??? There's nothing left! He can't be dead…no one with his kind of assets would die this way…he wasn't even home when the fire broke out? What? The house exploded!!! No way!!! A new nightmare had just hit in a horrendous and violent manner…what would they tell Suz? Oh, he just can't be dead…

The Swiss chalet and river stone style façade of the two-floor, steep pitched, and gabled roof of the gallery was decorated for summer and looked amazing. The steep pitched roof helped control the snow accumulation on the building in winter.

The open floor concept allowed for ample wall space for showcasing art, and a ginormous glass-encased, and perfectly lit up center island displayed carved wood, precious metal artworks, and one-of-a-kind gemstone jewelry.

Recessed lighting was abundant as well as spotlights for special showings. Many pieces were created by Kim as well as pieces on commission by local and area artists.

The modern, locked when-not-in-use cash register sat on a wooden freeform carved wood and attached-to-the-wall island, and access was difficult due to a locked wooden gate; hence customers couldn't get in without someone seeing it happen. In addition, an extension was added for having coffee on demand, a coffee bar with a suitable selection of individual coffees.

"Get down here now, Kim!" Nancy, a slim brunette with pixie cut hair and startling blue eyes, yelled up the stairs to Kim's painting studio, in her art gallery, The Art Gallery of Evergreen, in Evergreen, Colorado.

Upon hearing Nancy yell for Kim to come downstairs to the main showroom, her husband, Richard, peeked into a nearby playpen and saw their six-month-old son, Daniel, fast asleep, so he left the back room of the gallery, where he'd been carving a delicate 3-dimensional nativity scene, to see what had Nancy so excited.

Kim, with her long curly blonde hair flowing behind her as she made her way down the steps to the main floor, was curious about why Nancy wanted her. Her green eyes were lovely, and she glowed – a pure love and pregnancy glow. She was almost five months, and due to have a sonogram tomorrow.

"What's up, Nancy? You look shocked. What's happened?" Kim looked at Nancy's face, then Richard's face, and finally the large flat screen television on the wall announcing news about an explosion on the far north side of Evergreen, west of Genesee.

"Oh, my goodness! Wasn't that the house you sold to Dmitry, Richard?" Kim's mouth was open as she stared long and hard at the pictures and evolving news report.

"It's the house I sold to Dmitry! Wow. It's utterly all gone!!! I never imagined it would catch on fire and burn to the ground. Surely, Dmitry got out of it in time." He peered at Nancy, and she shook her head from side to side.

"It's not just a fire, Richard. The house exploded! The news is saying the house exploded! I'm not sure Dmitry made it out in time." Worry etched Nancy's bottom lip as she watched the screen. *Was Dmitry home at the time? Why can't 9News say if he made it or not?*

"I'm absolutely horrified! Dmitry was always the epitome of a nice, kind, and certainly rich Russian. Why didn't we hear the blast?" Kim implored Richard with a look, she wanted her question answered.

"That house was on the north side of the mountains, to Interstate-70. That makes it about thirteen miles from there to the gallery. With the slopes of all the foothills between us, it was hard to hear, I think." Richard surmised as Daniel cried out. "I'll go and get him."

"He's hungry, Babe." Richard handed Daniel over to Nancy and she sat down in the carved wood reading nook that Richard had built. Soon Dan was nursing away, oblivious to the commotion.

"Hi everyone!" Susan Davis, a 25-year-old young woman, tall with deep green eyes and curly red-hair came through the front door. She worked part time at the art gallery, and she was an artist herself, with a preference for using watercolor in her paintings.

Suz had set aside a block of time to enjoy watercolor painting in the art studio, on the upper level of the gallery, with the full natural light it offered in the afternoons.

"Why are all of you looking at me? Am I wearing a sign that says, 'Stare at Me' or what?" She laughed as she headed for the carved wood island with the cash register and coffee bar, stuffed her backpack in the back side of the counter, and out of sight. "Why is no one laughing with me?"

Kim grabbed her arm, "Suz, come sit with me and Nancy. Please?"

"Okay, did someone die? What is going on? You are all freaking me out right now! Just tell me!" Susan directed her slant-eyed gaze at Kim.

As gently as they could, Kim and Nancy explained what had happened at Dmitry Ivanov's home. Both knew Susan had taken a liking to Dmitry over the last few months, and they were concerned about her as neither of them knew exactly how deep that relationship went, as Suz had kept a lot of it to herself.

"But he wasn't there, right?" Suz stared at the television screen on the wall, looking at the video footage and listening to the news. Yet the news replayed Dmitry's photograph and his assumed loss of life.

"He just can't have been there at the time. No!" A tear rolled down Suz's cheek as she looked away and out a nearby window, not seeing the people, businesses, or the nearby lake.

"No! We had a date for tonight. We were…I was…I was finally going to let him show me his love for me…and mine to him…in bed. Oh my gosh, I just said that aloud. Please forgive me…my brain…the words. I'm so sorry." Suz wailed in tears.

Dmitry must be okay! I won't settle for anything less…this is simply not true… Dmitry was not at home…not a death by a fiery explosive inferno…Dmitry's NOT dead!!! I will see him, and we will make love…we will…I can't go on not knowing how our love would have gone in the most sensual of ways…and in the future…my soulmate gone…

"9News reports that they believe Dmitry perished in the explosion. We must wait and see. And you can't go to his house, all of it is cordoned off. I'm so sorry." Kim hugged Suz and handed her tissues to sop up some of her streaming tears.

"You are staying with Richard and me tonight, Suz. We don't want you to be alone right now." Nancy gave her a hug and squeezed her chilled hand. "We will all get through this, okay?"

Suz nodded her head, tears flowing down both cheeks. "We clicked; you know? Kim, you and Paul mesh together just like Nancy and Richard, and baby Dan. Screw my watercolor session; I can't even think about losing myself in art!!!" Tears kept coming; buckets of them. "Dmitry can't be dead!!"

"I'm closing the gallery now, it's only ten minutes early. Come on, let's get our things and head out. Suz will ride with you, Nancy." Kim instructed the others, so they gathered their things, and filed out the front door. She flipped the sign to 'closed,' turned off the lights, and locked up tight. *A solemn and somber group, indeed.*

Richard tucked baby Dan into his car seat as a tearful Suz got in next to him, followed by Nancy. Once everyone was buckled up, Richard skillfully backed their custom Red-Velvet Pearl-Coated Jeep Grand Cherokee Limited with all the bells and whistles, from its parking stall, then drove west past Evergreen Lake to their three-level, three bed, and three bath log and river rock home. Many homes in the Heart of Evergreen were built in this style.

None paid any attention to the wraparound porch with fairy lights strung throughout and the wooden outdoor furniture that graced the porch. The heavily treed home screamed welcome, any other day.

Richard carried Dan inside as he escorted both women ahead of him, up the steps, and into the wood accented entryway that led into a large, yet cozy, main living area with exposed beams.

Both women sat down on a large dark leather wrap-around sofa. Nancy put a throw around Suz's shoulders.

It was the 85-inch flat screen television above the large river rock fireplace that kept the attention of both women, the need for updates on Dmitry. Both women stared at the screen before them. Holding hands, Nancy prayed that 9News would have more to announce, and she hoped for news on Dimitry. News that never came.

Never mind, a matching loveseat and three matching recliners were grouped around a rounded coffee table topped with natural wood and three matching side tables.

Antler ceiling lights hung from above. Plenty of windows allowed natural light to filter inside. Adjacent to the main living area was a dining room that had a six-seat, carved walnut dining table topped with candles and summer décor.

Additional antler ceiling lights hung above the table and a matching carved walnut sideboard held more summer décor.

Richard carried Dan through an arched wooden doorway and into their fully equipped gourmet kitchen with wooden walnut cupboards and all stainless-steel appliances. Granite countertops, an additional wine fridge, and a breakfast bar area completed the open design.

Track lighting gave off a warm glow, and the pantry was large enough to feed a platoon of soldiers. Off the kitchen was a laundry and mud room and a back entrance led straight into the attached two car garage.

Richard took Daniel into the kitchen and secured him in his highchair. While he made grilled cheese sandwiches for the adults, Richard fed Dan his favorite pureed vegetable combo of carrots, sweet potatoes, and peas.

His happy and smiling son had no idea of what had happened that day. Nancy never saw how well Richard could multi-task, a smile never appeared on his countenance except when feeding spoonsful of veggies to Dan.

Once Dan was fed, Richard cleaned his cherubic face and hands amid sweet baby babble, then he changed his diaper.

Finally in the living room, he put his son inside a walker/bouncer combo with beads, buttons, plastic mirrors, and baby toys to occupy him as Nancy and Suz watched Dan, now out in front of them, and the television.

Richard brought out the grilled cheese sandwiches he'd made and a pot of chamomile tea. "I know you aren't hungry ladies but humor me and nibble on these while I pour the tea. I figured chamomile tea would help us relax a bit."

The evening was long and no further news regarding Dmitry was reported. Nancy put soft and cuddly baby bear patterned pajamas on her son, nursed him, changed his diaper, kissed him, nuzzled his dark hair, and tucked him in his crib. Dan was such a good baby and always slept through the night.

The guest bathroom was located off the main living area down a short hallway. Next to it was a linen closet and across from the guest bathroom was the master bedroom.

Nancy ushered Suz into their guest bedroom and gave her one of Richard's T-shirts to wear as a sleeping shirt. "I can lay beside you, Suz. You need not be alone." Suz refused the offer, so Nancy hugged her tightly, before she left the room.

Suz sank into the bed, pulled up the covers, turned onto her right side in a fetal position, and tears slid down her cheeks.

Both ignored the carved wooden spiral stair that led directly into a reading nook/library, on a landing that overlooked the main living space.

The room was fitted with a full mahogany bed set and matching furniture. Antler lights hung above the bed in her guest room and the guest room down the hall had a ceiling fan with lights. *The décor was just that...décor...all she on her mind as Dmitry...only Dmitry...Dmitry was gone...the man she'd come to love was gone...in an explosion...how does he even have a memorial service? Nothing left...he'd been so kind, gentle, and loving to her...she didn't care about his rich Russian oligarch money...she loved the way he was with her...now...nothing...she was alone again in the world...lost... scared...worried...no family left alive...she was totally alone...never to know the love she and Dmitry had, never a chance to show each other with tender and reverent touch and making love...*

Eventually, Nancy and Richard settled down for the night, holding each other and praying for the soul of Dmitry. Their ensuite master bedroom held a deep brown, carved walnut king size bed and deep brown walnut furniture along with one walk in closet. The bathroom included a walk-in shower and a jacuzzi.

"Suz loved him deeply, Richard. I'd no idea their romance was at that stage. I just don't know how to help her. I feel helpless in what to do or say." She turned and hugged her husband.

"Simply be yourself, Honey, be yourself, give her hugs and support. Be the family for her that she doesn't have. Be a sister to her. That's all we can do at this point." Richard then turned over and spooned with his wife, one arm around her waist, as they finally fell into a restless sleep.

When Paul arrived home at Pine Lodge, built in 2020, a rustic log and river rock four floor condo with fire resistant shake shingles on the roof, and built into the side of the mountain, he found Kim in the early sunset light from the kitchen windows highlighting her form and growing baby bump as she stirred a pot of what smelled like chili.

Nuzzling her neck, Paul asked Kim about her day and if she was excited about her sonogram in the morning, especially with her baby bump growing so fast. The last thing he expected was Kim crying as she turned around and faced him.

"Babe! Are you okay? Is the baby, okay? Are your spinal nerve stimulation wires not working? Is your back hurting? What has happened? Tell me now, please!" Paul enveloped Kim in his arms and led her to the dark walnut kitchen table.

I pray the two nerve stimulation wires are in place and working...receiving signals... blocking pain impulses to her brain...she'd been born with a birth defect... never surgically repaired...it had become worse and debilitating...and the nerve stimulation wires had decreased Kim's pain level by 80%! So thankful we have a personal elevator from the lowermost level and garage up to all three upper floors... Kim used that a lot...but why the tears?

"It's Dmitry. He's gone! Turn the kitchen television to 9News, Paul. He simply can't be dead!"

Paul turned the news on, then dished up the chili into two bowls and set them on the table along with two fresh glasses of water. Once seated, he looked at the television screen.

"Wow, Kim. None of this reached the neurology and spinal departments at the hospital in Lakewood." Paul was shocked at what was left of Dmitry's home. *Nothing...all wet ash...bent metal pieces...little pieces... reports stated the house simply exploded in a ball of fire...*

Kim knew she needed to eat for their baby's sake, so she managed most of her bowl of chili as Paul ate his.

As if robots, together they cleaned up the kitchen and loaded the dishwasher. Neither spoke as they were thinking about Dmitry and the way they'd met and how easy it had been to converse with him.

"Let's go to bed, Kim. We have an early morning, and we'll know more tomorrow as well. Come on, sweetheart, we both need rest." Paul suggested as he turned Kim around and they headed toward the master bedroom.

A huge king size bed dominated the room that was detailed in muted shades of rose and blue. Both changed into sleepwear and brushed their teeth.

Once cocooned in bed, they clung together lost in thought, elated to know the sonogram was in the morning, yet heartbroken and terribly sad that Dmitry was most likely dead. They held onto each other all night long.

Dr. Aaron and Sarah Leawood had seen the televised news while at work in the busy emergency room (ER) at the same hospital in Lakewood that Paul worked at.

Aaron was best friends with Paul and Sarah had her bestie in Kim. Nancy was now a bestie, too, with Richard rounding out the three young couples.

Due to their hours being a bit different in the ER, Dr. Aaron, an ER doctor who'd been a neuro and spinal doctor before switching to the ER, and his wife, Sarah, an ER registered nurse, drove separate vehicles home that evening.

Living in Lakewood in a beautiful multi-floored timbered and river rock home, nestled against, and into the side of a front range foothill mountain, with a small stream of water and a small lake on their property, was the sanctuary they called home.

Yet on the drive home, Sarah didn't feel like her home was a sanctuary, much less her white Cadillac Escalade. The spacious living room with a huge stone fireplace would be just that, the kitchen wouldn't be cheery or evoke a sense of home, the oak cabinets and granite countertops would be as cold as the center island countertop.

Just as cold as the granite stones marking Simon's grave…and John's grave…next to each other…her oldest strangled before birth…labor induced…sweet John strangled on his umbilical cord…Simon due to incompetent respiratory…never mind…*Oh Danny…I pray you are okay…and can handle the news about Dmitry…this would be a mother and son talk when she arrived home…****depressed, she was…in a funk…she couldn't breathe…just like after Simon died…it hurt to breathe…SHE…COULD…***

NOT...BREATHE...her lungs refused to let her breathe... only those who have lost a child know this feeling...she hurt for Danny...gripped in fear...scared...she relived the last moments of Simon's life...*think about home, Sarah, think about home... let the good thoughts in so you can breathe and be able to help Danny...*

The black and chrome appliances fit perfectly in the kitchen, the floor to ceiling picture windows with a view of two small cottages, some outbuildings, and a small, but entirely lovely, lake fed by a small stream was not serene in her mind.

Danny would be lost...no way out of that...he'd liked Dmitry...he'd loved his little brother, Simon...get it together, Sarah, think about your home...let it give you peace of mind...so that you can speak with Danny in a calm voice...at 13 1/2, Danny had seen too much sorrow in his life...Oh, Danny...Sarah loved the back deck behind the mud room where all things winter or summer such as skis were kept within reach...

The exposed beams in the vaulted ceiling gave warmth to the dining room, which was dominated by a large gleaming rectangular pecan dining table that sat twelve people with ease. Matching chairs surrounded the table that was decorated with candles and summer decorations, floral arrangement, gourds, and fake pine branches.

That's good...keep it up...flood your heart with warmth and coziness...Danny will be okay...keep that flood of warm feelings flowing...Danny would need that security...

The soft lighting above the dining table leant an air of coziness to the overall room. Family pictures graced the walls, and a set of bay windows surrounded a breakfast/reading nook, which easily seated five or six people. Soft rose-colored cushions created a perfect place to read, snack, drink coffee, or daydream. Oak herringbone wood flooring completed the spacious room. *Family meals...birthdays...holidays... scouting events...fun times...family...hugs...closeness...laughter...tears...keep the warm thoughts coming, Sarah...keep it up...*

Bedrooms. Our master bedroom on the main floor with an ensuite and a lovely fireplace. A king sized, carved, dark mahogany, four poster bed dominated the room, with matching carved tables on either side of the bed that was covered in a plush summer duvet, and decorative pillows.

Two walk-in closets completed the master suite, and the oak walls held photos of happy family times. *Her heart was slowly warming up again...Aaron was her rock...and she loved him...with her whole heart...*

Aaron's den, a full bath decorated in summer floral design, the kids' playroom also known as Family Fun Room, caused Sarah to smile. *This is working! Think about your home...and the love...the warmth and sense of family...keep it going...*

Ah yes. Near the entry, our gorgeous large, carved, and curved, mahogany staircase with the balustrade decorated in fake pine boughs and summer décor. The stairway was covered in light brown carpeting. *Oh Danny...he'd finally stopped sliding down the banister...a smile curved her lips...but how is Danny right now? Her smile disappeared...*

Four guest bedrooms with full pecan beds and matching dressers, summer duvets and décor, light carpeting, and writing desks with large closets took up most of the floor with both children's rooms on the same level. *Sarah smiled to herself...Kim and Nancy have stayed here in the past...Alice and Sadie stay over in severe weather...Danny and Lisa have their rooms on this level, too...Danny...*

Danny's room. Danny had it his way with a full-size bed, and he self-decorated it with racing memorabilia and all things Boy Scouts from memorabilia to trophies, badges, pinewood derby cars, and collections from scouting events, especially the National Jamboree he'd recently attended in Washington, DC.

The children liked having a full bath between their rooms. When they used it, they could lock both doors for privacy and personal space. *Danny had to have racing posters in the bathroom...of course he did...a small grin appeared on her face...*

And through the opposite door was Lisa's bedroom decorated in unicorns, pink, purple, and gold. At ten, unicorns were still her 'thing,' so she had a unicorn duvet and pillows on her magical full-size sleigh bed, unicorn posters and she'd added some music posters as well.

She was slowly losing the 'all unicorn only' theme and growing up...ten going on twenty-one...

Hmmm. Another full bath down the hall plus a set of stairs to the fully open attic with two dormer windows on opposite sides. That storage space was well used, and well loved.

*Home at last...she would go to Danny first...she had to prevent him from sliding down into that deep depression he'd suffered after Simon died...they both had suffered...she had to save her son! She would **NOT** lose her only living child to a state of deep depression again...and most certainly not a suicide! Sarah was determined to do everything Danny needed to get through this...Sarah knew she would give 2000% to see Danny come through this horrible traumatic news...*

Sarah arrived home first with Aaron not far behind. She walked inside to find her son, Danny, with dark hair and cobalt blue eyes, and daughter, Lisa, a curly blonde-haired and blue-eyed girl, crying on the soft wrap-around sofa with Grandma Alice's arms around both. Alice, a thin grey-haired, dark-eyed, smartly dressed woman, was Aaron's mother.

She was the best grandmother any child could hope for...both kids were fortunate that she was here when they needed their parents the most...Sarah was grateful...Thank you, Jesus, for Grandma Alice...but how is Danny doing?

They had seen the televised news regarding Dmitry, and it shook them. Danny, especially, was stricken with guttural sobs that tore Sarah's heart open once again.

The news had brought back memories of his baby brother, Simon, a towheaded boy of only four years, his horrid battle with cancer, and dying seven and a half months later at age five. *With no hair on his little head, his body a testament to the hard effects of chemo and radiation...How could that not affect Danny?*

Sarah enfolded Danny in her arms as she sat next to him, and his sobs tore her heart open further. The memories of Simon were in his head. She soothed Danny with soft words and rubbed his back until he finally hiccupped, and his tears stopped.

Sarah cried with Danny...only the two of them understood this special bond with Simon...no one else in the family could even begin to imagine...and Danny knew only from his child, and brother, perspective, Sarah as only from a mother's perspective...

"Why, Mom? Why was Dmitry killed? I don't understand. All I can think about are Simon and Dmitry!!!" Danny demanded to know why, and Sarah had no genuine answer for her son.

"It was his time. God called him home. Dmitry was taken instantly, without pain. He never had a chance to suffer any pain, Danny. He never knew what happened." Sarah comforted her son with the only words she could say. "No pain. It was a blink and poof; Dmitry was in Heaven." *She prayed silently that his soul was in Heaven...*

"Dmitry gave me that cool drone a few months ago. I'm going to place it in a 'place of honor' next to Simon's 'Golden Blonde-Haired Boy' photograph. When I look at Simon's picture and the drone, I'll know they are in Heaven without pain. And that's a good thing. Those memories are good ones to remember."

Danny was determined to keep his memories...the good ones...around him... hooray for Danny being positive suddenly...Danny would get through this...her smart son would be okay...Jesus would see to that!

"Sounds like a wonderful plan, Son." Aaron walked in and firmly agreed with Sarah. "Your mom is right, Danny. He never had a chance to suffer any pain. God called him home to Heaven."

Lisa ran over to her father, and he held her against him as she stopped crying. She'd known Dmitry, but not as well as Danny had known him.

The Leawood's housekeeper, Sadie, or Grandma Sadie to the children, a short grey-haired and green-eyed woman who loved to cook walked into the room. "I know you probably don't feel like eating but I've made meatloaf with mashed potatoes, gravy, and green bean casserole and it's on the table."

Seated together in the dining room, the Leawood family, Alice and Sadie ate their meal at first in silence. Then, memories of Dmitry were spoken, the children calmed down, and even laughed at some memories as did the adults.

Danny and Lisa were strong and resilient, they would both be okay, Sarah was sure of that, but she'd watch them like a hawk for some time. The children's mental and emotional health was a top priority.

Together, a prayer was said for Dmitry and the family readied themselves for bed. Goodnight was said, kisses given on the children's cheeks with a hug, and Sarah and Aaron went to their own room.

Alice and Sadie had each left earlier for their respective mother-in-law homes behind Aaron's home. It was a somber evening.

General Tilson had decisions to make, and he decided to sleep on what would be the plan moving forward with Dmitry.

Dmitry ate the roast beef with potatoes and carrots and a slice of chocolate cake that had been brought to him before he readied himself for bed in his new 'domicile' at the Federal Center. *He was safe and tomorrow would be a new day…he'd do his part fully…give all intelligence to both generals… and figure out his path going forward…without Suz…or his friends…he already missed them all…a lot…especially Suz…life would never be the same again…*

Chapter Four

What will today bring? Generals Tilson and Ness were fair men...trustworthy for sure...unlike some of his ex-comrades from his mother home, Russia... no longer his mother home...was it ever his mother home? He was dead to them... hopefully...9News did an excellent job on reporting the explosions and fire...the helicopters took great footage of the scene...a scene that Dmitry had a tough time looking at...his home...his life...his love...everything...wiped out instantly!

"Good morning, Mr. Ivanov. I see you've finished your breakfast. General Tilson would like me to escort you to the same meeting room as yesterday." Agent Hughes gave Dmitry a small smile.

"Certainly. I'm ready." Dmitry then nodded his head, and the two men walked in silence to the meeting room and Dmitry took the same seat he sat in the day before. The chair was comfortable, and the hardwood table gleamed.

Agent Hughes handed Dmitry a fresh cold bottle of water before he sat down next to him. Agent Thompson was already at the table and no guard was at the door.

They trusted him a bit more...or this was one of their tactics...it didn't matter...he was going to spill everything he knew...it wasn't like he was going anywhere anytime soon...

Generals Tilton and Ness arrived and took their seats. "Well, Dmitry, shall we get on with the rest of the information that you know and/ or suspect?" General Tilson asked.

"I need you to know that this meeting is recorded electronically and that I'm taking notes in my laptop." Then he placed the laptop on the table and turned it on.

"Yes, Sir, I understand," Dmitry replied. "Do you have a map of metro Denver and one of Colorado Springs?"

"Yes, we do. Agent Thompson, would you grab a couple from the cabinet along with some pens, pencils, and writing tablets please?" Supplies were kept in a tall, locked metal cabinet at the far end of the room.

"Thank you, Agent Thompson." General Tilson responded after his agent stacked the items on the conference table and sat back down next to Dmitry.

"First, there never was a hit on the president of the United States." Dmitry continued, "What was once the KGB, now known as the FSB (Federal Security Service of the Russian Federation) and the SVR (Foreign Intelligence Service), of which I *was* a member, never ordered any hit on your president. Was a member…was…in my old life…before yesterday…yet never really a faithful member…I acted the part…to see what they were up to."

His thoughts were spoken aloud…wow…well, that is what happens when one is honest…first time for everything, that's what they say, I think, in American slang…

"I just spoke my thoughts aloud… In answer to your question, why would they? He's the most protected, and most powerful, man in the world. They did spread that rumor as a ruse to keep agents busy in DC so that the sleeper agent Russian who'd infiltrated Homeland Security could gather intelligence to further Russia's cause."

Dmitry sighed, "That's not right; what I meant to say was to gather intelligence to further the rogue Russian oligarchs cause, and that includes a limited number of Russian oligarchs, of which I only know of a few, not all of them, and that number changes frequently. Their loyalties are fickle and that you can use to your advantage."

"And that cause would be exactly what?" General Ness asked Dmitry directly as he stared him in the eye.

"Colorado. More specifically Denver, DEN airport, the Federal Center, and NORAD (North American Aerospace Defense Command), the United States and Canada bi-national organization charged with the missions of aerospace warning, aerospace control, and maritime warning for North America.

"What about each one? I need you to be specific, Dmitry, or we can't help you." General Ness replied as he jotted notes onto his pad with a pen.

"I know, and I will tell you all that I know and, furthermore, what I suspect. A few of the Russian oligarchs have been set on living for the future, the New World Order (NWO) thing. They are not always with Russia's president, although they act like they are, yet they are a rogue group of Russian oligarchs bent on learning all things Denver and Colorado.

"They hire spies and assassins for their own gain. Allow me to elaborate, please, so you know their twisted thinking."

"By all means, please do continue, Dmitry," General Tilson encouraged him. "I'm taking notes, and this sounds like a conspiracy theory type of thing, right?"

"Yes, Sir, and no. Many facts are unknown to them, such as the computer chip that had been placed into a new frame to reframe at the art gallery in London, the one in a painting by Emma Pleasance, a small landscape painting. The unsold artworks were packed up too fast when they went back to the United States.

"I learned after the fact about the deaths of Mr. and Mrs. Pleasance (Kim's parents) when I read the newspaper article sent to me via email. The oligarchs don't care about loss of life; they want anything that will give them the power they crave! Mr. and Mrs. Pleasance were sadly taken out by vicious hired hit men for a piece of the money pie.

"Kim's parents. Those agents were sloppy, and they don't care about innocent lives. It's disgusting! They also ransacked the Pleasance home but found nothing. They were too late. Turned out, Kim already had that piece on display in her home in Boston.

"I don't remember the spy who told me in an email. Oh! I do remember as it was the same one who had infiltrated the covert operations center in DC. The same one who 'took himself out' in DC, due to depression, I think, or that was what your news coverage offered.

"It's always been about location, location, location to them. The rogue oligarchs don't care about anything but themselves, Denver, and the state of Colorado. It's always been about location as in Denver is situated in the middle of Colorado, and Colorado is in the middle of United States.

"They desire a place not easily reachable by other countries who might want to start war or use nuclear weapons; they think in terms of Cold War days. Those rogue oligarchs desire the four distinct seasons Colorado offers, too.

"They believe they can obtain what they want with imbedded spies and their many billions of dollars. What they should do is build huge, safe underground bunkers with amenities, food storage, and water storage for longer than a single year for themselves.

"But no, they want more than that. An oligarch does not run out of money like they did in the prior century in the 80s and 90s. Times have changed. When one has that many billions of dollars, nested in Swiss bank accounts, they earn interest money as fast as they can spend it.

"Most importantly, they desire the infrastructure here in this city and state. That is why they planted spies. For instance, they wanted intelligence on the Denver Federal Center. Unfortunately for them, Olga Pasternack was caught re-framing an art piece with a frame containing a second embedded computer chip at a separate London art gallery showing that had featured works by Emma Pleasance.

"That chip the United States intercepted, contained intelligence about the Denver Federal Center that the spy knew of and was suspicious of. The plan was to pass it on to an oligarch who was designated to buy that specific piece of art.

"They want the intel more than anything due to the power they crave. The blow of losing out on that intelligence chip took away one third of the power they'd planned to obtain.

"The conspiracy theory part is that not all intelligence is real as some are theories they read about or believe in, such as secret tunnels, yet now they will never have that needed intelligence of NORAD or the Federal Center, yet they won't stop trying.

"This can be used to your (the US) advantage for sure. If the last chips and infiltrators are caught, the rogue oligarchs are then left with nothing, and they won't try this type of 'takeover' again, not that it's a real takeover. I just don't see it as a real 'takeover' thing. It's a power struggle to be the one with the most to offer."

"I see. Yes, we did intercept that chip." General Tilson agreed. Thinking back on that computer chip, the general decided that Dmitry would be escorted back to his room for lunch, and they would resume later in the day or tomorrow.

General Tilson phoned Alice Leawood and canceled their dinner plans for that evening. They were now more than good friends. Who knew that two people nearing age 60 could fall in love? He'd make it up to her. He surely would.

Most people knew that NORAD existed...top-secret...inside Cheyenne Mountain...in Colorado Springs...built in the 1950s...the command-and-control Center was hard for long-range 102 Soviet bombers to reach during the Cold War...back to location, location, location...it housed more than a dozen different government and Department of Defense agencies...no one in the public sector knew about the top-secret agencies housed at NORAD...the in-depth and highly detailed information about NORAD was hard to believe that information got out...until General Ness figured out that his superior at the Pentagon had been the leak! Once found out, the general had offed himself at home in DC...the story put out that he'd been deeply depressed...then Jack Ness became the next general over his department in DC...the things we do to keep the public as calm as possible...until a threat is known...then they inform the public on what was learned, or what was done, such as when Osama Bin Laden was killed...the second chip with intel about the Denver Federal Center...how did that happen? How did that get out? Who did it? Did they have a mole? General Tilson realized that the list of employees required a great amount of checking each person out again...

Kim and Paul pulled up outside the art gallery in Kim's SUV. They were checking in on Nancy, Richard, and Suz before heading down the canyon for Kim's sonogram. Nancy and Richard had the gallery under control and Nancy kept Suz with them, so she wasn't alone.

"We are fine. Get that sonogram and tell us the details as soon as you can. I want to know! I want the low down on your little nugget! *Oh, don't worry about Suz…Richard and I've got this.*" The last part Nancy had whispered into Kim's ear.

They arrived 15 minutes ahead of schedule. Nancy had recommended her obstetrician to Kim and they both decided she would be theirs.

Dr. Tammy Harwell's office was located right off Bergen Parkway and Castle Drive in Evergreen.

After checking in at the front desk, Kim and Paul took a seat in the waiting room. Soon the nurse, Vicky Torres, dressed in scrubs with babies on them, called out for Kim.

After escorting Kim and Paul into the examination room, she took Kim's vital signs and weight. Vicky was a kind woman, and her 40 years had been kind on her Latino countenance as she had very few wrinkles.

"I need to weigh you, okay." Kim stood on the scale and Vicky wrote down her current weight.

Vicky escorted Kim and Paul into an examination room. "Do you need help to get on this exam table?" Kim stepped right up and positioned herself on the exam table.

"Oh good, you are so strong, Kim. The doctor will lift your shirt up when she comes in shortly. In the meantime, I will take your vital signs before she comes in as she will need to review them."

"Your blood pressure is great at 128/72, pulse is seventy-four, oxygen saturation 99% on room air. Doctor will be in shortly." Vicky smiled and out the door she went, busy on her way to the next task on her list.

Kim and Paul were holding hands when Dr. Harwell came in and introduced herself to Paul. "Are you ready for your sonogram? More importantly, are you ready to find out if it is a boy or a girl? I hear you are a doctor yourself, 'daddy-to-be'." She gave Paul a quick smile before she set about doing the sonogram.

"Yes!" Kim and Paul replied with full smiles on their faces. Kim giggled, and that caused Paul to laugh, and then Dr. Harwell joined in.

"Okay. Not to put things off, but I want to listen to your heart and the baby's heart first."

"I hear strong and regular heartbeats!" Dr. Harwell informed Kim, before she added that the ultrasound gel was pre-warmed in its holder in the sonography machine.

"Have you been experiencing any discomfort or morning sickness or spotting?" Dr. Harwood liked to ask this question early as new parents-to-be were usually too excited after their 'baby news' to remember.

Kim smiled and shook her head no. "I've had a good pregnancy all the way so far."

"Good to hear. I'll dim the lights now and we'll get started." The lights dimmed; she placed a towel down low below Kim's belly.

"The gel is warm, water-based, and does not stain clothing. It helps transmit sound waves more precisely than without."

She squirted warm gel onto Kim's baby bump and began to move the transducer over her stomach. "From the side, it looks like your uterus might be tipped forwards above your bladder. That is not unusual, but it does mean that the further along you get, the more often you will need the bathroom. Now let's check out that baby!"

Dr. Harwell smiled at both expectant parents before moving the transducer over Kim's abdomen again.

"Right now, I am taking measurements of your baby's head circumference and length. Do not worry, this is the first part of the ultrasound. I am checking placement of the placenta and a few other things such as your baby's heart, looking for defects." Using a wireless computer mouse, the doctor made lines on the monitor screen and froze some angles as pictures.

"The screen images look excellent," Paul commented. "Am I seeing what I think I'm seeing? Do you have a surprise announcement for us? Am I right?" *She took a lot of measurements, and I know what I saw...would Kim be ready for this? If she wasn't, then she had only a few months to get ready...I so love my wife...and this precious gift from God...*

"What, Paul? What announcement? Can you see the baby's sex? Boy or girl? Tell me now." Kim was so happy with the look of sheer, thrilled surprise, and happiness on her husband's face.

He kissed Kim, then answered her questions with a grin and a saucy lift of his right eyebrow. "I'm leaving this for Dr. Harwell to announce."

"Well, Kim, Paul, you are having twins!" Dr. Harwell grinned at both parents-to-be. "That's why your baby bump is bigger than normal for your gestation time."

Kim was dumbstruck! *Two babies...right here...in my tummy...we made two little humans...two little minis...I have no words...totally awestruck... TWINS! Can we even manage twins? OH. MY. GOSH. Two cribs...two of everything...oh...my...*

"Kim, are you okay? Or are you in dreamland?" Paul laughed at his wife.

"Sorry, so sorry, Dr. Harwell," replied Kim. "Are they both okay? Do they have good heartbeats? Are they okay? How do their hearts look? Any spinal deformities? I've got to know! I pray they don't inherit my spinal issues. I've got to know now!" Kim cried out in a wave of emotion. The fright on Kim's face was palpable and she was scared to find out. *Please be okay...Jesus, I leave this in Your hands...You have this...all praise and glory to you, Jesus...*

"Hold on, Kim. Calm down. Easy breaths in and out. Everything looks normal," she told both parents-to-be. "Almost done, just a bit more to go. Your babies are growing and developing normally, as expected. There are no spinal deformities, so they won't suffer the pain you've endured most of your life." Dr. Harwell stated as she smiled at Kim.

"I don't see any problems with your babies or their environment in your womb, and I see no congenital conditions or issues. Do you want to know the sex?" Dr. Harwell smiled as she questioned the new parents-to-be.

"YES!" Kim shouted in excitement; her eyes sparkled with supreme happiness. *Finally, a baby...two babies...*

"They are fraternal twins, so they each have their own amniotic sacs, and placentas in your womb. Both placentas are well placed and not too low. As for the sex, you are having a boy and a girl! Congratulations! It looks like you are due around September 12." Dr. Harwell smiled.

"We'll keep a closer watch on the twins as your pregnancy progresses. Oftentimes, twins are born a week or two early. No need to worry about that as it is completely normal."

Paul grinned at Kim, then he kissed her tenderly on the lips. Kim glowed! She radiated happiness. At age 27, she was finally going to be the mother she'd always wanted to be.

They would have a complete family with a boy and a girl. Jesus had gifted them with the most precious of all gifts. Dr. Harwood handed them four sonogram pictures of their babies growing.

The happy couple drove back to Evergreen in a glorious wave of love in knowing when the babies were due and having TWINS! After parking at Kim's art gallery, they walked inside hand in hand.

"I want the juicy details now," Nancy squealed and then she laughed. Soon Richard and Suz joined in on the fun. Suz had normal skin color on her face again, she held baby Dan and gave him sweet baby talk and kisses.

I'm due on or around September 12 and everything looks normal." Kim gushed with happiness and Paul gave her another kiss.

"Well, spill it! You are holding back on us, Kim! Boy or girl?" Suz asked with a smile.

"That's when things started happening faster than fast! Paul knew before me, as a doctor he knew what he saw on the ultrasound screen.

Doctors!" Kim looked sternly at her husband, rolled her eyes, then laughed.

"What happened 'faster than fast'?" demanded Nancy. "It wasn't bad since you are both glowing and grinning like you just won the lottery. Spill. The. Beans. Now!" Nancy snickered, then waited for more beans.

"We are having a baby boy…" Kim announced, but she was cut off by Richard.

"Dan will have a playmate when your baby is older. I can carve the crib in the style you both liked for a baby boy then, right?" Richard wanted confirmation from both parents-to-be.

"That's the thing, Richard. Tell them, Kim." Paul gave his wife another tender kiss.

"Tell us what? Spill it, Kim! The suspense is too much!" Nancy was overjoyed for her best friend.

"As I tried to say before Richard interrupted me, we are having a baby boy …and a baby girl." Kim laughed at the puzzled looks on her friends' faces. Then they realized what she meant.

"Oh!!!! Twins! You have twins growing in your tummy, am I right? Yes!!" Suz punched her fist into the air.

"We are, indeed," replied Paul. "Looks like two cribs are needed, Richard. Both designs we chose last week."

"Congratulations!" Richard replied and the others joined in. It felt like a full-on family event had just happened and Suz was part of it. She was family, too.

Family isn't who is related to you via blood; family are those people who feel like family. And Suz had fit in perfectly with their family.

"How are you, Suz?" Kim wanted to know if she was handling things better since the news of Dmitry's death.

"I'm sad, but not crying. I wish there were a way to have a service for him, but no body, no family to plan services, and what would those arrangements even be?" Suz lost her smile.

"We have it covered, Suz. Paul and I plan to get everyone together for a meal, and then then speak about Dmitry and our good memories.

A special memorial for all of us, including the Leawood family. That sound okay to you?"

"That sounds perfect, and a way to have some closure. Dmitry would be touched by that; I know he would be. Thank you for your amazing support." Suz gave Kim a tremulous smile and they hugged.

At the Leawood home that evening, both children acted like normal. During dinner, Alice informed everyone that Grandpa James couldn't make it for dinner due to unforeseen business at the Federal Center. No one questioned why as they all knew he was a busy man who had to keep most things top-secret and safe.

Chapter Five

*G*eneral Tilson was tired…and rightfully so…he'd been up late pouring over all the intelligence the United States had regarding Russian oligarchs…and the US had a lot…most Russian oligarchs believed a new world order was coming… as the largest private owners in Russia and the world, they were the cream of the 'elite' crop…they all possessed political power to influence their own interests…with Oligarchy, came a form of power structure in which power rests with a small number of people…Russia has that…so does China…since 1991, a new a class of Russian oligarchs had emerged…they controlled significant portions of the economy, especially in the energy, metals, and natural resources sectors and many maintained close ties with government officials…such as the Russian president…

"Excuse me, General Tilson? They are ready for you in the meeting room," his secretary or aide-de-camp, Cheri Banes, a dark-haired and dark-eyed woman of short stature, also known as a 'little person,' buzzed in on the intercom on his phone.

"Thank you, Cheri." I bet Cheri has my coffee waiting for me in the conference room.

Upon arrival, General Tilson saw that he was the last person to arrive. Already seated, General Ness, and General Tilson's top secret-yet-not-so-secret agents Hughes, Thompson, Mason, and Woods were present as was Dmitry. Cheri had just topped off his cup of coffee.

"Let me know if you need anything, General Tilson." With that, she left the room and closed the door.

No one stood guard. Dmitry wasn't going anywhere as he would not be able to leave the building with the guards on duty throughout, and he wasn't a threat to anyone in the room.

"Let's get started on this business. If any added information should come up regarding NORAD or the Denver Federal Center, we'll deal with that then. I would like to start with Denver International Airport (DEN)."

Maps of DEN were already in place on the hardwood table. "Before we get into this deeply, I want to state the past and current briefings given to the public, so we are all on the same page moving forward," General Tilson looked at each man and they nodded in full agreement.

"Denver International Airport (DEN) is an international airport, that primarily serves the Denver metro area and the front range mountains. It is the second largest airport in the world. We all know how large DEN is, the runways, and how busy they are since each of us have flown in and out numerous times.

"With over 40,000 employees, the airport is the largest employer in Colorado. DEN has ranked from the second to the busiest in the United States, and sixth busiest in the world. DEN replaced the overcrowded and insufficient Stapleton Airport in 1995. Since then, the airport has grown rapidly, adding counter space, runways, commuter rail service to DEN, and the RTD's A line.

"Renovations have always been ongoing, especially in the Jeppesen Terminal, changing the places of and adding more TSA security checkpoints from the Great Hall on Level 5 to Level 6 (East and West) while simultaneously updating and consolidating airline ticket counters/check-in for all airlines.

"Upgrades are ongoing and will not stop. Forty new gates have opened in the last five years, and with them new retail and restaurant tenants. DEN is expected to manage upwards of one hundred million passengers per year.

"The plan is to add four more new concourses with one hundred more gates east and west of the terminal by 2045. 'Operation 2045' will help support the airport's goal of serving over 125 million passengers annually by that time.

"The Teflon-coated fiberglass roof of Denver International Airport is unique and alludes to the Rocky Mountains. DEN is also known for a pedestrian bridge connecting the terminals to concourses with views of planes underneath them, the Rocky Mountains, and surrounding views of the area.

"Now, Dmitry, what can you add to this basic overview? What intelligence do you have? Try to be specific, please." General Tilson asked as he drank more coffee.

"Rogue oligarchs want DEN for themselves. Any country would love to have an airport like DEN that covers over 54 square miles, one that is bigger than many large United States cities, yet no country could sustain the amount of people and planes that DEN has, and with the New World Order, they believe that DEN would be their best option before a worldwide nuclear event could break out. Back to location, location, location." Dmitry poured himself more coffee and passed the coffee carafe to General Ness.

"These oligarchs could build a large base in Russia, but they won't; they cannot compete with DEN, nor do they want to do so. For them, taking control over DEN is their goal. Furthermore, they don't want the airport for making money, they have that, they want it for purely other selfish reasons."

"Please explain in detail what those "rogue oligarchs" think they can obtain with controlling DEN," General Ness asked as he looked over his map of DEN.

"They want what is below, they want those connections, they believe in every conspiracy theory they've ever learned or heard about. Even if a half truth, they want it. For them, a half-truth is part of a truth and that means power and status. It's all for power and status in Russia, especially, plus allies!

"One oligarch believes that the 'Illuminati Headquarters' exists underground at DEN. They believe that they can take over control of the Illuminati and become their own **'Oligarch Illuminati'** and eventually take over and control the world. The **'ultimate power factor'** is what they **want, crave, and demand.**

"Power and greed drive them. Rather, power, control, and living through a nuclear world event, in a safe and comfortable environment is the true driving force. **Yet, they know they can't take over the 'Illuminati Headquarters'.**

"Money can buy intelligence but not anything like DEN. If they know what's there, they gain a higher social standing in Russia." Dmitry sipped on his coffee, disgusted with his homeland oligarchs and how they never cared about humanity or human life.

"Please explain further. What other conspiracies do they think DEN has and/or controls? What intelligence do they have now?" General Tilson was curious. Many conspiracy theories have existed since construction had begun, and many still exist, between the artworks of children in paintings and murals, to gargoyles, and sculptures that intrigue people with different meanings or interpretations not always agreed upon.

"Secret tunnels. Secret tunnels are number one. Most people who fly in and out of DEN know about the tunnel system used to move luggage between check-in counters, airplanes, and baggage claim areas.

"The oligarchs believe that there are more tunnels than the ones used by DEN and known to the public. And that is the intelligence they want. They crave to know what is under DEN and Denver. They crave knowledge and intelligence, even though they know they cannot obtain it. Knowledge is power and power is the right hand of the Russian president.

"They want details about all the tunnels, both known and secret. They are trying to obtain that information via a spy in baggage control at DEN, and then secrete it to them via a computer chip. I honestly don't know who the spy is or the name.

"The safety provided by underground secret survival bunkers, special ones, for only the elite of the elite. Like a Super Yacht, they want a Super Bunker. They want their bunkers designed by the ones who designed their yachts. They want, and have the money, for that level of comfort."

"Excuse me, Generals, may I ask a question?" Agent Hughes asked both generals.

"By all means, Agent Hughes." General Tilson nodded in the affirmative.

"There are 'doomsday' bunkers located all over the world. For instance, Bill Gates has one at each of his homes. The same for the elite in the UK. Russian oligarchs have plenty of high-end bunkers built in their chosen styles with amenities; other countries have bunkers around the world. Why DEN? What is the lure factor? What is the key force that drives them? What is the key to receiving the power they desire?" The agent asked Dmitry. "I don't see them ever attaining DEN, of that we are all sure they cannot."

"Good questions, Sir. The oligarchs have special elite bunkers designed in the manner they desired – you are correct, nice, comfortable Super Bunkers, but they don't have the lure of what DEN offers. That's the tunnel system itself plus more, so I will explain in more detail. What is true or not, I've no idea.

"For the bunkers, they want luxurious 15 to 20 floor bunkers or 'Survival Condos' such as the one that's often in the news and located in the State of Kansas, near Concordia. That one was created inside an ICBM missile silo from the Cold War days and is fifteen floors. There are many of those in Kansas and around the US.

"The elite oligarchs are just that – elite oligarchs. They want the best of the best. The elite monitored what the designer and builder created in that silo in Concordia, Kansas.

"Yet they want more than that. Greed drives them to seek more power. They have water sources and nutritional means, but they want to outdo the US. To outdo the US bunker wise, is a feather in their cap, you say and is a huge power factor in Russia.

"One huge component they plan to incorporate into their bunkers is the tilapia aquaponic facility. Tilapias grow fast, they are harvestable at six months, and they reproduce so fast that one has a steady supply of fresh fish as a food/protein source.

"This bunker in Kansas includes vegetable gardens, a mini grocery store, library, gymnasiums, sauna, steam room, climbing wall, bar, three years of stockpiled food, and other amenities that oligarchs are used to having all the time. And the oligarchs have most of that in their own Super Bunkers, yet that is not enough for them.

"Also, the bunker in Kansas includes recreation such as sports areas and pool tables, a swimming pool, theater, music, libraries, miniature golf, tennis, and the like. The luxury of furniture, a wine vault, and 'windows' that are flat screen television/computer type screens, that electronically display multiple images for each of the four distinct seasons on a rotating basis."

"They want family and friends, kitchens, medical supplies, nurses, doctors, and surgical rooms. They want everything that the bunkers here have, especially the medical side, of utmost importance. They want the space, and the tunnel system DEN has; and space for schooling and having a community-like setting underground. They want what they think NORAD has."

"The oligarchs already have bunkers and some have the amenities you just described. No oligarch would be without their own secret Super Bunkers. People in metro Denver have private bunkers, and there are other bunkers in the state and all over the world. They have weapon storage and armories. What am I missing here?" General Tilson queried.

"That's the thing. Another huge component they want, especially if a nuclear war was to start: a shooting range for practice, a stockpile of armories loaded with guns and shells and all that the US stores in an armory, the military grade, plus a decontamination room, volcanic ash remover, and reverse osmosis water filtration system.

"The tunnels under DEN have ample room for dozens of armored vehicles, if not more, swat vehicles, and remote-controlled sniper areas around the outside of the complex.

"The tunnels alone, have many multiple heavy military grade steel doors, like NORAD has, and that is like candy to a child to them, especially a child who just had their first taste of chocolate.

"Most bunkers around the world can certainly withstand earthquakes and other such planetary events such as Yellowstone National Park going full on eruption and the destruction afterwards.

"Yellowstone would show signs of an impending eruption months or years before the actual event happened. When an eventual super volcano erupts at Yellowstone, the devastation would be worldwide. The entire US would be covered in ash. No one can breathe heavy ash and live. Climate change could last decades.

"The water, soil, everything would be contaminated, and the oligarchs knew they would have a superior system of fresh water every day, as DEN has that system. A ten-year or longer nuclear winter would be easy to get through."

Dmitry sighed, "I have more on conspiracy theories the oligarchs believe in."

"I'm sure you do, Dmitry, I'm sure you most definitely do. We thank you for all that you have given us. We've worked past lunch, and at this time, we will stop for the day.

"I cannot tell you what DEN has or does not have tunnel wise or conspiracy wise. Honestly, I have no idea what all DEN has or if any conspiracy theory is true or not. I do know a break is needed as well as sustenance." General Tilson announced.

The general nodded to his agent, "Agent Johnson, please escort Dmitry back to his temporary living quarters. Your meal will arrive, and we will take this back up on Monday morning. Watch movies, read a book, write down notes you think could be important, and get some much-needed rest. Nothing imminent is going to happen, that we do know for sure."

"Yes, Sir," replied Agent Johnson and after saluting both generals, he and Dmitry left the room with the others following behind.

The weekend would bring much needed clarity to the situation. He had a new mission this afternoon, and he sent Agents Hughes and Thompson to DEN to personally speak with the CEO and a planned phone call with General Tilson this afternoon at 3pm sharp! It was necessary to investigate the baggage handlers ASAP!

The current CEO took the business of a potential Russian spy working in baggage control seriously. Although the agents and General

Tilson could not offer DEN officials much detail, extra security officers were situated in the baggage control tunnels. Two agents under General Tilson dressed as baggage handlers for the weekend and on into the following week as needed until the Russian spy was caught.

Chapter Six

*D*mitry deserved a service...Kim and Paul had the right idea...holding the service with the entire group of close friends and family, in the Heart of Evergreen...that Dmitry loved...the heart of the place Dmitry had called home...the Heart of Evergreen they all called home...

Alice had personally phoned General James Tilson and informed him of the planned service the next day. The day was perfect for a picnic on the west side of Evergreen Lake. Since they would all be in attendance, the art gallery closed at noon.

The Leawood's arrived first, and Sarah placed blankets on the grass near a picnic table. Aaron was tasked with getting foldable lawn chairs set up and the kids, Danny, and Lisa, helped Grandma Alice and Sadie set up the table. No one dressed up and everyone wore summer attire.

Nancy, Richard, and baby Dan arrived with another picnic basket. Despite the purpose behind the picnic, sunny dispositions within each person remained.

Lisa and Danny played with baby Dan on a blanket. A constantly smiling and happy baby lifted the spirits of all.

Grandpa James arrived and brought yet another picnic basket with him. "Good to see you, Alice. I have missed you," he murmured into her ear before kissing her cheek.

"I've missed you as well, James. You brought fried chicken, and I know you didn't cook it yourself," she teased him with a smile.

"I may not have fried that chicken, but I do know the best places to buy fried chicken," James winked at Alice, and she smiled. Then he swooped in for a long and tender kiss and hug. *I needed that kiss...and seeing Alice always was the highlight for ANY day...*

"They are kissy-kissy, Dad. Grandpa James is kissing Grandma." Lisa squealed.

"I've told you repeatedly to let it go, Lisa. They have the right to kiss since they are dating, after all." Aaron smiled at Lisa.

Aaron hoped his mother and James would marry; they were so good together. The kids loved their "Uncle-James-turned-Grandpa-James," and he fit right in with the entire family.

Finally, a pregnant Kim arrived, escorted by Paul. Suz was with them. They'd walked together from the gallery on the northeast side to the west area of Evergreen Lake.

The picnic was relaxing, the food good, the dessert even better as both Alice and Sadie tried to outdo each other, all in fun of course.

Kim decided to talk about Dmitry first. She sat next to Paul in a lawn chair, and they held hands. "I remember the first time Dmitry walked into my art gallery. He was an impressive man. The charm he easily exuded was sinfully charming and noble. I never saw that change during his time here."

"I agree, Sweetheart. He was a true gentleman through and through." Paul gave his wife a tender smile.

"True," Nancy replied. "I was there when he walked into the gallery the first time. His charm and respectful manner were unique in a manner that wasn't USA-like. He held himself in an aura of his own, not being snobby, or anything like that, he was one of a kind. Maybe being Russian had something to do with it."

"He was naturally kind to everyone. I never dreamed he would end up fitting in like family when I first met him," Richard replied.

"In his own unique way, he did become family to all of us. I never saw that coming at all." Richard smiled at Nancy and leaned over to give her a sweet, tender kiss.

"Everybody kisses," Lisa rolled her eyes in exaggeration. Everyone laughed aloud at her comment and facial expression.

"Well, you all do kiss! I liked Dmitry because he took time to talk with me." Lisa wasn't about to let the kiss thing go.

"Newly double-digit ten and going on twenty-one. Guess for what are you in?" Paul joked to Aaron, who wasn't laughing as he'd just thought the same thing. *Oh yes...that will get him! The perfect comeback!*

"Well, Paul, just remember that you will have the same problem in ten more years!" After he smirked at Paul, Aaron turned his head away innocently. *I got him back...chalk one up!!*

"Dmitry was smart. He knew a lot about drones and different gadgets and topics. He always knew what the current headline news was around the world," Danny spoke out.

"He was smart about diverse cultures, too. I think he'd traveled around the world quite a bit before he moved to Evergreen. He always had a new topic when we talked. I'll never be that smart." Danny frowned for a moment.

"Don't sell yourself short, Danny. You have your entire life still to come and you can do anything you set your mind to do. Each one of us has diverse kinds of things we are smart at, good at doing. One of yours, Danny, is your perception of things and others. You hit the nail on the head every time." Aaron smiled at his son.

Aaron was proud of everything Danny had overcome in his life thus far and he knew his son would be successful.

Sarah was in full agreement. "You know, Danny, you help the other boy scouts in your troop. They look up to you. They all know that you will be an Eagle Scout soon, and that impresses them. Your mom is impressed, too." Sarah smiled at her son. *Danny was going to be okay...thank you, Jesus.*

"Hey, look! The elk are moving along the north side of the lake. Dmitry loved the wildlife here." Danny was happy the elk herd, which lived in Evergreen year-round, showed up. It was like Dmitry was with them in this time of memories.

They all watched the elk as they ate, drank, and moved around. The kids had been taught to give the elk a wide berth all the time, especially if they are female and have young babies, or if they are males and in the autumn rutting season.

If an elk should become agitated or fighting with another male elk during rutting season, the elk will charge anyone. Watch from afar and if they head your way, simply walk away normally in a non-threatening manner and all will be well. Unfortunately, many people who lived in Evergreen plus visitors ignore the signs posted, and incidents could happen.

"I thought Dmitry was especially courteous and amiable. Nothing fazed him. At first, I thought he was aloof, but that didn't take long to change and then I saw he was simply a unique individual." Sarah smiled at Suz and encouraged her to talk about Dmitry.

"He was kind, and the smartest man I knew. He was able to talk on any subject and he connected with me at first because he had no living family, just like me." Suz sighed, then continued.

"When he was with me, he was often funny. We could talk about anything. Our shared love of art, he loved my watercolor paintings, my art, we loved art. Of course, I still do. I found inspiration in his interpretation of artworks of all types. We bonded. We fell...," Suz gently wiped tears away from her eyes as she gathered her thoughts.

"We fell in love, real love, like all of you have. Now he is gone, but I will overcome this. Dmitry would want me to do that. He loved his fancy vehicles, clothing, gems, and art, but he also loved the simple things that life has to offer such as watching elk and other wildlife from inside his home, and he loved me. Dmitry loved me, the true love that you all have." Tears fell down her cheeks and Sarah gave Suz more tissues.

"You have a special relationship to always remember. No one can ever take those memories away from you." Nancy hugged Suz.

"Plus, you still have family. You're my Aunt Suz, remember," Lisa stated and Suz hugged Lisa for a long moment.

The rest of the afternoon was full of memories, and they made new memories in honor of Dmitry. Sometimes lost in thought, other times talking, or playing. The memorial service was one that even Dmitry would have been proud of.

Chapter Seven

I must tell Dmitry about the service...it will bother him greatly...but he must know...Dmitry has been truthful and up front with us...I must do the same... it will hurt him...but I must...

Monday morning came all too soon. General Tilson decided to go down and talk with Dmitry before they began further debriefing in the same meeting room.

General Tilson knocked on Dmitry's door at the Federal Center.

"Come in," answered Dmitry.

Good morning, Dmitry. I wanted a chance to speak with you alone.

"Did something bad happen? What can I do?" Dmitry was sure something had happened at DEN.

"Nothing has happened." The general sighed. "I wanted to tell you about Saturday afternoon. Everyone held a memorial service for you, Dmitry."

"What? Who did? How is that even possible?" Dmitry felt alarmed. His heart raced! They were on to him; they would find him! Or not. *He'd best listen to the general...don't get excited...remain calm and collected...hear him out...cool down...chill out...ignore the oligarchs for now...*

"It's okay, Dmitry. Please listen to me. Everyone you personally know, the Leawood, Smith, and Manse families along with Suz held a picnic and memorial service on the west side of Evergreen Lake."

"Oh…" Dmitry had no idea of what he to say. He was truly shocked they did this; it was unexpected. *That was a special thing for them to do...they cared...now he felt even worse that they believed he was dead...no one comes back from being dead in the espionage business...*

"I was there. You know that Alice and I are seeing each other. Each member of the families spoke about you, their special memories of you, and, near the end, a large herd of elk showed up and Danny decided that it was a sign of your approval of the service." Tilson had seen it as a sign, too.

Looking up, Dmitry asked, "How was Suz?" *He was afraid of what he would hear...I hope she is better...he'd never planned to hurt her...in time, she would love again...just not with him...*

"She feels your loss acutely. At the same time, she has been talking about you in positive terms, things we didn't know about you, not secret personal things, but she spoke of your love to joke around, and that was new to me. It was a perfect service." That was true. It had been public and open air, yet the most intimate memorial service he'd ever attended.

"Thank you for letting me know, General Tilson. I wasn't sure they had cared about me that much. I miss them all terribly and Suz most of all. This is my lot in life now, and I intend to make the best of it." Dmitry nodded his head.

"Shall we go up to the meeting room? I'll escort you today."

Dmitry agreed, and they made short work of riding two floors up via an elevator before walking to the conference room.

Both Generals Tilson and Ness, and Agents Hughes, Thompson, Woods, and Knight sat down along with Dmitry. General Tilson opened the meeting.

"For the record, Agent Woodson and another agent are currently out at DEN with the baggage handlers, dressed as baggage handlers, and extra security from DEN are in place. If we are fortunate, we will catch the spy. This is day three of trying to figure out which baggage handler is the embedded spy, and so far, nothing useful has come forth."

"Excuse me, General, I have more to say about the tunnels and the oligarchs' beliefs. I wrote a few notes over the weekend for this session; I did not want to forget something that could be important." Dmitry peered over at General Tilson's face.

"Okay, Dmitry. You have the floor," General Tilson replied. "Let's get started."

"Thank you, Sir. I have more intelligence on the tunnel system and what is true or not true I don't know. I only know what the rogue oligarchs want and believe."

After clearing his throat, Dmitry began. "Of all things, they are positive that tunnels lead to not only underground bunkers for the rich and elite, but they also believe that there is one large tunnel that an electric vehicle or light rail train can be driven, or ridden, that can take anyone directly to and inside of NORAD."

"Whoa! I had not heard that one before," General Ness commented. "It would certainly be handy if it existed."

Everyone laughed at that comment and then Dmitry began afresh, "So far, we have the bunker systems, main tunnels, side tunnels, and amenities under DEN and the local area.

"The rogue oligarchs believe that tunnels exist under the city of Denver itself. Not only that, but they think the tunnel system goes all the way here, to the Federal Center."

No one said a word. The facial reactions were a mixture of shock, disbelief, and puzzlement.

"How on earth did they come up with that one?" General Ness was first to respond. Oh, my...

And what if some of this was true? So much could be factual in parts...an entirely top-secret branch of the military could be a real thing...an entire chunk of the tunnel systems could be true...he'd never know...of that, he was sure...yet parts of many conspiracy theories have a basis in a small piece of truth...entirely mind boggling...it would be easy to have large bore machinery busting through granite... they'd been used before, and are still used...all the time in Colorado and elsewhere... a tunnel boring machine (TBM), also known as a 'mole' or a 'worm', is a machine used to excavate tunnels...and we have them right here in Colorado!

"I don't know. Like I said before, the rogue oligarchs change often, they are fickle, and only a few are in the group, they come and go, but all remain friends of the Russian president. Again, conspiracy theories factor into this entire situation.

"Somewhere in the tunnel system, they believe that a large prison type of encampment exists. Not only that, but they believe the Denver Mint is accessible from a tunnel. What they want with the mint, I've no idea.

"They use secret Swiss bank accounts under miles of umbrellas keeping what they have secret from each other. That, too, is fickle. They don't trust each other so that is why members come and go.

"A $750 million super yacht isn't enough. One would think they had other ways to spend their time and energy on. But, power, they want the most power they can get, any way they can get it! This whole tunnel system intrigues them to no end. I'm intrigued by the possibilities. Who wouldn't be?"

"You are certainly the most enlightening, and the most entertaining, Dmitry." Everyone laughed at that comment. General Ness continued, "They want to control what they desire, and they want the best of the best, right here in metro Denver. Denver is known for the best in that regard, true."

"For sure," agreed General Tilson. "The infrastructure here is worth more money in the world than all other countries in the world have in combined infrastructure. I say that as it is a commonly known fact. Canada is part of NORAD, Dmitry."

"True, Sir. They know that for a fact. But they want proof that the tunnel systems exist; if they don't, then they don't care about obtaining control of DEN and everything with NORAD, or the Federal Center.

"Back to location, location, location, and all the below ground tunnels and infrastructure are vastly superior to what the rest of the world has. Yet both NORAD and the Federal Center computer chips never fell into their hands.

"As for the Federal Center, the rogue oligarchs know that the Federal Center has at least thirty-four below the surface levels. Most of what they know are facts regarding the Federal Center. This place is home to more Federal agencies than anywhere else in the US except for DC.

"It's common knowledge that there are more than ninety buildings right here, and over four million square feet of office, warehouse, and other areas with different uses.

"Look at all the high-tech satellites, dishes, electronic transmission devices, and the zillions of huge solar panels that keep on multiplying at the Federal Center complex. Who wouldn't like to have all of that? Anyone can drive past the Federal Center and see these things from the street.

"The ice core lab samples from around the world intrigues them. Those samples intrigue me as well. These oligarchs consider the ice core samples to mean that other secret samples, all kinds of seeds, genetic improvements, and many specialized laboratories exist of all kinds, including germ warfare.

"They also believe that little green aliens reside in one bunker, that they live in some of the tunnels cohabitating with humans who live in and work in those same tunnels and bunkers! That seems extremely farfetched to me, but..."

Again, everyone at the table laughed aloud. *But then again, what truth could there possibly be?*

"Excuse me, Dmitry. There have been conspiracy theories circling around for decades about aliens. The rogue oligarchs are hoping for aliens. If one of them could provide proof to the Russian president, that oligarch would command the top position next to the president, or even become the next Russian president. That is the power they are fighting for, am I right, Dmitry?" General Tilson asked.

"Common knowledge is out that laboratories do exist. You can read all of that on the Federal Center's web site and even Wikipedia. The rogue oligarchs believe that more exists and is kept secret. They all know germ warfare exists, and the place in the US is the Federal Center. A few countries, including Russia, have their own germ warfare labs.

"Once they know the layout, they want to take over, yet at the same time they know they can't ever take over any of what the US has in Colorado. That goes back to power. The want to best each other in the ladder of who has the most intelligence and the most power, and then they become the second most powerful man in Russia, and the MOST powerful man in Russia.

"The thing about *ALL* oligarchs is simple. They all have and want, the best of the best, they can buy more possessions, but their power ranking remains the same. That leaves only one thing to outdo one another, rogue oligarch or not, *POWER*! Power is the only thing that drives them.

"While the knowledge is nice to know, I don't see the oligarchs attempting to take over any of what they desire from DEN, NORAD, or the Federal Center.

"They never received NORAD intelligence, so NORAD is completely out of this plan of theirs. The same with the Denver Federal Center, thus that intelligence was never received. That only leaves DEN. The intelligence on DEN is the cherry on top. The most desired intelligence.

"They have ZERO military of their own! It's difficult enough for Russia in their war with Ukraine and interference elsewhere around the world. Russia is not in league with the rogue oligarchs, nor would Russia be with them in the future, I don't think.

"So, the oligarchs pay for information, they plant spies just like Russia itself does, and all they have received is partial information. But they think money will win in the end.

"At best they are pompous idiots. There're self-important arrogance blinds them to reality in their quest for power and becoming the next Russian president.

"Seeing that no one else in the world has a structure anywhere close to what this facility, the Federal Center, has right now, none are even slightly comparable.

"What took many decades for the US to build, modify, remodel, add onto, you name it; the oligarchs want it all, yet they know they never will obtain and control this facility."

"Dmitry, you are right, that will never happen. We are too secure for that to happen, and no one gets in here easily. It doesn't matter what they learn, they still won't be able to obtain control over it. I can see the advantages they'd have, of course, in gaining power over each other, as this building will withstand any nuclear weapons, earthquake, or Yellowstone erupting; the same with NORAD." General Tilson was having other thoughts. *Russian games...for power...Russian games...everything fell right into place...Dmitry is not at risk...99.9% sure of that...I don't think he is at risk...time will tell...*

"What is on your brain," General Ness asked General Tilson. "I bet we are both thinking alike right now."

"This is purely a game of who can get the best intelligence in a power struggle among the rogue oligarchs for being the top favorite in Russia, and with their president. Money buys intelligence and the most intelligence buys the most superior of powerful positions. Dmitry is correct on all of this. The rogue oligarchs care zero about any human life; humanity doesn't even pop into their brains."

"That is highly probable and exactly what I was thinking," General Ness responded. "Time will tell if we are correct. It keeps coming back to power." *Power...Geesh! Kill who you want, just give me the intelligence! To them a game, to others, a death sentence...*

"Shall I continue?" Dmitry queried those at the table.

"Certainly, Dmitry. How much more is there?" General Ness was a curious man.

"Not much. General Tilson is correct. The rogue oligarchs spend money to gain intelligence. But they really can't use that intelligence themselves.

"They can, and do, use all intelligence in their power play. Your president has a vice president. The oligarchs love power, they love power play games, and that is exactly what they are doing now, no matter the cost or who gets hurt or killed.

"They know they can't ever take over DEN, NORAD or the Federal Center, but they can prove how useful they are to Russia's president if they have received great intelligence, and then gain control of enough power to one up the Russian president; even become the next Russian president.

"That is their game and their cause concisely. Plenty of money in the play against each other for one coveted position no matter who gets hurt or dies.

"This is shameful to me. Now, I'm no longer their pawn. The most I did was receive information on Olga Pasternack and her being caught and deported back to Russia, and the spy at Scotland Yard (Nikolai Romanova) having been caught. Those two things are what has been communicated to me."

"At this time, we will break for lunch. I'd prefer to begin again in the morning. Please escort Dmitry back to his apartment, Agent Hughes. Let us know if you need anything, Dmitry. A hot lunch will down shortly."

"Yes, Sir." Replied Agent Hughes and he saluted before taking his leave with Dmitry.

Chapter Eight

*One rogue oligarch hired assassins to take out people in their quest for intelligence and ultimately, power, because they don't care who they hurt to get the power they seek...assassins did track Kim and Nancy to Evergreen...but that was **driven by one spy's anger at the women over the loss of two top spies killed in the rollover crash while chasing after Kim**... that was pure anger in the spy and zero to do with the rogue oligarchs...so far, there is nothing against Dmitry...this will be interesting...I bet Dmitry **isn't on a hit list...he knows nothing of any use** to those oligarchs and **he's clearly not a threat to them**...I'll keep this to myself right now...must play the game out...I could be wrong...**my gut feeling has been right 99.9% of the time**...time will tell...*

Monday morning arrived right on schedule like always. General Tilson arrived a few minutes early for work and was looking over his notes for the day, thinking what steps are best now, when his secretary, Cheri, buzzed him to say that Agent Woodson was on the line. "Thank you, Cheri."

"This is General Tilson." He waited to hear Agent Woodson's voice.

"Good morning, General. We caught the baggage handler early this morning. I'll be headed to the Federal Center with him in custody for interrogation soon. He didn't put up a fight."

"Splendid work, Agent Woodson. Have you learned anything?" General Tilson hoped for good news.

"Well, Sir, the baggage handler/Russian spy was caught when he tried to get past a steel door that was in an area clearly marked no trespassing.

"He had electronic devices to both record and take photos. A search of his parked vehicle yielded nothing of interest in his car. I sent a team to investigate his home, and they are to report back to you."

"A superb job! Well done! I'll see you when you get here. You know where to take him for interrogation. Thank you, Agent." General Tilson smiled; things were looking up. *Not all Mondays were bad...certainly not this one...*

Generals Tilson and Ness walked into the interrogation room. This time Ness would do the interrogation. Agents Thompson and Woodson stood guard.

"I'm General Ness and this is General Tilson. What is your real name?"

"Victor (Vitya) Stepanov." He replied in a neutral tone of voice with perfect usage of the English language with a Russian accent.

"Who sent you to infiltrate baggage handlers at DEN and why?"

"Oleg Petrov woke me up a year ago, no longer a sleeper spy. Since then, you apprehended him and he died during interrogation in DC, or so I heard through the grapevine of sleeper agents.

"DEN hired me years ago to work in baggage handling, and I've been good at what I did for the airport. My job was normal. Oleg Petrov activated me right before he was caught.

"I'm a sleeper agent and you caught me. My mission, upon activation, was to gather intelligence about the tunnels under DEN and take photos of what I found. That proved to be impossible to do. DEN is locked up tighter than tight."

"What did you find? Please detail what you found and how you obtained the intelligence." General Ness remained as resolute as a cucumber. *I hope he tells me what I want to hear...*

An agent knocked on the door and asked for Generals Tilson and Ness.

Must be news on what was found in this sleeper agents' home. "We'll be right back," General Tilson spoke to his men.

Once the door was closed, General Tilson queried his agent.

"Mr. Stepanov is clean, Sir. No intelligence in his home. His smart phone was his only communication device, and it contained nothing of substance other than a couple phone numbers of now-suspected-sleeper-agents in the Denver area, and two photos of the military grade steel door he couldn't penetrate."

"Great work, thank you." General Tilson replied.

"Sir, I have more. We ran his fingerprints through our biometric fingerprint system, AFIS (a fingerprint system widely used by the US and other countries), and he came back clean."

Ah. First time this sleeper agent was activated. "Great work! Thank you! You may go now."

"Yes, Sir."

"What's your take on this?" General Tilson raised an eyebrow as he looked at General Ness.

"Let's go back inside; this will be wrapped up in ten minutes or less." The guard opened the door for both Generals to pass back into the interrogation room, then closed the door securely.

General Ness said nothing, but he stared at Victor Stepanov who was unfazed by his stare.

"You are a sleeper agent, you acted alone, you know of other sleeper agents in the Denver area, but you will deny knowing names. Correct?" General Ness inquired. *Not my first time doing this kind of rodeo...*

"Correct, Sir." Victor Stepanov wasn't going to deny that statement. It was true. Besides, he hadn't done anything truly illegal, the trespassing got him nowhere.

"I'm turning you over to the agents back in DC. What happens to you then, will be up to them. Trespassing is illegal at DEN, but you never got far enough to trespass and gain intelligence.

"DC will send you back to Russia simply because you are/were a sleeper agent, and your fingerprints are on record. If you were to ever try to come back into the US, you would be prevented from doing so." General Ness decided the straight truth was best at this point.

"I'll be on the same military transport back to DC." General Ness' work here was done. Time to go home.

"I'll have Cheri arrange for the military transport to DC. Until then, you stay in this room until they arrive." With that, both generals left the interrogation room.

"I'm glad you were here for this operation, Jack. I liked working together on this situation and the one last year." General Tilson knew that General Ness was an asset of the best, the cream of the crop, for the US.

"You know where I am in DC. Come over for a visit soon?" General Ness cocked one eyebrow.

"I'll keep that in mind. Now, I'm going down to talk with Dmitry. You need to pack for your trip back to DC. You know how to reach me if needed." The Generals saluted, shook hands, and went their separate ways.

Dmitry invited General Tilson into his quarters when he knocked on the metal door.

"Good morning, Dmitry. I know I'm late this morning. Sorry about that." General Tilson had come to like Dmitry during this time. Dmitry was intelligent, but not spy material.

"Good morning, Sir. Please have a seat. I was just going to pour myself another cup of coffee. Care to join me?"

"You bet! I take mine black, thanks." Dmitry handed a mug of steaming coffee to the general.

"Does your late arrival have anything to do with me?" Dmitry was curious. Something happened, he was sure of it.

"Do you know Victor (Vitya) Stepanov?" General Tilson carefully watched Dmitry's facial expressions and his tone of voice.

"I'm sorry, but I don't know him at all. I don't recognize the name other than it is a Russian name. Why do you ask?" Dmitry was curious if a new development had arrived. "Is there a new development in favor of the US? I hope so!"

"The spy who'd infiltrated DEN was a sleeper agent, Victor (Vitya) Stepanov. He'd worked at DEN in baggage handling for nine years before being activated."

"I see," Dmitry affirmed. "As you must be aware, there are thousands of Russian sleeper agents all over the US, living amongst us, having families, real jobs, friends in their work setting and neighbors, and waiting quietly until, and or if, they are activated."

"I certainly am aware of all that, Dmitry. I'm also aware that you don't personally know any of them. Only sleeper agents know other sleeper agents. The US certainly has thousands of them." General Tilson sighed.

"I know it gets lonely down here by yourself and I have work to do so I won't be down here as much. With that in mind, I'd like to have you start watching DVDs in the process of getting, and maintaining, a new identity. Are you okay with that?"

"Yes, Sir. I'll start the DVDs anytime. I'm thankful the US government is doing this for me." And he was. It wouldn't be his old life, but it was a life, and Dmitry was grateful.

I will do my best in my new life…and I must get past those I've left behind in Lakewood, Evergreen, and especially Suz…my one true love…

"Dmitry," General Tilson peered into Dmitry's dark eyes. "As of today, stop shaving. Your hair must grow out as well. Your new identity, when created, will require a new you."

"I understand, Sir. We are creating a new 'me' and that involves every aspect of my old self to be changed into an entire new persona." He understood, and the process had begun. He was alive!

The US wouldn't abandon him, and life could be good again...except for the loss of his friends and his love...Suz...

"This is not a work only situation, Dmitry. The guard outside your door would be fine if you asked him to watch a movie with you or play a game of chess. For that matter, the guards can share meals with you, and conversation is encouraged."

"Thank you, Sir. You have been kind to me."

"We are not a hotel by any means, but you are not a prisoner, either. The guards simply keep you from going into areas that are not meant for public eyes. This is necessary for the tour groups who come through here as well. As it is, you've seen more of the Federal Center than those in tour groups."

"Thank you, Sir. I'll remember all of that." Dmitry was relieved that he would start the training for his new identity. *He'd ask the guards to visit and play chess or checkers...watch movies...eat a meal...he'd never have his old life back...or sweet Suz...but he'd have a life...and he was grateful...the US was kind to him...*

With that, General Tilson took his leave.

Chapter Nine

Danny had worked hard on his Eagle Scout project…now it was ready to show the public…he'd chosen to build an octagon pine gazebo on the top of Lookout Mountain in Golden, Colorado…so much planning and talking with Jefferson County…gazebo design, placement, materials, volunteers to help build, all the hours Danny, and others, had spent planning for the gazebo and seeing it through to completion…my son was such a strong young man coming into his own…if only Simon had been here to do this together with Danny…both working on obtaining their Eagle Scout…what if all three boys had lived? Then Danny would have had his older brother, John, to look up to as well…but that was a pipe dream…it wasn't meant to be…

Danny, Lisa, several troop members and one scout leader, Jim, worked on the gazebo. Aaron and Richard also assisted, and everyone was on the top of Lookout Mountain today to complete the final touch-ups on the gazebo and to collect any trash in the area.

The unveiling (the gazebo wasn't veiled) was scheduled for this afternoon and a newspaper representative planned to be there for an article in our local newspaper.

It was easy to coerce the help of Alice and Sadie to bake cookies with me. The cookie baskets were filled and lots of fresh cold-water bottles were in ice chests. The excitement was infectious.

Every milestone Danny reached; I couldn't help not thinking about his brothers in heaven being cheated out of each event… Every single milestone!!! Any mother in my position would feel the same way…yet both boys are happy in heaven…surrounded with love…

The final touchups on the gazebo completed, and the gazebo was scheduled to be unveiled in two hours. I was nervous and excited. I chose to build a knotty pine gazebo not in Lakewood, but atop Lookout Mountain in Golden, Colorado. The gazebo would benefit the local community, metro Denver, and all vacationers. The knotty pine fits right in with the surrounding pine trees and mountain wildflowers and grasses.

Many hours went into this project, and it first had to pass the parks and recreation people and those involved with Lookout Mountain. A perfect spot was found under some pine trees with views of the Continental Divide, Rocky Mountain National Park, metro Denver, and the plains.

Each meeting and each step were documented, and the time required for each step of the entire process listed. Each challenge was documented. Mom and Dad helped with my project, and I even got Lisa to help. My scout friends and scout leaders were involved. Lots of 'man' hours involved and they added up fast.

The City of Golden had to review my proposed process, and they appreciated the details and the people who volunteered to help. They supplied lumber (mostly cut) and lead free, special outdoor clear sealant to protect the pine from the natural elements that was both user and wildlife friendly. I was able to obtain the cement for the foundation and all the nails and metal parts needed to complete my project were donated by the City of Golden.

Uncle Richard cut and carved the remaining lumber with my help.

He also helped me with the design at the top of the gazebo just under the roof.

Uncle Richard carves wood in both small and large pieces, and he had carved and built all the pieces and furniture he had in his old house, the one Dmitry had bought and was killed in. This gazebo would honor

Dmitry and my brothers in Heaven, but I kept that part to myself. *This gazebo would forever hold special memories of John, Simon, and Dmitry...*

I chose to build an octagon gazebo made mostly from knotty pine wood, so it matched the location and blended in exactly right. The aesthetics were important and had to pass the county, the city, and the mountain park area demands.

Rustic black shingles covered the slightly inclined gazebo roof, and I chose a 2 x 2 square railing leaving two of the octagon sides open for entrance. The railing gave a sense of seclusion and was sturdy enough that two knotty pine built-in benches were added.

The posts going up to the roof were also square to match the railing. The addition of carved pieces near the top gave a sense of natural elegance thanks to Uncle Richard.

The built-in pine floor fit the overall design, and the gazebo was built on a durable concrete base. I had enough cement to make one entrance ADA accessible (for those who have disabilities or elderly individuals), the other entrance was one single step up.

Representatives from the county, city, and my scout troop came. Everyone liked the look of the gazebo, and how it blended in. Everyone snacked on Mom's cookies and cold bottled water. She took a lot of pictures. Geesh! *Too many pictures...only Mom does that!*

Overall, when added up, just over 260 hours were spent on my project; surpassing the required 185 hours.

Well done, Danny, well done!" Dad was proud of me just like my mom, and Lisa thought the gazebo would be nice for picnics.

"Thanks, Dad. Your assistance helped me fulfill my plan and idea."

"That old saying...it takes a village...well, Danny, you chose the right people, the right project, and you got it all done. I'm so proud of you." Sarah smiled down at Danny.

"Thank you, Mom. I'm glad you are here to see it." Danny blushed slightly.

"Now when someone needs to get out of falling snow or rain, or just to sit down and relax, they can. Hikers can take breaks." Danny smiled.

"True, Danny. I'm honored to have been of help with your Eagle Scout project." Uncle Richard was all smiles.

When I turned around, I saw Grandpa James and Grandma Alice sitting on one bench inside the gazebo, whispering to each other.

I wonder...they are in love...I don't know anyone who got married in their sixties...they do belong together...I hope they get married...I know they are in love...

Aunt Nancy and baby Dan (he was named after me) came to see the completed project. Aunt Kim and Aunt Suz were working at the art gallery, and Uncle Paul was called in to help someone who had sustained a spinal injury in an accident, so they couldn't make it.

Wow...I just realized how many new words are common for me to use...medical words...dad was a doctor and so was Uncle Paul...mom was a nurse, Aunt Kim has two spinal nerve stimulator wires up her spine to help block out pain impulses to her brain...mom was right at Dmitry's memorial service...I do pick up on many things...my 'perception of things and others'...

Now locals and vacationers can take breaks at this gazebo. Lookout Mountain Park is the burial site of the internationally famous western frontiersman William Frederick "Buffalo Bill" Cody, and is listed on the National Register of Historic Places. Hikers climb a steep trail to the top of Lookout Mountain, and paragliders often use it when paragliding. The historic Boettcher Mansion offers a venue for events. The museum and preserve are cool! Plus, there is a lot more to do and see at the top of Lookout Mountain which is 7,500 feet. The impressive views!

Chapter Ten

*D*mitry was all in on the new identity project. He'd now become Sergey Vegorov. The new identity program was intensive, and Sergey worked hard to become his new persona. In a few more months, Sergey would be on his own, in a new state, a new city, a new job, his first social security number, and with ZERO contact with anyone from his old life. It was hard to watch this process as General Tilson knew his love for Alice was strong, and he knew Sergey had loved Suz just as much. A change is coming. Soon. That General Tilson was sure of.

"Now that was tasty, Alice." James smacked his lips. "Darling, you always outdo yourself cooking." He admired her homestyle cooking.

"No problem at all, James. You know I love to cook." After pouring a glass of wine for each, they went into the large living room area of her cottage behind the Leawood home.

For a stone and log cottage, she had three bedrooms and two baths – the main bedroom with ensuite, a large kitchen and dining area combination, and a large living room with a stone fireplace.

Sadie had the other mother-in-law's/housekeeper type of cottage like Alice's, and they were near each other but set back from the main house.

"What is on your mind this time, James? I know you can't tell me anything to do with work, but you look exceptionally tired. This should be an early night for both of us." She didn't want him to go back to his house in Lakewood.

She needed more, and for that she needed him in her home every single night...

"Things are a bit calmer now. I miss you so much on the nights when I can't come here and be together with you." James leaned over and kissed Alice with a sensuously sweet kiss that made her toes tingle.

"I miss you, too, when those evenings happen. You are taking early retirement at 64, right? In less than a year?" Alice wasn't sure about waiting until James retired as she wasn't exactly getting any younger herself, now at 62.

"True, but this isn't working. I don't like the half-in, half-out lifestyle we live." James smiled at Alice, and she blushed slightly. He never tired of seeing her blush.

"I've been thinking, and I think it's time. I want to be all-in, Alice. It's past time. Alice, will you marry me? Will you marry this old general who has strange hours now and then, but the same general who loves you to the moon and back?" His eyes bore into hers.

"I've been waiting for that question for months, James! You old codger, you! What took you so long? And, no, I'm not upset. You took your sweet time in asking me!" Alice doubled over she was laughing so hard.

James solemnly continued to stare into Alice's eyes. Finally, she realized... she never gave him an answer! "Yes, James. I will marry you on a couple conditions."

"Conditions? What strings do you have in mind?" James was bewildered as Alice was not the kind of woman who would want strings. *What is she up to now?*

"Yes, James. Two strings." Alice kissed him deeply. "But not what you think. I want a small and casual family only wedding near the lake outside the window. Is that a problem?"

"I'll marry you anywhere, Darling. You had me scared there for just a tiny second. Lisa's antics are rubbing off on you." James grinned, then lost his smile just as fast. "What's the other condition/string?"

"Would you be okay with living in this house? I don't want to leave my son and his wife or my grandchildren. You have been Grandpa James to them for a year." Alice peered into James' eyes.

"Hallelujah!" Then James kissed Alice deeply and withdrew a blue velvet jewelers' box from his pocket. He opened the box with the front facing Alice.

"Oh, James, it's perfect!" The yellow diamond sparkled in the firelight.

Gently, he placed the ring on her left ring finger. As if in agreement, they picked up their wine glasses, the wine bottle, and turned the lights off downstairs.

James kissed Alice's body in every spot imaginable and she nipped at him as well; hands gently stroked each other as they knew their love's most sensual places. Age meant nothing to them as they deeply loved one another in full and absolute need for each other. They were so in tune with one another and both cried out when they climaxed, after which they lightly stroked each other's body in absolute serenity in each other's arms.

Surrounded by plush rose and blue bedding, and more pillows than he could count, they finally fell asleep in each other's arms, fully sated from slow and sensual love making that bordered on a hunger neither would let go of. *Making love and sex doesn't stop at 60!*

On the evening of July 13, they repeated their vows with the minister from the Federal Center presiding. They gave each other matching yellow gold bands.

James had a yellow rose boutonniere pinned to his light grey suit jacket (no tuxedos allowed), and Alice held half a dozen yellow roses mixed with greenery and baby's breath that fit in with her tea length, yellow, multi-tiered, and light gauzy dress with matching sandals.

Next to James stood Aaron, who looked dapper in his green polo shirt, jeans, and black boots, while Sadie stood with Alice, in a lightweight ecru gauze dress and matching sandals, the first wedding she'd ever been a part of. Both were happy for the newlyweds.

Sarah wore a sundress in a mauve and pink floral design and sandals, Danny dressed like his dad, Aaron, and Lisa wore a cute pink and blue sundress and sandals.

The Manse family was present, and they all wore lightweight and comfortable summer casual wear, Richard in a polo shirt and shorts, and Nancy in a flowy midi skirt and white blouse, baby Dan wore a big grin on his face – he was now eight months old, and he grinned at anyone, anything, and everything.

Dan loved to scoot around on top of a blanket laid out near the ceremony, before being placed in a bouncer/walker for play time with Lisa taking over the duty of babysitting (her choice).

Not to be outdone, Paul and a very pregnant (seven months with twins) Kim wore a loose beige maternity sundress with flat heeled sandals, and Paul sported a nice button-down shirt and pants.

They had brought Suz with them and she sparkled in her loose but belted sundress in light green. Her red locks, green eyes, and light green dress complimented each other.

Everyone enjoyed a relaxed and catered picnic on the large deck and back lawn. A perfect small, casual, and family wedding. Just like Alice wanted.

Chapter Eleven

*S*ergey Vegorov was in the making! General Tilson was glad that the program was working out for him. Changing one's looks, name, and adding a new social security number used not only in the US but also abroad wasn't enough. The government created a new passport and driver's license for him. His new background included a faked birth certificate, and faked school records.

Sergey diligently used his new identity consciously, he became the updated version of himself through intentional actions, and his transition was easier for him. His new mindset had to be inked in his brain! If not, he would fail, and failing wasn't an option!

He had a limited paper trail, so it was easier to create a new image of a new man - Sergey. With his hair and beard grown out and his eyes changed to blue thanks to contacts, he did look like a new person.

Sergey understood that he would initially pay for most of his needs via cash that the government would set him up with once the new location was chosen.

Later, he would have use of his own money in his Swiss bank account, but his spending would have to match his new lifestyle, he couldn't simply spend some of his oligarch billions of dollars on a new house or new car. That would be a completely new learning curve he'd have to adjust to immediately. *And I will, he thought…he was sure of that!*

The US secretly changed the name on those Swiss Bank accounts to Sergey's new name, and a fake new umbrella corporation. The Swiss banks were happy to provide for both, no questions asked, since it was a military general in DC, not asking, but stating, with deliberate instructions followed to the letter.

Swiss banks understood when certain generals called to make certain arrangements, as they had a passcode and the bank president knew exactly what to do. Not just anyone could do this as Swiss banks were highly protective of their clients. Privacy for their clients was of the highest importance.

The mental preparation was difficult emotionally. All he knew before was unmentionable and he had to figure out five new things to be of interest in his new life, new hobbies, new collectables.

Decisions…the US was leaving no stone unturned…and he was grateful… extremely grateful…now he simply had to produce things that interested him the most…yet five new hobbies were difficult…

Books were a given as in general, most people love to read an informative book. Books provided entertainment and were a type of escapism and respite from dreary moments in life. This one was a given for Sergey, as he's always loved books and this was a basic item most people in the various identity protection programs chose this one first.

Sergey thought about what new things he would like to have around him, to be associated with. He felt like he was failing in this part of his new persona. *Books…that was all that came to mind…he had time to produce more ideas…this part was harder than he'd originally thought…think, Sergey, think!*

Photography! I will learn photography. I will learn to operate a digital camera and when I get a great shot, I will have created my own artwork! *Me? A creative person? Why not? I was a new human being, after all…I could sign my pieces with 'Sergey'…*

The US has an excellent and comprehensive plan for my new persona. Not only had my financial status changed, but the US also looked at social and logistical steps, plus medical!

I had to have my digital footprint and presence minimized, if not erased. Since I wasn't on any social media platforms, nor did I have online subscriptions, that part was simple. No need to delete my presence. No one could track my location or activities.

Every single day I grew into 'Sergey' more, and the staff at the Federal Center used my new name only. Becoming a new person doesn't happen overnight; yet becoming a new person with all previous identity wiped out as much as possible, well, the US knew the tricks to make this happen!

I miss Suz...and the rest...I still had a bit of Dmitry left in me...might always have a bit...but I had to be in the present and prepared for the future...Sergey...

I would have internet service when I reached my new location, and I would use a reputable VPN service the US chose for me, and it would have strong encryption protocols. The US wasn't controlling my life; they were creating a new life just for me. *Sergey... Sergey Vegorov...pleased to meet you...*

I'm fortunate the US is helping me and I'm happy they don't have a ton of work to do on my behalf, since I never had an American footprint with a long paper trail and family and friends all over. *I was an easy case for them, yet they did so much...grateful doesn't express what I feel...tomorrow would be a new day... and more to learn...one day at a time...*

General Tilson came down to talk with me. He couldn't do this every day, but he did make the effort to see me now and then.

"I hear good reports from Agent Jones. He is of the opinion that you are doing exceptionally well, Sergey." General Tilson smiled at his new friend.

"Thank you, Sir." That means more to me than you could ever imagine. "This new life? I want to succeed. I heard you and Alice got married. Congratulations."

"Thank you, Sergey. That's the attitude to stay in, to succeed. Please call me James, now. Do you need anything?"

"I've decided to start photography. I want to learn how to take great pictures with a digital camera. If I can get some nice shots, I could even sell one now and then and write "Sergey" on the bottom. What do you think?"

"That's a fine idea. I'll have Tim arrange for a digital camera and the set up. You can practice using it in here." The General smiled.

Sergey had found another thing to occupy his time and for his new life...a creative endeavor that would give him back his love of art, in a new manner...

"Do you need anything else, Sergey?"

"Other than the camera set up, I have all I need, Sir...James. I'm honored to use your first name. I never saw that one coming!" Sergey laughed, then frowned.

"I just can't get Suz out of my head. I love her and miss her so much. I'm heartbroken. I don't think this pain will ever get better." A single bitter tear ran down Sergey's right cheek and disappeared into his beard.

"I know, Sergey, I know. Have you spoken with Tim about how you feel? I ask as he is a special counselor to those who are creating a new life." *Tim can help Sergey sort out his sad feelings. I hope so.*

"Now that I know he is also a counselor who has helped others like me, I will talk with him. Thank you, James."

"Okay, then. Have a good day and we'll talk again soon." With that General Tilson took his leave. *I wonder...could there be a way? Highly doubtful...impossible even...but...possible...best to mull this one over in his head a while...for the best of all...the safety of all...*

"Everything okay, Kim?" Paul asked out of concern as Kim had a strange look on her face. She'd seemed a bit off that afternoon, and he knew something was up.

"I'm not sure. I just had a contraction. Let's wait and see if another one happens." Kim smiled at her husband, and she tried to not show fear in her features.

"Okay, Babe, I'm yours for the day." He cupped Kim's chin in his hand, and tenderly kissed her.

"Paul, that was another contraction, I think! Call Dr. Harwood so she can check me out. Clinic or hospital; I don't care!" Kim was more worried than she'd let on.

"Dr. Harwood is still at the clinic and wants to see you right away. Careful, Babe, we will go down the elevator and slip inside the Jeep please." Paul was deeply concerned, and he worried for both Kim and their babies.

At the clinic, they were taken directly to an examination room and Dr. Harwood came in immediately.

"Don't worry overmuch, Kim and Paul. I know. Easier said than done. I want to do an exam, and we'll take it from there." Dr. Harwood listened to both babies' heartbeats and did a vaginal exam.

"You are not dilating, Kim. That's good. Now, tell me what you feel when the sensations come to you, cause you to feel like you are in labor."

"It's happening now, Dr. Harwood! It's like my tummy tightens up fast. It's uncomfortable but no real pain. What's happening? I can't lose my babies! It's way too soon!" Kim's tears streamed down her face and Paul held her hand tightly as he silently prayed to God.

"Calm down, Kim. Listen to me. I know what's going on. Everything is going to be okay. It already IS okay." Dr. Harwood was able to get Kim calmed down enough to listen to what she wanted Kim to hear and understand.

"You are NOT in labor, Kim." Dr. Harwood's hand, gently laying on Kim's stomach, had just felt Kim's uterus tighten up. "You feel that, right?"

"Yes, doctor. What's going on?" Kim saw reassurance on her doctor's face, yet she was still worried.

"You are experiencing Braxton-Hick's contractions," Dr Harwood smiled, then added, "they give you a tight and uncomfortable sensation, but they aren't regular or intense like actual contractions. I just felt the tightness of your uterus from your baby bump. They don't last a long time or grow in intensity."

"Can we stop them? What do I do?" Kim was still worried, as she didn't know what to expect but Paul reassured her that Braxton-Hick's contractions were not labor before Dr. Harwood had a chance!

"What he said, Kim. What he said." Then she laughed. "There are a few things that I want you to try. Go home and relax, take a warm bath, and change your position when and if you get another one." Dr. Harwood's face was serene and comforting.

"Change your position each time and they will eventually stop. And, no, Kim, they are not harmful to your unborn babies!" Dr. Harwood gave Kim a wink and grinned.

"I'll run that bath as soon as we get back home, Kim." Paul gave his wife a gentle kiss on her lips and a second one on her tummy followed by a third one on her tummy so both babies received a kiss from daddy.

"Most of the time, a change in position is all you will need, but since this is your first pregnancy, and you are so worried, a relaxing bath is in order." She smiled at Kim. "You can go home now. All is well. Take the next two days off from work. No lifting anything heavier than ten pounds."

Once Kim was secure in a warm, coconut scented bath with bubbles, Paul called the art gallery, then placed his phone on speaker mode.

"The Gallery Loft of Evergreen. This is Suz. Is everything okay, Paul? The phone caller's ID let her know it was Paul.

"Hi Suz! Is Nancy nearby?" Kim wanted to speak with both if she could.

"I'll go get her now." Suz hurried to the office area and told her that Kim and Paul were on the phone.

Picking up the handset from the office phone, Nancy put it on speaker mode. "Hi Kim. Suz and I are in the office. What's on your mind?"

"I saw Dr. Harwood earlier this afternoon and she told me to take the next two days off from work. Will that be a problem for either of you?" Kim didn't want to add additional stress on either woman.

"No problem at all, Kim. What is going on? Your next appointment with Dr. Harwood is in two weeks. Why were you there today?

Nancy was determined to keep her best friend safe, and her two babies inside of her extra safe. Kim had yearned for children for so long, they simply had to be safe.

"In a nutshell, Kim had five Braxton-Hick's contractions. Those are not real labor contractions, but Dr. Harwood told Kim she had to take the next two days off from work." Paul told the women.

"Kim is okay, she simply needs to take it easy for the next two days. Everything is fine. She's in a warm, sudsy bath relaxing now." Paul smiled at his wife. She was radiant and glowing. *Pregnancy suited her to a T!*

"Are you two sure you'll be okay without me," Kim queried her friends. "Before I have these two babies, we need to hire another person to help out at the gallery."

"That's true. I should have thought of that myself, Kim. I'm on it. Suz and I are fine. Let Paul pamper you and leave the rest to us. We've got this!" Nancy laughed and told Kim she loved her.

"I'm positive Paul has the right hands to soothe your every aching need!" Suz snickered, then laughed. *Too funny!*

"What Suz said!!!" Nancy wasn't about to let that pearl go by. Both women laughed hysterically.

"Agreed, Kim! We are fine," Suz added. "Rest up. Goodbye." And they were fine. They worked together like a well-oiled machine.

"It's good to see you, Alice. That's never going to change." James pecked Alice on the lips, then she turned back to finish dinner cooking on the stove.

"I'm glad you are home. I miss you when stay over a bit longer than usual." Alice gave James a hug, then went back to stirring the bubbling pot on the stove.

"Tonight is a simple but creamy ham and potato soup with nice chunks of both ham and potatoes. I made a few slices of garlic bread to go with it." Alice beamed a huge smile at James. She knew this was his favorite soup, which was more like a stew, it was so thick and creamy, and the spices were a perfect complement to the soup.

"Afterwards we can relax with a glass of wine and brush our teeth to get rid of garlic breath." Alice winked at James, then she smirked.

"Or some 'warming lube' for my friable vagina? You know how I like you using that since I'm not on HRT (Hormone Replacement Therapy), James, hmmm?" Alice snuck in a kiss before grabbing two bowls for dinner.

"I know that look! We'll follow that wine and tooth brushing with taking a soapy, slick, sensual, sexy shower together before bed. You love shower sex, too, as I recall." James winked at his wife. Yes, this was living life to the fullest, with the woman of his dreams.

Love at age 64 and 62 (for Alice) was the best! How did I manage to snag her? My woman is off the market! Not that she is a piece of meat or for sale in a store...I best stop thinking and finish my wine...soapy sexy shower...let the night take us where it will...

Chapter Twelve

I would have to look for work and Tim would help me sort out a new work situation. That would be different. I've never held a real job in my entire life. Alarm clocks? That's a new one for me. My life would be vastly different. Once my new location was chosen, then I'd have to search 'help wanted' ads with Tim. Surely, I'd find something to do. At least part time.

Since I have zero possessions now, I didn't have to sell or give anything away. The explosion took care of that. My short paper trail was going to work, I was positive it would with nothing to follow.

Agent Timothy Jones, a dark-haired, dark-eyed, tall, and muscular man, has steadily collaborated with me on 'Sergey,' in creating the new me. He came most days during the week, and on weekends I practiced what I'd learned the prior week.

Tim was kind but he had to impress upon me the necessity of being 'Sergey' and cutting all ties.

When Tim arrived this morning, he carried three shopping bags. "A new wardrobe for you, Sergey. One that fits your new name and position in life."

Sergey looked in each bag. "You brought me jeans, a belt, shirts, a coat and hat, gloves, sleepwear, slippers, underwear, socks, and tennis shoes. That most certainly is a wardrobe change! Thank you, Tim."

"You need these for your new life, and I figured you were tired of wearing the scrubs that the doctor gave you to wear when we destroyed the clothing you had on when you arrived here." Tim lifted clothing out for Sergey to view.

"Plus, you can start wearing these clothes today. That way you are used to them when the time comes. Break in the new tennis shoes. Get into your new persona. Sergey style." Tim knew Sergey would be a success story.

Each person is different in this program. Some are in for a few days to a few weeks; others are in the program for life. Sergey would be a lifer person with government help until he died a natural death.

"After my shower later, I'll do just that. Thank you, Tim. You all think of everything." Sergey was happy that things were working out.

He could turn this into an adventure of sorts...a game of sorts...without Suz...he'd do the absolute best he could...Suz would have wanted that... if she knew...life without Suz is now, and would forever be different until he died... deep, true love...

"James said...I could talk with you. That you counsel people. I just can't get Suz out of my head. I love her and miss her so much. I'm heartbroken and I don't see this sorrow changing anytime soon." A single bitter tear ran down Sergey's right cheek and disappeared into his beard.

"Woah! James? You call him *James*? No way! I must call him General and Sir!" Tim exclaimed, then he thought about what Sergey had spilled forth from his gut.

"I know how much you miss Suz. I can clearly see that she was your soulmate. This is tough on both of you as she thinks you are dead. Time will help ease the pain, so they say. I hope it works out that way for you."

Tim understood how difficult this situation was in going from an oligarch to a regular 'Joe' was hard enough, and losing Suz had made it almost impossible hard on Sergey.

Today Tim and I worked on how my physical departure would work out. The logistics involved when I first stepped out of the Federal

Center and into my new life, I must maintain privacy and leave nothing traceable.

"The plan for you, Sergey, is to leave the Federal Center in a basic but comfortable car, with a NAV system. The car will be dependable, yet not new, around three years old, but it will have all new tires and a special license plate for the state and county that you will be moving to.

The registration documents and insurance will be in your new name. The plan for you is to drive away from the Federal Center during off-peak hours. You must drive on less traveled roads." Tim smiled. *Sergey would succeed...he was a determined man...and one that Tim would miss when he left...*

This part would be easy in my case. I would have several untraceable burner phones to use initially, before buying my own new phone once I was steadily working.

In addition, I would have cash for my needs and food, apartment, and for medical needs. I could only call James, Tim, and those who worked with Tim directly. Those three numbers were the only numbers in my new burner phones. *The US is great at details...they sure had this one figured out...*

Americans with paper trails must do a lot more. They must stay on less used roads (like me) or buy bus tickets with cash to get to their new location.

They must do a lot more work to cover up their paper trail, and sometimes they have people nearby watching out for them in criminal cases. Those people had to remain protected.

They had to make sure no clue of any sort was left behind. Sometimes, they even had to use voice modulators if their voice was distinctive, like James Earl Jones, for instance.

Tim gave me options for my new location. The best place would be somewhere new to me, with no previous connections. Starting fresh enabled me to have less of a chance of being traced back to my old life. Everything made sense.

I want to live somewhere in the mountains for sure...or have mountains close by...Washington State maybe...Idaho? Rustic cabin would be best...Washington

State is too expensive...Idaho it will be, I guess...Twin Falls...a bigger city...but doable...a cabin in the woods...maybe...more likely an apartment or rental home...

"Remember, Sergey, you must create a place that matches your lifestyle preferences and budget, which won't be 'oligarch' style at all. You must start anew with cash and a low budget to work with. I know you can do this."

Sergey would, indeed, as he would make it so while he trained at the Federal Center...Tim would see to that...Sergey had only one month left to go in his training...

"Tim? I want to work with car rental services. That would be the easiest for me to learn. A car rental agency in Twin Falls, Idaho. That's the job that would suit me the best, I think. What do you think?" Sergey hoped that Tim would agree.

"Hmmm...after giving it some thought, I think you are most definitely on track to a job that would make your work situation easier on you. Think about it over the weekend, Sergey."

"I will, Tim. Thank you for your formidable support." Sergey smiled as Tim went out the door.

"I'll be back on Monday, Sergey. Practice what you have learned this week, take breaks, read, watch television, eat dinner with your guard, and relax. Practice being relaxed all the time. And think about car rental services and Twin Falls."

After Tim left, I realized my time for leaving the Federal Center was coming up much faster than I'd realized. Nervous? *A bit... Relaxed? Not quite...Excited? A little...Scared? No...Practice, Sergey, practice...you can do this...you will succeed...do it for Suz...make her proud of you even though she'll never know...*

Nancy created a sign on a piece of vintage card stock and used her talent in the art of calligraphy to create a 'help wanted' type of sign. Instead of placing it in the window, she kept it near the cash register.

That way, she could briefly speak with customers and potential new help when they bought art pieces.

The day arrived for the Baden-Powell banquet for me and other new Eagle Scouts from my area. Baden-Powell had founded scouting. Mom, Dad, Lisa, Grandma Alice, and Grandpa James were present. When the moment came, I was ready to accept my new Eagle Scout trophy and gold card. *I did it!!!*

The final details worked out and Danny's Eagle Scout Court of Honor was coming up fast. I flip-flopped between being nervous and happy. Proud to have accomplished this feat!

Mom, Dad, and Lisa were proud of me. I wish Simon were at my side. Dmitry would have been proud of me. All my family would be present. Mom ironed my scouting shirt and neckerchief in preparation for my big day.

Kim and Paul had a busy day. He had back-to-back appointments all day in the hospital, plus his in-patients to see.

Kim was actively searching for a new person to join the staff at The Art Gallery of Evergreen.

"I can't get anything done, Nancy. Every time I turn around, I must tinkle in the bathroom. My breathing is easier now so that is a plus." Kim stretched her back and before she could seat herself in her chair Nancy was right there!

"Stay standing, I want to see your profile and baby bump. Nancy's orders girlfriend!" Nancy smirked at Kim and then took a good look from all angles.

"The babies have dropped, Kim. This is normal, but I want to drive you over to Dr. Harwood's so she can check you out. You're not in labor, but…you should be seen, I think."

"I'll call and let them know you're coming," Suz told her besties. "I'm fine at the gallery since Richard is in the back, he can help in the main showroom."

Suz called and let Dr. Harwood know that Kim was coming in and she let Richard know that she was working the front alone. Richard came out of the back room each time the door chimed, alerting them to a new customer.

"Good afternoon, Kim, and Nancy. I see you have dropped, Kim. I must do an exam, so we know what is going on with you babies. Don't worry. You are fine." Dr. Harwood spoke in a soothing voice.

Once in the exam room, Kim slipped on a gown and with help, she got up on the exam table. Dr. Harwood took Kim's blood pressure first. "If you should develop unusual puffiness in your face, hands or feet, you must call me or go to the emergency room."

"What is that? What does that mean?" Kim looked at Dr. Harwood, fear in her eyes.

"Mothers carrying multiples are at a higher risk for pre-eclampsia. I must know if you start to gain more than two pounds in a week or one pound in a day. Multiples usually make their presence known at 36 weeks. You're at 37 weeks now which means the babies are putting on weight and gaining some fat to help fill out their little bodies. Their lungs are ready for life outside the womb." She smiled at Kim and saw her relaxation when she realized that her babies were safe and already considered ready to be born.

"Kim, you are fine, but you need to hear this. If you get severe headaches, dizziness, or puffiness, I must see you. Pre-eclampsia is a special kind of high blood pressure that can happen in this stage of pregnancy, more often with multiple births. I'm going to do the exam now." Dr. Harwood smiled at both women.

"Your cervix is fine; you are NOT dilating. Please lift your shirt up so I can do an ultrasound." Dr. Harwood ran the gel and transducer around and, yes, one of the twins was headfirst, with head engaged, just waiting to be born.

"Both babies are fine. One twin is in position head down." She smiled at Kim. "You'll be a mama soon, within a week. I highly doubt you will make it to September 12 – your due date. Your labor could start any day now."

"What should I do?" Kim wanted Dr. Harwood to repeat what to expect at this stage of her pregnancy. Kim knew what to expect, but it was the reassurance that she needed.

"The babies are growing, and they are healthy. As I said before, they will be smaller when born since it is a multiple birth. That is normal." She smiled at Kim again as she cleaned the ultrasound gel from her patient's tummy.

"I want you to stop working as of right now. Limit your activities and get plenty of rest. Elevate your legs and have that handsome husband of yours pamper you! I'm not putting you on bedrest but no heavy lifting and take it easy."

"That's excellent news. I'll be stuck on you like the stickiest glue, Kim, if you don't follow orders. That means I'll be in and out of the gallery and to your home every single day checking up on you." Nancy smirked.

"No chasing 'Nurse Nancy' off!" Then Nancy pealed out in contagious laughter and Kim and Dr. Harwood joined in.

"Now is a suitable time to stop driving, too. Your husband and friends can help you out with that. Continue with your social activities like dining together in a restaurant or at your friends' homes. Life does go on, just take it a lot easier."

"I understand, Dr. Harwood. Since I can go out to eat, does this mean I can attend my nephews Eagle Scout Court of Honor? I would be mostly relaxing during the event, sitting for the majority, with my 'glue' next to me!" Kim rolled her eyes at Nancy.

"You sure can, Kim. No problem. You are good to go home now." Dr. Harwood reassured Kim once again.

"I don't know, Kim. That event is a 'scout' thing, and you know what happened at the last 'scout' event we attended. My water broke, and I went into labor at once at the Pinewood Derby event, and all those people and scouts saw my water had broken!" Nancy giggled, reliving the moment and the birth of baby Dan, now nine months old.

"That won't happen with me. I know my babies will come early, but I would never dream of allowing my water to break during Danny's Court of Honor! So there!" She gave Nancy the evil eye look.

Kim was determined that her babies would stay inside of her as long as possible as she adjusted the maternity pants she'd just stepped into and pulled them up with assistance from Dr. Harwood.

"Okay, ladies." Dr. Harwood grinned as she remembered what had happened when Nancy went into labor. "Go home!"

Chapter Thirteen

Today is my court of Honor and I'm nervous. It's one thing to collaborate with other scouts, work on badges, my Eagle Scout project, and the unveiling. Even my project essay was scary to write up and then my Eagle Scout review by the 'higher ups' in my scout council was scary to do; but it was done, and I did qualify to be an Eagle Scout, I became an Eagle Scout right after my Eagle Scout review by the 'higher ups'!!! Just like that! I'm an Eagle Scout!!! Today a bazillion gazillion people would be in attendance. On top of that, my church knew about my Court of Honor as an event room at church was rented for the event. I'm doomed...DOOMED!!! I'm not a speech person...I'm so doomed...I can't talk in front of people...

I dressed in my tan scout uniform shirt with all the required parts, such as rank and required patches, sewed to my shirt. Mom has stitched every emblem on each shirt as I've grown up. She even saved my old cub scout shirt and everything!

My scout sash and all the badges I earned were in place diagonally and my scout neckerchief was in place and held together with a scout slide. I added new denim jeans, my scout belt and black hiking boots. *I'm going to fail or succeed entirely today...hopefully I swim...*

Mom did so much work, behind my back, to get to today, things I didn't know about until I started to receive postal mail every single day. Jaw dropping mail. Mom caused this to happen!

She'd found time to notify many hundreds of people about my Eagle Scout Status. She mailed out who knows how many letters on my behalf! I was honored, yet nervous, but happy...yet I was afraid to ask her who she sent letters to...

Congratulation letters signed by the current US president, all past living presidents, the vice president, other state and national figures and officials, and signed letters of congratulations from every single state except for Florida. Florida sent me a letter stating that the governor only signs congratulation letters for Florida scouts. *They wasted postage on that one!*

Mom sent out letters to other famous people, too, including the Pope! Our bishop sent a congratulation letter, and others such as Jay Leno. Jay Leno supports all scouts. *His letter was fun to read. He's also really into cars of all kinds. He's a 'gear head' and I felt like I was, too. Cars and all vehicles catch my eye.*

Mom found a list of suggested people to send letters to from the boy scout website. They included famous people who supported scouts and scouting, and she must have gone bonkers doing all of this, mailing out notices of my achievement while working as a busy ER nurse and being a mom and a wife!

Each letter and card were slid into a plastic sleeve and then into a white four-inch binder. That binder was full of signed letters and cards. Unbelievable!

Two large tables covered in white cloth and decorated in yellow and blue streamers and balloons were laid out just for showing my awards and mementos since a little cub scout.

I placed my opened binder of letters and cards, trophies, awards, pinewood derby cars, sailing regatta ships, and all my personal mementos I'd kept throughout the years.

My collection from my scout jamboree in DC required a lot of space. I was meticulous and nervous about how the arrangement looked.

In special honor, I placed my Eagle Scout trophy and the associated pictures of events from the dinner.

Mom ordered from the grocery store fruit, vegetables, cheese, crackers, and dips as no one had time to make the platters and she ordered a large sheet cake covered in white frosting and then blue and yellow for decorations and the words. Sadie made me a smaller, special cake for me to cut later when we were back home.

The food was placed on another large table with paper plates and plastic cutlery. Iced tea, coffee, and various sodas with plastic cups and ice were at the far end.

The last Sunday in August; soon to be 2pm, and more people arrived and sat in chairs at the round white tables in the large open space. Our priest came! My friends' mom, who is a newspaper publisher, came! Too many things were tossing around in my brain. *Brain overload! And I was still doomed...*

"You are cordially invited..." yes, Mom sent out the announcements to everyone. Would we even have enough snacks? *Before I knew it, my Court of Honor was about to begin....*

Of course, our entire Leawood family, Grandpa James, Grandma Alice, and Grandma Sadie sat together. Grandpa and Grandma hugged with a quick kiss before they sat down.

I wasn't sure if I should be embarrassed or not! PDA with two people in their sixties? At home, it is not important. But here? Nobody paid much attention to them.

Aunt Kim and Uncle Paul held hands and sat together at the next table over, and Aunt Nancy, Uncle Richard, and baby Dan sat at the same table. They'd brought Aunt Suz along and she played with little Dan.

Aunt Suz looked sad off and on...she misses Dmitry...we all do...I wished he'd lived, but I was happy that we all got to know him in separate ways...

It looked like a lot of people from town, relatives, and scouts from my troop were here today.

Before I knew it, my Court of Honor began...

My scoutmaster began the ceremony by greeting everyone present, and that was followed by an Opening Flag Ceremony that other scouts in my den provided. The same ceremony when we started any regular den meeting. *So far, so good...*

All the scouts recited the Scout Pledge followed by my den master giving a short presentation on the highs and lows in my path to becoming an Eagle Scout. Some of what he said made everyone laugh. *That helped my nerves...some was embarrassing...but people laughed...*

Did you know that only four percent of all Boy Scouts earn the rank of Eagle Scout? My den leader told all of us this fact! He also said it amounted to 0.522% of the entire US male population! My scoutmaster had all the numbers and the details. Wow! I had no idea!

Lisa's mouth opened from where she sat, and she was amazed. Her mouth didn't close for a bit as she intently listened. It was funny but I couldn't laugh. She finally understood a lot of my path to get to today. I had to laugh inside myself, and that was hard!

My scoutmaster then called me up front and he presented me with my Eagle Scout Badge and Pin, and we shook hands, scout style. Then he asked me to turn around and face those in attendance, and everyone clapped their hands. *I was happy and embarrassed...*

Mom and Dad were asked to come to the front by my scout master, and I pinned each of them with the special pins for moms and dads of new Eagle Scouts. Then another scout escorted them back to their seats. Respect and decorum all the way through so far.

Decorum...great word...but I'm losing mine fast! Oh boy...here it comes...I'm doomed...the dread...I can't do this...yet I have no choice...I chose this path, and I would get through it one way or another...Jesus, help guide me in what I should say. Amen.

It was time for me to make a short speech about scouting and what it has done for me, the benefits of scouting, and the experiences I had during all my years of scouting.

By the time I was done, the younger scouts were in awe of me. *For real!!* I didn't see that one coming!!! I think I might have impressed them and they will work hard and become Eagle Scouts, too. *That would be so cool and impressive!*

Oh no!!! Did Aunt Kim 'tinkle' on the floor? She had to go to the bathroom all the time now...that's embarrassing...wait...what? No...no way...not again!!! Aunt Kim just had to do what Aunt Nancy did during my last Pinewood Derby...and I was prepared to help her get inside her Jeep...those twins would be born one week early... mom had told me twins usually arrived a bit earlier...I had to help Aunt Kim...

"Paul. My water just broke." Kim whispered to her husband with flaming red cheeks.

"No problem, Babe. I'll bring the Jeep around to the door, then I'll come back inside and help you get out of here and into the Jeep. Okay?" Paul knew they would have their babies soon. *Soon!*

"What's going on?" Nancy asked quietly. "Never mind, I see it on the floor. You just had to do what I did, didn't you, Kim? All the attention on you, right?" She giggled and winked at Kim and remained sitting beside her best friend as Paul left to bring the Jeep around to the door.

Uncle Paul came back inside, and I walked over to them. "I'm going to help you get into your Jeep, Aunt Kim. My scout speech is done so you had perfect timing. Uncle Paul and I will both help you out the door and into your SUV. Don't be embarrassed. Mom said that to Aunt Nancy when her water broke." All would be okay. *Jesus would make it so…*

I wanted to console her and make sure she knew that an Eagle Scout was helping, just like I helped Aunt Nancy when her water broke, and baby Dan was born.

Halfway to the door, Aunt Kim screamed out and doubled over, having a hard labor pain.

Oh boy. Everyone knows now!!! My new cousins were about to make a grand entry! Mom and Dad only smiled when they saw what was happening. Our priest was about to say a closing prayer after my speech, but he nodded his head at me and waited until I was back inside to continue with my Court of Honor.

Our priest did a closing prayer which was then followed by a Closing Flag Ceremony. Afterwards, everyone filled up their plates and snacked and chatted.

The reception was nice. It was fun to talk with everyone and when it ended, mom and dad helped me pack up all my awards and scouting memorabilia and I helped them with leftover food and drink.

Earlier in the reception, Aunt Nancy and I had cleaned up the area where Aunt Kim's water had broken, so no one would accidentally slip and fall.

Once the tables were cleaned, the candles blown out, the floor swept, and trash removed and discarded in a dumpster, we got to go home. *What a day! Looking back, I realized it was a momentous day, and my nervousness, well…part of growing up, I guess…*

Paul and Kim were not at the hospital all that long before the twins were born. Between contractions, Kim changed into a gown with Paul's help. She lay down on the birth bed and Paul snatched a quick kiss and whispered, "You got this, Babe."

One nurse barely got an IV inserted when Kim yelled again. Another nurse placed telemetry pads on Kim and took her vital signs. Dr. Harwood came through the door, and she performed a vaginal exam.

"You are fully dilated, Kim. It's time for Mom and Dad to meet their babies. When the next pain comes, I want you to push, Kim. Push hard!" Kim nodded in understanding.

With the next contraction, Kim pushed as hard as she could, and the baby's head crowned. "One more hard push with the next contraction and a baby you will have!" Dr. Harwood loved this part of being an obstetrician. It never got old, at all.

"Okay, Kim, now push as hard as you can!" Lily Kymber was born first at 5:02PM and Paul cut the umbilical cord. Lily gave out a lusty cry and was handed over to a nurse who did a quick APGAR score to evaluate the newborn's health.

The nurse then placed the tiny baby girl on Kim's chest, skin-to-skin, a warm blanket over both. The nurse kept one gloved hand holding the little bundle, so she didn't slide off Kim's chest.

"Hello there," Kim spoke to Lily, amazed at what she saw. *I finally have a baby!!!* "We have a baby, Paul!" *Thank you, Jesus. All glory and praise to You!*

Paul smiled down at Kim and Lily, the two most beautiful people in the world. He marveled at Lily, tiny yet healthy. Her little fist held onto his finger.

"Stop admiring and counting fingers, baby boy is crowning now. Push hard with the next contraction." Dr. Harwood instructed Kim.

The nurse took Lily to a neonatal bed with a warmer and another nurse joined in cleaning up their baby girl, checking her five-minute APGAR score, weighing, measuring, adding matching hospital bracelets, and creating baby footprints for the new parents.

"Just one more push, Kim. Now. Push hard!" and then Jonathan Paul presented himself to the world at 5:13PM.

Paul cut his cord, too, and another nurse took their baby boy and did a quick APGAR score, before placing him on Kim's chest. *Three most beautiful people in the world...*

Kim and Paul were elated! Jonathan was taken to another neonatal bed with a warmer and a fourth nurse joined to clean the tiny baby boy, do the second APGAR score, weighing, measuring, and creating more baby footprints.

Both babies' APGAR scores were seven. That was a normal number for babies. In the end, Lily Kymber, and Jonathan Paul both came in at 17 ½ inches long, with Lily weighing five pounds and two ounces, and Jonathan weighed five pounds and one ounce. Each had vivid blue eyes and a slight smattering of blondish – brown hair.

Kim and Paul were both over the moon. Now Paul was on official family leave from the hospital for the next 12 weeks.

They happily called friends and family later that evening with their joyous news. Two days later, all four of them went home as a new and complete family.

The new family of four had their first week as a family to themselves, as planned prior to the babies' birth...no visitors...

Chapter Fourteen

*M*onday came around and I knew it would be an intense day. Tim would surely inform me of what was left for me to learn. Then we'd look at the map and finally choose my new location...my new Sergey home...I would miss, Tim...and James...and Suz...all of them...especially Suz...my love...my heart broken and shattered...my love for Suz only deepened each day...the chasm of not having Suz in my life engulfed me...yet my love for her...never wavered...

James knocked on my door before Tim arrived. I invited him inside and offered coffee which he accepted. We sat down in the kitchen to talk. *Soon, I would no longer have these conversations with James...and I was already missing that...*

"How are you doing, Sergey?" Concern was written all over James' face. *He's here as my friend right now...I can tell as plain as day...he is visiting a friend...I'm honored...and saddened...*

"I'm doing okay. I know I'm well prepared for my new life. You and Tim will be only a phone call away if I need anything. And Tim also told me that others on his team are also only a phone call away. So, I'm safe. Tim said there has been no 'chatter' about me these last two plus months." Sergey smiled.

"But I'm still sad at losing all of you as friends, and then I'm overwhelmingly heartbroken without Suz...the true love of my life. I never knew that kind of love existed, until Suz."

James let out a long sigh, "I know, Sergey, I know. I can't fix that situation, but on the other hand, I can give you updates on your friends. Danny had his Eagle Scout Court of Honor yesterday afternoon."

"I knew he'd be an Eagle Scout. You must be proud of your grandson. I would be if I was his grandpa. As Sergey, I am proud of him." And Sergey was proud of Danny. He'd liked that young teenager when he first met him.

"Kim went into labor one week early with twins! It started near the end of Danny's Court of Honor yesterday afternoon." James smiled at the memory.

"Happy news! Are they okay?" Sergey was anxious. Twins could be very tiny and need medical help.

"Yes, they are. They will all be home in no time." James added.

"Tim is right, there has been zero 'chatter' about you at all. I honestly don't think anyone is actively searching for you. Think about it, Sergey.

"You never knew actual intelligence, no one received the intelligence since we intercepted both computer microchips, and you only know what is available on the internet and official websites. You don't know the assassins, and you never did." James peered at Sergey, as his mind was going over the facts.

"You gave us their motive and the power-hungry oligarchs who want the top spot. Those things that their billions of dollars can't buy outright, only through covert and corrupt means. That's not top-secret news. Russia has been operating like that for decades."

Tim knocked on the door and was welcomed inside. "Good morning, General, Sergey," followed by a salute to his general.

"Good morning, Agent Jones. I'll leave you to it with Sergey." James' return saluted his agent, and with that, James left. He had an idea in his head, and he had to find out if it would work out. *Lives were riding on this issue...and two more lives were added yesterday to compound his idea...*

"Okay, Sergey. Today you will practice your voice modulation, learn more American Slang, and a few other pointers so you are safe when you drive to your new home." Tim smiled.

"Most of this you know or figured out already, if not, it doesn't hurt to repeat anything. Your new home – that must be decided on this week."

"Twin Falls, Idaho. That's where I want to go."

"Great. I'll let the staff know this now." Once he'd spoken with the staff, Tim turned back to Sergey.

"The final details for your new persona such as driver's license can be finalized once they find an apartment for you. Normally, I tell those in our program that towns with lower population densities or small towns are best, and that is especially true for those in witness protection.

"In your case, you aren't as restricted. There has been zero chatter about you. No one has even looked at where your house once stood. We have a special camera sensor that sends out an alert when anything is near your old home's debris, and so far, the techs have only seen elk and other wildlife that set off the sensors."

Tim's mobile phone rang, and he answered. "Great news! I'll tell Sergey."

"You will have a house and not an apartment. Upon arrival, you will go to the rental house that was just set up for you. Your landlord lives in the red brick house on the right of your yellow brick house. Introduce yourself to your landlord, get your keys, first month's rent and deposit are already paid, and the house is furnished. You will receive a packet containing all this information to take with you.

"Act natural, be Sergey, adopt a low-profile type of lifestyle. In your case, simply be the nice gentleman you've always been, but don't do anything to draw attention to yourself. This keeps your new identity secure.

"Again, you have oligarch money, but your lifestyle will be down low. No lavish spending or anything that could make you stand out in your new community. Be kind, act normally, and blend in with the community in a low-key manner.

"No social media, Sergey. None."

"Tim, you forgot that I told you I've never had a single social media account. I used computers for research, viewing paintings and email." Sergey laughed. *That would not be a problem, at all.*

"You will have a computer and internet service, and we will set you up with an email account before you leave here. Integrate into your new neighborhood slowly, and don't reveal too much.

"Not that you can, really, since you are a new person without much of a paper trail, but you can't describe your prior years in much detail.

"The other side of that is you cannot become a hermit and isolate yourself. Try to get a sense of belonging in your new neighborhood. You love books, the local library is nice, and you will meet like-minded people there.

"Also, find a community activity or group activity to join. Twin Falls has an amateur photography group, and you have been practicing the usage of your new camera, so..."

"That sounds perfect, Tim! I'm happy about that. I know I will learn at my own pace like the other's and each time we meet, I will get to know more people." Sergey had a real smile on his face for the first time. *A library, a camera, and an amateur photography group...who knew?*

Tim was thrilled to see Sergey have true happiness for the moment. Life had flipped on him, and he was finally interested in what his future held. *A simple life for an exceptional man.*

"Sergey, you will start your new job the second week you are there. You must always maintain your new identity. Keep practicing your new signature. Keep your identity as your persona is now. Your mail will arrive at a local PO Box to maintain your anonymity.

"Keep private yet a bit open to others. Be open, yet 'bookish,' private, yet laugh when others laugh in the photography group or at work.

"Neighbors will associate you with books if you sit on your front porch and read. Smile and say hello, good morning, etc. as they walk past your house.

"It will be stressful, but you have resources to call when needed. Remember, one of us will always be on call from my team, and we treat mental health just as important as physical health.

"I'll be back on Wednesday, Sergey. Practice your signature and your handwriting in general."

"Thank you for all you have done for me, Tim. See you Wednesday."

"It's been a week, Nancy. What if we check to see when we can stop by and visit Kim and the family?" Richard was excited to meet his new niece and nephew.

"I love the way you think!" Smiling, she texted Kim and patiently waited for a reply as she hung up a new watercolor Suz had painted – a serene landscape with two toddlers, a boy and a girl, playing in wildflowers with butterflies, on the west gallery wall.

Suz walked up and placed a card on it that read, 'For Show Only' and 'Not for Sale.' This one was a surprise gift for Kim and her family.

Nancy's phone beeped, alerting her that she had received a text message. *Yes!* Right after the art gallery *'closed'* today and *'bring Suz,'* too. Nancy was going to get her new *'baby smells'* in today!

"At closing time, Richard. We are to bring you, too, Suz!" Nancy smiled at both, patted Richard on his right cheek, then went and peeked in at Dan, sleeping in his playpen in the backroom.

Now nine months old, he was good for getting into anything and everything, he was a fast crawler, he stood up holding onto furniture every chance he had and would be an early walker.

With the gallery locked up tight for the day, the quaking aspens were just starting to turn golden for autumn. It was early September after all, and Richard drove all four of them to the home of their friends, less than three miles away.

Catching sight of Richard as he pulled into the driveway, Paul opened the front door in a warm, welcoming manner and he sported a huge grin on his face. Nancy held Dan as they met Paul at the front door.

"Come in and have a seat in the living room. Kim, Lily, and Jon are in there." Paul welcomed his friends. *God has so blessed me...with Kim, both babies, a happy life...and wonderful extended family...thank you, Jesus!*

Kim was seated on a leather sectional with her feet up. Lily and Jon were asleep beside her nestled in their twin bassinets.

Immediately, Nancy took first peeks at her new niece and nephew sleeping contentedly. *Wait...what? One week old and Lily was smiling in her sleep!*

"Sure, Kim," Nancy whispered. "Lily already smiles while sleeping. Only you would have contented twins." The two women hugged each other, then brought Suz into their hug.

"Remember, Suz, family isn't always blood; family are those people who you can be related to and those you are not. Everyone in this room is family. You have a new niece and nephew." Kim smiled at Suz, happy to see some color in her cheeks, since Dmitry had passed away.

"Besides, you are the best aunt for babysitter duty." Nancy replied to Kim and Suz with a smirk. "You are so good with Dan, and he adores you."

Richard peeked at the twins, and he smiled. "You have two little 'bundles of trouble' when they get older, 'old man'."

"No, you are wrong." Paul replied. "They are both 'bundles of trouble' already. Twins are challenging work."

Baby Jon started to cry, and Kim gently picked him up. After checking his diaper, she grabbed a new disposable diaper from the baby bag near her feet and baby wipes.

She was almost done with Jon when Lily started crying. "This is not contentment. Paul, please make two bottles of formula."

Nancy took Jon from Kim, and then Kim picked up her daughter. Lily needed a diaper change, too.

Richard brought two lukewarm bottles back with him, and Kim took one for Lily. Nancy held her hand out for the other bottle. Side by side they fed the twins just over one ounce of formula, then burped them.

"With 'double trouble' nursing just wasn't for me. They both received my colostrum (the first nutrient-dense milk from a new mother's breast and high in antibodies and antioxidants); then straight to powdered formula before we left the hospital." Kim looked at Nancy to gauge her reaction.

"What? I'm certain that I fed Jon correctly and burped him. Oh... no, Kim. I'm not judging you at all. Just because I nursed Dan, doesn't mean that my way was the only right way." She handed Jon to Suz' waiting arms.

"Your twins are contented, and they are filling out. Your babies are thriving, and Paul gets to share the feeding duty with you, which is special. Richard didn't have that initially, until I started pumping."

"True, she is indeed. But I did watch." Richard snickered, raised one eyebrow, then laughed. "Dan's too young to hear this." And they all laughed.

"Your brain is always in the gutter, Richard! Baby Dan will hear about this when he's older! Men have no shame whatsoever! Were you two born in the gutter?" Kim laughed, and then all laughed hysterically. *True statement...*

Paul brought cold, bottled water into the room, and everyone grabbed one. The visit was perfect, and Kim was updated on the gallery news. "I'm still looking for the right person to help out." She felt it in her bones that the right person would pop in soon.

They only stayed for just over an hour before heading home. A perfect family centered visit.

Everyone had received happy endings, except me...the Leawood Family, the Manse Family, the Smith Family...James and Alice...but Suz...she did not...I want my happy ending, too...no happy ending for Dmitry...and not for me...Suz finally fell asleep...exhausted from missing the smartest man she knew...the love of her life...

Chapter Fifteen

*J*ames wanted his idea to work out. Special consideration was of the utmost importance. General Ness would arrive at the Federal Center early this morning to help with a new plan or keep the current plan in place. Tim didn't know yet, but he would soon enough. Maybe…it could work out…if rules were followed to the letter…especially with the children…most especially the children…

Cheri buzzed his office to let him know General Ness had arrived.

"Thank you, Cheri. Please bring in two cups of coffee, thanks." He stood up and General Jack Ness walked into his office. Both saluted each other and then sat down.

A knock at the door, and Cheri was right on time, bringing in two cups of hot coffee. "Thank you, Cheri." Cheri was a godsend for him. Not the coffee, although that was always nice.

Cheri tackled any task and she made it look easy, even when it was strong. She knew how to keep top secret things top secret. She was tough. Small and tiny stature, she could win against any man.

"Anytime, General." Cheri quickly left the office so the men could get down to business.

"It's good to see you, Jack. How is DC?" James was curious if anything new had sprung up regarding the rogue oligarchs.

"No chatter; continued silence. I honestly don't think anyone cared about or was looking for Sergey (Dmitry). I seriously doubt he was ever of real concern to them, as he never knew actual intelligence to begin with. What are your thoughts?" Jack queried.

"All Sergey knew was to find the chips, if possible, and get them sent to Russia. One chip was found here, in a frame in Evergreen. That chip detailed NORAD with more intelligence than either of us knew. Those oligarchs took a hard blow on not obtaining that chip! Their loss.

"The second chip was caught by Scotland Yard when the spy was reframing a specific piece of art that was to be bought by a specific oligarch. We have that chip. They failed in obtaining intelligence on the Federal Center. Their loss, again.

"Sergey knew of no intelligence on either chip. We both looked them over carefully.

"No third and final chip was created as the baggage handler who'd infiltrated DEN was caught before he could obtain anything." James questioned Jack with his eyes.

The rogue oligarchs failed a third time…all three goals failed…a total perfect failure…their plan foiled…

"Sergey never knew real intelligence, only the facts on the internet, our websites, plus the DEN website, but no real intelligence. Sergey certainly gave us a lot of intelligence on the suspicions and theories the oligarchs believed in. He gave us entertainment and laughs, for sure.

"Life is highly significant, but for the rogue oligarchs, Sergey was, and is, insignificant. Back to you, James." Jack replied with a smirk.

"Essentially, Sergey was a 'go-between' of sorts. No one benefitted from Sergey. At this point, I'm 100% certain that they have more important things to fight over in gaining power. I do know, and believe, that Sergey felt he was in danger when he arrived here at the Federal Center unexpectedly."

"He was frightened, that was obvious, James. The assassins were real in Boston, and in Colorado. But their agenda was revenge at losing their top two spies in a motor vehicle accident as they chased Kim. With zero intelligence to buy, those rogue oligarchs are fighting for position and power in Russia." Jack took a long sip of his coffee.

"The war with Ukraine doesn't help, and I believe they are also looking at the race for President of the United States." James sighed. "This is a delicate situation, but only for the affected people here."

"Agreed," Jack responded. "That said, it's past time to take care of the real estate Sergey owned, and the house remains need to be taken care of. Or has that been done, James?" Jack lifted one eyebrow.

"I had agents dressed as City of Genesee employees, and they helped the city clean up the debris, nothing of importance found in the ashes, all nicely worked out with the city administrator, and a bonus for the workers.

"It's all open space park now with no plan to change, ever. The open space now belongs to the City of Genesee, as the land was donated, and animals and walkers/hikers have free use."

"Fantastic! That is great to hear." Jack grinned. "Yes, we do make a pretty good team, indeed." Both men chuckled.

"As you know, Tim has been working with Sergey. He understands the reasons behind his new persona and that he needs to follow them. His deep depression over the loss of his friends and Suz are still in the acute stage.

"Tim has reported to me, that he also feels like we do, that Sergey was not, and is not now a true risk to the Russians. The deep love he had, and has, for Suz all but consumes him. But Dmitry can't be resurrected." James sighed.

"One more cup of coffee, Jack?"

"Of course, you know I was on a military transport flying to Denver overnight. Jet lag on those planes suck."

James buzzed Cheri at her desk. "Cheri, could you please bring in two more cups of coffee, thanks."

Cheri immediately knocked on the door, then came in with two large cups of coffee, "Is this fast enough, Sir?"

"Thank you, Cheri. You read my mind. I don't know how things would get done around here if you weren't on top of everything. You are a gem."

"Thank you, Sir," and she quietly left the office and closed the door behind her.

He never treated her like a 'coffee girl' or anything demeaning. He was kind and he, and she, knew her value to him, a true asset. She kept on top of things. Everything remained private. She was a tiny person, but she was capable of anything that needed doing. Too bad some workplaces were not the same. That was a shame. Little people are people, too. We have feelings, too. She knew she was blessed in the position she held.

After school today, we took Danny and Lisa, and Alice and Sadie up the mountain canyon to meet their new baby cousins. The children were excited.

"Do you think I can hold one of the twins, Mom?" Lisa wanted to hold a tiny baby so bad.

"We can ask, Lisa." Sarah laughed with her husband, Aaron.

"Uncle Paul and Aunt Kim will tell us what we can do, Lisa. Ask nicely and accept their answer. They are Lily and Jon's mom and dad, so they are the boss." Danny informed Lisa.

"I hope I get to, for a little bit." Lisa was all smiles and full of hope. The temperature had dropped a bit by the time they reached Evergreen, a breezy 44 F. They all wore light jackets and reached the condominium safely.

Paul answered the door and welcomed everyone inside. They hung up their jackets on the wooden coat rack in the hall and Paul whispered that the babies were asleep and to be quiet.

"I want a hug," Aunt Kim told the children. They complied, and then she hugged Sarah and Aaron.

"Come meet Lily and Jon, your new cousins, only two weeks old." The twins were sleeping side by side in their bassinets.

"Wow," Lisa whispered. "They are tiny."

Danny peeked at both, then he smiled and gave Kim another hug. "The twins look happy, Aunt Kim. I'm so happy for you and Uncle Paul."

"Please sit down. Paul is bringing out hot chocolate and a meat and cheese tray with crackers." The large leather sectional and multiple matching chairs seated everyone.

Kim was telling Sarah how much the twins weighed now when Lily began to cry. She picked her daughter up, checked her diaper, and made fast work of changing her. Before she finished, Lily was crying full-on.

"Here, Babe," Paul handed Kim a warm bottle of formula as he placed a second bottle on the table. Lily greedily sucked at her food.

"And that new cry would be Jon. When one gets hungry, the other one is not far behind. Who needs sleep? I mean, sleep is highly overrated in our home." Jon was in his arms just as fast as his daddy could pick him up.

"Daddy has diaper duty this time." Kim laughed at her husband.

Paul did his diaper duty perfectly and then started feeding Jon. Two weeks old and both mom and dad were pros at diapers and bottles.

"Both are filling out nicely." Sarah was happy to see the babies thriving so well. "You two make the cutest boy and girl babies."

"I think they resemble Kim more than me," Paul laughed, and Aaron joined in.

"Because you aren't 'cute,' Paul. So, they must take after Kim!" Everyone laughed at that comment.

Alice and Sadie simply soaked up all the love and family time. Both their faces wore contented, happy smiles.

Soon Lily burped and was a happy baby again. Lisa had closely watched Aunt Kim with Lily, looking at how she held her, how she was gentle, how she supported Lily's head, and sure of each part of her daughter's care.

"Aunt Kim, may I hold Lily, please?" Lisa softly asked.

"Come sit next to me, Lisa. I'm going to carefully put Lily in your lap, hold her head like I position her, and snuggle together. Lily loves cuddles. Keep her head supported." Kim glowed when she smiled at Lisa being a little mommy.

Danny held Jon's hand as Paul burped him. Before he knew it, he was holding Jon. Danny kept on smiling at Jon, playing with his little hand, and thinking that Uncle Paul trusted him to do what Lisa had just been taught.

At 14, Danny had grown into a wonderful young man, who was now an assistant den leader with his old boy scout troop.

Chapter Sixteen

Both James and Jack had decided now was the time to talk with Sergey. It wouldn't be easy, but it had to happen. Sergey had to know. It wouldn't be easy for him to hear, but Sergey deserved to know the true facts. Then he could make his own decision about his future life moving forward.

General Tilson knocked on Sergey's door. Sergey welcomed both generals inside and offered coffee to them, which they accepted.

Tim saluted both generals and then sat back down when James said, 'at ease.' He'd been sipping a cup of coffee and chatting with Sergey. Tim knew what was coming. *Hopefully, Sergey will understand.*

"I hear things are set up now in Twin Falls, Idaho. I know it's a beautiful area. It's about time to see you off on your drive to your new home. How do you feel about that? Are you ready?" James studied Sergey's face.

"From what I've seen, Twin Falls is beautiful. I enjoy seeing places I've never been. I'm good with all of that. Tim can tell you the same if he hasn't already." Sergey responded and smiled. *The smile didn't reach his eyes, and all four men knew it.*

"Yes, Sir. Sergey is ready. I can't teach him anything more." Tim agreed.

"Good to know." James thought about how he would mention this next conversation as gently as he could. *I don't want Sergey to feel like no one in Russia cared about him.*

"What's on your mind, James? Why are you both here?" Sergey could tell that something was troubling his friend.

"Wait a minute. You and General Tilson are on a first name basis now? Of course you are. You are a nice and kind gentleman, Sergey." General Ness was glad to see the tension had worn off a bit with his comments.

"Well, what is it?" Sergey wanted to know. "What happened to bring two generals down to see me?" Sergey looked at both in turn.

"All right, we have intelligence, or lack thereof, from Russia. General Ness and I are of the same opinion and so is Tim. We aren't hiding anything from you, and we aren't talking about you behind your back. That didn't come out quite right. I'm sorry." General Tilson gathered his thoughts.

"What I meant to say is we do talk about how you are doing in the program - this new mission for you – your new life, and where you need to be, but we don't talk about you in a demeaning manner." General Tilson explained himself better and Sergey nodded his head.

"I understand that General. I will call you both 'General' or 'Sir' as we talk. Much easier for me to do it like Tim does with both of you here. Please, do go on." Sergey smiled at General Tilson.

He genuinely liked James...his honest and real friend...those rogue oligarchs could learn a few things from James...

"Understood, Sergey. I want you to know that we aren't trying to hurt your feelings or be nasty to you. But this discussion must be done, as it would not be fair to you if we don't." James smiled at Sergey.

"I'm confused." Sergey's face showed it, too.

"Well, I'm just going to say everything in a factual manner. Okay?"

"Yes, Sir." Sergey was ready to hear more.

"We've had zero chatter, only continued silence regarding 'Dmitry.' No one has investigated your death." General Tilson stopped.

"What do you mean? I have no family, so no one to inherit from me. Or is there more? No one from Russia looked in on my death?" Sergey was curious.

Both General Ness and I, please don't take this badly, we don't think anyone has cared to investigate your death. What I'm trying to say is that we don't think you were ever a target for them at the time you showed up here." *Whew...he got one hard part out.*

"Why would you think that? What are the facts? Do you have proof?" Sergey was confused. "I feared for my life. I knew they could take me out for my failures in getting them the intelligence they wanted."

"The 'facts' come together so please hear me out. You were tasked to locate the computer chip in Evergreen. If you obtained it, you were to send it straight to the oligarch who wanted it. You never obtained even one of those chips.

"Furthermore, you never knew what intelligence the chips contained. All you knew was one on NORAD, one on the Denver Federal Center, and one on DEN. The oligarchs failed, not you, Sergey. You won and they knew you didn't know the chip contents."

"What are you 'driving at'," Sergey inquired. *Could it be?*

"I'm impressed. You really have American Slang down well." General Ness chuckled. He wanted Sergey to know this, and it was true.

"Thank you, Sir," Sergey looked back at General Tilson.

"Scotland Yard obtained the second computer chip before the oligarch could buy the painting. Those oligarchs failed a second time. You had no knowledge of what the chip contained, and the one who did have the intelligence is dead.

"The oligarchs must have known by then that what they wanted wasn't going to happen. They needed all three chips to give them more power. Do you understand what I'm saying?" General Tilson smiled at Sergey.

"They needed all three chips to obtain the power they desired. They received none. That is what you are saying, correct?" Sergey questioned.

"That is part of it, Sergey. You will understand completely when I'm done. The third computer chip was never created. The baggage handler was caught before he could obtain any intelligence and place it on a chip for them.

"Correct me if I'm wrong, but you never knew any actual intelligence, did you?" General Tilson asked Sergey.

"No, I didn't. I tried to find the frame that contained the chip in Kim's art gallery in Evergreen. Only the spies who obtained the intelligence and created the chips knew what they contained. But you already know that, right?" Sergey responded. *Get to the point, James…*

"Yes, you are correct. I will continue since we are all in agreement. I will get to the main point, but the reasons why we think as we do will be clearer if explained in an orderly fashion.

"Please don't let this next statement hurt you. Your life is significant, Sergey."

"Sir, I know you believe that and so does everyone I've met. I believe it, too. I came down here to the Federal Center so I could be up front and honest from the start. I certainly wanted to live, and still do, as well. Despite missing my friends and especially, Suz."

"We know, Sergey, and this is hard to say but I must. For most people in the United States, life is highly significant, for criminals not so much.

"As for the rogue oligarchs and possibly others, you were insignificant." *Now the second hard part is out. No one wants to be considered an insignificant person, unloved, the works.*

"No one benefitted from you. They couldn't as you knew nothing. Yet, you were frightened when you arrived here, and that was obvious to all of us. You feared for your life, and we weren't about to let them take you out."

"Yes, Sir, that is true. What does my action in coming here back in May have to do with me now? We are four months past that." Sergey was hopeful, yet unsure. *He hoped, and he prayed silently.*

"Russia and the 'powers that be' of the rogue oligarchs is tied up. Between the war with Ukraine, confiscation of their super yachts, and trying to interfere with our upcoming presidential election, well…

"You were never a risk to them in the first place. None of us realized that when you arrived here. It came about as you provided intel on the rogue oligarchs and what we, the US, was able to obtain since then."

"I see. That does make sense. I hadn't thought of it in that manner. My situation has changed, but I can't go back to being Dmitry. Is that what you are implying?"

"Correct. Dmitry is buried. You helped bury him. The open space that your home was on in Genesee was cleared of debris and donated to the City of Genesee for use as an open space park for wild animals such as elk, and for those who like to walk and hike. What do you think about that?"

"I loved watching the wildlife and sunsets. Keeping that space open and maintained is wonderful." Sergey smiled thinking of the views he'd had when he lived there.

And the ones he'd shared with Suz. Their talks...everything she said had been meaningful and she listened to what he thought on numerous subjects...and kissing...soft and gentle or hot and needy...holding Suz in his arms...her love for him... and his for her...

"Earth to Sergey. Are you lost in space?"

Sergey looked back at General Tilson. "Sorry, Sir."

"I understand your excitement. Only you can make this next decision. You are completely set up for Twin Falls, Idaho, should you want to continue that path. However, there is a way for Sergey Vegorov to remain in Colorado."

"Tell me how, General." Sergey was excited and it showed on his face!

Could this really be real...James wouldn't say it if it weren't...but, where in Colorado...could he see his friends...what about sweet Suz...his true love...his soulmate...

"You would have to keep your new persona, forever. You would need to maintain a lowkey style of living initially and get a job. You could even live in a home in Evergreen."

"Really?" Sergey wasn't sure what he meant by 'Evergreen.' He didn't want to get his hopes up. But he hoped he meant Evergreen, Colorado. *How many 'Evergreens' are there in Colorado?*

"Yes. The only safe way is to have all your friends, including Suz, come down here, to the Federal Center, to learn about Sergey Vegorov." General Tilson smiled at Sergey.

"Of course, I would have to explain to them the how and the why, the reason and the cause...without much detail...and no one could ever mention the name Dmitry Ivanov again." General Tilson sipped his coffee as his throat was dry.

"After that shock registered with them, then Tim could bring you in to see your friends and the love of your life. So, Idaho or Colorado?"

"I'll take Colorado for $1000, Alex," Sergey joked, and everyone laughed at how he'd used 'Americanism'. He was on cloud nine. His hopes came true, and it was only a matter of time until Suz was in his arms once again.

"Okay then. It'll be a few weeks before this can be set up. In the meantime, remember you are Sergey Vegorov and you will remain Sergey Vegorov the rest of your life.

"Once settled, you will have access to all your money in your Swiss bank accounts. Evergreen is known for pricey real estate. One home is priced at $19 million right now. You would need to buy one for around $1 million to maintain a low-key lifestyle.

"Suz may live in a big enough home..." General Tilson was interrupted. Sergey's excitement and happiness was palpable and infectious to everyone present.

"She has a four bed, three bath home. Sorry, Sir, for cutting you off." Sergey apologized. He had not meant to cut off his friend.

"Apology accepted. I hear that the Art Gallery of Evergreen is looking for some help. You might be able to work in the environment that you love, should they hire you." James noticed an even bigger surge of happiness in Sergey's features. *We did the right thing...this would work out...*

"Perfect, simply perfect! Thank you, James." Sergey grinned, his perfect white teeth gleamed.

"Back to James again, is it?" General Ness laughed aloud with the others.

"General Ness and I will leave now. You need to talk with Tim so you can sort your feelings out before your friends are told any news. We do take care of mental health as well as medical needs." The officers saluted and James and Jack left.

Tim and Sergey talked into the early morning hours. Hope and faith do make a dramatic difference...thank you, Jesus!

Chapter Seventeen

It took a lot of finagling, but everyone was able to meet at the Federal Center on the third Sunday in October. 20 October 2024 would change everyone's lives once again...in a clever way. Curiosity ran furious and even Alice couldn't get James to tell her what was going on. Between the twins, work hours, the hospital hours, school schedules, and the art gallery, this was the date the group had decided on. Had they known, it would have been immediately. The meeting was set for 2PM.

The first to arrive were the Leawood family, Dr. Aaron and wife, Sarah, children Danny and Lisa, housekeeper Sadie, and James' wife, Alice. They were escorted to a large meeting room and a table was set up for self-serve drinks and snacks.

"I missed you, Alice. I know, I saw you at home only two hours ago, but I still missed you." James hugged his wife.

"I missed you, too, James. Soon you will be retired and then we will be together much more." Alice kissed James on his cheek before he sat down next to her. The Leawood family sat across from them.

"What's up, Grandpa?" Danny wanted to know why they were once again at the Federal Center. He was worried that they might have hit men after them once again, and he planned to help if anyone tried to hurt his family or friends – the Eagle Scout was ready!

Yet Danny was also timid...surely no one was after them...if so, they would have been driven down to the Federal Center in armored SUVs like before.

"I'll begin once everyone is here. Don't worry. No one, no assassins are after any of you. If any were, we'd have brought you in via armored military SUVs with guards." James smiled at Danny.

His grandson, the one he didn't know he needed...one who remembered the details of the time when assassins hunted them...no child should ever have that fear...yet children the world over are intentionally hurt...destroyed...raped... killed...every single day...

The Manse family, Richard, Nancy, and baby Dan - just over 10 and 1/2 months old, arrived. Richard had carried in Dan's favorite walker with toys. They sat across from James and Alice, and to the right of the Leawood family after choosing snacks and drinks. Dan had a sippy cup already.

"What a mysterious gathering," Nancy looked at James with a slanted eye.

"All in good time, Nancy, all in good time." James offered Nancy a sassy look and she rolled her eyes twice.

Only a few family members left to arrive...and they had 'double trouble' coming along for the ride...my family are here...he felt good about the decisions Sergey had made.

Finally, the Smith family arrived, Dr. Paul, his wife Kim, and their twins, Lily, and Jonathan, aged two months, were in their carriers asleep. Suz was with them.

He'd made sure with Paul beforehand that Suz wouldn't drive down here alone. They sat across from the Manse family leaving one chair open next to Suz. A placard had been placed so that the seat would be open.

No way would he have allowed Suz to drive after what was coming...she would stay the night at the Federal Center anyway...

Fifteen family members had gathered. *It was time...who knows how they will take what he was ready to announce...Cheri had placed several boxes of tissues on the table before she had left on Friday...*

"Shall we begin? What I'm about to say CANNOT be spoken of again. Two words CANNOT be spoken by any of you again. Dmitry Ivanov. No one can say his name again. Do you understand?"

"What? Why?" Suz didn't understand. *The man she'd loved, she could never say his name again – why would James say this? What is going on?*

"Grandpa James, you know we want to always remember Dmitry. This is wrong! Aunt Suz loved Dmitry!" Lisa wasn't about to let this happen. At age 10 and having been once in the past at the Federal Center, she was tuned in to the feelings of her family.

"Lisa, let grandpa talk, okay?" Aaron asked his daughter. "Let grandpa say everything first before you make a judgement, please." Lisa nodded her head yes.

"As you are all aware, the last three years have been traumatic to say the least. That goes for each person here, including me. Things were done to protect you, bad men tried to kill some of you. Yet you all made it through. You were, and still are, strong." Everyone's eyes were glued on James' face.

"That said, I have no easy way to say the following, but you must listen carefully and follow it without question." James looked around and everyone nodded their heads in the affirmative.

"A large part contains top secret details and those I CANNOT divulge, so don't even try to ask me. The reasons were right and remain that way. Dmitry Ivanov's name cannot be mentioned again as of *RIGHT NOW*. That is one top secret detail and of the *HIGHEST IMPORTANCE*."

Suz was confused, grabbed a few tissues to swipe a tear away, and remained quiet. *Something is going on, something extremely important...*

The best way for me to say this...is to come right out with 'Sergey Vegerov' is alive...from the start...

"Don't ask questions until I'm through. You will understand by the time I'm done, and it won't take long." James looked around the table, all faces were on his.

"Mr. Sergey Vegerov is alive and well...," before Lisa interrupted.

"Who is...," Lisa stopped herself from saying more.

"As I was saying, Mr. Sergey Vegerov is alive and well. My team and two other teams have poured over all information possible, and more than once. We honestly believe that Sergey's life is no longer at risk.

"Sergey loves his new name." Ah...they are starting to understand. "He does love his name, Sergey, and he has been happy to have had sanctuary here for a few months.

"Think back to the time when the Federal Center was your temporary home. We had to do the same for Sergey. He needed protection and NO ONE could know he was alive." James took a fortifying breath.

"No one was hurt or killed in the explosion in Genesee. I won't say more about Genesee other than the news was shocking, but there was no choice. I'm sorry it went down that way." All eyes were glued to James.

"Moving forward, Sergey is safe and so are all of you, but you must follow what I say. Think Sergey. Say the name Sergey. Get used to it. You can all say the name 'Sergey' now." James smiled at his family.

"Sergey...Sergey..." they all said the name more than once.

Suz was crying, but they were happy tears. Her love was alive. They could still have a happy life, but with changes. *His name mattered not...she loved his person...*

"Sergey has missed all of you a lot, especially you, Suz. That man loves you to the moon and back. Danny would say a gazillion times, but he is quiet and listening to this new phase in all your lives including mine." James grinned at Danny and he grinned back!

By this point even James had a certain dampness in his eyes.

"Who wants to meet Mr. Sergey Vegorov?" Everyone raised their hands and shouted 'me' immediately.

"Sergey has longer hair and a short beard, otherwise he is unchanged. His eyes are the same, and you will recognize him right away, yet most people would not."

"Open the door, Tim." Tim held the door open as Sergey rushed inside, picked up Suz, and held her close to his chest. Both were crying together – tears of happiness. They clung to each other tightly.

Everyone was excited and happy for Sergey and Suz...Many happy tears were shed...the entire family stayed together reacquainting with each other...tears... shock...relief...amazement...and more happy tidings for over an hour before James announced they would have to go back home...only Suz was allowed to remain at the Federal Center and both Tim and Sergey walked her to his temporary living quarters.

True love was a real 'thing' for Suz and Sergey. They loved and cuddled with each other the entire night. When they finally made love, both knew they fit together as was meant to be...the most exquisite love they'd ever known...as only two people in deep love understand...his reverence for her body and soul...her reverence for his strength and love...it was all consuming...

Chapter Eighteen

Things are looking up, indeed. Everyone was safe and happy, retirement coming up soon. He was ready to retire and spend time with Alice and his family.

The next day (Monday), General Tilson escorted Suz and Sergey to Suz' home in Evergreen. Sergey had all his paperwork and his new persona details with him before they left for Evergreen, and the documents listed Suz' address as his home on his faked new documents.

Once they were safely inside Suz' home, James drove back to Lakewood via a detour, stopping at home to spend quality time with Alice. *Soon he would be home all the time...*

When they finally stopped hugging, Suz showed Sergey around her four bed and three bath home. It was modest by Evergreen's means, and Sergey loved the charming mountain home overlooking part of Bear Creek and golden aspen trees.

Wildlife was abundant, and plenty of light filtered inside the dark wood sided home with a nice open space bilevel design.

Both Sergey and Suz wanted to get married soon and start a family. Life was too short, and they intended to live theirs to the fullest. House hunting started and Nancy hired Sergey to work three days a week at the art gallery, the same days Suz worked.

Sergey fit right in, not surprising with his keen eyes and known love of art. When he showed them his photography skills, they knew they had another artist to feature on the gallery walls.

Sergey quietly obtained $3 million of his billion(s) in private funds so he and Suz could buy a new SUV, one that featured safety over luxury, yet still had a few bells and whistles. In time, he'd transfer more money to the US and buy a fancy car in a few years.

The traumas they'd all endured had taught them that life was fragile and to treat each day as a new gift from God.

Sergey obtained an entirely new family, he had siblings, nieces, and nephews. James was even his 'dad' now.

Sergey made it known to all that he would be funding University education for all his nieces and nephews. No one challenged him on that score. He was a billionaire and they knew he wanted to spend money on worthy causes as well. But he still led a low-key lifestyle.

The rest of the money was placed into a savings account except for the money spent on basic mountain man type of clothing like Richard wore. Surprisingly, they were the most comfortable clothing Sergey had ever worn!

A mountain style home was found the first week of December. Located in Evergreen but tucked away from the road, a rustic style, three-bed, four-bath, log, and river rock home was perfect.

Exposed beams complemented the interior's large, open floor plan with log walls mixed with native stone. Two fireplaces made of native stone fit in the floorplan scheme. The master ensuite bedroom was large and airy, just like the main living room and bathroom nearby.

The home highlighted panoramic window views, and a large outdoor space surrounded the home. Perfect for watching wildlife saunter by.

The kitchen had built-in stainless-steel appliances and granite countertops matched the center island. The dark wood cabinets matched the exposed beams, and a pantry off to the right side of the kitchen was large and would hold everything they needed.

The lower level had a built-in two vehicle garage, and two bedrooms, a bath, a family type room, and fireplace.

Behind the laundry room was a mud room that led out to a large back deck, perfect for sitting or standing when the weather allowed. White twinkling lights adorned the rails.

The home sold unfurnished, so they planned to use the furniture Suz already had, buy a few carved pieces from the gallery Richard had created, and Richard decided to carve a few new pieces as a wedding gift. For a couple who wanted to marry as fast as they could, no date had been set yet.

The couple were able to buy the home with cash and move in right away. Between the art gallery and the house, not to mention Christmas wasn't far away, they were busy. Sergey felt invigorated to be living a real life, not an oligarch lifestyle. Things are just that. This was a thousand times more.

Everyone was invited to their housewarming on Saturday, 21 December 2024. It was a low-key affair, nothing special, and family only. Libations were available as was soda and hot chocolate. Finger foods were served.

Once the Leawood family, the Manse Family, and the Smith family were situated and fed, the home lost all power, leaving the fireplaces as the only source of light besides scattered candles.

In the stillness of the evening, a familiar voice spoke up asking for everyone to stay seated.

What is James up to this time, Alice wondered. Ah, yes, he did become licensed to perform wedding ceremonies.

James started the ceremony with a traditional welcome, and then the couple made their intentions known to all those present.

"Mom, they are wearing regular winter type clothing!" Lisa whispered into Sarah's ear, and everyone heard her and laughed.

"Hush, watch, and listen. People get married in all kinds of clothing." Sarah smiled down at Lisa, who was now holding a happy one-year-old baby, Dan.

Suz and Sergey exchanged heartfelt vows they'd written themselves, and then exchanged rings. After James pronounced them as spouses, the lights came back on, and everyone congratulated the 'housewarming newlyweds' before them.

They did it their way, low-key, without fanfare…stress free…nothing to plan or clothes to buy…happily blessed…

Epilogue

Christmas was another family affair held at the Leawood's home. Aaron and Sarah loved having a house full of family and love. Relaxed and no strain on anyone.

Danny and Lisa played with little Dan, yet it was the conversations that kept half of their interest. Baby Dan was running to each person in turn. He ran, not walked. Only Nancy would have a runner rather than a walker.

Alice and James simply cuddled off and on and soaked up the happiness along with Sadie.

Even the food was low-key and buffet style, make-your-own-sandwich with veggies and hummus. Only pecan pie for dessert. It seemed like everyone wanted to have a low-key, low stress Christmas.

Nancy and Richard announced that they were expecting again, and her due date was 31 August 2025. They were over the moon happy, and it showed. Congratulations were given to the happy family.

Kim and Paul's twins were now four months old, and they could sit up by themselves. Both were mesmerized by the Christmas tree lights and decorations. Everyone took a turn holding them up to see the pretty lights.

Suz and Sergey mostly sat back and enjoyed the ambiance and soaking in the scene. Finally, they decided to make an announcement. It was early stage, but they were pregnant, too! Suz was only two weeks overdue, but she had the signs and symptoms, and her early home pregnancy test was positive. She would be due sometime in September. Another round of congratulations and more happy tears. A perfect ending for the entire family. This was the best Christmas ever…

Note: Russian spies are located all over the United States. These spies blended seamlessly as part of the USA culture. They live and work among us, as neighbors *and co-workers. They fit the ideal of an American family. Many often lived in pairs so they could, 'live amongst the enemy and blend in and not stand out' and they often used Morse code in reporting back to Russia. Current estimates place the number of Russian spies operating in the USA between 2,000 and 3,000, which could be much higher. This is the society in which we live.*

City of Spies: DC Is the World Capital of Espionage. The Denver Federal Center was harder, by far, to infiltrate.

Biography

Mary L. Schmidt writes under the name of S. Jackson along with her husband, Michael, pen name A Raymond, and Mary L. Schmidt. She grew up in a small Kansas (USA) town and has lived in more than one state since then. At this time, Ms. Schmidt and her husband split their time between Kansas and Colorado (they love the mountains and off-road 4-wheeling). Traveling is one of their most favorite things to do and she always has a book or even three books to read, in the same week. Books have always been her thing. It seemed like every time she turned around, a new library card was needed due to the current one being stamped completed. Diving into a delightful book made any day perfect and you would be surprised at the number of books she has read over and over. She drew paper dolls and clothes for them, and with watercolor as her medium when painting scenes, especially flowers. She continued with art in high school exploring a wide variety of arts and loved it! Her creative side loves to be an amateur "shutterbug" and they have an online art gallery. In college, she went into the sciences of all things and received a bachelor's degree in the Science of Nursing. Her nursing career was phenomenally successful, and she hung up her nursing hat in December 2012.

S. Jackson is a retired registered nurse; a member of the Catholic Church and has taught kindergarten Catechism; she has worked in various capacities for The American Cancer Society, March of Dimes, Cub, and Boy Scouts, (son, Gene, is an Eagle Scout), and sponsored trips for high school music children. She loves all forms of art but mostly focuses on the visual arts, such as amateur photography, traditional, and graphic art as her health allows.

She has written fifty-four books with others in various stages of production, and she is included in four anthologies.

A. Raymond is a member of the Catholic Church and has helped his wife with The American Cancer Society, March of Dimes, Cub and Boy Scouts, and sponsored children alongside his wife on music trips. He devotes his spare time to fishing, reading, playing poker, Jeeping, and traveling adventures with his wife. Spending time with their grandson, Austin, and granddaughter, Emma, happens to be another favorite past time.

Memoirs

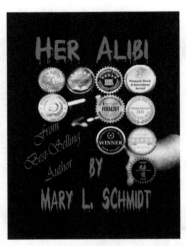

Visions of her Cherokee grandmother, Cordie, flashed through Mary's mind as her mother, Marguerite, informed her that her stepfathershot himself and was in the hospital. Oh no!

No! This can't be! Not after the joking around at my home last night. NO!!!!Did she use me last night? She'd never use her scapegoat child. No, she couldn't! Even Marguerite wouldn't sink that low! Or would she? Marguerite had always been abusive and vile to most people,and especially to her children and husbands, but would she shoot Harold?

Yet, here I was, and I had to tell the police that, yes, my mother was at my home all evening and into the night. How despicable that my mother connived her way into using me as her alibi. Her insanity unchecked and never stopped.

This book is a true memoir drawing upon the locals and inspiration of the areas in which the author lives and works. Names of towns, places, facilities, and people are real except for three men. Any resemblance to persons living or dead is not coincidental in nature and places where events take place are from her life growing up and as an adult.

Visions of her Cherokee grandmother, Cordie flashed through Sarah's mind as her abusive husband brutally raped her repeatedly shortly after giving birth. He took what he wanted, leaving her bloody body to be filled with years of physical pain and emotional scars that led her to believe she was worthless, and a happy life was hopeless. Sarah tried many times to leave but that was always futile. She felt useless. Her life was shattered once again when her oldest son, John, died at birth and Simon, her youngest endured a horrific cancer battle. With her only living son, Daniel she felt renewed strength knowing Cordie was watching over them always. She finally had the courage with the help of Cordie's visions from the spirit world to leave her abusive husband and make a new life for her and her son. Her new oath to her and Daniel was that no one would ever hurt either of them. Romantic love never existed for Sarah, although she had room in her heart for love. Life taught her to be wary, until the day an old friend from her past, Aaron came back into her life. Would she finally find and know true love? Could Aaron break through the walls that surrounded her? Dare she hope for love once?

Children's Books

A dog and her squirrel friends!

Teach the difference to your child!

"Love the parent and educator guide in the back. Teach your child good touch/bad touch, and body ownership!"

"Take a stand today and build up your child's self-esteem! Stop bullies and child suicide!"

"Disability and differences are treated with positivity and a refreshingly direct approach."

"Fosters your child's creativity and spark discussions! Help children with language and learning social skills."

www.ingramcontent.com/pod-product-compliance
Lightning Source LLC
Chambersburg PA
CBHW071254040125
19925CB00015B/979

ARCHON:
An Architecture for Multi-agent Systems

> The copyright for the front cover photograph has been wrongly assigned to Atlas Elektronik GmbH and the University of Porto. The copyright for this photograph Lies with EA Technology, Capenhurst.

ELLIS HORWOOD SERIES IN ARTIFICIAL INTELLIGENCE
Series Editor: Professor JOHN CAMPBELL, Department of Computer Science, University College London

Aiello, L.C., Nardi, D., Schaerf, M.	REASONING ABOUT KNOWLEDGE
Anderson, J. (editor)	POP-11 COMES OF AGE: The Advancement of an AI Programming Language
Andrew, A.M.	CONTINUOUS HEURISTICS: The Prelinguistic Basis of Intelligence
Al-Attar, A.	KNOWLEDGE ENGINEERING
Beal, D.F.	ADVANCES IN COMPUTER CHESS 6
Bergadano, F., Giordana, A. & Saitta, L.	MACHINE LEARNING: An Integrated Framework and Its Applications
Bläsius, K.H. and Bürckert, H.-J.	DEDUCTION SYSTEMS IN AI
Campbell, J.A. (editor)	IMPLEMENTATIONS OF PROLOG
Campbell, J.A. and Cuena, J. (editors)	PERSPECTIVES IN ARTIFICIAL INTELLIGENCE, Vols 1 & 2
Carter, D.	INTERPRETING ANAPHORS IN NATURAL LANGUAGE TEXTS
Craig, I.D.	FORMAL SPECIFICATION OF ADVANCED AI ARCHITECTURES
Davies, R. (editor)	INTELLIGENT INFORMATION SYSTEMS: Progress and Prospects
Evans, J.B.	STRUCTURES OF DISCRETE EVENT SIMULATION
Farreny, H.	AI AND EXPERTISE
Forsyth, R. & Rada, R.	MACHINE LEARNING: Applications in Expert Systems and Information Retrieval
Frixione, S.G., Gaglio, S. and Spinelli, G.	REPRESENTING CONCEPTS IN SEMANTIC NETS
Fútó, I. & Gergely, T.	ARTIFICIAL INTELLIGENCE SIMULATION
Gabbay, D.M.	ELEMENTARY LOGICS: A Procedural Perspective*
Gardin, J.-C.	ARTIFICIAL INTELLIGENCE AND EXPERT SYSTEMS: Case Studies in the Knowledge Domain of Archaeology
Gottinger, H.W. & Weimann, H.P.	ARTIFICIAL INTELLIGENCE: A Tool for Industry and Management
Gray, P.M.D. & Lucas, R.J.	PROLOG AND DATABASES: Implementations and New Directions
Hawley, R. (editor)	ARTIFICIAL INTELLIGENCE PROGRAMMING ENVIRONMENTS
Herik, J. van der & Allis, V.	HEURISTIC PROGRAMMING IN ARTIFICIAL INTELLIGENCE 3: The Third Computer Olympiad
Hodgson, J.P.E.	KNOWLEDGE REPRESENTATION AND LANGUAGE IN AI
Hoek, W. van der, Meyer, J.-J.Ch., Tan, Y.H. & Witteveen, C.	NON-MONOTONIC REASONING & PARTIAL SEMANTICS
Kopec, D. & Thompson, R.B.	ARTIFICIAL INTELLIGENCE AND INTELLIGENT TUTORING SYSTEMS: Knowledge-Based Systems for Teaching and Learning
Levy, D.N.L. & Beal, D.F. (editors)	HEURISTIC PROGRAMMING IN ARTIFICIAL INTELLIGENCE: The First Computer Olympiad
Levy, D.N.L. & Beal, D.F. (editors)	HEURISTIC PROGRAMMING IN ARTIFICIAL INTELLIGENCE 2: The Second Computer Olympiad
Lopez de Mantaras, R.	APPROXIMATE REASONING MODELS
Lukaszewicz, W.	NON-MONOTONIC REASONING: Formalization of Commonsense Reasoning
McGraw, K. & Westphal, C.	READINGS IN KNOWLEDGE ACQUISITION: Current Practices and Trends
Mellish, C.	COMPUTER INTERPRETATION OF NATURAL LANGUAGE DESCRIPTIONS
Michie, D.	ON MACHINE INTELLIGENCE, Second Edition
Mortimer, H.	THE LOGIC OF INDUCTION
Obermeier, K.K.	NATURAL LANGUAGE PROCESSING TECHNOLOGIES IN ARTIFICIAL INTELLIGENCE
Partridge, D.	ARTIFICIAL INTELLIGENCE: Applications in the Future of Software Engineering
Ramsay, A. & Barrett, R.	AI IN PRACTICE: Examples in POP-11
Ras, Z.W. & Zemankova, M.	INTELLIGENT SYSTEMS: State of the Art and Future Directions
Saint-Dizier, P. & Szpakowicz, S. (editors)	LOGIC AND LOGIC GRAMMARS FOR LANGUAGE PROCESSING
Savory, S.E.	ARTIFICIAL INTELLIGENCE AND EXPERT SYSTEMS
Savory, S.E.	EXPERT SYSTEMS IN THE ORGANISATION
Shanahan, M. & Southwick, R.	SEARCH, INFERENCE AND DEPENDENCIES IN ARTIFICIAL INTELLIGENCE
Sparck Jones, K. & Wilks, Y. (editors)	AUTOMATIC NATURAL LANGUAGE PARSING
Smith, B. & Kelleher, G. (editors)	REASON MAINTENANCE SYSTEMS AND THEIR APPLICATIONS
Torrance, S. (editor)	THE MIND AND THE MACHINE
Turner, R.	LOGICS FOR ARTIFICIAL INTELLIGENCE
Vernon, D. & Sandini, G.	PARALLEL COMPUTER VISION: The VIS-à-VIS System
Wallace, M.	COMMUNICATING WITH DATABASES IN NATURAL LANGUAGE
Wertz, H.	AUTOMATIC CORRECTION AND IMPROVEMENT OF PROGRAMS
Yazdani, M. (editor)	NEW HORIZONS IN EDUCATIONAL COMPUTING
Yazdani, M. & Narayanan, A. (editors)	ARTIFICIAL INTELLIGENCE: Human Effects
Zeidenberg, M.	NEURAL NETWORKS IN ARTIFICIAL INTELLIGENCE

* *In preparation*

ARCHON:
An Architecture for Multi-agent Systems

Editor: Dr THIES WITTIG
Atlas Elektronik GmbH, Bremen, Germany

ELLIS HORWOOD
NEW YORK   LONDON   TORONTO   SYDNEY   TOKYO   SINGAPORE

First published in 1992 by
ELLIS HORWOOD LIMITED
Market Cross House, Cooper Street,
Chichester, West Sussex, PO19 1EB, England

A division of
Simon & Schuster International Group
A Paramount Communications Company

© Ellis Horwood Limited, 1992

All rights reserved. No part of this publication may be reproduced, stored in a retrieval system, or transmitted, in any form, or by any means, electronic, mechanical, photocopying, recording or otherwise, without the prior permission, in writing, of the publisher.

Printed and bound in Great Britain
by Bookcraft Ltd, Midsomer Norton, Avon

British Library Cataloguing in Publication Data

A catalogue record for this book is available from the British Library

ISBN 0–13–044462–6

Library of Congress Cataloging-in-Publication Data

Available from the Publishers

Table of Contents

Preface 7

1 Introduction 11
    1.1 A SHORT HISTORY OF DAI 11
    1.2 THE APPLICATION CHALLENGE 12
        1.2.1 Archon Applications 12
    1.3 THE SYSTEM DESIGN ASPECT OF ARCHON 14
    1.4 ARCHON AGENTS 15

2 The Problem Definition and the Functional Architecture 17
    2.1 INTRODUCTION 17
    2.2 TWO ROLES OF COOPERATIVE AGENTS 17
        2.2.1 When to cooperate? 18
        2.2.2 How to choose the Cooperation Type? 19
        2.2.3 Cooperation decision making 20
    2.3 FUNCTIONAL ARCHITECTURE 21
        2.3.1 Functional Structure of the Archon Layer 21
        2.3.2 Archon's Position in the DAI field 22

3 The DAI Functionality of the Architecture 25
    3.1 THE INTERFACE TO THE APPLICATION SYSTEM 25
        3.1.1 Reconceptualisation 27
        3.1.2 The "Intelligence" of an IS 28
    3.2 FUNCTIONAL REQUIREMENTS 30
        3.2.1 The Knowledge Required 30
        3.2.2 Cooperation Knowledge 32
    3.3 FUNCTIONAL BLOCKS AND ARCHITECTURE 39
        3.3.1 Overview of architectural options for Archon 39
        3.3.2 Functional description by message flow analysis 42

4 The Communication Functionality of the Architecture 53
    4.1 GENERAL REQUIREMENTS 53
    4.2 HLCM AND SESSION LAYER 55
        4.2.1 The Session Layer 55
        4.2.2 The HLCM 57

5 The Information Modelling within the Architecture 59
5.1 INFORMATION KNOWLEDGE AT THE ARCHON LAYER 59
5.1.1 Overview of the Problem 60
5.1.2 The Agent Information Management module: AIM 62
5.2 AGENT MODELS 66
5.2.1 Information contained in Agent Models 67
5.2.2 Types of Acquaintance Models in Archon 68
5.2.3 Functionality of Agent Models 69
5.2.4 Attributes of Acquaintance Models 70
5.2.5 Summary 75

6 The HCI Requirements and Components of the Architecture 77
6.1 RANGE OF POSSIBILITIES FOR THE USERS OF ARCHON 77
6.2 A METHODOLOGICAL FRAMEWORK FOR HCI 79
6.2.1 Application Analysis 80
6.2.2 User Analysis: Development of the User Portrait 81
6.2.3 Task and Transparency analysis 83
6.2.4 User Interface specification 84
6.2.5 The User Agent's AIM 86
6.3 USER MODELLING ISSUES 87
6.3.1 The need for a user model 87
6.3.2 Types of User Models 87
6.3.3 Representation of the User Model 88
6.3.4 An Archon User Modelling example 89
6.4 CONCLUSIONS 91

7 An Implementation using Blackboards 93
7.1 UPShell FOR COOPERATIVE AGENTS 93
7.1.1 Main Goals 93
7.1.2 UPShell Description 94
7.1.3 Implementation 96
7.2 COOPERATION BETWEEN ARCHON AGENTS IN THE UPShell 97
7.2.1 Introduction 97
7.2.2 The Decision Making Module Structure 98
7.2.3 Knowledge for the Decision Maker Module 98
7.2.4 Global System Coherence 102

8 The Application Demonstrators 105
8.1 INTRODUCTION TO THE APPLICATIONS 105
8.1.1 Iberdrola demonstrator 105
8.1.2 EA Technology Demonstrator 106
8.2 ANALYSIS OF THE APPLICATIONS FROM A DAI APPROACH 107
8.2.1 General Constraints 107
8.3 THE IBERDROLA APPLICATION 108
8.3.1 Information used by the Iberdrola Demonstrator 108
8.3.2 Generic Tasks in the Iberdrola Demonstrator 109
8.3.3 Agents in the Iberdrola Demonstrator 110
8.3.4 Cooperation Overview of the Iberdrola Application 111

TABLE OF CONTENTS

  8.4 CIDIM - THE EA TECHNOLOGY APPLICATION 114
    8.4.1 Information used by the CIDIM Application 114
    8.4.2 Generic Tasks in CIDIM 115
    8.4.3 Agents in CIDIM 116
    8.4.4 Cooperation Overview of the CIDIM Application 118
  8.5 CONCLUSIONS 120
    8.5.1 Related work 120

9 Glossary of Terms **123**

10 References **127**

FIGURES:

Fig. 1.1	A classical control scenario	15
Fig. 1.2	The Archon approach	16
Fig. 2.1	Decision making for cooperation	20
Fig. 2.2	The Functional Modules of the Archon Layer	21
Fig. 2.3	DAI Dimensions	23
Fig. 3.1	The different viewpoints on information	31
Fig. 3.2	Knowledge Models	35
Fig. 3.3	Abstract Cooperation Scenarios	36
Fig. 3.4	The Archon Agent Architecture	40
Fig. 3.5	Message Type 1	43
Fig. 3.6	Message Type 2	44
Fig. 3.7	Message Types 3 and 4	45
Fig. 3.8	The Planning and Coordination Module	49
Fig. 6.1	The setting for Archon applications	78
Fig. 6.2	Interface design and development	80
Fig. 6.3	The Integrated Framework for Analysis	82
Fig. 6.4	Transparency of systems	84
Fig. 6.5	Architecture of the dialogue component	85
Fig. 7.1	The UPShell	94
Fig. 7.2	Structure of Decision Maker	97
Fig. 7.3	Two Sets of KSs	99
Fig. 8.1	The Iberdrola Application	111
Fig. 8.2	Information Flow in the Iberdrola Application	112
Fig. 8.3	The CIDIM Application	117

Archon:

The highest magistrate in Athens. The government was originally monarchical, but after the death of Codrus (about 1068 BC) the Athenians resolved that no one should succeed him with the title of king, and therefore appointed his son Medon with the title of archon (ruler). Later (683 AD) the number of archontes had been extended to nine, three of them playing a special role but without very clear cut responsibilities and duties. Thus these nine archontes can be said to have formed a loosely coupled system with fuzzy boundaries for ruling the state.

ARCHON:

An **AR**chitecture for **C**ooperative **H**eterogeneous **ON**-line Systems

Preface

The ESPRIT Project ARCHON which is funded by grants from the Commission of the European Communities under the ESPRIT-Programme, reference number 2256, is a five year project that started in January 1989.

ARCHON is a large consortium involving 14 organisations with several workers within each organisation. The full list of those who have made technical contributions to the ARCHON project is given overleaf.

This book is based on an internal report (compiled by Abe Mamdani as the responsible work package leader) of the project which synthesized into a single document all the diverse strands of the work. It showed the status at the half-way stage of the project which was reached in June 1991. The project was required to make aspects of that work public. At the same time several requests have been received from other ESPRIT projects for information on ARCHON's achievements. This book is the result of these requirements. As the technical leader at the prime contractor organisation, I have undertaken to edit this book. The book's sole purpose is to make public the results achieved by ARCHON. No attempt has been made to attribute that contribution to individual members who form the ARCHON team. ARCHON workers have produced several publications on their own contributions. These are also publicly available as technical reports of the project. A full list of these reports is given at the end of this book and can be obtained from Atlas Elektronik. I, as the compiler of this book and all my colleagues within the ARCHON project who have contributed the technical material presented here, hope that readers will find this material informative and helpful in furthering their own work.

Thies Wittig
December 1991

The contributors to this book are:

Jochen Ehlers	*Atlas Elektronik GmbH, Bremen, D*
Jutta Müller	*Atlas Elektronik GmbH, Bremen, D*
Thies Wittig	*Atlas Elektronik GmbH, Bremen, D*
Francois Arlabosse	*Framentec, Paris, F*
Erick Gaussens	*Framentec, Paris, F*
Daniel Gureghian	*Framentec, Paris, F*
Jean-Marc Loingtier	*Framentec, Paris, F*
Abe Mamdani	*Queen Mary and Westfield College, London, UK*
Nick Jennings	*Queen Mary and Westfield College, London, UK*
Claudia Roda	*Queen Mary and Westfield College, London, UK*
Nicholas Theodoropoulos	*Queen Mary and Westfield College, London, UK*
Robert E. King	*Amber, Athens, GR*
Evangelos Lembessis	*Amber, Athens, GR*
David Cockburn	*EA Technology, Capenhurst, UK*
Andrew Cross	*EA Technology, Capenhurst, UK*
Javier Echavarri	*Iberdrola, Bilbao, E*
Jose M. Corera	*Iberdrola, Bilbao, E*
Juan Perez	*Labein, Bilbao, E*
Inaki Laresgoiti	*Labein, Bilbao, E*
George Stassinopoulos	*CNRG NTUA, Athens, GR*
Tryofon Tsatsaros	*CNRG NTUA, Athens, GR*
Marina Spyropoulos	*CNRG NTUA, Athens, GR*
Alessandro Saffiotti	*Universite Libre, Bruxelles, B*
Frank Tuijnman	*University of Amsterdam, NL*
Hamideh Afsarmanesh	*University of Amsterdam, NL*
Eugenio da Costa Oliveira	*University of Porto, P*
Long Qiegang	*University of Porto, P*
Rui Camacho	*University of Porto, P*
Ronald van Riet	*Volmac, Utrecht, NL*
Rob Aarnts	*Volmac, Utrecht, NL*
Vincent van Dooren	*Volmac, Utrecht, NL*
Onno de Groote	*Volmac, Utrecht, NL*
Paul Skarek	*Cern, Geneva*
Joachim Fuchs	*Cern, Geneva*
Elena Wildner	*Cern, Geneva*
Nicholas Avouris	*JRC Ispra, I*
Marc Van Liedekerke	*JRC Ispra, I*
Lynne Hall	*JRC Ispra, I*

The Archon team acknowledges the time, effort and interest our Project Officers *Brice Lepape* and *Patrick Corsi* from the CEC in Brussels have spent in long discussions and debates to get the project off to a good start and make sure it stays on the right track.

The book consists of the following chapters identifying the organisations that have contributed technically and hence produced the written text:

1. Introduction, 11
Atlas Elektronik
Queen Mary and Westfield College

2. The Problem Definition and the Functional Architecture, 17
University of Porto
Queen Mary and Westfield College
Atlas Elektronik

3. The DAI Functionality of the Architecture, 25
Queen Mary and Westfield College
Framentec
IRIDIA-Université Libre Bruxelles
Atlas Elektronik

4. The Communication Functionality of the Architecture, 53
CNRG-NTUA
Queen Mary and Westfield College
Atlas Elektronik

5. The Information Modelling within the Architecture, 59
University of Amsterdam
Queen Mary and Westfield College

6. The HCI Requirements and Components for the Architecture, 77
JRC-Ispra
University of Porto

7. An Implementation using Blackboards, 93
University of Porto

8. The Application Demonstrators, 105
Iberdrola
EA Technology
Labein

9. Glossary, 123

10. References, 127

1

Introduction

1.1 A SHORT HISTORY OF DAI

Archon aims to establish an architecture for 'Multi-Agent Systems' (MAS) for industrial applications. MAS is a term used in the field of Distributed Artificial Intelligence (DAI), itself a subset of the general field of Artificial Intelligence. Before we go into any detail of the Archon approach, we will give a brief overview of evolution of DAI.

Although it appears that DAI has come into 'fashion' only recently, it has in fact been around for quite some time already. In the middle of 1980 the first workshop on DAI took place at the MIT, trying to "establish an informal consensus on the meaning and scope of the term" [Davis 1980]. Many of the ideas presented at that workshop resulted later on in a number of papers. One of them, trying to address this subject in a more general manner and putting some emphasis on planning tasks, was by Nilsson in 1981, describing DAI as a network of loosely coupled systems. Another basic paper of that time is by Smith and Davis, 1981, dealing with cooperation in distributed problem solving, defining to some extent the terms 'loosely' and 'tightly coupled'.

But only five years later, in 1985, on the fifth workshop on DAI, the first system developments in this area were presented. Since that time the number of prototypes, architectural frameworks, languages, etc. for DAI has been increasing rapidly. At the same time more fundamental discussions on a taxonomy of DAI began. The "informal consensus" which had evolved over the years had to be turned into a more formal definition. This was the aim of the 1986 workshop on DAI and Sridharan 1987 has produced an excellent review with a first classification of DAI (see 2.3.2). While his suggested dimensions are quite helpful to understand the internal structure and the scope of DAI systems (in terms of Distribution, Problem decomposition, Autonomy, etc.), they only implicitly touch the organisation of agents in a cooperating community.

The more introspective view on DAI systems gradually widened to a perspective on the problems that DAI could tackle and what impact certain problem domains could have on the structure of an DAI system. Bond and Gasser [Bond et al 1988] in their introduction to 'Readings in DAI' define a distinction between Distributed Problem Solving (DPS) and Multi Agent Systems (MAS), terms that suggest different architectures more suited to specific application needs as, for example, in distributed planning or distributed control. In DPS agents generally share an overall global goal, they have a common language and semantic. Moreover, a single agent is never able to solve the given problem alone but only the agent community as a whole can accomplish that task. In MAS agents are much more independent, they share the same environment, but they are competing about limited resources (e.g. time, space, tools), they have to coordinate for efficiency reasons (benefiting from other agents results, assisting other agents) and they have to avoid conflicts. In the extreme case they could solve the given problems individually. Since they do not necessarily have to speak the same language, they have to cope with the problem of translation and mapping into the individual representations.

This may appear as a neat definition and distinction but at a closer look one realises that there is not such a clear boundary between these concepts. Many DPS systems can be said to contain some elements of MAS and vice versa. Furthermore, new terms and concepts emerge, like Cooperating DPS as a distinction to Black-board based DPS.

1.2 THE APPLICATION CHALLENGE

In this evolving and still unsettled field Archon aims to contribute with an architecture for Multi-Agent Systems with its foundations derived from the merging of application demands with DAI concepts. Most of the existing DAI systems deal with (over-)simplified application scenarios. Much like the first Expert Systems used toy problems to derive their concepts and only recently have found their way into real applications, DAI appears to be still in a similar early phase.

AI - and its subarea DAI - is an applied science lacking an integrating theoretical framework. Thus, it depends on observation and examination of the real world to abstract concepts and theories from specific cases, and it is quite natural that researchers start with simple, sometimes even constructed problem cases. The often encountered problems in scaling up the techniques derived from such simple examples to full-size, real-life problems are even more difficult to solve in distributed, cooperating systems. Here, we are dealing not only with one AI system for a single problem area, but with several such systems that moreover require 'intelligence' for their cooperating behaviour. The effort involved in the attempt to design and build a DAI system for real applications is tremendous and beyond the capability and capacity of a single R&D team. In this respect the Archon project is in a rather exceptional situation: over five years more than 30 researchers and system developers have the opportunity not only to conceive new concepts and methods in DAI but also to apply them to real problems through the application partners integrated in the project team.

1.2.1 Archon Applications

In the early definition phase of the project we were looking for suitable real applications. Before we made our decision, a number of candidates were discussed, among them:

Air Traffic Control: A favourite amongst DAI applications, but for the time being confined to theory and paper. It will still take a number of years from now, before any real system development with a good chance of real applicability becomes feasible.
CIM: Also a good, however very complex candidate. But since none of the industrial companies involved in the consortium was developing products in this area, it was skipped as well. That this is a very promising application area for DAI has been demonstrated by several projects, one described very extensively in [Meyer 1990].
Vessel Operation: To integrate the variety of different systems on board a ship to increase the automation level for higher safety and economy through a cooperative framework has definitely advantages over the hierarchical approach [Wittig 1992]. However, since there is no single equipment supplier for the control and supervision

systems for ships, it would have made coordination with developing companies difficult.

In the end the decision was made for:

Electricity Management: Although this may not be the most obvious application for DAI, it has a number of advantages. The most prominent ones are:
i) The application problem as seen from a DAI point of view is 'balanced', i.e. it is not too simple but also not too complex. A number of subsystems exist in such applications, each with a specific task but sometimes with overlapping capabilities. In the two specific applications we chose already a number of knowledge based systems had been developed or were under development at that time. This meant that we could really concentrate on the important part of coordination among these systems.
ii) The application domain was familiar to some of the research partners who had previously developed Expert Systems in this area [Arlabosse 1987, Wittig 1986].

There is of course a danger in focusing entirely on one application domain. In order to ensure generality of the architecture, we additionally included so called 'application studies'. These are smaller exercises in applying the emerging concepts to quite different applications. The ones we are looking at, but which are not described in this book are:

Robotics: Application of the Archon framework in the area of intelligent Robotics with the objective to implement a Flexible Production Cell. The subfields for cooperation are: Robot control, Sensing (proximity sensor in the robot arm), Planning for Task Assistance, and Vision/Scene Analysis (3D scene analysis and flexible modelling of objects). The UPShell that is described in Chapter 7 has already been applied to this application [Oliveira, Camacho, Ramos 1991].
A second, closely related application study will be carried out for a robot arm with six degrees of freedom in a laboratory environment. The arm is equipped with a variety of sensors, including a vision system and force sensing. The control hardware consists of a VME crate containing a variety of processors, connected trough a LAN to a SUN workstation. This system in particular will allow testing the Archon software in a real-time environment, which is relevant to later process control applications.

Cement production Control: Again, the purpose of this application study is the coordination through cooperation of the various control systems of a Cement Production process [King 1982 & 1988]. Individual controllers assisted by Expert Systems exist, tied together by a hierarchical and tightly coupled system. The current set-up for an Archon approach consists of the agents that play the core role in the production process: The Precalciner, the Kiln Burner, and the Clinker Cooler, each controlling a number of tasks that have to be coordinated amongst the three.

Fault finding and operational help in the control system for Particle Accelerators: Particle accelerators have been developed to create high energy beams of particles to investigate the subatomic world and the fundamental nature of all matter.
The Proton Synchrotron (PS) accelerators at CERN are one of the world's most

sophisticated high energy research tool. The PS complex is the heart of CERN's accelerator and experimental facilities, serving many users in a time-sharing fashion and acting as injector for the bigger accelerators, the Super Proton Synchrotron (SPS) and the huge Large Electron Positron (LEP) rings.

The CERN PS complex comprises particle accelerators of different types, accumulation and storage rings and beam transfer lines, controlled through a large computer network of about 20 minicomputers and 150 microcomputers, interfaced by CAMAC to the components of the accelerators, like power supplies for bending magnets, RF cavities for acceleration and complex beam measurement devices.

Running an accelerator is like controlling a large industrial process. Fault finding and repair in the PS control system has become time consuming and difficult, and it consumes a lot of man power: soon ideas have been developed to move from traditional methods to AI-based ones [Malandain and Skarek 1987]. The systems to be integrated for cooperation comprise a large relational database, a control system consisting of a large computer network and several separate expert systems. The domains are: beam diagnosis and control, control system diagnosis, and alarms treatment. The task of these expert systems is to find faults in the control system to help maintenance and control of the accelerator. Most of the static knowledge for the expert systems has to be read from the database and dynamic information has to be read on-line from the control system to be diagnosed.

1.3 THE SYSTEM DESIGN ASPECT OF ARCHON

Large systems are built in a distributed fashion in order to master complexity. Ideally this should mean a separation of control and execution to make the control part more explicit and maintainable and thereby reduce the complexity. Like high level programming languages have been developed to make control structures explicit that were only implicit in assembly languages; at a higher level Knowledge Based Systems aim at a similar reduction of complexity by making the implicitly contained knowledge of a programmer in a conventional software system explicit. Consequently, the next level to explore is System Design. Complexity of systems has two different aspects: It refers to the solution of the primary application problems, which determines the functional requirements of a systems and, on the other hand, it refers to issues such as security, maintainability, flexibility and adaptability to changing requirements during the life-cycle of the systems. These are issues the establish the non-functional requirements of a system.

Essentially, these non-functional issues are the ones addressed by the cooperative systems approach like Archon. It means splitting up a system into several smaller and dedicated ones whereby not only the execution becomes distributed but - most important - the control becomes decentralised. Obviously, the control part of each of these dedicated systems has to deal with the solution of its own problem domain. But additionally it has to control the coordination with the other systems, a task that was dealt with centrally in the non-distributed, monolithic system. By distributing this control and assigning it to the individual systems, allowing them to control not only themselves but also the way they interact, we believe that the control complexity has been reduced.

1.4 ARCHON AGENTS

To describe what is referred to as an 'Agent' and an 'Intelligent System', we will use a simple analogy of cooperation among operators in a control room. Let us assume a control room for supervising a complex process by means of several, independent supervision and control systems, each pursuing its own, dedicated task. Each of these systems is controlled by an operator. While each system only has its own specific goal, the operators have an overall goal. To achieve this they have to coordinate their individual control tasks, in other words, they have to cooperate. Figure 1.1 shows such system set-up

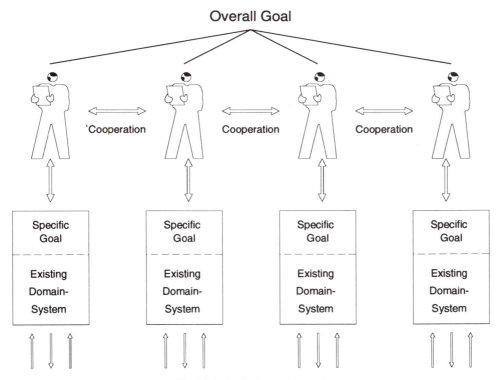

Fig. 1.1 A classical control scenario

This level of cooperation is addressed by the Archon approach. In terms of this analogy, to replace the individual operators by an additional layer, we have to introduce a functionality which we call the 'Archon Layer' (see Fig. 1.2). Amongst other things this layer will contain a representation of those parts of the Overall Goal that are relevant for the specific subsystem. The existing domain system together with this Archon Layer (AL) now constitutes an AGENT. These agents will have the ability to communicate and through this communication they will coordinate their tasks much in the same way as the human operators did.

This Archon Layer has to interact in two ways and thus has to maintain two different views of the system: Firstly it has to interact with the Domain System and, secondly, with the other agents in the community. These Domain Systems will mostly be Knowledge Based Systems and therefore they are called Intelligent Systems (IS). However, as the

Archon architecture is an open one, these systems do not have to be all Expert Systems. So the abbreviation 'IS' can also stand for Industrial System (see also section 3.1.1 "The Intelligence of an IS")

Since Archon deals with heterogeneous systems, there is a need to translate information from the specific representation of one IS to that of another. This will be achieved by a global information modelling formalism, as described in Chapter 5. However, to exchange 'knowledge' different mechanisms are needed. So far, Archon is following the discussions on Common Knowledge Representation [Ginsberg 1991], but the development of a Knowledge Interchange Protocol (KIP™) is one of the long term aims of the project that will be addressed at a later stage.

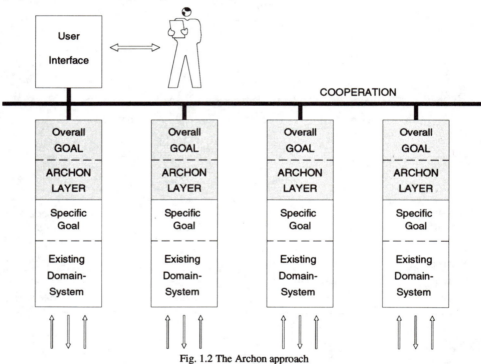

Fig. 1.2 The Archon approach

2
The Problem Definition and the Functional Architecture

2.1 INTRODUCTION

Unlike PGP framework (Partial Global Plans) to dynamically coordinate agents in Distributed Problem Solving system, [Durfee et al, 1987]), the Archon approach does not require the agents to have compatible local goals and it allows each agent to detect the needs for cooperation, to be aware of its own and other agents' capabilities, and to dynamically choose an appropriate cooperation type. More importantly, this approach explicitly represents the domain-independent cooperation knowledge which can be generally used elsewhere.

Agents in multi-agent systems need not only to consider how to cooperate with the others, they must also control themselves locally so as to correctly achieve the committed tasks. Archon investigates the relationship between these two different levels intended for cooperation (dealing with other agents and with itself) relating incoming messages and agents' local task scheduling behaviours. Inter agent cooperation does not directly involve specific tasks but refers rather to the agents capabilities and states as visible to the outside world. Intra agent coordination is based on the assumption that each agent can execute one or several local tasks and mainly addresses scheduling issues. Four kinds of local task scheduling behaviours have been identified:

o   restart a task under execution
o   redo an already executed task
o   task swapping and
o   multi-task execution

In this section these two alternative roles that agents play in a cooperative multi-agent system are discussed. From both points of view, we describe why and how cooperation can take place.

2.2 TWO ROLES OF COOPERATIVE AGENTS

In any cooperation type, not all the agents involved have the same motivation to cooperate. Two possible answers to the question, "Why do you cooperate?" show the difference:

" I cooperate since I need the other's help. "   and
" I cooperate since the others need my help."

Moreover, the agents involved in a specific cooperation are not at the same position. To answer the question, " Why do you cooperate with agent A in this type?" exhibits the difference:

" I choose this type due to the following reasons ..."
and
" Agent A expects me to cooperate in this type."

Therefore, in any specific cooperation, the agents may play different roles: cooperation initiator and cooperation respondent. The cooperation initiator is the agent that initiates the cooperation from its own needs and views. This may include to ask for help or to supply help voluntarily. Clearly, in the task-sharing cooperation type, the initiator is the one who cannot execute a task locally and tries to find help from the others. Whereas in result-sharing, the initiator is the one who sends results to the other "interested-in" agents so that these can share the results. The cooperation respondent is the agent that responds to a cooperation initiated by the others. That is, it is the external force that drives it to cooperate. Cooperation respondents will accept or supply help. In a task-sharing cooperation case, the respondents are the ones who consider to share the others computational load. For result-sharing, the ones who consider the arriving data are respondents.

Having distinguished these two different cooperation roles the questions is "When to cooperate?" and "How to cooperate?" from each role's viewpoint.

2.2.1 When to cooperate?

Being situated in the dynamic environment, each agent ought to detect the needs for cooperation according to its local view or to its partial view of the overall system. That is, the agent must identify the circumstances under which it should initiate cooperation or respond to cooperation requests.

From the cooperation initiator's point of view, the reasons to initiate cooperation are:

I1: Needs help.
     The initiator itself can not achieve a task.

I2: Can supply help.
     To supply the data to the others so that it can be shared.

Whenever either of the two reasons is present, the agent will then become a cooperation initiator and try to establish cooperation with the others.

From the respondent's point of view, the reasons to respond to cooperation demands are:

R1: Can supply help.
     The respondent can solve the task which is needed by the others.

R2: Accepts help.
     The respondent can use the data supplied by the others to improve its own solution.

Whenever either of these reasons is available, the agent becomes a cooperation respondent and involved in the cooperation. These two roles are dynamically assigned to the agents, and one may play the two roles for different cooperations at the same time.

It is evident that the reason R1 only applies to reason I1, and R2 to I2, respectively, so that only two rather than four combinations are possible.

2.2.2 How to choose the Cooperation Type?

Having detected the need for cooperation, the agents then need to determine how to cooperate with the others. For this purpose, the following two decisions must be made in sequence:

1) Which cooperation type (e.g. task-sharing, result-sharing, etc.) to choose?
2) Which coordination policy (e.g. Client/Server, Contract Net) to employ?

A cooperation respondent cannot make such decisions since it just reacts to the cooperation demand issued by the initiator. Therefore, the cooperation initiator must take the responsibility to make these choices. From the initiator's point of view, the reason to initiate a cooperation can determine which cooperation type to choose. If it is because the initiator cannot solve a problem by itself, then it will choose task sharing to ask help from the others. In case it finds some data to be useful for the others, it will try to suggest the others to share those data by initiating cooperation in the type of result-sharing. Nevertheless, whether or not the initiated action will be followed will depend also on the respondent.

After choosing the cooperation type, the initiator then needs to determine a coordination policy in order to send out cooperation demands. Coordination policy is the way to achieve the cooperation of the chosen type. To do so requires the knowledge about the overall system. If, for example, the initiator finds out that only one specific agent can solve the task that cannot be dealt with locally, it should try to establish Client/Server protocol between itself and that agent. If, however, the initiator finds out more than one which can supply help, it then should use a contract net policy to determine the most appropriate one.

Even if the initiator can determine the cooperation type and cooperation protocol, there still exists a need for the respondent to make the decision on how to cooperate. This need derives from the situation that the respondent may face more than one cooperation demand at the same time. Under this circumstance, the respondent must decide which one to respond to, i.e. which one to help or which help to accept. The following information is helpful when making such choice:

1) The Cooperation Type

   It is useful to give priorities to cooperation types. Clearly, if one initiator is trying to establish a Client/Server cooperation while another is trying contract net with the same respondent, the responder should give priority to the first.

2) The Cooperation "Effect"

   If more than one cooperation request of the same type exists, the respondent should choose the cooperation which will be most beneficial from its point of view.

This may be evaluated from the two perspectives:

o   to contribute to the local goals as much as possible, and
o   to contribute to the other agent's work as much as possible.

2.2.3 Cooperation decision making

Figure 2.1 summarises the previous discussion by stating the following main steps involved in Decision Making about Cooperation:

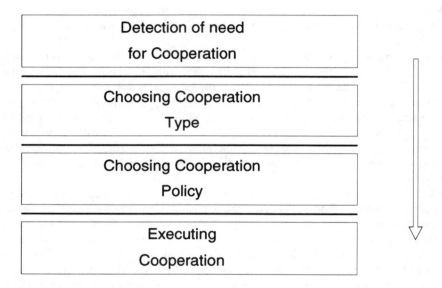

Fig. 2.1 Decision making for cooperation

Cooperation may be performed in a small number of steps or may involve a potentially time consuming, even infinite procedure. In this case special mechanisms at the initiator and/or responder should detect the need to terminate the cooperation.

2.3 FUNCTIONAL ARCHITECTURE

2.3.1 Functional Structure of the Archon Layer

Before we go into the detailed description of the Archon Architecture, we will outline the functional structure of the Archon Layer (Numbers in curly brackets refer to numbers of chapters that give a detailed explanations). This is shown as a set of functional modules in Fig. 2.2. Each Archon Layer has two I/O channels: one to the underlying domain system which we call the Intelligent System, and one to other agents in the community. This reflects the two views of an agent mentioned in the Introduction, one on its own application solving the tasks the domain system was designed for, the other on coordinating its own activities with those of the rest of the community. To deal with its own IS is the responsibility of the *Monitor* {3.3.1, 3.3.2}. It monitors the IS by checking the states of the different tasks that may be active in that system, by receiving requests for information and forwarding these to other modules of the Archon Layer. Furthermore, it controls the IS by starting or stopping specific tasks, by supplying data from other agents or the user.

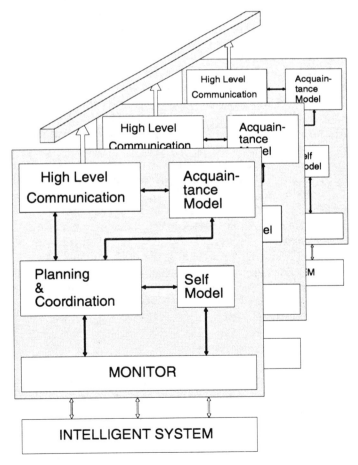

Fig. 2.2 The Functional Modules of the Archon Layer

In order to reason about the state of its own IS, the Archon Layer needs some model of its IS reflecting its state. This is called the *Self Model* {5.2.2}, and it is maintained by the Monitor. This Self Model is not just a 'status record' of the IS, it also contains plans on how to control the IS. These are partial plans, called *behaviours* {3.1, 3.2.1, 3.2.2}, which are used by the Monitor and can be updated by other modules of the Archon Layer.

In the same sense the Archon Layer has to model the other agents in the community if it actively wants to coordinate its actions. Other agent, or Acquaintances of an agent, are modelled in the *Acquaintance Model* {5.2.2}. This model reflects both static information like skills and interests of other agents as well as dynamic information such as the current state a specific other agent is currently in. Agents not only coordinate their activities, they also exchange domain information. As long as such information is of small size, it can be sent to all interested agents through the normal communication channel whenever it becomes available. But if this is massive information like the state of an Electricity Distribution Network, which can be some MBytes, it does not make sense to send this around just in case some other agent is interested in some bits of it. A more economic way to deal with that is to keep this information where it originated, let interested agents know that it is available, and provide the agents community with an information access formalism through which they can obtain those parts they are interested without copying the entire set of data. This is achieved through the *Agent Information Management - AIM* module {5.1.2}, a distributed data-base in which the Acquaintance Model is embedded. By not making AIM a separate entity, but blending it into the Archon Layer we ensure access through the same inter-agent communication link.

At the beginning of this chapter we explained the two cooperation roles an agent can play and what decision are necessary to actually enter into a cooperation with another agent. This functionality resides in the *Planning and Coordination Module - PCM* {3.3.1, 3.3.2}. It is a central part of the Archon Layer and, in contrast to the Monitor, it reasons about other agents in the sense of when and how to cooperate. It can initiate new cooperation and it has to respond to cooperation requests from others. Obviously, it has very close connections with the Monitor, directly to quickly deal with exceptional situations either in its own IS or in the overall community, and indirectly through the Self Model.

Since all cooperation in Archon is based on communication, the Archon Layer contains a *High Level Communication Module - HLCM* {4.2.2}. It is based on an implementation of the *Session Layer* {4.2.1} following the OSI standard. The HLCM is called High Level since it provides services such as intelligent addressing and message filtering to the Archon Layer modules. For example, whenever the PCM decides to send information coming from its IS to other agents, it just informs the HLCM to send it to all agents interested and leaves it to the HLCM to find out who these agents are.

2.3.2 Archon's Position in the DAI field

As we mentioned in Chapter 1, Sridharan has produced an excellent review of the 1986 Workshop on DAI that presents a classification of DAI. In order to classify this work, Sridharan suggests 8 dimensions for the evaluation such as GRAIN, SCALE, INTERACTIONS etc. These dimensions are to some extent correlated, for example, fine granularity often implies large scale of processing components.

The work on DAI encompasses an extremely broad range of implementations from fine grained, large scale connectionist implementations to a collection of coarse grained independent systems. In between these two extremes are found almost classical blackboard systems and work on concurrent object type implementations. The latter, particularly has wider appeal then just within the context of Artificial Intelligence. It represents the essential on-going work on concurrent processes. A good appreciation of research on concurrent objects can be gained from the book by [Agha 1986].

Instead of merely reproducing Sridharan's classificatory dimensions we will review them in the light of the Archon architecture and add some further important features to them (see Figure 2.3).

MODEL: Nearest description of Archon's model dimension is that of a "society" model in which relatively complex agents cooperate.

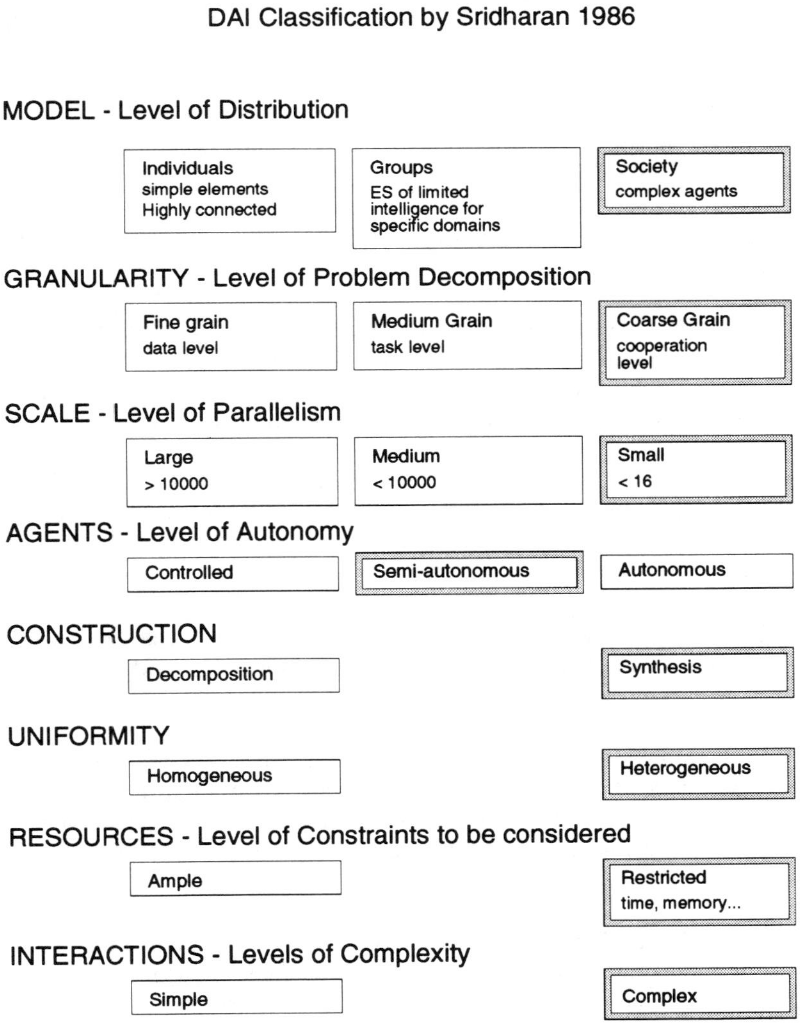

DAI Classification by Sridharan 1986

MODEL - Level of Distribution

| Individuals simple elements Highly connected | Groups ES of limited intelligence for specific domains | Society complex agents |

GRANULARITY - Level of Problem Decomposition

| Fine grain data level | Medium Grain task level | Coarse Grain cooperation level |

SCALE - Level of Parallelism

| Large > 10000 | Medium < 10000 | Small < 16 |

AGENTS - Level of Autonomy

| Controlled | Semi-autonomous | Autonomous |

CONSTRUCTION

| Decomposition | | Synthesis |

UNIFORMITY

| Homogeneous | | Heterogeneous |

RESOURCES - Level of Constraints to be considered

| Ample | | Restricted time, memory... |

INTERACTIONS - Levels of Complexity

| Simple | | Complex |

Fig. 2.3 DAI Dimensions

GRAIN: Archon typically represents a coarse grained system.

SCALE: The scale of computing elements to be employed is seen as small. This dimension correlates with the grain size as well as the model of the system.

AGENTS: Controlled or autonomous. Archon in a sense considers both characteristics. At the top most level, the cooperation is seen between semi-autonomous agents. However, each such agent includes controlled 'sub-agents', in our terminology the Intelligent Systems, as its part. Sridharan possibly confuses several dimensions here; further dimensions to be considered here are:

CENTRAL vs. DISTRIBUTED CONTROL of computing resource: Central control of computing resource may be the easy way to ensure time-critical operation, but ,as we said in the Introduction, this may increase the complexity of the overall control of the system.

INDEPENDENCE of rationality and responsibility: In which each system is capable of arriving at a decision on its own if necessary. Cooperation in such a case helps to improve the quality of decisions.

INDEPENDENCE of problem domains: In which each agent is designed to operate within a well defined domain.

> The above three dimensions are not necessarily correlated. Central control may still devolve independent responsibility to the agents. Some of these agents may be composed of sub-agents, each designed to be an expert in its own domain, but requiring close mutual cooperation to arrive at a common goal.

CONSTRUCTION: Whether the total system is synthesized or decomposed top-down is another one of the dimensions considered by Sridharan. In Archon, synthesis is seen as the key way to construct the total system. Cooperation between hybrid systems is established through the Archon Layer.

UNIFORMITY: Whether the agents are homogeneous or heterogeneous. In Archon the predominant view is that of heterogeneity, allowing not only different expert systems but also conventional software systems to inter-communicate.

RESOURCES: Sridharan, in his review admits that dimension also represents several dimensions based on memory, bandwidth, complexity of information exchanged etc. Archon predominantly considers the constraints placed by limited resource because of the time-critical nature of the applications for which Archon type system are in tended.

COMPLEXITY OF INTERACTIONS: This dimension correlates with bandwidth resource. On the other hand, coarse grained, "autonomous agents collected in a contract net have relatively complex interactions" (Sridharan). In Archon, therefore, this is a trade-off dimension.

3

The DAI Functionality of the Architecture

3.1 THE INTERFACE TO THE APPLICATION SYSTEM

Archon is dealing with Multi Agent Systems applied to the field of Industrial Control. Intelligent Systems (IS) are industrial control and supervision systems both acting and observing the parts of the real world concerned by an application. Once encapsulated within agents, these ISs will benefit from the communication, cooperation and information management provided by the Archon Layer. The fact that the IS level is regarded as layer indicates that the Archon Layer is reasoning about the IS, and actually using the control part of the IS, that reacts and reports on the information coming from the real-world.

This is an important division of responsibilities: by keeping all domain related reasoning at the individual IS level, the community, i.e. the various Archon Layers, does not have to deal with constraints or untractable models coming from the characteristics of the dynamic and complex real-world - like irreversibility of the actions or representation of unstable transient states. It is well known that mixing different levels of knowledge abstraction and logic - related to interactions with the real world and related to interactions among systems - may lead to undecidable situation. However, once having identified the need for this separation, this has an impact on what is expected from an IS and its internal control: the "Ideal Archon IS" must have certain characteristics in addition to its own constraints and skills, in order to make use of and to be used by the services provided by the Archon Layer.

A list of the "ideal" expectations or constraints one is likely to find in such a typical IS is:

General features of an IS:

- Information System

   It processes information given by the other agents in the community in order to execute actions or generate further information. It processes information coming from the world, and from itself, (e.g. exceptional situations due to the world or to the internal processing) in order to react and report to the Archon Layer. The first implies goal driven control, the latter an event driven mechanism including for example: filtering of unstable information and, if the IS is a KBS, explaining how it has achieved a result or why is has not.

- Conventional Industrial System
    The information processed as well as the processing itself are in the industrial control area, linked with the "system under control or supervision", e.g. snapshot messages from an electricity network. This "system under control/supervision" is dynamic and in general too complex to be totally predictable or even fully observable. The processing itself is linked with the general functions one expects to find in industrial control:

    situation assessment: system's state, hypotheses generation, validation, external conditions, alarm-generation;
    planning: of control actions on the system, of manoeuvres, of resources, of inspection/repair actions;
    control: execution of plans; and
    simulation.

- Complex System
    The "coarse grain" assumption of an Archon community implies not only few but also complex agents. This complexity is determined by the IS of an agent. The internal knowledge representation, world model and reasoning mechanism of an IS generally will be too complex or too specific to be shared by the Archon Layer without using another abstract, domain related representation, and to be modelled in a sufficiently detailed way at the community level.

- Control System
    The IS is not only acting or observing, it is also collecting and reacting to events coming from the world. Due to the nature of the "system under control/supervision" these events have to be considered as partly predictable in terms of time, order and context.
    Conflicts that arise between intentions or current plans of the agent and the information collected by the IS have to be solved at the Archon Layer.
    Actions or observations of an IS may be conflicting at the level of their impact on the real-world or of their viewpoint of it. At the first glance this aspect has to be dealt with where the proper knowledge resides: at the IS level. On the other hand, however, these conflicts are typical examples of needs for cooperation - needs that are tackled and organised at the Archon Layer.

Specific features of an IS:

- Interceding Functionality
    It will provide the agents with the information and results they need through a goal driven interaction with the real-world. Conversely, the event driven interaction will provide the agents with filtered events, avoiding unstable or irrelevant events.

- Instrumental Functionality
    In order to get things done in the IS, the Archon Layer needs to be able to plan and launch tasks within the IS. These tasks are primarily the ones the Industrial System was meant for but could also encompass diversion of some of these tasks to obtain a result that others may need independently from the final function the IS is solving.

- Reactive Functionality
    An IS has to be ready to react to real-world stimuli at any time. These reactions may be of no interest to the Archon Layer above if they are corresponding to normal execution within the running task, but they may also stimulate action such as situation assessment and backtracking within the Archon layer. This would typically be the case in an exceptional situation. In such a case the IS is expected to report to the Archon layer and following subsequent control from there.

Integration of these features at the Archon Layer:
These three facets - interceding, instrumental, and reactive - are what are called in Archon *low level behaviours* of an agent. Behaviours are modelled in the Self Model of the agent and used by the Monitor and the Planning and Coordination Module (PCM), as will be explained later. They represent the link between a situation analysed at the Archon Layer and the control facilities residing in the IS. They are not modelling all the internal reasoning and information processing capabilities of an IS but only an external and logical description of their Archon related steps, results and data requirements. In order to execute such behaviours, the control part of the IS must allow separate access to the tasks it can perform, it must recognise exceptions and pass them to the Monitor, and it must filter information and delegate control to the Archon Layer in case of conflict generated by external stimuli.

There is one additional, important aspect of a typical IS: it may well have been built independently as a stand-alone system. In fact, this is the typical situation for an Archon application, which intends to integrate various already existing systems in a cooperative framework to increase the overall efficiency or robustness of the application. Although the existing systems have not been designed in order to meet the requirements and constraints of an Archon IS, it is possible to partly re-conceptualise their control as outlined in the next section.

3.1.1 Reconceptualisation

Any supervision and control system processes a well defined input into an expected output (nominal result) by sequencing a set of interdependent tasks. To achieve this it may create communication and scheduling constraints for other systems. Usually, an independently built system offers only few additional interworking possibilities outside of these communication and scheduling requirements.

A more sophisticated class of systems can deal with incomplete input: it can produce so called 'contexted' results, i.e. either a partial result, labelled with belief factors or containing default values.

To migrate from an independently built system to an Archon Intelligent System the above mentioned separate access to its tasks is necessary in order to be able to:

- run separately each of the sequenced IS tasks in order to benefit from intermediate results, to adopt a different sequencing depending on the situation, or even to divert one of these tasks from its original role in the sequence to obtain a result that can be useful for others (diverted results),
- run these tasks with incomplete input information to get some preliminary result at an early stage (partial, contexted results).

Furthermore, all situations (exceptional and nominal) have to be analysed and modelled in terms of behaviours. The control has to be adapted so that the reporting and delegation to the Archon Layer is ensured.

3.1.2 The "Intelligence" of an IS

The term "Intelligent System" implies that this system exhibits not only some form of intelligence (in the Computer Science / AI sense) but also that the Archon Layer, sitting on top of it, makes use of this intelligence. Archon is about "Cooperating Expert Systems" which assumes the existence of AI at two different levels:

(1) AI-based systems at the "nodes" of a distributed application. These systems deal with specific domain problems, their view is entirely on that subset of the real world where they have to solve a problem.
(2) AI at the cooperation level, i.e. "intelligent" coordination of the way two or more systems can work together. This requires knowledge that the underlying ISs would not have in the first place, being designed as isolated systems - at least in terms of a community. As in any other problem area, this knowledge could of course be hard-coded for any specific application or specific system community. But in the same way as Knowledge Based System technology strives to provide generic solutions, the same attempt should be made at this level.

The question now is:
Is there any relation between the Knowledge of an IS and the Knowledge of the cooperation level, i.e. the Archon Layer ?

Or, put in other words:
Does the behaviour of an IS as seen from the cooperation level differ if it is a KBS or just a conventional problem solver or information system ?

As we have seen before, the IS delivers its results (domain-problem solutions according to its tasks) to the Archon Layer which then determines what to do with them. As long as just results are passed up, there is no difference between a KBS and a conventional system. A KBS may produce better results, but for the AL the technology or methodology the IS employs is of no concern. There is, however, a difference between a KBS and a conventional system: at least theoretically a KBS can not only explain its results but, more importantly, is able to explain why a certain result could not be achieved. Since any KBS reasons explicitly it should be able to provide this justification.

A simple example to illustrate this:

Say, there are two ISs, one for data processing (non KBS, complex signal processing or state estimation for electricity networks) and one for interpreting these data to identify possible overloads and to establish a restoration plan (KBS). The data processing goes along a standard procedure which will give the best possible results (as input to the interpreter) for average quality data. The KBS would then produce a list of possible interpretations (hypotheses), each attached with a certainty factor (CF). As long as the CF of one interpretation is significantly higher than the rest, everything is fine. However, if they are all more or lest the same it is up the user to find out why and see if some different data processing procedures could yield a better result. If instead of the user a cooperation level was introduced in this example, then there are two possibilities to find out about the problems of this insignificant interpretation results:

(1) The cooperation level could contain sufficient domain related knowledge to find out what information should be provided for a better result and, subsequently, ask the Data Processing IS to try and achieve it. Most likely a good deal of the domain knowledge incorporated in the Interpreter would be duplicated on this coordination level.
(2) A more generic approach would be for the intelligent Interpreter to explain why its results were not significant. Through its explicit reasoning process it can not only derive "good" results and explain how it has achieved them, but can equally well derive information about missing or bad input data. It would then pass this explanation up to the cooperation level which then - in a generic way without needing domain knowledge - can inform the Data Processing unit.

Not surprising, the second approach is the one taken by Archon. But it still does not fully answer the question above. When talking about "Cooperating Expert Systems", one tends to assume that these systems get actively engaged in a cooperation with each other. The basis of such cooperation would be their knowledge about their own application, their own capabilities, needs, goals etc.; their knowledge about the capabilities of the other Expert Systems; and some additional functionality allowing them to reason about sharing their tasks and results with other systems. However, the Archon philosophy postulates that the domain related systems (the ISs) do not commit themselves to any cooperation activities. This is handled entirely by the Archon Layer on top of them. Thus, it may appear that Archon is not dealing with "Cooperating Expert Systems". However, at closer inspection, Archon provides exactly the 'additional functionality' mentioned above in order to provide a generic framework which deals with all cooperation related tasks, imposing only minor changes to systems incorporated into the Archon community.

Finally, the answer to the above question:

Whether an IS is a KBS or a conventional data processing system does not make any difference to the *architecture* of the Archon Layer. It does, however, make a difference to the *specific instantiation* of the AL modules. A Monitor, for example, serving a KBS has to be able to deal with symbolically expressed responses in order to derive actions or requests to other modules and, in the end, to other agents.

3.2 FUNCTIONAL REQUIREMENTS

3.2.1 The Knowledge Required

We have introduced Archon as a framework for multi-agent systems, where in each agent three layers can be found:

o   Real world interaction layer ("Intelligent System"),
o   Cooperation layer ("Archon Layer") and
o   Communication layer.

The Archon Layer is the place where the cooperative and information exchange functions will reside. These functions will process information received from other agents through the communication layer as well as information received from the IS layer. The result of the processing follows the same external (i.e. to other agents) and internal (i.e. within an agent) split: messages passed to the community, instructions and information passed to the IS. The processing itself uses knowledge on how to handle information and how to act accordingly. The functional description of the processing involved is described in section 3.3 Within Archon we have made a distinction between two main areas of knowledge: Cooperation Knowledge and Information Knowledge.

Cooperation Knowledge

This knowledge refers to the cooperation with other agents, i.e. the protocols that can be used, the detection of a need for cooperation, and its execution. Furthermore, it is linked with the IS's control, it is behavioural knowledge and generic cooperation knowledge.

Information Knowledge

This is structured knowledge about domain dependent information, knowledge about various viewpoints of the process domain, and knowledge on updating, retrieving and querying this information.

Whatever knowledge area, the objectives of Archon (building and modelling layered multi-agent system for industrial and dynamic application, as well as providing a framework to a future designer using Archon architecture, functions, constructs, models, paradigms) give different viewpoints on how to analyse, acquire, elicit, and describe this knowledge. These viewpoints are summarised in Figure 3.1.

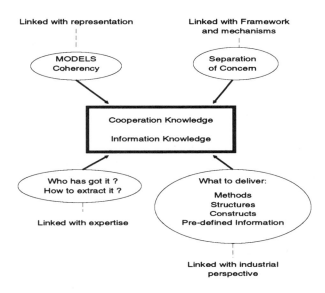

Fig. 3.1 The different viewpoints on information

The Viewpoints

- Models, Coherency

The knowledge on information or cooperation embeds modelling of the various interactions and coordination that can take place both within an agent or at the community level, and models for representing knowledge about an agent itself and about other agents. These models should also reflect coherency: coherency between the modelling of an agent's viewpoint on the others (acquaintances) and its self-model, coherency among the different models of domain dependent knowledge within each agent, and coherency between the modelling of what an agent offers to the community and what it can "personally" do. These coherencies are mainly static, i.e. acting as design constraints.

- What to deliver

In the end the Archon project will deliver a framework to be used by systems designers to develop an Archon application, i.e. to benefit from the added value that such a framework will offer. It certainly will encompass design methodologies and constraints, but also tools, modules, and predefined functions. Regarding knowledge, the question is how one can go about delivering explicit Archon related knowledge that can be used directly, and to what extent only constructs, rationales, and examples can be proposed with which the designer will encode his own knowledge.

- Separation of concerns

An essential aspect of the Archon architecture is to separate the main functions of the modules. This separation affects how information and cooperation knowledge is allocated and manipulated.

- Who has got the knowledge, how to extract it

The expertise needed to acquire and model the knowledge is manifold: expertise on the application itself, expertise on the Industrial Control domain, and expertise on the Archon systems design. The latter will only evolve as Archon partners are developing the framework. A good deal of literature surveys exist, but expertise based on these is mainly reflecting various trade-offs between abstract viewpoints on cooperation or information modelling, and our application partners' expertise.

3.2.2 Cooperation Knowledge

The Needs of the Developer
A fundamental question addressed in Archon concerns the nature of the resulting development environment we want to deliver to the designer who wants to build cooperative systems. At one end of the spectrum the Archon designer could be provided with a language and a set of mechanisms (such as agent models and communication facilities) from which the entire application would have to be developed. Using this approach, agents would be purpose built for each and every application, there would be little generality and the system designer would be faced with a long and onerous job of building a cooperative application almost from scratch. The other extreme is that the designer is given a framework in which all the control knowledge needed to build a cooperative application is present and all that has to be done is to instantiate the self models of each agent. Each agent within the community would then be capable of automatically building up models of other agents and of participating in cooperative problem solving based on the general control knowledge embodied in the system.

While the latter option may appear attractive it is unlikely that such an approach would be feasible or have the necessary expressive power for any sufficiently complex application, whereas the former certainly has the expressive power but lacks generality. The problem is then to find a sufficiently general approach which retains the expressiveness necessary for real-size applications. Right from the beginning of the project we had the notion that the architecture of an individual agent should contain both a model of itself (self model) and models of other agents with which it is expected to interact (acquaintance models), these structures would then be manipulated by a sufficiently general control mechanism. This approach was devised as a solution to the expressiveness/generality problem: the control mechanism provides the generality whilst the sophisticated agent models provide a sufficiently rich structure which allows the complexities of real-scale applications to be expressed. In this way a wide range of general behaviours could be specified and then an actual behaviour would be obtained by applying the general behavioural descriptions to the specific information about the problem (contained in the agent models).

Having gone along the route of generic control knowledge and sophisticated agent models the next question is: how far can this approach be extended? Based on the current separation of concerns expressed within the architecture, three major areas can be identified:

o   control of the underlying intelligent system
o   assessment of the agents local and community role
o   support cooperative interaction

As a result of our experiments it appears that the knowledge maintained to aid the processes of situation assessment and cooperative support can be manipulated using predominantly generic knowledge. It may be the case that a small amount of domain-specific knowledge may be needed to augment the generic knowledge, however this appears to be a relatively infrequent requirement. With regard to controlling an underlying system, however, it appears that this is a highly domain specific task and writing using general knowledge to define this behaviour is less profitable. The reasons for this being that task interleaving, obtaining results, backtracking and other such functions which would be tackled at this level are intimately related to the underlying system. Therefore a more specific approach which is mainly event driven is required at this level and 'behaviours' have been found to be appropriate for this task.

Models and Separation of Concern
In the context of "cooperation knowledge" , we have five global functions to fulfil within each agent :

(1)   Global Situation Assessment

in the sense of how an agent views the flow of messages received and sent in the community, in particular to set a context for (re)actions within the agent.

(2)   Local Situation Assessment

in the sense of both assessing the IS activation/control in the context of a multi-agent interaction - the goal driven path - or assessing the IS reaction/control as possibly conflicting with that context - the event driven path.
All situation assessments are targeted at:

o   Choice/selection of acquaintances to work with and for what purpose
o   Choice/selection of cooperation protocol to use
o   Interaction with the IS (scheduling of tasks within the IS)

It is not the purpose of this section to refine these functions, but to outline the cooperation knowledge models, their coherency, and their conceptual "location".

Within these global functions three functions relate to types of knowledge modelling:

(3)   Low Level Behaviours Model

These low level behaviours represent the link between a situation analysed at the Archon Layer and the control facilities and constraints residing within the IS. They are modelled in the form of pre-compiled partial plans representing the possible combinations of an IS's tasks. They provide tracking points in order to obtain the desired results from the IS in the cooperative context of the agent. Two sub-types of these low-level behaviours can be identified:

- dependent on the specific IS of the agent, e.g. representing the specific results and processing organisation of this IS
- dependent on general features of an IS, e.g. representing general schemes like the "task suspension before a result arrives", "multi-tasking execution", "stepwise execution", "feedback of contradicting reaction from the IS", and so on.

All low-level behaviours are stored in the Self Model of the agent.

(4) High Level Behaviours Model

In addition to describing purely localised activity, behaviours may be used at a more general level of abstraction (i.e. relevant in more than one situation or application). This contrasts with the low level behaviours described which are intimately related to a single, particular situation. At present there are two areas where such higher level behaviours may be employed:

- Cooperation protocols
  Where a cooperation protocol follows a well established convention, it may be possible to model such interaction using behaviours. So, for example, with the contract net protocol for distributing tasks: one agent sends out task announcements to a group of agents and then waits until they have all replied before deciding which one will be chosen and then informing that agent of the fact. This well defined and general interaction could easily and efficiently be modelled using behaviours.

- Typical agent interactions
  Within the domain of industrial systems it is possible to define well established interactions between different classes of agents (e.g. between a diagnostic and planning agent, between a diagnostic and control agent, etc.). At a certain level of abstraction such interactions may be described using behaviours. These descriptions may facilitate reasoning about the behaviour of the community (or at least a subset of it) and may be used to guide interactions. However to retain flexibility and generality it is important that these descriptions are suitably high-level; so for example the cooperation protocol, the agents involved, and so on will be instantiated at run-time by the dynamic knowledge model component.

The design of the behaviours of the last sub-type are obviously an on-going work which is linked with the last knowledge model ("Dynamic knowledge") and will benefit from the on-going experimentation with the application. These behaviours are stored in the Agent Acquaintance Model (AAM) of the agent.

The low level behaviour model can be represented by the "transaction" paradigm, a concept supported by the ALAN language [Loingtier 91] and introduced by Agha in 86. The high level behaviour model can, at least for some parts, also be represented in that way, but to achieve sufficient flexibility in the interaction with other agents a more declarative style, allowing opportunistic reasoning using rules or knowledge sources is advocated.

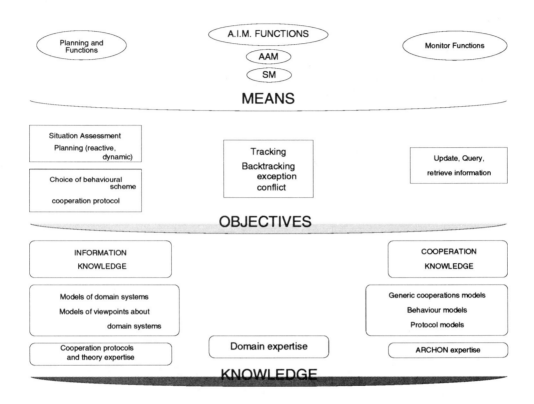

Fig. 3.2 Knowledge Models

(5)   Dynamic Knowledge Model

This knowledge, expressed as heuristics, is stored in the self and acquaintance models and covers various fields:

o   Both types of situation assessment. Either to choose a behaviour depending on the situation or to detect a need for cooperation which does not correspond to a high level behaviour. This includes conflicts that may occur either because conflicting requests are sent to an agent or because an exception disturbs the actual cooperative situation.
o   Selection of the agents to be involved in a joint behaviour or of the agents to receive some information.
o   Selection of the protocols.
o   Dynamic planning of cooperation, if no behaviours are known in the occurring situation.

This dynamic knowledge model is at the moment foreseen to be expressed through the generic knowledge concept described above in the "What to deliver" paragraph.

It is clear that the elicitation as well as runtime interaction among these knowledge models is still an on-going major issue in Archon. At the moment a first initial view is represented in Figure 3.2.

Abstract Cooperation Scenarios
In order to illustrate the possibilities of cooperation between different agents, the following selection of abstracted cooperation scenarios is given. Chapter 8 contains a number of real cooperative situations found in the main Archon applications. Figure 3.3 broadly depicts a community of agents with specific tasks and capabilities. Cooperation is conceivable:

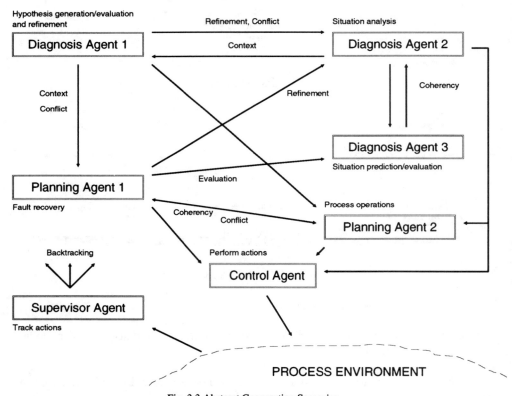

Fig. 3.3 Abstract Cooperation Scenarios

o   *Between the Diagnostic Agent 1 (D1) and Diagnostic Agent 2 (D2):*
    D1 may need the situation analysis from D2 in order to make certain assumptions or to refine hypotheses. Conversely, the hypotheses made by D1 may focus the attention of D2. They may even conflict with information D2 acquired while D1 was reasoning.

o   *Between D1, D2, the Planning Agent 2, and the Control Agent:*
    D1 and D2 may be in an undecidable situation: to access some information some actions have to be taken on the process and its environment.

o   *Between D1, D2, D3 and the Planning Agent 1 (on fault recovery):*
    To start fault recovery planning, the planning agent needs hypotheses concerning fault locations. They should be provided by D1, but while the planner runs some new hypotheses may be generated which either can speed up its work or enable it to abandon some of the hypotheses it is currently working on: both D1 and the planner could benefit from this cooperation.
    The planning agent may be in an undecidable situation which could be solved by getting clearly focussed information from D2.
    Some of the planned action may have a high uncertainty attached to them. In this case a prediction of their effects would be useful which could be provided by the diagnostic agent D3.

o   *Between the Supervisor Agent and the rest of the community:*
    While tracking actions, the supervisor may detect some exceptions, i.e. critical situations the application is about to enter. It would then alert all the other agents of the community in order to jointly reason about emergency actions.

Uncertainty and Knowledge
The Archon Layer constitutes part of its own application domain, quite apart from an agent's IS, where the domain to be modelled and dealt with is normally a pre-existing fragment of the physical world. The question "Is our domain knowledge uncertain?" does not make sense in the case of the Archon Layer. Rather, the correct question to ask is "Is it worthwhile to model this or that type of knowledge in the Archon Layer as uncertain knowledge?".

Our attitude, therefore, will consist in identifying the places where uncertainty may be made to show up, or, to put it differently, in identifying the places where modelling Archon Layer knowledge by taking uncertainty into consideration may produce useful benefits.

"May" and "could" refer to the fact that the choice of actually considering (or ignoring) uncertainty should be made, we believe, by the Archon system developer, based on the characteristics of the environment the Archon System is to be applied for. In the following, we report some notes on the possible locations of uncertainty in Archon Layer knowledge. Also, we try to split these locations between potential uncertainty producers (i.e. where we may want to generate uncertain knowledge) and potential uncertainty consumers (i.e. where we may want to consider the uncertainty affected the used knowledge).

One first and very general type of knowledge in which we may want to consider uncertainty is the knowledge related to situation assessment. Specifically, knowledge about the status of partners' agents, about capabilities of acquaintances, about the cost of getting certain information from a particular agent, may be affected by uncertainty. Again, the real point here is not to establish if this knowledge is or is not, in itself, uncertain; but rather to see if it is worthwhile to represent it as uncertain knowledge. We illustrate this point by an example. Let us suppose that agent **A** has requested agent **B** to execute a goal **G** (based on the fact that **G** is a capability of **B** in **A**'s AAM). Let us further imagine that agent **B** rejects this request. We probably want this experience to be reflected in **A**'s deleting of the capability **G** for agent **B** from its own AAM. However, we may want to be less drastic, and just reduce the confidence **A** has in **B**'s holding capability **G**. This implies that we may want to model agent **A**'s AAM as a set of (possibly) uncertain beliefs, dynamically (but smoothly) updated as new information about the Archon system status arrives. Similar considerations apply to the knowledge about the IS of the agent itself.

If we regard the knowledge in the AAM as an uncertain set of beliefs, we are introducing uncertainty in the Archon Layer knowledge by performing uncertain situation assessment: knowledge about other agent's status and capabilities becomes one source of uncertainty.

Who is the consumer who uses this uncertainty? There are a number of points during a cooperative situation in which an agent must choose among alternatives in its cooperative behaviour. The most apparent examples include:

- choosing among different potential suppliers of a needed information
- choosing among different suppliers of a needed service
- deciding whether to perform a goal locally, or to ask another agent to do it

These are typical instances of decision making problems. We know from the literature in this field that uncertainty may be worth considering in (at least part of) these decision processes. As an illustration, we continue the above example of the "rejected goal". Suppose a new need for goal **G** to be executed arises in agent **A**. **A** will consider all the possible agents who are believed (by **A**) to possess capability **G**; let's suppose they are **B** and **C**. For each of them, we will measure how much **A** believes it to be a good candidate. In measuring this belief in the case of **B**, **A** will have to consider the diminished belief in **B**'s holding capability **G** (cf. above). **A** will then select the agent whose candidacy it believes most strongly (**A** may possibly weight its belief by some "cost function"). If **C** never refused a request of **G** from **A**, and supposing that this is the only relevant parameter of choice, **A** is likely to prefer **C** to **B** for executing **G**. We want to emphasise once again that the above does not mean that there is an inherent uncertainty in the selection process, but rather that we may want to use uncertainty to better model it.

From the above discussion, an important requirement follows for a suitable uncertainty reasoning tool to be used in the Archon Layer. Because both sources and consumers of uncertainty are sparse (i.e. only some functionalities may consider uncertainty, while most of the others will not), it is important that uncertainty be an optional characteristic of some piece of knowledge. This means that it must be possible to represent and use most knowledge in the non-uncertain way, but allow for uncertainty in some fragment of it. Moreover, the sparse "uncertain" parts of the overall knowledge, and the "categorical" ones, must interact in a clean way.

3.3 FUNCTIONAL BLOCKS AND ARCHITECTURE

Based on the functional requirements identified in the previous section, this section will provide an overview of the architectural options and the functional blocks identified so far. The previously identified knowledge will be mapped to the respective functional blocks. The interworking of these blocks will be explained in terms of message flow and a more detailed specifications of the Archon modules in terms of functionality will be given.

3.3.1 Overview of architectural options for Archon

In this section we will describe the functionalities of the "interacting modules" in the Archon Layer. This framework reflects two main design decisions: decentralisation of control and local environment.

Within the chosen decentralised control regime no agent is allowed to be designed in such a way that it prescribes the activity of another agent. Through interaction, agents can influence each others' activities. However, as each agent has an internal focus of control, such interaction may be ignored. A decentralised control regime allows high levels of autonomy, avoids communication and computation bottlenecks [Davis, Smith 83] and enhances hardware and software fault tolerance since it facilitates error confinement. On the other hand, in a distributed control environment, it is harder to achieve global coordination and it is necessary to have control over the uncertainty caused by decentralisation [Lesser, Corkill 81 and 87]. Local environment means that each module can only access local information. No shared variables exist, the only way to interact is via explicit messages. The message addressing paradigm has well understood semantics [Decker 87]. Furthermore message passing increases generality because no shared memory between agents is required[1].

In the following we will describe the modules of the Archon architecture in terms of their functional properties. This should not be confused with implementation aspects or software design issues. As an exemplar of the realisation of such architecture Chapter 7 of this book describes an implementation in which these functional modules are built using the well-known blackboard paradigm embedded in Prolog. Other activities in the project are working on different implementations based on the object oriented paradigm, using CLOS and LISP. Whatever implementation is chosen, the functional entities in the architecture, both knowledge and services, are the same.

The Functional Archon Architecture
Several modules constitute the building blocks of the Archon Layer:
The Agent Acquaintance Module (AAM), Self-Model (SM), High Level Communication Module (HLCM), Monitor, the Planning and Coordination Module (PCM) and the Agent Information Management Module (AIM), as shown in Figure 3.4.

---

1. At the first glance this may appear contradictory to the Information Sharing Architecture (ISA), we will present in Chapter 5, which proposes to share information among the agents through the means of a distributed data-base. But firstly ISA is object-oriented so the access is based on the message passing paradigm and, secondly, locality is preserved as any access to ISA objects goes through the appropriate Archon layer modules.

40 THE DAI FUNCTIONALITY [Ch. 3

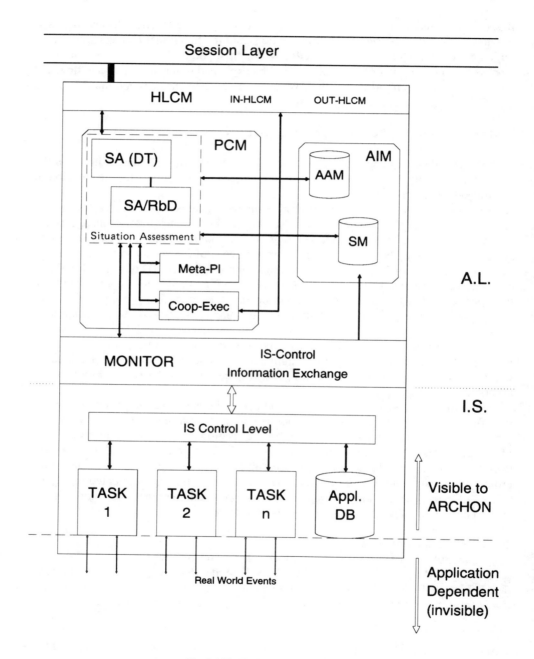

Fig. 3.4 The Archon Agent Architecture

Agent Acquaintance Module (AAM): This module contains acquaintance models, which are partially dynamic data structures containing most of the domain specific information needed by the other modules, that allow them to be primarily domain independent. Such information may include acquaintances, skills, interests, relevant problem solving states and operational stages (see Chapter 5).

Self-model (SM): This is an abstract data structure containing descriptions of the underlying intelligent system - it specifies the names of procedures that can be invoked, information needed by these procedures, results produced and so on. Whereas there is only one self-model per agent, the number of other acquaintances modelled can vary between zero and the whole community. Each agent accommodates the models of exactly those community members which it is "interested" in. A subset is defined of those agents which have similar interests/capabilities or the ability to provide services that the local agent cannot perform (e.g. solve certain goals or furnish particular pieces of information). As agent models only represent appropriate properties and because they have different interests, it is likely that several different models of a particular agent will exist within the community.

High Level Communication Module (HLCM): This is defined as the layer allocated between the Session Layer and the rest of the Archon modules. The HLCM functions allow agents to establish meaningful dialogues necessary for decentralised problem solving and coordination. Archon supplies both generic communication functions (e.g. "send this message to all agents which are interested in it") as well as physical communication functions (e.g. classical send and receive) to the multi-agent system builder. The three key services provided by the HLCM are: intelligent addressing, filtering and message scheduling.

Intelligent addressing allows agents to send messages to "relevant" acquaintances. The relevance of a message for an acquaintance is decided on the basis of parameters supplied by the Monitor or the PCM and on information contained in the Acquaintance Models.

Filtering allows agents to receive only relevant messages - "intelligent addressing" can be seen as filtering outgoing messages. For instance, an agent can use filtering facilities to receive messages only from certain acquaintances or about certain subjects.

The HLCM scheduling mechanisms allow agents to receive messages in a specified order. The order may be based on the message type (e.g. messages carrying an answer to a previous question, messages carrying information spontaneously supplied by other agents or messages carrying requests from other agents) or on the abstract description of the message's content.

The need for message abstracts representing domain knowledge occurs in all the three services: filtering, intelligent addressing and scheduling of messages. An example of the use of this knowledge is the "Timeout" service which aborts a communication when a message becomes obsolete. The evaluation of the timeliness [Durfee, Lesser, Corkill 1987] of a message is related to its meaning in the domain of the application.

These services are provided by the HLCM in the current stage of development. Nevertheless not all of these services will necessarily be used in all applications. It is up to the designer of the application who instantiates the Archon Abstract Machine if filtering of messages will be done at the HLCM level, on the PCM level or on the Monitor level. A more detailed specification of HLCM services is given in Chapter 4.

Agent Information Management module (AIM): This provides an object oriented information management model, a query and update language to define and manipulate the information and a distributed information access mechanism to support the remote access and sharing of information among agents (see Chapter 5).

Planning and Coordination Module (PCM): This provides all functionality that is related to global situation assessment, planning and supervision of all cooperational behaviour the Archon community of agents is supposed to have. In particular, it will deal with Dynamic Planning. This feature will be carried out on the basis of the status and control information exported by the other agents and should also have its own synthetic view of the activity performed locally within the agent. Reasoning taking place at this level encompasses the assessment of the main stages in the execution as well as detection of possible conflicts between actions or plans of actions between the agents.

Monitor: This is a layer between the IS and the rest of the Archon Layer and serves as the highest control instance of the IS. For the rest of the Archon modules the IS is hidden and represented by the Monitor. It will schedule and interleave IS tasks (e.g. for providing services to other agents) based on the information provided by the Planning and Coordination Module (PCM). Vice versa it provides the PCM with information about the status and requests of the IS. The Monitor provides a local situation assessment. The Monitor is responsible for a considerable amount of control concerning its IS, which typically belongs to the field of process control. Essentially, the Monitor is a Reactive Planner, in charge of the nominal and flexible control of the IS: the global situation assessment required will be delegated to an upper level (the PCM) and passed through what we call the global context knowledge. Reactive means that the link between situation assessment and the choice of actions (either basic actions or plans of actions) is not a complex reasoning task because the low level task interleaving may be partially encoded in a precompiled plan. However it is still an open issue if very simple relations between the assessed situation and the action (this relation being possibly defined in a look-up table) are sufficient, or if more sophisticated situation-action constructs with environment/contexts passing and/or constraints checking on the fly are necessary. Reactivity is required to abide to response-time constraints in industrial applications. Reactivity will hence be a major mode of execution at this level although some local dynamic planning of task interleaving may also be achieved in predefined situations (e.g. if a non mandatory optimisation task is lacking one of its inputs).

3.3.2 Functional description by message flow analysis

This section will identify message types in an Archon System (i.e. between agents) and will give a rough outline on how these messages are handled by the Archon Layer modules. Again, the purpose of this exercise is not implementation oriented but to explain the functional relationships and dependencies.

Message types

Two classification clusters have been identified: data messages vs. negotiation messages and expected vs. unexpected messages. Four types of (high level) messages are expected to arrive at an Archon agent:

1) information from an agent consisting of an update concerning its status, acquaintances, etc. *[unexpected data]*.
2) unexpected information (e.g. results achieved by an agent and volunteered to those it has registered as 'interested_in' in its AAM) *[unexpected data]*.
3) expected information (requested by its "cooperation-execution" functionality) *[expected data or expected negotiation message]*.
4) inquiries from other agents to enter a cooperation *[unexpected negotiation message]*.

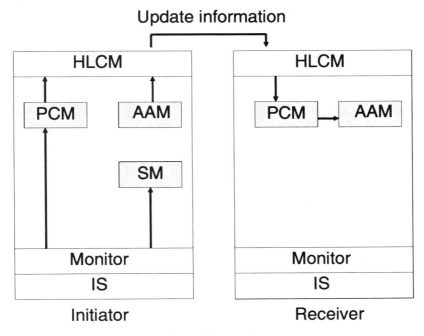

Fig. 3.5 Message Type 1

Information flow scenarios

This section describes the responsibilities of the Archon Layer modules (like AAM, SM, HLCM, etc.) by analysing the data flow of the above mentioned message types. By this analysis a clearer view of these modules concerning (a) their functionality, (b) the knowledge they have to provide and (c) their interaction, will be achieved.

Message Type 1

Update information for the AAM of an 'interested_in' agent will be routed by the HLCM of the receiving agent via the PCM to its AAM. The update information is generated in the sending agent either in the PCM (in case the interested-in type is concerned) or in the

Monitor (in case abstract descriptions of processing states are concerned). In both cases the message is sent to the HLCM. The HLCM of the initiator knows which agents are interested in this information by consulting the AAM. The receiving HLCM directly passes this information to its AAM. The Monitor of the initiator takes care of updating the SM within its own Archon Layer.

Message Type 2

Unexpected information has been sent by an agent (its PCM) that thought the information is important for other agents as well. All information produced by an IS will be passed by the Monitor to the AIM module where all local results are stored. The PCM will look into the AAM which contains a list of all parameters the other agents are interested in. From this information is it able to judge which other agent is interested in that result.

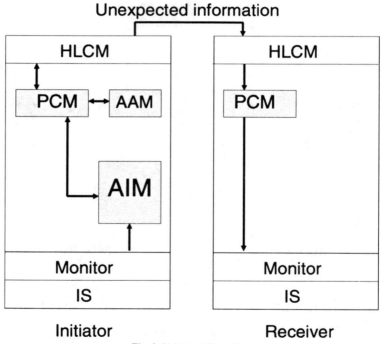

Fig. 3.6 Message Type 2

Agents can be interested in the entire result of a task of an IS, or in just a part of it. In the latter case the AAM will contain a 3DIS query expression which selects a part of the result. For example, if an agent is not interested in the entire black out area, but just whether the transformer at a specific location, e.g. at Hernani, is inside the area, the query expression would be:

INTERSECTION (PICK_R(RETRIEVE(black-out-area, has-element, ?)),
(PICK_D (RETRIEVE(?,has-name, transformer-hernani)))

This expression is sent by the PCM to AIM after the result has been stored there. The response of AIM to the query, if any, is then transferred to the PCM again. In both cases the information, classified as unrequested results, are passed to the HLCM for sending it to the respective agents.

All unexpected messages arriving at the receiver will be passed by the HLCM directly to the PCM. The PCM decides whether to pass the information to its Monitor (e.g. for IS task scheduling) or to ignore it (filtering). Unexpected information might be a trigger for "cooperation" (initiator part) as well. In this case it is up to the PCM to take this information as a trigger for further activities. In "nominal situations" these unrequested results might be also triggers on the Monitor level for local planning and acting.

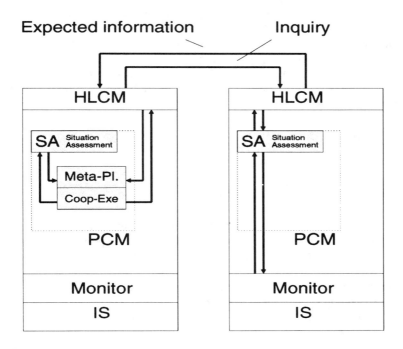

Fig. 3.7 Message Types 3 and 4

Message Type 3

Expected information is always the "answer" to an inquiry sent by the agent itself, i.e. the PCM has realised a need for cooperation, chosen a cooperation type (Client-Server, Contract Net, etc.) and has taken over the responsibility for the cooperation and finally initiated the inquiry.

A simple example: If the Monitor detects that a certain information XYZ is needed but not locally available, it passes this request (get me XYZ) to the PCM. The PCM asks AIM. AIM either provides the result (by establishing a query to the respective other AIM) or not. In the first case the result will be passed to the Monitor and the task is completed. In the latter case the PCM will choose the coordination type "client/server" that looks into the 'capability'-slot of the AAM and pass a suitable inquiry via its HLCM to the respective agent. The answer to this request will be passed directly via the HLCM to the PCM of the agent that has initiated the cooperation.

Message Type 4

An inquiry of another agent, i.e. an unexpected negotiation message, will be routed by the HLCM of the receiving agent to its PCM. The inquiry will be rejected or postponed by this PCM if answering will conflict with other plans of higher priority (e.g. PCM is going to launch an important and time consuming task in short). In all other cases the PCM will pass the inquiry either to the Monitor if the inquiry is about providing information or initiates further investigations in this matter if conflicting plans are concerned. There is no use in asking AIM to provide this particular information, because the initiator has done it already before (see section above) in vain.

The Monitor has the ability to reject the inquiry, if either the IS is too busy or executing the inquiry would endanger the underlying process, the IS has to take care of. Otherwise the Monitor establishes a local plan about how to schedule its tasks for providing the information it has been asked for. The Monitor sends the information back to the PCM which hands it over to the HLCM.

Figure 3.7 illustrates the message flow of message type 3 and 4 for the simpler type, an inquiry about providing information.

Detection for the need for cooperation

A cooperation with another agent will be initiated by the PCM. The following situations might lead to the necessity to initialise cooperation:

1) Plans or actions of two agents are contradicting or tend to contradict
2) The Monitor needs information that only another agent can provide
3) Due to an exceptional situation an agent may require the assistance of another agent

The detection of the need for cooperation and its initialisation is an important task of the PCM. Although, through a number of experiments, we have a good understanding of this functionality, it will still be a subject of further research in the project. Detection of the need for cooperation due to conflicting plans, to missing information or to task sharing possibilities (according to the definitions of [Smith, Davis 81]) will be of main concern.

The Planning and Coordination Module PCM

The principal tasks of the PCM are:

o *The surveillance of other agents activities:* Each agent receives from the other agents results, control and status information. The reasoning for dynamic planning of high level actions will hence be dependent on the type of information exchanged between the agents. This information will either be sent on request by a remote agent, or it will be automatically sent for update purpose of the agent models.

o *The choice of a communication protocol:* It is up to the PCM to set the proper protocol for information exchange between the agents. These protocols may themselves define the encapsulation of the messages as well as synchronisation points.

o   *Relevance/Adequacy of external requests:* Requests provided by other agents should be selected along the following criteria:
Internal capability and availability of the agent (this information is contained in the Self Model), and Compatibility with the current plan.

o   *Detection of global conflicts:* Tasks requested by another agent could require the use of non-sharable resources already allocated within the IS. Rejection of a request in such case must be properly forwarded to the requesting agent.

o   *Backtracking for non-nominal situations:* If a global conflict is detected between actions already scheduled and actions or plans of a remote agent, it may be necessary for the PCM to bring the system back to a safe state, unwinding if possible the effects of actions already executed. Different backtracking capabilities will depend on the IS, Monitor and PCM implementation ranging from a simple reset of the current IS to very fine backtracking capabilities allowing suspension of the Monitor and IS tasks and update of the current environment.

o   *Assessing the need for cooperation:* The need for a cooperation may be classified in two types related to their origin:
Exogeneous needs: conflicts between external plans or duplicated plans or sub-plans are exogeneous needs, and Endogeneous needs: examples of such needs may be a possible lack of input for a planned or executed IS task, need of additional information for Monitor or PCM reasoning, need of synchronisation between tasks distributed among several agents.

The Planning and Coordination Module (PCM) is responsible for all global situation assessment, planning and supervision. Archon has chosen a distributed Planning and Coordination Module. Every agent contains its own PCM, and by this Archon did not follow the numerous attempts in DAI with a "mediator" (e.g. [A.Satie, M.S.Fox 1989] among others), being responsible for all coordination ('mediation') of a community of autonomous agents as an external module. This decision has been made to achieve greater flexibility and avoid communication bottlenecks. Furthermore, it will provide an easy way to maintain the agent community (e.g. if another Archon agent enters the community). A consequence of the last aspect is reflected by one of the main architectural paradigms of Archon: to design the Archon Layer such that its basic services are identical for all agents and no hierarchy exist. The function of this module is threefold: It will provide services for monitoring (situation assessment), meta-planning and coordination of agents.

On the level of monitoring, the main task is the assessment of the global situation. The PCM has to monitor the activities of the agents, both the agent that this particular PCM belongs to and the other agents. This shows the main difference between the level of monitoring inside the PCM and the Monitor: The Monitor schedules ("monitors") its IS, the PCM monitors the agents. The PCM is in charge of coordination of semi-autonomous agents, while the Monitor acts as a controller of its underlying IS. The PCM contains all knowledge concerning assessment of the agent's local and community role and concerning support of cooperative interaction. The Monitor contains all knowledge concerning control of the underlying system.

The level of monitoring of the PCM consists of two distinct parts: A Reasoning based Detection (RbD) facility and a Direct Triggering component (DT). These two mechanisms will exist in parallel. The former is in itself a knowledge based system. For instance, it has to detect if plans of its agent contradict with the plans of other agents in the community. The latter is in principle a simple triggering mechanism for supporting "nominal" cooperation. The RbD facility is a dynamic planning system while most of the Direct Triggering component will end up in reactive planning. The output of both mechanisms on this level is the status of the agent, i.e. either 'idle' or an abstract description of the need for cooperation. The latter will be achieved by matching the current situation against generic cooperative situations.

Activation of the PCM module can be done either by direct request by one of the agents or as a result of the situation assessment by the PCM itself, e.g. the inconsistency of the plans of two agents will be detected by this functionality.

It is assumed that cooperation on the level of computation, which is mainly about providing a particular bit of information from another agent, will be initiated by direct triggering. More sophisticated forms of cooperation will be handled by the Reasoning Based Detection. For example, when agents are competing about limited resources, or trying to harmonise contradicting local plans. The principles of Reasoning Based Detection are still under investigation and will be subject of future work. For the time being, certain messages are used as triggers to initiate cooperation on the level of Situation Assessment in the PCM, which matches a "behaviour" as a reactive planning mechanism on the lower level of the PCM, i.e. the level of coordination.

After the PCM module has realised that there is a need for cooperation, a plan for the cooperation has to be established. This is the level of meta-planning. On this level the main task is to make a choice about which cooperation type fits best the need that has been detected.

In the following, some examples will be given to illustrate the principle of the Meta-Planning facility. If the PCM of Agent X knows by means of its AAM that Agent Y has some helpful information, a simple request to that Agent will be submitted to the DT facility of the PCM of the receiving agent. No further meta-planning is necessary. If the Situation assessment facility of the PCM gets a certain predefined pattern of information, a "behaviour" will be instantiated. Behaviours to be selected and instantiated will be: Negotiation by Game Theory, Contract Nets, or Argumentation Protocols.

On the level of meta-planning the PCM has to contain an abstract description of these Cooperation Types (= Behaviours) as well as an abstract description of the cooperation-scenarios they are supporting, in order to match these against the problem description handed over by the level of situation assessment.

The execution of what has been decided on the planning level is performed and supervised on the level of coordination. Coordination of agents will be performed by submodules, that have been selected and triggered at the level of meta-planning. The research community in AI is currently working on identification of further modes for cooperation. Archon, therefore, will not restrict itself to a set of cooperation types, but provide a framework for integration of different cooperation modes that can be activated dynamically on the level of meta-planning in the PCM. The coordination of agents, performed by these submodules, requires strategic cooperative knowledge and the authority to initialise a cooperation. A reference implementation of some of the possible submodules will clarify the view of the project on how this authority will be granted.

Since each agent contains a PCM module, it may happen that different PCMs are triggered by their Monitors at the same time. In every cooperative situation at least two agents are involved, one agent acts as the "initiator" while the other is triggered and acts as "respondent". Due to this design choice it is possible that one PCM acts as an initiator and as a respondent at the same time but for different problems. The different levels of the PCM are shown in figure 3.8.

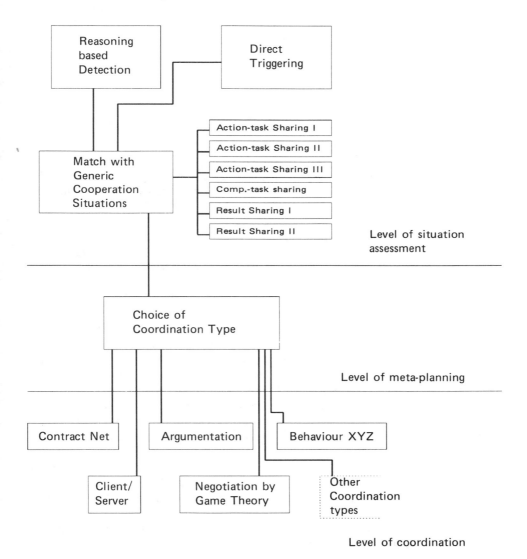

Fig. 3.8 The Planning and Coordination Module

The Monitor
The Monitor is the only link between the underlying system and the other parts of the Archon Layer. As such its main role is to be a remote control of the underlying system. The IS tasks at the level of granularity defined during the design should be triggered, suspended, rescheduled or killed by the Monitor itself. The adjective "remote" is to stress the fact that the Monitor will communicate with the IS through messages and is not an

integral part of the IS. All messages flowing between the IS and the Archon Layer should hence be generated or received by the Monitor (e.g. scheduling messages such as starting a task, suspension, or abortion, as well as requests and error/control messages generated by the IS). Hence, the main decisions concerning the control of the IS will take place within the Monitor, while the decisions it is not able to deal with should be made by the PCM in the upper part of the Archon Layer.

The main functionalities of the Monitor are:

o   *Perception of the Information*: The information that will be used for this functionality comes from multiple sources :
    - The underlying IS.
    - The higher level of planning.
    - The other agents.
    Update of this information is asynchronous (e.g. messages may be generated by the IS and received within the Monitor and in the meantime the global context may be updated by the PCM).

o   *Access to the Self Model*: To access the Self Model content, read and update mechanisms are provided. As the Self Model will be a local structured memory of both dynamic and static information, the Monitor will have to decide on Self Model updating for further use of this information.

o   *Situation Assessment*: Characterisation of a local situation is done by dynamic checking and clustering of the information contained in the messages. Heterogeneity of the knowledge used requires typing conventions to be shared between the sender and the receiver of the message and a pattern matching mechanism to be used by the perception functionality to recognise these types. The types of the messages sent should hence be known beforehand. In the nominal cases (outside of exception or stepwise refinement), the situation assessment provides sufficiently accurate information for the reactive planning functionality to choose and instantiate the plans. The asynchrony of the information occurrence quoted above leads to a design choice for the assessment of the global context:
    - The context provided may be assessed continuously. This allows the Monitor to react on-line to new global situations generated by the PCM or the other agents. A possible draw-back may be the inconsistency caused within the Monitor by interrupting the reactive planning.
    - The context may be assessed periodically: functions in the Monitor will take into account context changes at pre-defined points in time.

o   *Update of Local Information*: Local information is analysed and clustered for local decision making of the reactive planning activity but also to allow higher level of assessment (carried out by the PCM). The decisions made for the local reactive planning and the status information of the IS/Monitor are passed to the PCM either directly or through the Self Model (stability of these information is a criterion to determine the proper location).

o   *Description of High Level Goals*: In non-nominal situations the context received may encompass the description of high level goals. For instance, the result of global exceptional conditions may force the Monitor to drastically change the current activity of its IS (e.g. quick rough diagnostic of the network). In this case the goal and the other information transmitted through the context will be defined with the same granularity and synchronously updated. This goal-oriented dependency between the Monitor and the PCM is a way to increase the autonomy of the agents during the development phase of an application. If the situation characterised by the PCM is expressed in a more informative manner than hierarchical dependencies between actions, backtracking among environment will be easier to install.

o   *Decision/Action Planning*: Situation analysis will allow to instantiate the behaviour and make a choice among the actions and actions plans. These plans refer to available IS functions and their synchronisation constraints (e.g. two tasks updating the same data structure should not do it concurrently).

o   *Execution Tracking*: Analysis of the message flow (input and output of a task, error and warning messages, intermediate results) between the IS and the Monitor should allow a tracking of the execution. There are many situations that are difficult to determine beforehand and which should be tracked during the execution:
- Incompleteness of an input needed for executing one IS function.
- Inaccurate or incomplete output of the IS function execution.
- Warning or errors produced by the IS if it encountered a problem during execution (like resource deficiency).

In case the IS is unable to generate auto-diagnostic messages, the tracking should be fully delegated to the Monitor. Therefore, the Monitor itself must contain a richer model of the IS behaviour including all the required conditions listed above.

o   *Re-planning*: Local or global exceptions and situations of incompleteness may force the Monitor to re-plan its actions and/or trigger the level of reasoning in the PCM. A replanning may hence locally trigger a dynamic reasoning. This will be in charge of re-building the plan of actions taking into account characteristics of the local control, the messages, or the IS status, either obtained already or expected.

In order to bridge the gap between these functionalities and the IS control facilities, the Monitor will make extensive use of the behaviours. The self model will be used as a storage structure for these behaviours.

4

The Communication Functionality of the Architecture

4.1 GENERAL REQUIREMENTS

In order to cooperate agents must be able to interact. They may interact either by acting (and recognising their acts) on the real world or by communicating. In industrial applications communication is the most common means of interaction since it facilitates coordinated and flexible behaviour which would otherwise be impossible to achieve. Furthermore community members are normally physically distributed over several hardware platforms, meaning that efficient and reliable communication is a prerequisite for a sophisticated cooperation environment.

For achieving cooperation between different expert systems, an 'open' communication has to be used, which allows not only the transfer of data in the conventional sense, but the interchange of knowledge and the solution to problems formulated on a high abstraction level. In Archon the OSI (Open Systems Interconnection) layering concepts intended for a communication system have been extended to a cooperating system. While OSI has been considered as a starting framework, deviations from and alterations to its concept have been made. In Archon there is a need for communication between cooperating agents to be carried out with a sufficient amount of embedded intelligence. This has been achieved by altering some of the conventional OSI Layer protocols and by incorporating a higher level module (HLCM), where much of this intelligence resides.

Driven by these deviations an Archon Reference Model analogous to the OSI Reference model has been introduced. The scope of the Archon Reference Model is also analogous to the scope of the OSI Reference Model, i.e.

a) to specify a universally applicable logical structure encompassing the requirements of Archon.
b) to act as a reference during the development of new ideas and the definition of the corresponding procedures
c) to enable different agents to cooperate by encouraging the compatible implementation of cooperation and communication features.

The proposed Archon Reference model reflects a salient difference not encountered in conventional OSI systems. In general, OSI provides a protocol stack for communications protocols to serve predefined higher level distributed applications. Lower layer functions, some also addressing communications, exist and are used in Archon with hardly any alterations. It is the higher layers which are newly developed here and which take a supervising and coordinating role to existing intelligent systems.

Hence the Reference architecture has been drastically influenced in this reverse relationship between new and preexisting functions in Archon and traditional OSI systems. As in OSI, the Session Layer in Archon is above the actual application (Archon Layer) and below the transport mechanism used. A decision was made early in the project to rely on ready available facilities for transport mechanisms (e.g. TCP/UDP Unix internetworking communication). We have thus excluded the more elaborate transports protocols of OSI.

The Session Layer comprised an entirely new development for Archon and is incorporated in the so called Communication Platform. The need to deviate from OSI was mainly based on the existence of one-to-one and one-to-many communication possibilities. The latter has not yet been standardised in OSI. For Archon, Session Layer means the layer where communication facilities are offered and tailored to their users, i.e. to the upper layer in the Archon Reference model. We have followed a common approach to incrementally cover more sophisticated communication needs.

However, the Archon Layer modules normally do not access these services directly but through HLCM services. This further layer allows the reasoning modules to avoid evaluations such as which type of connection to establish, when to retransmit a message, how long to wait for an acknowledgement and so on. Furthermore, the HLCM supplies other services more related to the "aim" of communication. In particular, the reasoning modules may ask the HLCM to send messages to "agents which are interested in the message" (this is an example of intelligent addressing), or to receive only certain type of messages (filtering) or to give priority to certain messages (scheduling). It is important to note that the HLCM itself makes no decision about receiving/sending messages. So, for example, if the Monitor wants to receive only messages from agent X about subject Y, it will have to set all the necessary filters. This can be done at run time. The rationale for this separation of concerns is that the HLCM has no knowledge about the type of cooperation which has been established among agents, therefore it can only offer services but not take decision. One can imagine the HLCM being an efficient secretary able to perform tasks such as dispatching information to all interested persons, selecting which phone calls to pass to his boss, etc.

We can summarise the quality requirements for communication at the Archon Layer with the following:

o   optimal exploitation of hardware and software communication resources supplied by the lower layers
o   increased reliability
o   hiding of low level communication problems to the A.L. modules

The functional requirements are:

o   message filtering
o   message scheduling
o   intelligent addressing
o   routing of messages into the A.L. (It is generally recognised, however that the messages from the HLCM to the Archon Layer will have to be addressed to certain modules rather then generally to all the Archon Layer modules.)

4.2 HLCM AND SESSION LAYER

The HLCM is the High Level Communication Module as seen from the Archon Layer. It provides services on the level required by the PCM, the Monitor, and the AAM. The HLCM, however, requires further services to establish the communication with other agents in the Archon community. These services are provided by the Session Layer. The following section first describes the services provided by the underlying Session Layer and then those provided by the HLCM.

4.2.1 The Session Layer

Connectionless point to point services
Rationale
There are cases where the communication needs are limited to a mere exchange of messages between agents, where one agent sends a message to a single destination. It is obvious that the advanced features offered by the point to multipoint software are not adequately used and so there is no reason to pay the cost of using such a sophisticated piece of software with a great degree of complexity which implies an increased resource consumption and overhead.

Furthermore if the data exchange is spread across time there is no need to have the overhead of creating, maintaining and releasing a connection each time that a relatively small amount of data has to be transferred. The next sub-section will present the design of the connectionless point to point services.

Design
In order to meet such requirements the communication schema is structured as follows:

o   There is only one type of session entity

o   This entity enables the session user to send to as well as receive messages from any other "known" session user residing in the same network, including the user itself.

o   There is no connection establishment neither connection release phase. From the time that a session entity is created and if it is "known" to the community of entities, it can send and receive messages without any other connecting procedure. By the time that a session user does not need the session services any more it can shut down the session entity. This does not have any effect on the communication carried out by other session users.

o   A session entity has a name (assigned by its user) that enables the distinction between entities. A session entity is considered "known" to the community, if its name appears in the session configuration file that is local to every active session entity.

Connectionless multipoint services
Rationale
We have mentioned previously that in order to use the advanced features offered by the connection oriented point to multipoint session services, one has to pay the overhead introduced by the complexity of such a software piece. Furthermore, this complexity

seems at present to create problems with the LISP interface.

A solution to the problems stated in the previous paragraph could be the following: we could simply build a new sublayer over the existing connectionless services that have been tested and proved to interface with lisp successfully.

The new sublayer will be "transparent" as it concerns the services already provided by the connectionless point-to-point Session Layer. This means that if one is interested in using only the services provided by the connectionless Session Layer he will have only the small overhead introduced by the low complexity of this layer. Only the more demanding users that want to make use of the services of the new connectionless point to multipoint sublayer will have the overhead caused by the greater complexity.

Design

The connectionless point to multipoint services are meant to be used in situations that the simple point to point connectionless services are not adequate. It is evident that since the more efficient way to exchange messages between two agents is to use the appropriate point to point connectionless service, the new sublayer should offer a set of more complex services, and for the sake of efficiency should be used only when those services are needed.

Connection-oriented point to multipoint services
Rationale

The state of research in the communication aspects of Archon assumes the existence of a special Communication Agent on the Session Layer which will serve as a "Communication Mediator" for the communication between agents. It will provide storage and retrieval of messages in a common data storage area, establish multi-end-point sessions or broadcasting. The previously described connectionless multipoint services can be enhanced to connection oriented ones. In fact this has been previously defined during years 1 and 2 of the Archon project. By explicitly identifying connections the overhead during the actual data transfer phase can be reduced. The connection oriented services are more reliable than the connectionless, however this has not been found an important factor during the software testing phase. Hence the connection oriented services remain for the present in the background and will be reused later in the project. For complexness we give a brief outline of the connection oriented point-to-multipoint services.

Design
The communication schema is structured as follows:

o   There are three types of session entities named as: a source entity, a communication mediator and a sink entity. The source entity together with the communication mediator have the responsibility of a session connection. The source can update the common data storage area of the communication agent and it can initiate the release of the session connection. The sink entity can read from the common data storage area, ask to attach itself to a session connection, and abandon from a session connection.

o   There is a connection establishment phase, a data transfer phase and a connection release phase. For example, during the session connection phase the connection services can be used.

The session connection phase enables the session user (HLCM) to be connected with other users (HLCMs) through a session connection. The user has to create a source and a communication mediator and to connect itself to the source session entity by sending an S-CONNECTION-REQUEST primitive.

4.2.2 The HLCM

The aim of the HLCM module is twofold, on the one hand it supplies advanced communication services such as intelligent addressing, message filtering and message scheduling. On the other hand it ensures the efficient use of the services supplied by the Session Layer (e.g. selection of connection oriented or connection less services). The service structure of the HLCM is designed following the OSI services conventions (recommendation X.210). Each service is normally implemented via four primitives:

1 Request (from source user to HLCM)
2 Indication (from HLCM to destination user)
3 Response (from destination user to HLCM)
4 Confirm (from HLCM to source user)

Where a user is a software module that calls upon the HLCM services. This structure may be modified (in particular response and/or confirm may be avoided) by the user using the commands provided.
The services provided by the HLCM to its users are the following:

o ASK: Via this service the source user informs one or more of the agents in the community of a request. The HLCM keeps track of these requests and it is able to associate the request with its answer(s) when the appropriate TELL (see below) is issued. The user may specify if it wants to receive all the answers at the same time or one by one as soon as they arrive.

o ASK-NEGOTIATE: This service supports the bidding and assignment phases of the contract-net protocol. The HLCM service users indicates its request and the parameters (e.g. time, accuracy, etc.) over which the receivers are to bid.

o ASK-SINGLE-VALUE: This service is used in order to inform a set of agents in the community of a request of the source user. The HLCM keeps track of the request and selects one answer (TELL) on the base of a procedure specified by the source user. Example of such procedures are: "first-value" (the HLCM returns the first answer that arrives and concludes the dialogue), "highest value" (the answers must be numeric and the HLCM returns the highest one), etc.

o TELL: this service is used in order to supply an answer to a previous request which another agent has made via an ASK service. The user of this service is requested to specify the identifier of the ASK to which it is answering. The message may be distributed to other agents which did not issue an explicit request.

- o TELL-UNREQUEST: through this service a user may supply unrequested information to other agents in the community.

- o CIRCULAR: using this service a user may circulate a "modifiable" message among an ordered set of agents until a specified condition on the message becomes true (e.g. until the message changes, the content is equal to a given string, etc.).

This is not an exhaustive list of all the possible services that the Archon Layer modules may require from the HLCM. The HLCM is designed so that new services may be added whenever necessary. For all the above mentioned services, the HLCM service user is allowed to specify the destination of the message using the following language which abstracts from name and addresses:

```
l_des  ::=      <agents identifiers list> |
                interested in <list of subjects> |
                workload less then {<value> | average}
                sharing interests agents |
                everyone |
                and l_des |
                or l_des
```

The HLCM service users may also use a set of commands which modify the HLCM behaviour. Examples of these commands are:

- o SET-CONNECTION-FILTER: adds one filter for connection establishment. Each filter may specify conditions on the source and/or type and/or abstract of the message. Before accepting a connection request, the HLCM of a receiving agent, checks if that message should be rejected by looking at the connection filters.

- o REMOVE-CONNECTION-FILTER: removes the specified filter from the list of existing ones.

5

The Information Modelling within the Architecture

As pointed out in Chapter 3, the agent community has to deal with two different types of knowledge: the Cooperation Knowledge (how to interact and cooperate with other agents) and the Information Knowledge (how to represent and exchange information). This Chapter concentrates on this Information Knowledge, which again has to be seen under two different aspects:

(1) How to model, access and exchange domain related information that originally resides only in the ISs of the agents.
(2) How to model and represent information about the agents that is necessary for the Archon Layer functions to reason about and to establish links with other agents.

At the first glance, these two aspects may not appear to be much related. But if, for example, one agent urgently requires some information for its IS, it has to know which other agent can possibly supply this information (Aspect 2), it has to find out if that agent already has that information available (by accessing it), and if it is available it has to exchange it (Aspect 1).

This Chapter describes how these aspects are realised in the Archon framework from a conceptual point of view. As this book does not go into details concerning the implementation, it is worth pointing out here that the Agent Models described in the second section will be implemented in the distributed information sharing architecture, thus providing the required union of the two aspect mentioned above.

5.1 INFORMATION KNOWLEDGE AT THE ARCHON LAYER

Archon is a framework for embedding a collection of software systems (ISs) in a single cooperative architecture. Each IS (Intelligent System) has the information knowledge on different aspects of a complex problem domain. However, in general each IS has only partial information knowledge with respect to the entire problem domain, and some overlap of information knowledge exists among ISs.

In a control environment for example, some ISs may be controlling parts of an external physical system, or they may support and advise human operators who are controlling parts of an external physical system. These cooperating software systems are initially decoupled from each other. This means that ISs may use different local mechanisms to represent their information knowledge, they may associate different structures and semantics to the represented information, as well as employing different local control mechanisms.

A global framework such as Archon must provide appropriate means to represent and access the common part of these possibly diverse information models. It should contain:

(1) An *object-oriented information modelling formalism* to model and represent the complex static and dynamic information of the ISs within the agents.
(2) An *object-oriented query and update language* to support the sophisticated access, query, and update of data and meta-data of Archon ISs.
(3) An *object-oriented information knowledge access and sharing technique* to support the exchange of information and negotiation on access rights among autonomous agents.

This chapter in some detail the different kinds of information knowledge to be represented at the Archon Layer and how the above stated requirements are met.

5.1.1 Overview of the Problem

Within a system of cooperating ISs a large variety of information is manipulated. Some of this information describes the world that the system acts on, some is used to control the cooperation, and some defines the relation between other information and the elements that process information. The problem of information exchange among cooperating ISs is due to the following facts. Typically, each IS independently (locally) defines its own model of information, data structures, and operations to process the information.

On the other hand, sharing of information among ISs usually involves large volumes of complex structured data. Therefore (without an information management framework), data sharing within an Archon community would be performed in a completely adhoc manner. For one IS to receive some data from another it must also receive all the structural information and semantics defined on this data. Also, the entire task of interpreting and filtering the received data to make them suitable for use must be performed at the receiver IS itself. This makes the transfer of information quite costly. Furthermore, consider the case where there is neither a global data exchange mechanism, nor a global information modelling formalism to be used by ISs. Then, the details of the structural information (namely, the information representation, semantics, and operations defined on the information, and the distribution of information among ISs) must all be known to ISs involved prior to information exchange. It would be partly included in the application programs and partly in users' minds. As a result, the structural information is redundantly stored within the Archon community of ISs, and the exchange of information becomes quite vulnerable. Another drawback of this redundant storage is the consistency problem that emerges when ISs modify their structural information.

The main goal of embedding independent semi-autonomous ISs within one system is to obtain a single environment composed of loosely-coupled software systems that cooperate to achieve better performance in handling tasks and responding to users requests. Archon will provide a universe of discourse to support the cooperation among these ISs. Each IS represents some pieces of information (results) that it is able to produce and it contains a description of the information it needs to receive (this information is produced by other ISs). Furthermore, it incorporates mechanisms to receive that information, and it has its own local control knowledge. In order to support the cooperation among ISs, the Archon architecture introduces the Archon Layer for each IS. An Archon system is then defined as a collection of interrelated Agents, where each agent is an IS together with its Archon Layer. Archon agents use heterogeneous models to represent their information which in turn complicates the exchange of information.

A requirement to solve this problem is to develop an appropriate formalism in which the information that an agent produces, or needs to receive, can be described. It is necessary to support data models and higher level representation mechanisms in which the information of agents can be expressed more concisely. Modelling constructs supported by the framework must be general enough to represent the information common to the Archon application domain and at the same time capable of representing the specific information of agents.

Exchange and sharing of information among cooperating agents can be organised in two different ways. One way is to provide a number of functions, specific for each agent, that return some predefined selection of all the information an agent has (or can generate). The main disadvantage is that these functions encode detailed knowledge about the information needs of other agents. If these needs change, these functions have to be changed as well. Furthermore, different agents may have varying needs. To reduce the total number of functions, and to reduce the chance that they will have to be frequently adapted, the designer will be tempted to return a superset of the information needed, so that an agent can select upon receipt what it is really interested in.

The second way is to define a global information access/sharing mechanism that uses a global data model to represent the information of each agent, and provides a global language (such as a relational, functional, logical, graph-based, etc.) defined on the global model to support the agents' interactions. The second way approaches and resolves a wider spectrum of communication problems among agents:

(1) It establishes a common framework among the agents to define information structures and for manipulating them.
(2) It is more flexible, so no changes are needed in one agent if other agents need to access different parts of its information, or if they need to access its information in a different way.
(3) It supports the philosophy of loosely-coupled systems where we do not want to fix agents' interaction (in this case the access of information) in an a priori manner.
(4) It supports the efficiency. If an agent is interested in a small subset of information (e.g. a few elements out of a large set), it is much better to perform the selection at the site of the agent where the set is stored, rather than transfer all the data (most of which is not needed), and let the receiving agent perform the selection. Also, where no simple query language is available, one would have to introduce new message types for all commonly used queries.

Such a global formalism and framework can be included within the Archon Layer and supported by it. The Archon Layer can then offer support to cope with the representational differences between semantically compatible structures defined in different ISs. A major advantage of this global formalism is that the information structures that reoccur in many systems can be made to look identical at the Archon Layer. This is the approach taken for the Information Sharing Architecture (ISA). As such, the availability of a global formalism and framework forms a non-biased starting point for designing the structure of information exchange and agents' cooperation, for which it provides a minimal set of constraints. Furthermore this approach provides a proper framework for addressing some specific requirements that have been identified by the Archon applications. These are:

(1) Logging of results. Logging of results is needed to support a retrospective analysis of critical situations occurring in an application (e.g. a disturbance in the electricity network) and the way the Archon community of agents reacts to them. Since the information requirements of this analysis cannot be predicted in advance a model of all results and a language to flexibly select elements is needed.
(2) Flexible and dynamic selection of information for the user. For the user interface a tool (language) is needed to allow the user to define which information he is interested to receive and in which information he is not interested in.
(3) Exchange of highly complex datastructures. Within a robotics application this problem is particularly pressing since here we encounter commercially developed ISs, such as vision systems and CAD modellers, that generate highly complex datastructures such as edge adjacency graphs and boundary representations of objects. Typically, two agents that use the same information, especially if they are developed separately, will define the structure differently. This leads to problems in the exchange of information, where conversion is needed and in maintaining the consistency between the different structures when they are modified. The ISA approach facilitates the design of each agent if the agent is free to choose the representation that is best suited for its needs, without being concerned with the needs of other agents.

5.1.2 The Agent Information Management module: AIM

ISA serves to provide a framework for interconnected agents in which they can maintain their autonomy in modelling and sharing the information, yet it supports mechanisms for a substantial degree of complex information sharing, and while minimising the central authority. Therefore, the architecture of the AIM module is an approach to the coordinated sharing and interchange of computerised information among autonomous, loosely-coupled agents. Applying the principles of Archon (loosely-coupled, semi-autonomous agents) to ISA, we can state the following requirements:

(1) Agents cannot be forced to provide information to other agents.
(2) Agents can determine their own view of existing data. (There is no global schema, describing the information produced by all agents, rather, each agent builds its own schema).

Components of ISA

To realise this approach to information exchange by ISA, the following components are needed:

(1) A *global information modelling formalism* in which an agent can describe both the information it wishes to share with the community and the information it wishes to receive from the community.
(2) A *global query and update language* to access the available information, to be used by all agents in the community.

(3) A *global information access method* by which agents can know about the information of other agents and by which they can request and access that information remotely.

A main requirement for the global information modelling formalism is that it should be possible to easily model the complex information of agents and express the concepts that agents communicate among each other. A main requirement for the global language is to at least support the basic primitive query and update operations as well as being capable to support higher level operations specific to certain ISs.

In the remainder the choices that have been made for its components will be presented. It should be emphasised that no exhaustive search of 'all' possibilities to find the ultimate 'best' answer has been carried out. Rather, the goal has been to find solutions that are adequate and well tuned to each other, but sufficiently simple to be feasible within the scope of the Archon project, and which are roughly as good as (a decision that was based on our expertise in the area) the other alternatives. A commercial implementation of Archon is bound to make different choices, but this would not affect the architecture, nor how it is used by the applications.

The global information modelling formalism used for ISA is the 3DIS (3 Dimensional Information Space) an extensible object-oriented information management model. The global query and update language used for ISA is the 3DIS/ISL (3DIS/Information Sub-Language) developed on top of the 3DIS model.

The design of a global distributed information access method for ISA, called 3DIS/DIA (3DIS/Distributed Information Access), is based on the Federated Information architecture developed by [Heimbigner 85]. The Federated Information architecture was originally designed for integrating local databases in an office environment, while allowing complete local control over each of them. The 3DIS/DIA formalism developed in ISA provides mechanisms for sharing data and operations on data, and for combining information from several agents to facilitate the coordination of activities among autonomous agents.

The 3DIS: The Information Modelling Formalism of ISA

The information modelling formalism chosen for ISA is the 3DIS (3-Dimensional Information Space), [Afsarmanesh 89]. The 3DIS is a simple but extensible object-oriented information model. It is defined in terms of objects (a subset of which are mapping-objects) and relationships defined among objects. Objects are referred to by a unique designator, or by their value if they are atomic objects (e.g. strings, numbers). Relationships are simple triples of the form "(domain- object, mapping-object, range-object)".

Some basic reasons for choosing the 3DIS are:

(1) 3DIS is simple, and a simple implementation can support it, so no major implementation effort is required.
(2) 3DIS has successfully been used for engineering and design applications, [Afsarmanesh 89b]. This makes it more likely that it will be easy to express the concepts of the application domain of Archon.
(3) 3DIS integrates well with the architecture for information sharing, which is used to access the remote information.

A 3DIS model of application is a collection of interrelated objects, where an object represents any identifiable piece of information, of arbitrary kind and level of abstraction. The 3DIS unifies the view and treatment of all kinds of information as objects. The uniform treatment applies to both data and the description and classification of data (also called meta-data) that is usually treated differently in object-oriented data models. Therefore, types are also objects and their properties are modelled by relationships.

This makes it easy for database users to model, view, access, and query the structural information and the data content of databases. It also simplifies the user-database communications by unifying the data-definition and data-manipulation languages into a single database language. A single database language permits the same database language constructs to be used in querying and updating both the schema and the data content of the database.

The 3DIS data modelling formalism is a base on top of which the structures and the operations specific to an application environment (schema) can be defined. This, however, does not have to be done in one step. Instead a hierarchy of concepts can be developed where the concepts closer to the ROOT of the 3DIS-kernel define more general structures common to many application environments. Concepts further away from the ROOT will support increasingly narrow application domains. The 3DIS-kernel is the base on top of which 3DIS-schemas specific to applications will be defined.

The 3DIS information modelling formalism is extensible in the sense that Abstract Data Types (ADTs) specific to applications can be easily defined and supported using the 3DIS modelling constructs. Previously, in applying the 3DIS information model to certain engineering and design applications, several domain specific ADTs are developed in terms of 3DIS modelling constructs. Among these, the definition of ordered sets, multilists, binary trees, and the hierarchic definition of design components in terms of 3DIS modelling constructs can be mentioned.

The 3DIS/ISL: The Query and Update Language of ISA
The 3DIS/ISL is an object-oriented query and update language defined on top of the 3DIS model. This language provides a set of primitives to uniformly define, access, retrieve, modify, and activate (for procedural objects) the structural (meta-data) and non-structural (data) content of the 3DIS information-bases.

The 3DIS/ISL includes a small set of simple but functionally powerful object-oriented primitives, called the "Object Specification Operations". These operations support the data definition and data manipulation of the 3DIS modelling constructs. In specific, the operations allow users to add new objects (that may be of the kind atomic, composite, or type), to remove existing objects from a database, to create and destroy relationships among existing database objects, to retrieve objects and relationships among objects, to invoke behavioural objects, and to display objects on appropriate devices.

The object specification operations contain "basic operations" and "extended operations". The basic operations are primitives to query and update the 3DIS information-bases, while the extended operations are somewhat compound operations (defined on top of the basic operations) to assist the programmer (user) of 3DIS/ISL language. For instance, set manipulation operations and the iteration of a command on the elements of a set are supported as extended operations.

The set of object retrieval operations supported by 3DIS/ISL language is "complete" in the sense that it provides the same expressive power as a relational calculus. Later to better support ISA, we will extend the 3DIS/ISL language. A possible extension is the addition of a command to support the recursive search of related objects in a 3DIS-schema to answer a query on the existence of a relationship between two 3DIS objects. Such a primitive command is also needed to be defined to support the recursive search of connected nodes in a graph to answer a query on the existence of a path between two nodes. Such a query cannot be expressed with the current definition of the 3DIS/ISL language. Additional extensions to 3DIS/ISL are foreseen to support the 3DIS/DIA mechanism of information access and information sharing.

The 3DIS/DIA: The Distributed Information Access Formalism of ISA
The 3DIS/DIA (3DIS/Distributed Information Architecture) is a model and mechanism developed to support the distributed information sharing among loosely-coupled semi-autonomous cooperating agents within Archon. 3DIS/DIA uses the 3DIS information modelling formalism and the 3DIS/ISL language as the base. The 3DIS/DIA formalism is still at the design and modelling stage. Specifically, the design of the Archon community dictionary and the type and map derivation operators are incomplete. We expect our study and experimentation with the Archon application domain to help us determine what is required to be supported by these components of the 3DIS/DIA formalism.

For each AIM module a "private schema", an "export schema", and an "import schema" is to be developed. The private schema represents the structure of the private information stored in the AIM module. The export schema represents the structure of the information an agent wishes to share with other agents. The import schema represents the structure of the information an agent wishes to receive, which is exported by other agents.

Any exchange of information is done after the establishment of a negotiation between two agents. This negotiation involves determining which information to be exchanged and which rights are associated to the receiver agent with regards to which part of the information (rights to read, rights to write, rights to transfer these rights to other agents, etc.).

Using a predefined negotiation protocol, agents can contact each other directly to negotiate the export and import of information on types and maps. Once the negotiation on a type (or map) is completed a contract will be established, further access to the information content of this type (or map) is direct and without the overhead of negotiation.

It is important to notice that the actual transfer of data occurs when the importer (receiver) tries to access the instances of the type (or map) which is dealt with the same way as accessing the content of the type locally within an agent. For example, a query given to the AIM module of agent A that refers to a type exported by the AIM module of agent B will in fact retrieve information from the AIM module of agent B. The negotiation contract between two agents guarantees that the exporter will not modify the definition (structure or semantic) of the type (or map) unless it informs the importer. Later modifications to the contract, initiated by exporter or importer, may also be performed through the negotiation protocol.

A set of type and map derivation operations are also introduced to be applied to derive (and define) an agent's import schema based on other agents' export schemas. The derivation operators are essentially set operators from the relational calculus domain. These were chosen because they make it possible to resolve a large class of conversions of structural information (description and classification information), while at the same time being sufficiently simple to implement.

Development and Implementation Strategy of AIM

The main design decision was to decide that shared information is stored in the AIM module, and that the query is interpreted by the AIM module. This means that the AIM module, and therefore the Archon Layer as well, performs the function of a distributed information system. Information that an IS wishes to share with other agents will be copied to the Archon Layer and gets updated when necessary.

This approach has the following advantages:

(1) Immediate access can be guaranteed by the Archon Layer, since every time an information request arrives it can be processed immediately, without waiting for the IS.
(2) Distribution of information, maintaining local copies, performing broadcasts, etc. is all under the control of the Archon Layer, and can therefore be optimised by Archon.

The alternative would have been to translate 3DIS queries to the language of the IS and to let the IS execute the query. This was considered too complex, though not impossible.

5.2 AGENT MODELS

In order to participate in cooperative activity, agents need to be able to reflect about their role and also that of others within the community. This leads to two distinct types of knowledge being maintained: knowledge about local beliefs, desires and intentions (stored in the self model) and knowledge about other community members with which the local agent may have to interact (stored in the acquaintance models).

As well as representing information about different entities, there is a clear distinction in the way in which these two types of model are obtained. The agent's self model will be predominantly completed by the intelligent system designer and can be regarded as an abstract description (it only needs to represent those features which are relevant to the Archon Layer) of the underlying system. The models of acquaintances, on the other hand, need not be so detailed and accurate, as they are used for cooperative purposes rather than for detailed control. Therefore it is possible that these models may be built up in a more dynamic manner (such as during the course of interaction or by negotiation, for example).

The exact nature of the information which should be maintained about agents is one of the major open issues in contemporary DAI. The term **acquaintance** was introduced to the Distributed Artificial Intelligence (DAI) community by the ACTORS work [Agha 85, Agha 86]. In this early work, acquaintances were defined as other agents known in the environment and **acquaintance models** were confined to representing the name and location of acquaintances.

More recently these models have been extended: an acquaintance model now corresponds to an agent's view of the world in which it resides - "it provides an environmental model by representing explicit models of other agents in the world" [Gasser 87]. These extensions permit agents to incorporate models of the behaviour and capabilities of their acquaintances, and allow them to reason about their actions.

A corollary of the above definition is that agents will not necessarily maintain models of all community members; it is more likely that each agent will merely model a subset of the total community. This subset is constructed on the basis of similar interests/capabilities or the ability to provide services which the local agent cannot perform (e.g. solve certain goals or furnish particular pieces of information).

Another defining characteristic is that they are **explicit representations**. This means that they are an integral part of the structure of an agent and that their contents are open to inspection.

At this stage there have been few attempts to define, in a rigorous manner, the type of knowledge needed to support cooperative interaction; therefore like many other authors (e.g. [Avouris 89, Brandau 89, Gasser 88]) we have defined it through experimentation.

5.2.1 Information contained in Agent Models

Before we give a more detailed presentation of the Agent Models in Archon, we first describe the information contained in them by a higher level classification:

o   State Knowledge

   Indicates the activities which are currently being carried out, how far they have progressed and when they are likely to be completed. This knowledge is highly dynamic in nature, therefore appropriate mechanisms must be employed to ensure communication channels are not swamped with state information, e.g. each agent maintains a description of the tasks it is carrying out and their status (executing, finished, waiting for information, etc.).

o   Capability Knowledge

   Knowledge about actions which can be performed, how they are combined to achieve particular results, the information they require, the results which can be expected. This knowledge will typically be fairly static in nature unless community members are capable of transferring capabilities as well as data between themselves.

o   Intentional Knowledge

   Contains a high level description of the targets an agent is working towards or will be working towards in the near future. They are fairly stable in nature as they represent the systems longer term objectives. Complex agents are likely to have several intentions active at any one time and an agent's intentions may conflict with those of others within the community.

o   Evaluative Knowledge

   When faced with several alternatives for achieving the same objective, evaluative knowledge provides a means of distinguishing between them, e.g. tasks T1 and T2 may both produce result R, however one may produce the result in a faster way than the other. All things being equal, an agent would usually use this information to select the task which can produce the result fastest.

o   Domain Knowledge

> Facts and relationships which hold true of the environment in which the agent is operating. For example, never do task T1 and T2 in parallel, task T1 is more important than T2 in most circumstances and so on.

5.2.2 Types of Acquaintance Models in Archon

Within Archon, acquaintance models are dynamic data structures which contain most of the domain specific information needed by the other components of the Archon Layer. This repository of domain dependent information allows the components to be primarily domain independent.

Models are dynamic in the sense that as community interaction progresses, new information may be added (e.g. a new interest of an acquaintance may be discovered) or existing information may be modified (e.g. an agent's rating of punctuality may be altered to reflect the modelling agent's experiences).

Two types of model exist: an agent's view of itself (The Self-Model SM) and an agent's representation of its acquaintances (The Agent Acquaintance Model AAM). This is a conceptual rather than structural distinction: the two model types embody similar types of information although they are used for fundamentally different purposes.

Self Models

Self-models are an abstract description of the underlying intelligent system - they specify the names of procedures which exist in the intelligent system, information needed by these procedures and so on. Obviously there is a very tight-coupling with the underlying system, therefore a synergy between intelligent system development and self-model specification is required.

The motivation for maintaining a self-model is that it enables the Archon Layer to reason about the capabilities and activities of the local intelligent system. Without this model the Archon Layer would not be able to influence the activity of the underlying system as it would be oblivious to any of its characteristics.

It is envisaged that Archon will provide tools and techniques to aid the construction of these self-models, although at this stage it is difficult to state exactly what form these will take.

Models of Acquaintances

Whereas there is only one self-model per agent, the number of acquaintances modelled by an agent can vary between zero and the whole community - a completely domain dependent factor. A further difference is that models of acquaintances may be built up dynamically as a result of interaction, self-models will probably have to be specified in advance by the intelligent system designer and offer little scope for run-time adaptivity.

Each agent maintains models of exactly those community members which interest it. Models will not necessarily embody all an acquaintance's facets, only those of direct relevance - e.g. a modelled agent may posses many skills, however only the pertinent ones will be represented.

As agents only represent the appropriate properties and different agents have different interests, it is likely that models of the same agent may vary within the community. Models of the same agent may also differ even if they represent identical attributes, because agent's tailor their models to reflect their personal experiences. For example, if the competence of an acquaintance for a particular skill is quantified, the rating will be based solely upon the modelling agent's experiences of invoking that skill, hence it is likely to vary between different community members.

5.2.3 Functionality of Agent Models

Archon acquaintance models provide the primary mechanism for focusing inter-agent activity. Without such models, messages or activities could not be focused. When requesting aid with a goal or requesting information, agents would be unaware of capabilities of other community members, hence a general broadcast would be required. However, if models are maintained, agents have some notion of the capabilities of their acquaintances, meaning that requests can be directed to appropriate agents.

Aiding Cooperation
Acquaintance models can aid the cooperation process. For example, during execution of a goal, agents may generate information of potential benefit to other community members. Using the interests slot of its model, the agent generating the information can ascertain the set of acquaintances to which this information may be of use and then send it to them. This information, although not specifically requested, should be of benefit to the receiver - hence this is a form of cooperation.

Global Coordination and Coherence
In any multi-agent environment the possibility of mutual interference arises, leading to the possibility of harmful and undesirable interactions, such as: the spread of misleading and distracting hypotheses, multiple agents competing for or trying to access resources simultaneously, one agent unwittingly undoing the results of another and the same actions being carried out redundantly. In general terms, the agent community may fail to act as a coordinated, purposeful team.

Coordination could be guaranteed if every agent had complete knowledge of all community members, however this is unreasonable at least because of the excessive burden on communication resources. It is also important that such policies do not consume more resources than benefits accrued from the increased coherence. Therefore, a balance between problem solving and coordination is required, so that the combined cost of both is acceptable. As a result of these constraints, each agent has a limited perspective and bounded rationality [Simon 57, Fox 81], hence greater emphasis is placed on achieving an acceptable level of performance within the community, rather than optimising activities [Lesser 87].

Within the aforementioned restrictions, coordination can be increased if agents have some expectation about the character of interaction and some knowledge of their acquaintances' capabilities and status - precisely the type of knowledge encoded by acquaintance models.

Self Reasoning
The primary role of an agent's self-model is to facilitate self-reasoning - reasoning by the agent about itself. This self-reasoning will in fact be undertaken by the Monitor, but will draw heavily on self-model information. It's level of sophistication may vary enormously: from a simple look-up to a complicated examination of the agent's current state.

Self-models will probably contain a representation of the local agent's skills and plans. So when a request to satisfy a particular goal or plan is made (either by a general broadcast, via a proforma or by a specific request from another agent), the agent will examine it's self-model to determine whether it posses the necessary capabilities. If not, a message may be returned indicating the unsuitability of the receiving agent, enabling the originating agent to update it's model of that acquaintance.

Before goals can be executed, it is usually the case that certain (pre-determined) information is required - similar to the parameters needed for procedure invocation. The nature and location (e.g. local or remote intelligent system) of this information is also stored in the agent's self-model.

Similarly if a request to supply a particular piece of information is received, the local agent must evaluate whether it is capable of supplying it - determined by examination of the Knows-About slot in it's self-model or by inspection of the results produced by the skills it posses.

More ambitious forms of self-reasoning are possible, but have not yet been evaluated with respect to the Archon project. These include:

o   Determining whether the agent has sufficient resources to complete a goal by the specified deadline, before taking responsibility for it.
o   Determining whether a goal ought to be allocated to an acquaintance even if the local agent has the necessary skills (e.g. because acquaintance is better qualified or less busy).
o   Determining whether a piece of information generated during the execution of a goal should be passed back to the originating agent in the form of an interim report.
o   Determine whether a particular goal ought to be allocated to single or multiple agents.

5.2.4 Attributes of Acquaintance Models

This section details those attributes which are incorporated into Archon acquaintance models. This taxonomy has still to be finalised; meaning that further information types may be required and that modification of existing ones may be necessary.

It is not envisaged that all the proposed features will be required in every application. To achieve maximum flexibility and generality both in system design and application areas, only the fields essential for system operation will be declared *mandatory*, all others will be *voluntary*.

Acquaintance model information may be further classified according to whether it is *dynamic* or *static*. An agent's identifier, for instance, will remain unchanged throughout the system's lifetime, whereas its current workload is likely to be a highly dynamic parameter. This is not a pure binary classification, some features may vary but only intermediately. The goal is not to provide an absolute categorisation, as this would be highly domain dependent; it merely offers a general indication of the relative variability of the model's attributes.

Existing DAI research provides an indication of some features which may be stored in acquaintance models. Further sources of information include the requirements of the other Archon Layer components and the needs of the envisaged applications. Much of the following information is needed in any multi-agent environment, although it is often implicit in the system design.

Identifiers

Each acquaintance will be uniquely identified by it's name. Hence Archon messages will specify the agent's identifier and the communication facilities [Tanenbaum 89] will convert the mnemonic to a physical address and handle the routing.

Skills - *Representing Capability Knowledge and Evaluative Knowledge*

Knowledge of acquaintances' capabilities is one of the most important features represented in these models. At present, it is assumed that a skill is a goal which can be completely satisfied by the agent's underlying intelligent system without aid from any acquaintance.

Modelling agents will not represent all an acquaintance's capabilities, only those of direct relevance. The rationale being that models should be as compact as possible, in order to reduce storage overheads and search times. Capabilities are represented by **skill-descriptors**, one for each relevant skill an acquaintance posses.

The first element of a skill-descriptor is a skill identifier; the name of a procedure in the underlying intelligent system which can be invoked to satisfy the goal.

Accompanying the skill identifier is a list of information needed to satisfy the goal, analogous to parameters in a standard procedure call. Three main sources of information have been identified:

o Constant Data (which can be stored directly in the skill-descriptor).
o Knowledge known at the intelligent system level of the local agent.
o Knowledge known by some other agent (including the user).

Some of these parameters will be essential for skill activation, whilst others merely serve to enhance problem solving. It is also conceivable that not all the required parameters will be known when the goal is invoked, in which case default values may be used. These defaults may be updated if the sending agent subsequently receives information which enables it to provide better estimates.

A rating of the perceived level of competence may also be associated with each skill. This rating will be based upon the modelling agent's experiences of using the skill, and will be unique (personal) to each agent. In order to update this value, the local agent must have some evaluation mechanism. Such ratings can be used to differentiate between conflicting information and influence task-sharing. If, for instance, multiple agents offer conflicting results for a particular goal, the agent with the greatest level of expertise should be favoured. For task-sharing, if multiple agents are capable of completing a goal then the one with the highest level of expertise will normally be chosen.

If deemed appropriate, the skill rating may be further qualified. Such qualifiers could state conditions under which the skill rating may vary and how to act accordingly. For example, one agent may be particularly good at producing quick, approximate solutions to a particular problem; whereas, another may take considerably longer, but produce significantly more reliable results. Another possible use is if particular agents are good/bad at handling data with different characteristics. One agent may be good/bad at handling uncertain or incomplete data, whilst another may be virtually unaffected. Again these factors may be taken into consideration when evaluating information and making decisions.

Another skill-descriptor component may be an indication of punctuality; again a metric personal to the modelling agent. Obviously in hard real-time environments

[O'Reilly 85, Stankovic 88], in which processes have to be served before the specified deadline, such an attribute is redundant. However in soft real-time systems [Lesser 88], in which a probabilistic guarantee is given that the processes are served in time, this attribute may be useful. It would indicate how often an acquaintance missed deadlines for goals requested by the modelling agent involving particular skills. This information may influence the scheduling of time-critical tasks - if a task has to be completed by a specified deadline, then it ought to be delegated to an agent which has a good past record of satisfying time constraints.

A skill descriptor should include an indication of any results produced whilst executing a particular goal - this provides an indication to the Archon Layer of results produced by the specified goal. Such information may be useful for information dissemination and also for satisfying data requests from acquaintances.

Finally, it may be desirable to include a measure of an agent's reliability. This would indicate the reliability of the forthcoming results to be provided by the modelled agent or the reliability with which the modelled agent performs the delegated goal. It may be possible for the Monitor to carry out reasoning on the returned results in order to establish their credibility. Again this criteria requires a standard metric against which the results can be evaluated.

Skill Descriptor:
- Description: ....Goals which can be completed by the modelled agent's underlying intelligent system.
- Quantity: ....One for each skill the modelled agent posses which is of relevance to the modelling agent.
- Status: ....Mandatory, Intermediate
- Skill Identifier: ....Mandatory, Static
- Knowledge Required: ....Mandatory, Intermediate
- Expertise Level: ....Voluntary, Intermediate
- Further Qualification: ....Voluntary, Intermediate
- Punctuality: ....Voluntary, Intermediate
- Reliability: ....Voluntary, Intermediate
- Results Produced: ....Voluntary, Static

Plans - *Representing Intentional Knowledge*
At present plans correspond to a list of goals which need to be achieved, together with an indication of their partial ordering. It is assumed that not all plan steps need be performed by the local agent, in fact the local agent may have insufficient expertise to complete the specified steps and that individual plan steps may themselves be plans.

In the DAI community, it is recognised that in order to achieve coherent coordination, agents may require some knowledge of the actions of acquaintances and also the ability to reason about the effects of these actions [Georgeff 84]. For this reason, agent's may model the plans of their peers. In the RAND ATC work [Cammarata 83], each agent (aeroplane) needs to know the plans of other agents as well as their speeds, headings, fuel levels, destinations and emergency statuses.

MACE agents represent plans as a partially ordered collection of goals or skills, interspersed with plan points. Plan points are partial contexts from which the agent can resume computations when other agents have fulfilled their commitments to do some work. This notion of plans is perhaps the most appropriate for use in Archon.

Workload - *Representing State Knowledge*
Working in a time-critical environment may require agents to represent the resource behaviour of their peers. Knowledge of an acquaintance's workload may influence the information sent to it and may also provide an indication of when solutions can be expected.

Estimates of acquaintances' workloads may be used to influence communication with them. It is pointless sending low priority messages containing highly perishable data to already overburdened agents - the information will simply be out of date before it can be processed. At present, it is unclear exactly how an agent's workload can be quantified.

Information concerning an agent's workload can also influence goal delegation. It is best, in the vast majority of cases, to balance the computational load between agents. Under normal circumstances, given a choice between several agents with approximately equal expertise, the one with the lightest workload should be selected.

An agent's workload may be broadcast to all acquaintances when it changes (**data-driven**) or only sent on request (**demand-driven**). The former method may be communication intensive if an agent's workload changes frequently. However, if most agents have relatively stable workloads, then this method is ideal as it minimises communication.

The latter method ensures that information is only updated when strictly necessary, but slows down processing as it requires at least two messages to be sent - a request for the workload and a reply. If the workload is stable then this method may involve several consecutive requests which return the same unchanged value, burdening the communication channel unnecessarily.

For full generality, both data and demand driven modes are provided in Archon.

Modelling Solution Progress - *Representing State Knowledge*
This field tracks the progress of goals which the modelled agent has taken responsibility for. At present, this attribute consists of:

Solution Progress:
    Description: ....Modelled agent's problem solving state.
    Quantity: ....One for each goal the modelled agent has undertaken on behalf of the modelling agent.
    Status: ....Mandatory, Dynamic
    Goal Name: ....Mandatory, Static
    Time Started: ....Mandatory, Static
    Time Due: ....Mandatory, Intermediate
    Information Passed: ....Mandatory, Intermediate
    Progress Reports: ....Mandatory, Dynamic
    Interrupt Status: ....Voluntary, Intermediate
    Storage Options: ....Voluntary, Intermediate

---

The first seven options are self-explanatory, however the notion of progress reports needs to be explained in greater detail. There are two types of progress report, as occurs in the

Contract Net formalism: interim and final.

If agents produce information which they consider to be important, then it can immediately be communicated to the agent which spawned the goal, using an **interim report** - rather than waiting until the goal has been completed. It is up to the originating agent to evaluate the report's contents and take appropriate action. This early sending of information is desirable because it facilitates integration of generated information into the receivers problem solving activity at the first opportunity.

The other report type is the **final report**. Its purpose is to indicate goal termination and also to convey any relevant information generated by the process.

If the modelling agent is particularly busy, then it should possess the capability of disabling these interrupts (interrupt status slot either set to **enable** or **disable**). Such a mechanism would simply stop the modelling agent's processor being interrupted by incoming interim reports, although final reports would not be blocked. Depending on the perishability of the data, these unseen messages may be stored for later inspection or simply discarded (storage option slot set to **store** or **discard**).

Interests Representing Capability Knowledge
Explicitly stating areas of interest enables agents to evaluate whether any information they generate or receive will be relevant to their acquaintances. This sending of information which is expected to be useful, but which has not been explicitly requested, is one illustration of cooperation in a multi-agent environment.

Initially a very simple, tuple-based formalism can be used to represent an acquaintance's interests. This states that if information concerning X is generated then $Agent_1$ and $Agent_2$ should be informed.

$\quad$ interested-in($Agent_1$,[X,Y,Z]).
$\quad$ interested-in($Agent_2$,[X,Y]).

This slot facilitates coordination and coherence, by avoiding duplication of problem solving activity. This is because agents will automatically be informed of relevant information generated elsewhere in the system without explicitly requesting it. If this facility was not available, agents may ask acquaintances to generate information which has already been derived elsewhere in the community.

Has Supplied Representing State Knowledge
This slot maintains a record of the information which acquaintances have supplied to the modelling agent. This information is maintained in order to speed up problem-solving and reduce communication overheads. If a piece of information outside the local agent's domain of expertise is required in order for the current goal to progress and if an acquaintance has previously supplied this information then a fresh request need not be generated. This reasoning will be undertaken by the Monitor but will be based upon acquaintance model information such as rate of information ageing, information reliability and so on.

This slot also provides facilities for default reasoning; in certain situations it may be possible to start a goal with the information provided in this slot and simultaneously issue a request for an update. When this update is received, the new information can be incorporated - again a facility overseen by the Monitor.

The present structure of an agent's self-model is very similar to that of a model of an acquaintance. The main difference being that the self-model refers to attributes of the local agent rather than to those of an acquaintance.

The other difference is that the self-model may have to contain "house-keeping" information; that is, information private to the local agent which does not alter the model's functionality.

5.2.5 Summary

There exists a tradeoff between computation and communication costs, in addition to the ever present considerations of problem solving speed and efficiency. The more complete the models, the more local computation required to maintain them, but the lower the communication overheads (as much of the wastage is removed through greater focusing).

Models vary enormously in completeness from the very simple actor acquaintance model [Agha 85, Agha 86] to the very rich PAN [Wesson 81] models. Archon's models will fall between these two extremes, although it is envisaged that most of them will be towards the complete end of the spectrum.

In the actors formalism knowledge is segmented so that agents are specialists in one particular aspect of the overall problem-solving task. The advanced behaviour displayed is as a result of predefined interactions between tightly-coupled, simple processing elements. Each individual has very little knowledge of the global problem solving task or of the general communication and cooperation techniques. Hence, agents are unable to operate outside the context of other agents in the system nor outside specific communication and cooperation protocols specified in advance by the system designer.

A further point in favour of comprehensive models is that they facilitate system reusability and generality of system design. If an agent's knowledge of it's acquaintances is limited, then greater emphasis is placed upon domain specific reasoning mechanisms - e.g. for selecting which agent to ask to complete a goal or for disambiguating conflicting hypotheses. This dependence on the underlying domain means that each system will need to be re-implemented for each envisaged application. In summary, an individual model embodies all the modelling agent's knowledge of an acquaintance.

6

The HCI Requirements and Components of the Architecture

In terms of Human-Computer Interaction, two major problems have been studied in Archon :

1) The identification of the key features of the end-user interface of future Archon applications and the process of designing this interface so that it will enable the users to interact effectively and efficiently with the complex multi-agent system;
2) The challenges that the Archon multi-agent system will set to the application designers and developers in terms of human computer interaction, taking into consideration the distribution and concurrency of the system and the multitude of domain expertise areas involved.

In this chapter emphasis is given towards the first problem considering its importance for the use of Archon applications, with particular focus on a framework of principles which enable the development of Archon application interfaces.

The decision to define an abstract framework was due to the fact that in this way all Archon applications could be covered. This framework covers all areas of application interface development, but a special emphasis is given towards the user analysis and the architecture design phases. The design of the interface architecture is based on the concept of the User Interface Agent (UIA) which is described here. Issues related to User Modelling are also considered.

Previous research on user interaction with multi-agent systems has focused on individual applications. Within Archon there is the initial attempt to define a generic framework within which to consider human computer interaction with such systems. From the possible users of an Archon application we select in this study the end-users (operators) as our focus, given their importance for the use of Archon applications.

6.1 RANGE OF POSSIBILITIES FOR THE USERS OF ARCHON

Archon applications exist within process supervision and control. Results of research in this area and the study of the main Archon demonstrators have provided us with some valuable insights into the characteristics of the "operators in the control room" situation.

Archon systems will be introduced into control rooms, as in figure 6.1, in which an industrial process (for example a power distribution network or a particle accelerator) is monitored through an automatic monitoring and control system. The operators have access to a control panel which gives them a view of the state of the process and a control console through which they can act on the process.

Previous research on the tasks of control room operators [Hollnagel 91], has identified several groups of generic user tasks: (a) routine procedures like information collation and planning of routine maintenance work, (b) steady state monitoring, (c) monitoring and diagnosing disturbances, (d) response to disturbances and restoration actions. In other work, an analysis of the key characteristics of user interaction with the industrial processes under discussion is made: under normal conditions the intervention of the human operators is not needed for control operations. Therefore the monitoring and routine operations can become tedious, since nothing appears to be happening. The operators and the control engineers are called to perform some complex cognitive actions only in abnormal situations, often under time pressure while they have to inform themselves about the nature of the malfunction, the process context and network's state and so on. The task is made difficult by the complexity of the system, the avalanche of process and control data generated during fault conditions and by the psychological stress faced by the operators.

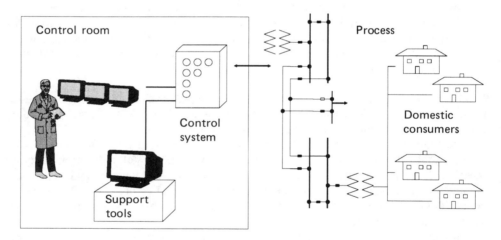

Fig. 6.1 The setting for Archon applications

In order to cope with such problems within control rooms there is an increasing use of support tools such as knowledge based systems (KBS) in performing these tasks. KBSs can be used for several different purposes, for example they can be applied to control complex devices, to ease the operation of complex devices by taking over some tasks of the operator, thus providing an intelligent front-end to the device, or to support the operator in his tasks, not by taking over his tasks, but by providing him with adequate support for his task execution, like diagnosing malfunctioning components and planning modifications to a network.

These tools are currently fragmented and often not related to each other. Archon aims to provide an architectural platform for the integration of these tools. The role of these existing systems however might change with the introduction of the integrated Archon platform. Also, through the Archon system extra aids are going to be introduced to the Control Room. The Archon applications are expected to facilitate the operators monitoring and supervising tasks in various degrees with the introduction of this technology in the control room.

The problem in relation to the integration of such tools is the provision of an interface which enables the operator to interact with a diverse range of tools. The various roles that these systems are expected to play and the various needs in terms of interaction and of operator's participation in the problem solving which the user interface should support are the result of the analysis which is performed for each application. The result of this analysis then should drive the design of the system interface.

Therefore a feature which demands consideration is the way that the system will be designed in relation to the user's participation (sharing of cognitive tasks between the user and the system in order to achieve a certain goal) in the problem solving. User participation in the system's problem solving is expected in cases when:

o   information technology has not yet reached the level to automate the complete task of the operator, or the costs for such a solution are high.
o   the importance and the uncertainty of the data or problem solving methods require that a human operator takes the final decisions.
o   human operation is necessary but the operator can make serious errors which are detectable.
o   updating and refreshing of operator knowledge is desired.

As can be seen from this brief introduction to this area, the design of the interface to promote user participation and to enable user interaction is a complex task. The analysis framework which is proposed in the next paragraph attempts to provide a structured way of arriving at the interface specification in order to be able to provide clear answers to the above questions for the future Archon applications.

6.2 A METHODOLOGICAL FRAMEWORK FOR HCI ANALYSIS & DESIGN

An interaction analysis and interface design methodology provides a collection of procedures and techniques which enable the interface to be constructed in an organised manner. The novelty of multi-agent systems, and the dimensions which these possess with regard to user interaction, in that users are expected to interact with intelligent multi-agents in the solution of problems, demand a new approach. Existing methodologies like User Centred System Design [Howey 89], with its focus on user involvement, and the Modality Framework [de Greef 88], which considers user-KBS cooperation, include those which have been taken into consideration.

An integration Framework for analysis and design of a user interface to Cooperating Expert Systems was initially proposed in [Hall et al 90]. A revised version is presented here. The assumption made is of modular design and of clear separation between the interface development and the application development in a user interface management system (UIMS) fashion. The relations between the application developers and the interface developers (dialogue and presentation components) is shown in figure 6.2, adopted from [Hartson 89].

The framework covers the phases of analysis of human-computer interaction and design of the user interface. A schematic description is provided in figure 6.3. The end result is a full specification of the user interface which can be supplied to the next phases: the user interface implementation and integration into the rest of the system.

In the diagram of figure 6.3, three major stages of the analysis and design are highlighted: The analysis of the application which determines the key application functionalities. This is followed by the user task and transparency analysis which produce the user conceptual model and the system task network. The result of this is the detailed interface functionalities specification through the task structure definition which leads to the User Interface Agent architecture and the dialogue design. This is followed by preliminary prototyping and testing with the users in an iterative fashion, until a stable and satisfactory interface specification can be produced, which can be developed in real scale and integrated in the system.

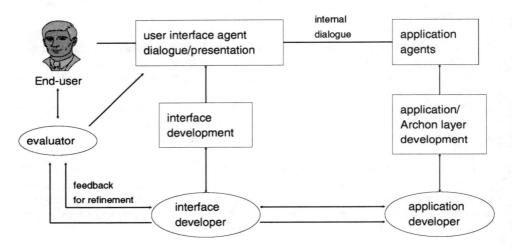

Fig. 6.2 Interface design and development
in the system development lifecycle.

6.2.1 Application Analysis

The analysis of the multi-agent system is initially conducted. This takes the form of the external requirements analysis (in KADS terminology, see [Hickman et al 1988]). The domain experts and the specification of the existing systems are the key inputs of this study. As a result of this analysis the "System Specification" is produced which contains:

1) The characteristics of the system as a whole. This can be achieved through an analysis of the broad tasks of the system, for example intelligent advice and support or problem solving.
2) The attributes of the individual Expert Systems, partly out of pre-existing domain analyses and modelling and partly out of the new cooperative role they are expected to perform. These can be considered models of the problem solvers, as suggested by the Modality Framework, within the multi-agent system and the methods used by these agents in problem solving activity. The environment within which the user will interact is thus determined, as are the characteristics of the individual agents within the system.

6.2.2 User Analysis: Development of the User Portrait

The focus of this lies on the analysis of the user in terms of their existence in parallel to the multiple expert system environment. Whilst it is felt that it is necessary to analyse user tasks etc. it is also felt to be of benefit to analyse the user in isolation prior to building any interface structure. This form of analysis should result in a detailed profile of the user and their environment, which can then be used to determine the requirements that a specific class of users will impose on the interface to the system. The user analysis phase of the framework considers the user as a problem solving entity, comparable to the other agents within the problem solving environment. This new analytic viewpoint of the user aims to consider and model the user in such a way as to provide a detailed analysis of the user which is comparable to the specification documents which are available for the agents within an Archon system. This analysis seeks to answer three fundamental questions relating to these users, firstly who the users are, secondly what the users do and thirdly how the users will interact with the application.

In relation to these three questions a two stage analysis, followed by the development of a user requirements specification (the user portrait), is proposed. This relies heavily on a number of other methodologies, for example, User Skills Task Match (USTM) [Macaulay et al 1990] and the Modality Framework. The analysis of the users in this situation should provide a user portrait which can be used in the later stage of trying to determine task allocation. Three stages, which are described in the following sections, are suggested in the development of this user model.

Stage 1 : Identification of User Population
The very first stage of the user analysis provides an identification of the user groups which must be considered. The identification of a primary user group provides the stereotype group which will be described.

Stage 2 : User Characteristics Analysis
The second stage of the analysis provides a body of information from analysing user characteristics. Users are analysed in three forms: Workgroup, Generic User and User Tasks; from three perspectives: Organisational, Social and Occupational. This provides a consideration of a minimal set which is use in terms of the development of a portrait. A major difficulty has emerged in that many of these characteristics are hard to scale. However, even with these problems, in following this type of structure it does become possible to provide information with which to develop a user portrait through which to understand user needs in relation to the interface.

Stage 3 : The User Portrait
An extensive amount of information is obtained from performing a user characteristic analysis, this is then used to develop the user portrait, which is used to help structure the interpretation of knowledge which has been obtained through knowledge elicitation.
The information obtained in this analysis and which is used to form the user portrait is high-level and does not deal with more specific interface design factors such as cognitive capability. This portrait and the analysis takes factors from a number of areas, primarily the USTM methodology [Macaulay et al 90] and work related to the computational user model. However, in order to avoid confusion, the term user portrait is used, meaning the model of the user when used for analysis, and not the model of the user which is pro-

grammable and is used by the system to support flexible interaction with the user.

Although the development of a user portrait is for analysis, many of the considerations used within user modelling are equally valid. The justification for this is that the information elicited and analysed for a computational model provides the same level of information even though at the end the actual model is not programmed. Thus the user portrait developed within this framework like the user models within computer systems should enable designers to be aware of users and to create a system which is appropriate to their needs and sensitive to their characteristics.

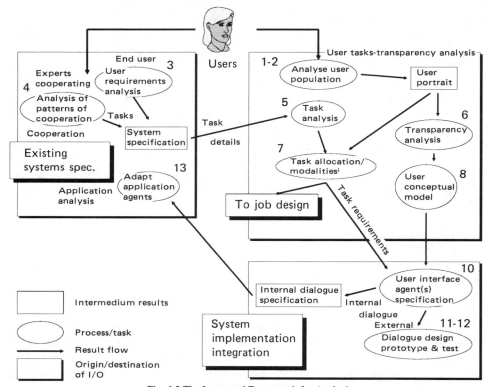

Fig. 6.3 The Integrated Framework for Analysis
and design of Archon applications user interfaces

The computational user model enables a system to infer a body of useful information about users based on a small number of facts, and this is also the effect of the user portrait. The term user model has been used in many different contexts, and thus has been used to describe a diverse range of concepts and entities. Kass and Finin [Kass 1989] provide the following definition of a user model: "A system knowledge source that contains explicit assumptions on all aspects of the user that may be relevant for the dialogue behaviour of the system." The manner in which user models have been constructed and implemented reveal that this definition provides an ideal rather than a realised objective. However in terms of the development of a user portrait it is hoped that the following definition will be achieved "a designer knowledge source that contains explicit assumptions on all aspects of the user that may be relevant for the design of the interaction between the user and the system." It has been suggested by Berry and Broadbent [Berry

1987] that the types of information which an ideal user model should contain include knowledge about the user's level of domain expertise and their interests, values, aptitudes, goals, expectations and assumptions. A further extension of this is provided by Kass, where it is stated that in the creation of a user model the following knowledge about the user is required:

1) user specific information - includes user goals, plans, preferences, beliefs and knowledge.
2) domain related information - in relation to the domain user modellers need to know concepts and terms which user understands and is comfortable with so that explanation to the user can use these so as not to confuse the user.
3) real world knowledge - information about what the user knows beyond the application but which still influence that domain
4) model of other entities

The information which makes up the user portrait contains the first three of these whilst the fourth aim is provided by the system specifications.

Thus the outcome of this phase is a user specification which provides a model of the user which can be used for the interface design.

6.2.3 Task and Transparency analysis

The user and system specifications are then used for performing the task allocation between the user and the system and developing the user conceptual model. The means for achieving these are the detailed task analysis and the transparency analysis. Since the Archon agents are fairly independent in terms of their tasks it could be that the user's view over the system is based on a clear identification of the agents and possibly other details of the architecture, like the inter-agent negotiation/cooperation schemes as concepts which then will be included in the user conceptual model. The replies to these questions are provided by the transparency analysis (item 5) which is based on the detailed task analysis and the user specification. System Transparency in the User's conceptual model is defined as the degree to which the user perceives the underlying system. The dimensions which have to be determined in the transparency analysis are multiple. In figure 6.4 the dimension of distribution transparency is highlighted.

Other dimensions of transparency are:

o   Knowledge and reasoning explanation,
o   Inter-agent and user-agent control,
o   Communication,
o   Negotiation and conflict resolution,
o   Agent heterogeneity.

These dimensions are interrelated and dependent upon parameters like the degree of user participation in the problem solving.

The result of the transparency analysis should feed into the design of the User Interface Agent, and especially onto the modules that implement transparency, like the AIM module for the User Self Model and Acquaintances Models.

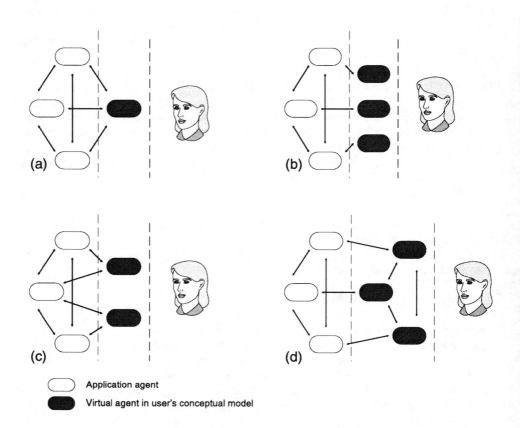

Fig. 6.4 Transparency of systems
(a) Opaque system, (b) sectionalised conceptual model, (c) clustered, semi-transparent model, (d) fully transparent system

6.2.4 User Interface specification

The detailed interface design specification is expected to be the result of this phase. The architecture of the interface should be determined here. It is expected that the control of interaction should be handled by one agent for each user, which is called in the Archon literature "User Interface Agent". This UIA should be specified at this stage. The complexity of the UIA depends on the application requirements. The interface design covers also the presentation system, the parts of the intelligent systems that handle direct interaction with the user and the parts of the agents which support UIA interaction. The key elements of the UIA for dialogue control are shown in figure 6.5.

The main functionality of the UIA is to control dialogue between the user and the agents. The user can interact with the system only through the I/O devices which create events (display information and input or select information etc.). The graphic and windowing system are services provided in the environment and are controlled by the UIA. An operation of the user on a screen, like selecting of an item or issuing a command has to be interpreted and directed to the appropriate destination. So the functionality associated to this communication is the filtering and direction of information.

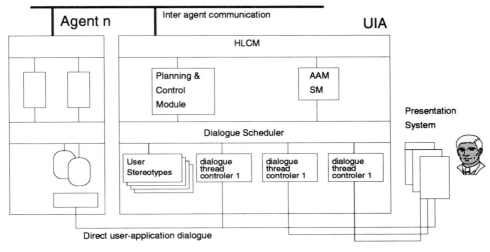

Fig. 6.5 Architecture of the dialogue component
The UIA of Archon

The specific language spoken by anyone of the Archon agents does not have to be known to the user. It is the UIA who performs the translation. The transparency analysis performed earlier in the interface design has produced the relevant specifications on agent translation by the UIA so the functionality of uniform and consistent interaction with the user can be satisfied. The same applies to the agents addressing the user. They do not need to know anything about either graphics and presentation system in general, or the user's involvement in the problem solving. The user model as distributed through the agents plays the role of interpreter at the local agent level.

An example of the mapping of agents language to presentation system objects:

The Agent: {fault in Transformer-1 }
　　　　　　　-> (Translation)
　　　　　　　　　　　-> *The UIA:* {Draw red circle at point x,y }

The implementation of this filtering should be done through the AIM module of the UIA and the agents directly interacting with the user. The AIM module developed for each agent is built in order to support the sharing and exchange of information among ISs while preserving their autonomy. As such the AIM module is a part of the Archon architecture useful to the end-users. The parts of the Archon architecture which are used in a particular way in the interface specification phase are the AIM module and the User model which can use most of the semantics introduced for the acquaintance modelling. These two aspects of the architecture are given some special consideration here.

6.2.5 The User Agent's AIM Module

In relation to the user interaction with Archon, the AIM module can perform a major role. The role played by the AIM module is three-fold. First, AIM acts as the vehicle for representing and accessing the IS knowledge to the Archon user in a coherent way across the community of the agents. This resolves the confusion in information sharing caused by the multiple representations and semantics associated to the IS knowledge. The AIM module of the UIA should contain the import schema for all the data exported by other agents and of possible use to the end-user. An import schema does not import data. So the AIM module of the User Interface Agent will not store the data generated by other agents. It will provide an interface to the AIM modules of the other agents, and thereby to the information stored there. The creation of an opaque view by hiding the distribution of information (not showing the end-user which information is imported from which agent), which can be requested at the transparency analysis phase above, can thus be achieved. The fact that some schema has been imported from agent A, and some other schema from agent B, is not relevant when querying the information. Therefore only the schema shows that the information comes from A or B, while the query to access that information contains no explicit reference to either A or B. So a query made by the user, or the IS of the UIA, to the AIM module in the UIA, does not (have to) contain the name of the agents that have provided the information. Second, the AIM module developed specifically for the UIA agent contains the information about overall representation of the sharable information in the Archon community of agents. For instance, the import schema of UIA contains the information about the agents involved in the community, what information each agent is willing to share and who are the agents receiving it. Therefore, it can provide an overall picture of the sharing of information and the agents involved within the Archon community if requested.

Thirdly, the AIM module of the UIA can be used to provide information to other agents. Whenever the user participates in the problem solving, the information produced by the user can be modelled in the export schema of the UIA, and stored in its AIM module, so that the other agents can access it. The alternative could be to let the user update information generated by other agents. This can be done by allowing the user write access on information produced by agents (e.g. by modifying the order of the hypothesis generated by the AAA (Iberdrola))

The AIM module can on the other hand support both the end- users of Archon accessing and manipulating the information of ISs and the Archon system developers who design and develop agents and their interconnections to Archon. Here we study the first.

The end-users who wish to access the information stored in ISs can directly interface to the IS's AIM module using the 3DIS/ISL language (the query and update language supported by AIM). It contains a set of basic specification and retrieval operations that are relationally complete (same expressive power as a relational database language). In addition a browsing interface is planned to be introduced and possibly used if requested by the analysis.

6.3 USER MODELLING ISSUES

As discussed earlier a result of the user portrait definition could be if the complexity of interaction and the multiplicity of user characteristics require it, the specification of a computational component representing the key features of the user, called "User Model".

The User Model should contain a representation of the user characteristics that may be relevant for his interaction with a computer system. Such model is useful and exploitable if it consists on a formal description of knowledge from which it is possible to derive potentially interesting assumptions for each specific on-going human-computer interaction.

6.3.1 The need for a user model

The UIA as a user system dialogue handler has two qualitatively different ways of communication: (i) one with the operator, the operator channel, (ii) the other with the rest of the system, the system channel through which the external and internal dialogues take place.

The UIA, seen through the system channel by the other agents, shall model the operator as an important part of another agent, although a special one (with skills, limitations, interests, permissions, priorities and levels of authority attached). The UIA, seen through the operator channel by an operator, will model the rest of the system in the way determined by the conceptual model of the user. The role of the user also depends on the functionality of the distributed system as stated in the introduction. The need for a User Model in the UIA is particularly evident in the case of a participative role of the User where he can be asked to assist some agents in the problem solving. This implies that the User has to understand the internal reasoning process of that agent, may expect appropriate explanations and needs to be accepted by the system as an authorised agent concerning that specific matter. In order to exhibit an adaptive behaviour regarding each specific user, the UIA should modify, format or enhance, the information passing through it, according to specific user characteristics.
These features can be responsible for :

o   filtering, focussing on appropriated topics,
o   hiding or displaying some particular windows,
o   providing (or not) a-priori explanations to the user,
o   choosing the level of detail of advice to give
o   different presentations of warnings.

The components of the UIA responsible for adapting the interaction capabilities to each specific user and situation, is the User Model.

6.3.2 Types of User Models

Traditionally, User Models can be classified along some dimensions: Users of the typical industrial Archon applications will be in a restricted number and authorised to log in by means of a password. Therefore, a certain amount of knowledge about their profiles can be accessed whenever each specific user logs in.

Profiles may be seen as Frames in a Knowledge Base and are composed of two main parts:

1) a static part containing permanent information, such as interests, responsibilities, operating permissions etc.;
2) a dynamic part which has information about the User's skills which may be updated in each session.

User Models inside the UIA can also have two components:

1) the short term component containing information about the topic currently under focus and the overall goal being pursued;
2) the long term component based on the profile of the current user. This latter component becomes active whenever the user logs in.

The short term component may be used in two different ways:

1) during an interaction to detect changes of context and together with the long term component to guide the performance of the system.
2) to update the dynamic part of the long term component at the end of each session. From the short term component, explicit inferences based on the user's input and behaviour, will be drawn.

6.3.3 Representation of the User Model

There are several formal ways of representing the intended relevant knowledge about users. Linear parameters and Overlay techniques are proposed respectively by Rich [Rich 79] and Sleeman [Sleeman 86].
Overlay techniques are useful for representing the system's assumptions about:

o the expertise of a user in a given domain;
o the concepts that a user is familiar with.

Overlay techniques imply that for each individual concept (and relationship) in the system's knowledge base, there are two parameters:

o information about the concept (known, not-known, no- information),
o strength of belief with which the system holds its assumptions about the user's familiarity with that concept.

The User Models, must reflect the choices made on the Archon Layer architecture. If the User is to be seen as an underlying capability and component of the UIA, the User Model should be reflected in the Self-Model of the UIA's AL. Therefore main conclusions follow :

o A component of the UIA's Self-Model will be based on a model of the current User. Therefore, such model gathers the User profile according to what must be described in the Self-Model. This includes User interests (slot "interested in").

o   The Acquaintance Models of the other Agents who interact with the user will also be generated taking into account the interests and capabilities of the specific user specified by the UIA Self-Model.
o   The control modules (Monitor and PCM) will have rules or procedures to operate on that knowledge. If we follow the Blackboard architecture for the Archon Layer, the uniformity of representation is accomplished by means of special Knowledge Sources about the exploitation of User Model by the UIA. The set of stereotypes which are going to be the basis of the User model as described in the next paragraph, can reside in the Intelligent System of UIA, driving the dialogue with the user (deciding which dialogue threads are suitable for the particular user etc.).

If a complex user model is selected with a dynamic component, there should be made provision for a user modelling component whose function is to infer new information about the user during the interaction. These inferred features, in each session, will instantiate the short term component of the user model.
This short term component will be used, at the end of the session, by the user modelling component to update the dynamic part of the long term component.

It is expected that the user modelling component will be able to infer information about users either directly or indirectly (by inference on possible user plans). The decision for the use or not of a user modelling component and the selection of the appropriate user modelling technique are left to the designer of the specific Archon application. However in the following section an example of a specific technique to build up User Models which is included which demonstrates the above ideas.

6.3.4 An Archon User Modelling example

Given a specific application domain, the goals of the system, and known information about their users, it is possible to build up stereotypes, which are collections of important characteristics to classify groups of a set of dimensions along which it is possible to describe the users behaviours relevant for an efficient interaction. These characteristics may include the level of user expertise regarding the system as well as tasks and concepts of particular interest to each group of users. Each stereotype (model of a group of users) consists of a set of triples:

Attribute:	the name of the user characteristic;
Value:	the degree to which this attribute characterises any user of the system;
Rating:	the confidence that this pair attribute-value fits any person of this group.

All knowledge expressed in stereotypes can be used to predict, to a certain extent, future behaviours an individual user may exhibit. Nevertheless, in order to use this mechanism of prediction, it is necessary for the system to be able to associate with a specific user one or more stereotypes. Therefore, the user model building component will use a kind of triggers which are events that index appropriate stereotypes. Each trigger consists of a triple:

Event: user's behaviour that suggest the appropriateness of a stereotype;
Stereotype: the name of the stereotype associated;
Rating: the confidence on stereotype appropriateness, based on the occurrence of this event.

The idea is that the system will check, along the interactions, for the occurrence of these events. Different situations may occur within the interaction of a user, so there can be many triggers that are associated with the same stereotype. Whenever a trigger is activated, predictions made by the associated stereotype should be included in the model of the user. When a trigger is activated 3 situations can occur:

1) This trigger has been activated before. In this case nothing should be incorporated in the user model.
2) This trigger hasn't yet been activated, but the stereotype associated with it has been instantiated before by the activation of another trigger.
The quadruples of the user model that have attributes predicted by this stereotype should have their value, rating, justification updated.
3) Neither the trigger nor the stereotype have been instantiated before.

Some of these features are considered next in the frame of the EA Technology application (for details see Chapter 8. The following Agents are involved: LVDA, HVDA, SVA, AVA (The UIA of this application), WEATHER, INFORMATION; Two nearby faults have occurred within a difference of minutes of each other. Let us consider two possible different Users :

1) The operator whose User Model specifies that he is only "interested in" location and time of permanent faults;
2) The control engineer whose User Model specifies interests in all the transitory and the permanent faults as well as weather information(possible causes of faults) ;

The Visualisation of the System response will be different for each one of the two Users:

1) To the Operator, only messages from the Advisory Agent will be displayed, e.g. :

......12:01:01 Permanent fault at line 1 at 12:00:00 due to lightning, severity 7. Loss of supply to Substation 1.
......12:40:59 Permanent fault at line 1c at 11:55:00 due to lightning, severity 3.

2) To the Control Engineer more information will be displayed.

Other than the Advisory Agent also the Weather, LVDA and HVDA will be responsible for providing more information about:
- the occurrence of lightnings (Weather Agent)
- fault clearing messages (HVDA) despite the on-going diagnosis(LVDA, HVDA);

Moreover, different display windows presentations and dialogue threads will be associated with these qualitatively different information.

6.4 CONCLUSIONS

The scope of the work on HCI within Archon has considered a number of areas. Two distinct user groups have been identified: The application developers and the end-users. These two groups have distinct requirements from the Archon user interface. The developer requests a representation of the multi-agent concurrent system through multiple views related to the domain tasks, communication, control, knowledge etc. On the other hand the end users do not necessarily need to view the system details, but they need a clear mapping of the concepts they are familiar with during the execution of their tasks on the interface and the dialogue control. The design of the User Interface Agent (UIA) who implements these requirements have been described in this chapter 5. In particular an Integration Framework for cooperating Expert Systems (IFCES) has been proposed within Archon with which to consider the analysis and design of the UIAs for future Archon applications. The basis of the framework, that is the conceptualisation of the user as an integrated entity in the multi-agent system and the introduction of transparency as a key issue during the design provide important and novel issues for HCI. In the frame of this design methodology, issues like user modelling in multi-agent systems have also been tackled: Provided that the systems can demonstrate adaptive behaviour regarding each specific user, it is necessary to represent computationally the key characteristics of the individual user. The first phase of the analysis should create the generic user portrait which then can be used as an input for the user model. The User Model is distributed in nature, one part responsible for adaptive system interaction based on the UIA's Self Model and another part responsible for adaptive behaviour of the agents towards the user residing in the agents Acquaintance Models. The general remark is that the concept of acquaintance modelling which is strong in the Archon architecture is useful for user interaction and user modelling.

A concluding observation is that a multi-agent system architecture like Archon promotes modular design of the applications which, as far as interface design is concerned, mean separation of the interface part from the domain related problem solving part. This is in line with the current trends in interactive complex systems design. The implementation of this principle results in the definition of the User Interface Agent, whose key characteristics and design methodology have been presented here. The UIA functionality maps on the general architecture of Archon agents. In the specific case of the developer interface the user agent is expected to be more complex with more requirements in terms of distribution and control transparency. The design of such an Agent for the Archon development environment is the projection of this work into the future.

7
An Implementation using Blackboards

This Chapter describes a Cooperative Distributed Expert Systems Shell that has been developed at the University of Porto. UPShell is able to transform a set of generated Intelligent Systems (ISs) into a community of Distributed Cooperative Agents. They can be committed to pursue an overall complex goal which requires the simultaneous contribution of different kind of expertise. Application independent knowledge involved either in Cooperation and in Local Task control, as well as the Agent internal Blackboard based architecture are reported and discussed in the second section of the chapter.
An exploratory prototype has been built which demonstrates the Archon Layer functionality but implemented using the Blackboard paradigm. Unlike a number of approaches in DAI the Blackboard paradigm is not used for communication and cooperation among agents but to coordinate the task within the Archon Layer of an agent. Many concept demonstrated with this prototype have been described in earlier chapters and have strongly influenced the evolution of the Archon architecture.

7.1 UPShell FOR COOPERATIVE AGENTS

This section is a general overview of a Cooperative Expert Systems Shell prototype called UPShell. It includes a description of UPShell Architecture, its principal aims, features and limitations. UPShell generates Expert Systems which may be seen either as separate Intelligent Systems (ISs) or as working parts of Agents in a cooperative community of Systems sharing their own specific domain knowledge.

7.1.1 Main Goals

The UPShell may be used either by domain experts in order to generate specific Intelligent Systems or, in a consultation mode, to deal with complex applications. In the first case, different ISs may be generated and, if needed, the Shell can be instructed to build up a Cooperative System out of several different ISs. In order to make this possible, special modules including additional knowledge must be automatically derived for the use of the cooperative community. In this case, ISs are transformed into Cooperative Agents. In the Consultation mode, the shell provides the means for user interaction with either a separated IS or a set of Agents pursuing the overall goal.

Our main intention in developing UPShell was to provide an environment to generate and use different Intelligent Systems that have intrinsic capabilities to deal with applications which require different, separate and distributed types of expertise. Electricity Distribution Network Management and Flexible Assembly Robotics [Oliveira et al, 1991] are two paradigmatic examples of applications for a Cooperative community of Expert Systems.

7.1.2 UPShell Description

In Figure 7.1 we see both the UPShell modules corresponding to the distinct capabilities of generating and consulting Cooperative Intelligent Systems (ISs) which are represented on the right hand of the figure. These Agents are composed of several modules for communication, cooperation (AL) and the IS itself. Each one of the ISs embeds different kinds of domain knowledge (facts, rules, structural knowledge) plus the inference mechanism (Rule Interpreter including an Explanations Generator and some time bounded reasoning facilities) inherited from the shell.

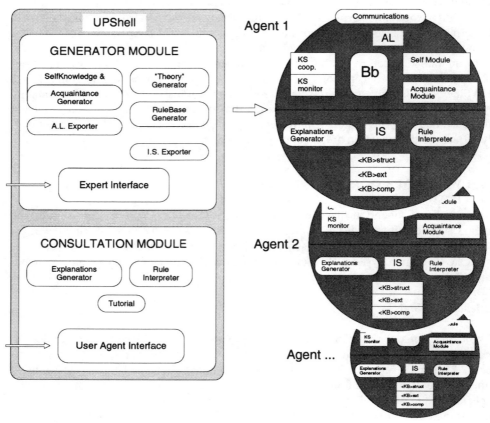

Fig. 7.1 The UPShell

From the ISs two important modules of the Archon Layer are derived: The Self Model and The Acquaintances Model needed for the intended Agents cooperation. In addition, each generated Agent includes modules for the Cooperation Planning and Coordination (PCM) as well as for IS Monitoring, displaying some important features which will be described later in the chapter.

Generation Module

One of the two main modules of UPShell is the Generation Module. It is responsible for the generation of the Intelligent System Knowledge Base - Structural Knowledge, Comprehensive Knowledge, Extensive Knowledge - on the basis of an interaction with the expert, by means of special acquisition protocols.

UPShell is capable of structuring all domain knowledge into different representational structures like rules, frames and predicates. It is primarily devoted to the development of Expert Systems for diagnosis and data interpretation. These Expert Systems are seen as the Intelligent Systems included in each Agent. Each IS is a combination of newly created files plus some functionalities which migrate from the shell itself into these new ISs. Therefore, different Cooperative Agents (which include ISs) use different copies of the inference engine as well as other capabilities offered by the Shell. Only the User interface still remains exclusively in the shell main program.

A complete description of the generated Intelligent Systems, all the UPShell features regarding knowledge Representation and time bounded reasoning capabilities as well as a detailed tutorial can be found in [Oliveira 1991].

Generation of the Self Model

UPShell is not just another Rule Based Expert System Shell. UPShell is able to automatically derive, on demand, important information to be used whenever these ISs are to be integrated into a cooperative community of Agents. A Self Model file (a kind of simplified abstraction on IS expertise) for each Intelligent System is derived from the already acquired knowledge and is mainly composed of the following information slots:

o Who_Am_I
o Is_My_Goal (Goal)
o Needs_of_Goal (Goal,Needs)
o Goal_Plan (Goal,Plan)
o Goal_Result (Goal,Result)

Generation of Acquaintances

The Acquaintance Model is another file attached to each specific Agent which is automatically derived by the Shell. The Acquaintance Model embeds knowledge about the others belonging to the same community, which is supposed to be of interest for the Agent under consideration (see Chapter 5.) This knowledge is mainly grouped into the following slots :

o Who_is (Agent,Machine,Path)
o Skill (Task,Plan)
o Knows_about (Agent, Attribute, Concept)
o Interested_in (Agent, Attribute, Concept)

The Consultation Module

Our intention was to give Cooperative Agents the capability to deal with resources which may be under constraints. These resources, which need to be shared by the community are time, communication channels and the other Agents themselves. We briefly address here the problem for an IS to reason under time constraints.

Time criticality results mainly from the possible existence of a deadline associated together with the overall goal. This implies that tasks may also have attached specific deadlines within which they have to be executed. In other words, to give to the Agent AL the possibility to reason about resources (like time) implies that ISs must have resource (time) bound reasoning capabilities.

Whenever the AL charges an IS of a task with a deadline attached, it is up to this specific IS to manage time in such a way that it will be able to respond in due time to external requests. In order to manage resources when they are limited (specially time) we thought of two general policies:

o   an incremental policy taking advantage of approximate processing techniques [Lesser et al 88];
o   a second one in which time slices are distributed to the possible computations (execution of rules) according to the constraints.

In the incremental reasoning policy, a first solution will be rapidly reached by doing approximate computations followed by a "second step" of solution improvement until resources are exhausted. The second possibility consists in a dynamic evaluation of the resources (time) availability after which the "best" distribution of time quantum is done among the rules and premises. While the first policy has the advantage of providing some answer at any time, the second policy allows for some "approximate" planning of resource allocation to the overall task and thus generates a better result than the "first step" outcome of the incremental policy. The UPShell incorporates in the present version the first approach. A full description of the implemented mechanisms can be found in [Oliveira, Camacho 1991].

After having specified the number and name of the ISs, Self-Models of each one are consulted and all acquaintance models are built up and saved. The Cooperative Agents are then ready to be launched. The user may enter commands to the community of agents through a simple command interpreter available at the user terminal (the user window). If no destination Agent is specified, the Acquaintances Module of the User is consulted in order to find out all possible destinations.

The user as an Agent may also interact with other Agents making requests, supplying unrequested information and, of course, collecting answers and reports on agents interaction.

7.1.3 Implementation

The UPShell Cooperative Expert Systems toolkit is written in Prolog and C. It runs under Unix operating system and the consultation module uses the X-Windows. Each Agent creates its own window using a special Prolog X-Windows Graphic Interface. For the time being only UPShell created agents may run in this environment. Systems generated by other tools have not yet been considered.

7.2 COOPERATION BETWEEN ARCHON AGENTS IN THE UPShell

7.2.1 Introduction

When and how to cooperate is an issue of great importance for an Archon agent. Each cooperative agent should be able to know when it is necessary to cooperate with the others. How to cooperate, i.e., what cooperation strategy to use, is another problem at another level. Here, we try to discuss these two problems by distinguishing the two different roles agents may play in cooperation. Starting from this point, we then construct a framework based on Blackboard paradigm [Corkill et al 88] [Lesser et al 83] [Hayes-Roth 87] to support the agents on detecting the needs for cooperation and to dynamically choose appropriated cooperation protocols.

In the introductory chapter of this book, some issues related with the cooperation concept have been presented. How to implement those defined concepts using Knowledge Sources and the Blackboard paradigm is presented in the next section. We also refer to other needed information items in order to enhance the global system's coherence.

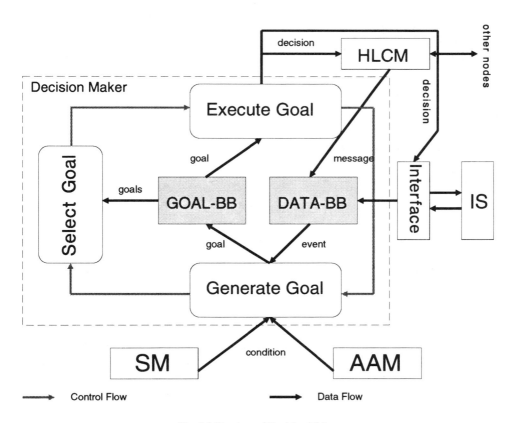

Fig. 7.2 Structure of Decision Maker

7.2.2 The Decision Making Module Structure

UPShell generated Agents incorporate a Blackboard-based Decision Making Module including the main features of PCM and Monitor. What we are arguing here is that this decision maker can take, with some advantages, the roles which have been recognized as those of PCM and Monitor as explained in their functional descriptions in previous chapters. The rational behind this approach, the use of one uniform mechanism to support these two kinds of reasoning - cooperation decision and local task scheduling - lies in the fact that they are indeed strongly related.

It is worthwhile to emphasize that the Blackboard paradigm is not used as a communication and cooperation framework between different Agents, which is definitively not its best use but entirely for Agent internal purposes, i.e. to enable each Agent to deal with all the information needed to make appropriate decisions on cooperative and local work. Here, the Data Blackboard (Data-BB) is the place to put the messages coming both from other agents through HLCM and the IS. Since the messages about the other agent's and own IS's state (busy/free) are directly used to update the AAM or SM, only request and data messages will be immediately put on the Data-BB.

The role the Decision Maker plays in our framework determines the contents of the Goal Blackboard. Two kinds of control decisions have to be made: decisions on interacting with the others (e.g. how to decompose a task) and decisions for local task scheduling (e.g. what task the IS should do now). Therefore, the Goal-BB encompasses goals to make these two kinds of decisions. Execution of a goal means either to ask the IS to send some messages through the HLCM to others for cooperation. In order to select the appropriate goal, all the goals on the Goal-BB are attached with a status flag and a dynamic changing priority. A goal in "wait" state can not be selected for execution since not all conditions for that goal are satisfied yet. Only the goal in "ready" state with the highest priority will be chosen and its state is changed to "executing".

7.2.3 Knowledge for the Decision Maker Module

The DMM at work
The Decision Maker, seen as a coordination module, has a relatively simple control mechanism - a three-step loop:

   Generate Goal
   Select Goal
   Execute Goal

It is widely recognized that control may be a kind of planning. Agents in multi-agent systems cannot fully know and anticipate others Agents behaviour and therefore cannot completely determine its own "long-term" plan. Under such circumstances, planning for control must be engaged in a cycle of plan generation, execution, monitoring and re-planning. Clearly, execution of a plan is achieved at the Execute Goal step. Whereas the other three actions -- plan generation, monitoring and re-planning -- are all implemented through the mapping from Data-BB to Goal-BB at Generate Goal step.

Actually, due to the fact that both other agents' reaction and IS's results (intermediate or final) are all put on the DataBB, and any change on this DataBB will be reflected on the GoalBB, the Decision Maker hence can modify its intentions (goals on GoalBB) according to the incoming messages, and as a result, can monitor the plan execution.

The key problem then turns to be how to map the incoming messages into the changes on the GoalBB. Intuitively, these changes are made by the set of Knowledge Sources linking the two blackboards at the Generate Goal step. Triggering one of them may cause such change on the GoalBB such as:

o   the generation of a new goal,
o   the state change of a goal, or
o   the change of a goal's priority.

At the Select Goal step, the Decision Maker chooses the most appropriate goal in terms of goal's priority and state. At the Execute Goal step this chosen goal will then trigger the corresponding KS to execute it. It is worth pointing out that executing a goal either activates the HLCM or the underlying IS, since the Decision Maker is only a control mechanism.

These three steps obviously represent three different kinds of actions related with decision making: intention generation, situation assessment and execution of intention.

Two sets of Knowledge Sources
The Decision Maker has two different sets of KSs corresponding to cooperation-decision-making and local-task-scheduling as shown in Fig. 7.3.

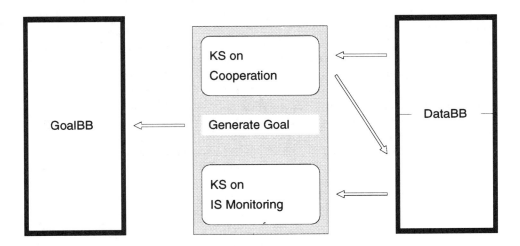

Fig. 7.3 Two Sets of KSs

According to this approach, Cooperation KSs have three kinds of abilities: detection of need for cooperation, choice of Cooperation Type and execution of chosen cooperation policy. This set of KSs is then the primary responsible for the agent's cooperation behaviour and maps into PCM. Another set of KSs has to control the underlying IS and, therefore, it determines the agent's local problem solving behaviour (Monitor functionalities).

These two sets of KSs can communicate with each other via the DataBB. For example, when one agent has decided (by means of the cooperation KSs) to execute a task in order to help another, it will put an event on the DataBB which, as a consequence, will trigger a task-scheduling KS to generate a goal on the GoalBB and commit the IS to execute it.

In the following, we will discuss how the Decision Maker deals with these two kinds of reasoning within the same uniform mechanism.

Supporting Cooperation
Reasoning Based Detection
Reasoning Based Detection is used by the cooperation organizer to detect the need for cooperation. Two KSs are defined: task-KS and result-KS.

The Task-KS, using other Agents' request messages as triggers, will consult the SM to see how to decompose the incoming request. According to the different conditions existing when a request arrives at an Agent (all inputs needed are available, some of them missing from the outside or some still to be supplied by the IS) three different rules belonging to this Knowledge Source can be activated.

The Result-KS, triggered by the results produced by the IS, will consult the AAM to see whether the others may benefit from these results. If so, it puts an appropriate flag on the DataBB: result-sharing(Data) to control the HLCM.

These two KSs help the organizer Agent to detect the need for cooperation and its type (Task or Result Sharing).

Direct Triggering
From the respondent's point of view, the mechanism it uses to detect a cooperation need is Direct Triggering. So far we have considered two different possibilities of establishing cooperation protocols between Agents for task sharing: Either by negotiation (Contract net) or by a more tight relationship (Client/Server). In order to use contract nets, there is a task-announcement KS which is triggered by the task-announcement message sent by the organizer. Whenever triggered, it is obvious that some Agent desires to establish a contract with this one as a respondent. Hence, there is need for cooperation.

A task-KS is used by the respondent to detect the need of the other type of cooperation. If one agent decides to assign a task to another using Client/Server relationship, the respondent can sense this request by means of this KS.

Likewise, in order to respond to a result-sharing cooperation demand, KSs are needed which are sensitive to the incoming data. Data-receiving and data-checking KSs have been developed for this purpose.

The trigger of the data-receiving KS is any new incoming data on the Data-BB. Whenever receiving data, this KS is invoked to check whether this data, together with that already existing, meets the input requirements for a certain task. If this is the case, the Decision Maker puts a pending goal in "ready" state on the Goal-BB in order to control IS to execute that particular task. Thus, when a cooperation organizer is trying to establish result-sharing cooperation, the respondent will consider this request by activating this KS.

The data-checking KS is another important one which is used to facilitate result-sharing. This KS, like the result-sharing KS, is also triggered by the incoming data. Its purpose is to check whether the incoming data is part of the input for a task under execution or a task already executed, and, if this is the case, whether it is more reliable than the previous data. If this is the case, a pending goal to control IS to restart or redo the corresponding task is put on the Goal-BB. This KS allows agents to use partial results in order to produce its own hypothesis until reaching consensus.

These three KSs constitute the Direct Triggering mechanism which is used by the Agent playing the respondent role whenever detecting the need for co-operation.

Choosing the cooperation protocol
It is up to the organizer to decide how to choose possible respondents. Two KSs are needed: for-task-sharing KS and for-result-sharing KS. For-task-sharing KS, triggered by the flag task-sharing(task), will consult the AAM to see which other agent can execute that specific task. If there is only one Agent who has this capability, then it generates a goal to initiate a Client/Server relationship. If more than one is able to execute the task, then it generates a goal to initiate the Contract Net.

The function of for-result-sharing KS is similar to the for-task-sharing KS, the only difference is that this KS will consult the AAM to see who may be interested in the data rather than to see who can execute a task.

Responding to an organizer
To be able to choose between possible cooperation demands the one to respond to, the respondent also needs some kind of knowledge - as pointed out in the Introduction of this book. In order to execute the chosen cooperation protocol and eventually establish the cooperation relation, each cooperation protocol must be complete. Therefore, in addition to the task-announcement KS, the following KSs are needed for contract net:

o   bid-KS which is triggered by a bid message evaluates it and sends an award message.
o   award-KS which is triggered by award message and sends a task announcement message.
o   termination-KS which is triggered by termination message and terminates execution of the contract and all related subcontracts.

Local Task Scheduling
We have identified four possible kinds of task scheduling of the Intelligent System, other than normal task conditional initialization:

o   *Task Swapping* During the execution of a task in the IS, whenever an urgent request (task) arrives, the Decision Maker controls the IS in order to suspend the current execution and to swap to execute the new arriving task. When the new task has been concluded, the IS then will continue the previous execution from the breakpoint.
o   *Restart Task* During IS's execution of a task, if more reliable or recent data related to that task arrive, the decision maker will control the IS to restart the task's execution.
o   *Redo Task* If more reliable data related to an already executed task arrives, the decision maker will control the IS to redo that task and control HLCM to send the newly produced results to those agents that are interested in it.
o   *Multi-task Execution* If the underlying IS has the ability to run several tasks simultaneously, the decision maker should be capable of monitoring the execution of several tasks at the same time.

As pointed out earlier, any new arriving data will trigger the data-checking KS which may put a goal to redo/restart a task on the Goal-BB. This goal, whenever selected at the "Select Goal" step, will trigger the Decision Maker to control the IS to execute the intended action at the "Execute Goal" step.

To redo a task is simple, however, in order to suspend the IS's execution so that a task can be restarted, we developed a step by step plan-execution mechanism. Unlike conventional approaches, the Decision Maker (here in its function as Monitor) does not send the whole task to the underlying IS and then waits for the final results. Instead, the Decision Maker itself follows the plan to execute that task and it only sends one primitive action (Basic Process Element) of the plan at a time to the IS. These task plans are predefined as the goal-plan in the SM. The knowledge source called plan-execution KS will be triggered by the IS message context(Task, BPE) and, as a consequence, the decision maker will consult the GoalPlan slot in the SM to find out the next appropriate BPE of this task and generates a goal (on the Goal-BB) to execute this BPE.

Task swapping may be caused by several reasons:

o   an urgent request from the other agents arrives;
o   a goal with higher priority which was in "wait" state now becomes ready due to the arriving of new data;
o   the deadline of a task is arriving.

Whether or not it is possible to execute several tasks simultaneously depends on the capabilities of the IS. Monitoring more than one task execution will not cause any confusion in the decision maker since each context(Task, BPE) message definitively determines the next BPE the IS should execute for this task.

Redoing an executed task or restarting a task under execution with more reliable data can guarantee that each agent's contribution to the global task is positive. Task swapping gives the agent the capability to process the task in due time. Multi-task execution can reduce the total amount of time the whole system needs to finish the global task. The KSs presented above are obviously application-independent, quite in accordance with the philosophy of the Archon framework.

7.2.4 Global System Coherence

In order to enhance global coherence, we suggest to add two specific information items to each agent's AAM:

agent_agenda (agent, task) and good_for (data, task).

Agent_agenda is an information to be dynamically maintained. It represents what the other agents intend to do. That is, whenever an agent has added a task to its local agenda, it should also inform the others about this intention. In the Blackboard-based decision maker, the local agenda consists of those IS goals that are still on the Goal-BB.

Good_for is a static and predefined attribute. It represents what sort of data may be useful for which task. Using good_for(data, task) - in a sense a finer grain 'interested_in' - together with already existing interested_in(data, agent) allows to dynamically determine Agents who may be interested in the data.

Keeping the others' agenda can contribute to cooperation due to the following reasons:

a) Using good_for(data, task) and agent_agenda(agent, task), each agent can evaluate the importance of its own tasks, e.g. how many agents may benefit from the execution and subsequent results of a certain task?
b) If one agent is free and it finds it can do a task which is in the other agent's agenda, the agent should do it in order to share the community workload.[2]
c) For result-sharing, each agent should first try to produce the data that can be shared with the others in order to reduce the other agent's solution search space as soon as possible.
d) It can help to decide whether or not to wait for the data from other agents.

We believe that for each agent to keep the information about the other's intentions is of great importance for the sake of global system coherence.

---

2. Such scenario assumes the existence of agents with similar capabilities. They can reduce the overall computational load of a system by exchanging tasks. In the applications described in Chapter 8 this would only be possible for a few tasks.

8

The Application Demonstrators

8.1 INTRODUCTION TO THE APPLICATIONS

8.1.1 Iberdrola demonstrator

Domain description

The first demonstrator involves Iberdrola S.A. [Corera 91], a Spanish electric utility partner in the project. Iberdrola is the largest electric utility of Spain in terms of market share and second in terms of power generation. It is interconnected with eight different companies.

The HV transmission network controlled by Iberdrola extends over an area of about 100,000 km^2 and consists of 120 substations, 300 lines and 300 power transformers in the voltage levels 132 kV to 380 kV. Data is acquired through Remote Terminal Units (RTUs) located at the substations, and is transmitted through different media to the Central Power Dispatch Centre (PDC), where the application will be located. The SCADA (Supervisory Control And Data Acquisition) system provides information on the status of 20 000 elements - breakers, switches and protective relays - with a polling cycle of 10 seconds maximum; and the value of 2000 analogue measures - power flows, voltages, frequency - which are frozen at maximum every 20 seconds. All this information is stored in the central computer, accessible to the application in different ways. In addition 4000 items can be remotely controlled from this computer.

Management of the electric network performed by the operator in the control centre consists mainly of topology changes - operation of breakers and switches - generation scheduling and control.

However, management of the same network in emergency situations becomes very complex due to the large number of constraints to be taken into consideration and the insufficient quality of the information arriving at the control centre. An emergency situation can typically be originated by a short-circuit in a line, busbar or transformer, and can be worsened by equipment malfunctioning (i.e. a breaker failing to open) or subsequent overloads (like a "house of cards": tripping of a line overloads other lines, which will also trip). The situation can become worse due to power stations triggering, with the subsequent power imbalance. Actions to restore service must be taken rapidly and accurately, as in this situation the network is less tolerant to operational errors. Actions will basically consist of breaker operations, topology changes and activation/deactivation of automatisms and protective relays. For large disturbances actions on power plants will also be required.

Objectives

The application has to aid the operator giving a coherent picture of the situation and suggesting measures to be taken. It should be able to:

- detect the existence of a disturbance
- detect the cause and type of the disturbance, and permanent effects caused, such as equipment at permanent fault, damaged breakers, etc.
- analyse the situation of the network once it reaches a steady state.
- prepare a restoration plan
- monitor the evolution of the network and the performance of the plan.

8.1.2 EA Technology Demonstrator

Domain Description

In England and Wales, (the situation is slightly different in Scotland), there are separate transmission and distribution companies and CIDIM is designed as an aid to the Control Engineers of the distribution system. In England and Wales there are twelve Regional Electricity Companies and the CIDIM system has to be able to be used in any of them - this should require only limited modifications.

Electricity is received from the transmission network at 132kV and is transformed down in stages, 33kV and 11kV, as it is distributed across a region. 132kV and 33kV are referred to as High Voltage (HV) and 11kV and below as Low Voltage (LV) in this document. Domestic customers receive their supply at 240V and some large industrial customers can take their supply at either 11kV or 33kV.

Since a fault on the High Voltage network can potentially cut off supply to more customers and the network 'fans' out from the HV to LV, it is sensible to spend more money on this network to protect continuity of supply. This is done in two ways; by providing alternative supply routes - so that if a line is off supply customers are not necessarily affected; and by use of telemetered automatic protection devices. Automatic protection devices are placed at strategic points in the network and are set up to open in response to faults isolating the smallest possible area of network (some protection schemes are more complex though this need not be discussed here). This reduces the damage to the network and keeps the area off supply to a minimum. The automatic devices can attempt to reclose in case the fault was transient, if the fault is in fact permanent they will reopen. Transient faults outnumber permanent faults and can be caused by the weather, e.g. wind or lightning affecting overhead lines. The telemetry system enables the actions of the automatic devices to be reported back to the Control Room where it is the Control Engineers (CE) job to ensure continuity of supply to customers as well as supervising maintenance and restoration work. On the Low Voltage network there are less alternative supply routes and protective devices tend to be non-automatic e.g. fuses, and untelemetered switches.

Generally, the last telemetered automatic protection device will be positioned just after the point where the voltage is transformed down to 11 kV; this is called the source circuit breaker. The operation of this device tells of a fault somewhere below it. If the fault is permanent then one of the fuses could have blown but the only way the Control Engineer will know of this is if customers telephone the Control Centre to complain of loss of power or if he is informed by his colleagues in the field, Field Engineers. Even at HV not all equipment is telemetered. This means that the Control Engineer has to take into account a number of factors when diagnosing faults: the telemetry from telemetered plant, telephone calls, and possible operations of untelemetered plant.

Although important, diagnosing faults does not take up a lot of the Control Engineers time. Maintenance and repairs have to be performed on the network and before this can be done the network has to be made safe to work on. Working to strict regulations the Control Engineer makes a Switching Plan, i.e. a list of all the operations needed to safely isolate a region of network, this plan will include opening switches and earthing the network. Some of the switches can be operated from the Control Room, some the Field Engineer has to operate manually. It is the Control Engineers job to ensure the Switching Plan is safe, a plan checked for safety is referred to as a Switching Schedule, and to sanction over radio links the operations the Field Engineers is to perform.

Other duties of the Control Engineer include restoration of power when this is possible by switching operations from the Control Room e.g. switching in an alternative route and ensuring that the network operates securely. This means that for all switching operations the Control Engineer has to be aware if customers will loose supply and if the network will become overloaded.

Objectives
The objectives of the CIDIM system are to provide assistance to the Control Engineer in the tasks described above, this includes:

o   Fault diagnosis at both HV and LV
o   Security analysis - performed automatically or on request
o   Help with creating safe switching schedules
o   Automatic rechecking of these schedules before the work is to be carried out
o   Collation of information - e.g. reporting that a new fault has occurred that will affect maintenance work which has already been planned
o   Greater availability and cross referencing of information

8.2 ANALYSIS OF THE APPLICATIONS FROM A DAI APPROACH

The selection of the number and type of agents that compose the application is not trivial, and should take into account issues such as what generic tasks are to be performed, what information is required by each task and what is available, what internal representation is needed, when parallel execution is possible and what interworking between agents can take place.

8.2.1 General Constraints

a) Limited Modelling of the Network
It is not possible to model the network to the level required for accurate reasoning, as the size of the resulting system would make it useless; in addition some of the data is unavailable. Information not modelled is:

o   Individual characteristics and settings of protective relays and automatic devices. Instead, they are grouped in a few types. This degrades slightly the diagnosis of the disturbance.

o   Historical performance of equipment in previous disturbances.

Correct modelling of the network events would require:

o   A short-circuit load-flow, instead fault-propagation heuristics are used.
o   Stability study on line, to test transient effects. Instead some pre-calculations are carried out, to in order to set limits to the actions that can be taken.

In the EA Technology application this does mean that the network can be modelled in a qualitative way rather than quantitatively, which reduces the model complexity and increases its generality.

b) Uncertainty Handling.
Most uncertainties, apart from those derived from imperfect modelling, come from inaccurate timing of the information (for example, in the Iberdrola application a fault is cleared typically in 0.5 sec, while time precision in alarms is +/- 5 seconds), and incorrect and lost information.

In the EA Technology application telephone calls will be used to diagnose Low Voltage faults. The link between the customer and the network from which they are supplied will be derived from the customers postcode. Relating customers to network in this way is not always correct and in some instances there will be uncertainty as to where a customer receives his supply from. There is also uncertainty about the exact time of power failure and there are delays in reporting it.

The telemetry system can sometimes mal-operate causing temporary cessation of telemetry from part of the network this can mean that the Control Engineer is unsure of the exact state of the network.

c) Actions Taken Affect the Whole Network.
Events in the network can affect the entire network. Therefore intensive computation is required to evaluate those effects. A numerical load flow must be employed.

d) Fast and Accurate Answers are Required.
There is no chance for trial-and-error approaches, as the situation can be adversely affected by wrong actions. Simulated 'what-if' actions could be useful if the capability to perform them quickly was available.

8.3 THE IBERDROLA APPLICATION

8.3.1 Information used by the Iberdrola Demonstrator

The distribution of the tasks within the agents of the application cannot be carried out without considering the characteristics of the information available. This is the big constraint for the application, and the use of redundant information together with cooperation between the agents is required for good overall results. Briefly, the information the application uses is:

Alarms	Including operation of breakers and protective devices; their time reference is not precise (+/- 5 seconds), but they are produced as soon as the control centre is aware of the operation through the SCADA system.
Chronological Alarms	They contain the same information as above, but their time-tag is much more precise; the disadvantage is that they are produced at the substation, and arrive at the control centre after a delay.
Snapshots	Including breakers and switches status, and selected analogue measures (i.e., busbar voltages and power flows); each snapshot is a relatively consistent picture of the whole network; the disadvantage here is that the operation of breakers which return to the same state (i.e. open and close) taking place between snapshots is lost.

8.3.2 Generic Tasks in the Iberdrola Demonstrator

In order to address the issue of splitting the application into agents, generic tasks responding to the objectives of the application are classified (Table 1).

TASK	Network Representation	AI/ Conventional	Numerical	Input Information	Time Response
1) Detection and classification of the disturbance	NO	CONV	NO	alarms chrono	10 s
2) Diagnosis of the disturbance	YES	AI	NO	alarms chrono	1 m
3) Black-out area identification and follow-up	YES	CONV	NO	snaphots	20 s per cycle
4) Restoration planning	YES	AI	YES (load flow)	snapshots	3 m
5) Restoration monitoring	YES	AI	NO	snapshots	20 s per cycle
6) Human Computer Interface	YES (graphics DB)	AI	NO	tasks 1-5 output	1 s

Table 1

8.3.3 Agents in the Iberdrola Demonstrator

First Considerations with Tasks and Agents

A first consideration is that the size and computational load of the application are very large. Therefore distribution in several agents is convenient, and parallelism encouraged.

A critical issue when designing the agents is the connectivity between elements in the internal representation of the network, which must be kept coherent with the information received. Taking into account that alarms are nearly immediate and that chronological information suffers a delay of several minutes, it is not reliable to update the representation with both. The same applies to snapshots: an agent doing the update with both snapshots and alarms would not be reliable. The first conclusion will be not to assign to the same agent tasks using information in different groups. Task 3 can be performed in parallel with task 4 and 5. Taking advantage of the fact that Task 3 does not require AI techniques means that it can be performed by a single agent, the BAI. The BAI communicates its results to another agent, the SRA, which performs tasks 4 and 5, which are sequential. The load flow execution within task 4 can be allocated to a slave machine, in order not to saturate the agent and block the main reasoning.

Task 2 can be assigned to two agents as the information available is not compatible for joint processing, but is highly complementary - chronological information arrives later but is more precise. Therefore two agents, named AAA and BRS, will analyse alarms and chronos respectively, with strong interaction between them to improve each others results.

There are two functions that apply to all tasks, these are Control System Interface and the Human Computer Interface; both are assigned to individual agents, due to their complexity. The former does not require complex heuristics and has been implemented conventionally. Task 1 (from Table 1) is also implemented conventionally and since it uses similar information it has been allocated to the same agent.

Descriptions of Agents

There will be 6 agents within the Iberdrola application [Laresgoiti 90] as shown in Figure 8.1 below:

CSI   (Control System Interface) Interfaces the application with the control computer, filters alarms and chronos and snapshots, detects disturbances and provide services such as load-flows. Runs distributed in two machines, UNIX and VMS, coded in Fortran and C. It does not keep a network representation.

AAA   (Alarms Analysis Agent) Uses alarms to diagnose a disturbance: first it calculates the hypotheses, then models them to get a complete analysis of all element operations, and finally tracks subsequent alarms to detect permanent faults. Coded in a rule-based shell ART from Inference - 60% coded in Lisp - and running on a Unix machine. Uses complete object oriented network representation and employs a Viewpoint mechanism to process simultaneously several disturbances.

BRS   (Breakers and Relays Supervisor) Same tasks as the AAA, but using chronos. Implementation same as above, but does not use Viewpoints.

BAI   (Black out Area Identifier) Evaluates the black-out area and tracks it in 20 seconds cycle, based on snapshots. Also watches for critical elements getting out of service. In the beginning of the disturbance, it receives the alarms to evaluate the area initially isolated. Same implementation as BRS

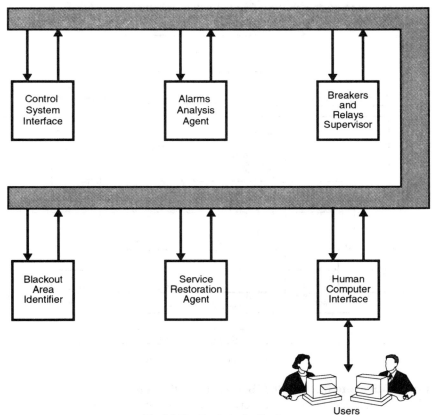

Fig. 8.1 The Iberdrola Application

SRA   (Service Restoration Agent) Prepares a restoration plan and tracks its execution. Implemented in Lisp on a Unix machine, and keeps an object oriented representation of the network at several levels of detail, from element to electric node.

HCI   (Human Computer Interface) Interfaces with the user of the application using text, menus and drawings. It is interactive so the user can suggest changes to the agents.

The main information flow is shown in Figure 8.2.

8.3.4 Cooperation Overview of the Iberdrola Application

As could be expected for a "large coarse" distributed application, cooperation between agents takes place along a "limited" number of interactions - what "limited" means will be understood after reading the further examples -, and using information with a high degree of abstraction involving complex reasoning at Intelligent System (IS) level. Most of it is identified as result sharing: partial or final results are either interchanged between agents - to check coincidence of results between "overlapping" agents - or provided to another agent to reason on these "added-value" results.

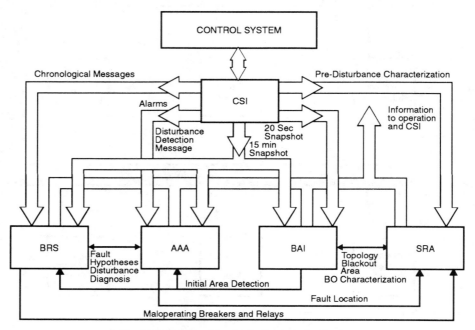

Fig. 8.2 Information Flow in the Iberdrola Application

Cooperative Situations in the Iberdrola Application
More detailed and extensive descriptions of cooperative situations for this application can be found in the appendix.

Cooperation between AAA and BRS

> These two agents diagnose the disturbance based on alarms and on chronological information respectively, following very similar reasoning steps. The AAA will be always ahead in its reasoning, which is good, to give to the operator an answer as soon as possible. The AAA sends its results to the BRS so that the BRS can skip several steps in its reasoning process, for example, if the BRS receives the AAA's hypotheses it can skip selecting from its own and therefore arrive at the final result earlier.
> The BRS can arrive at a more accurate diagnosis, and it will communicate it to the AAA. In case of disagreement they have to interchange partial results and reason on them. As an example, the BRS can detect that a tripping that was signalled as instantaneous, was in fact delayed: it will tell this fact to the AAA, so it can modify its conclusions. The AAA can also help the BRS: there is a risk that a substation is not on time, and therefore the chronos coming from that substation are not on time; it is

difficult to find then the right sequence of actions; however, the AAA which is prepared to reason independently of time can guess the sequence of the alarms: this is valuable to the BRS, that can order the chronos consequently.

Another feature of the AAA is that it processes simultaneous disturbances in different areas of the network by using Viewpoints, also called "Worlds": all the analysis is performed independently and simultaneously for both disturbances. Therefore each disturbance is followed and further reclosing operations are easily related to that disturbance.

The BRS is not prepared to do that: each disturbance is included in a window of 1 second, and processing is reset between blocks. The AAA can give it valuable information to relate one block to another.

As a conclusion, cooperation between these two agents results in a response that is faster and that improves with time.

Cooperation of AAA and BRS with BAI

The BAI will help the two agents in reducing the candidate faulty elements, by doing a connectivity analysis with breaker alarms; following the principle that the element at fault must be isolated from the healthy network. This agent is specialised in evaluating the black-out area, but this should be done when the network is in a steady state. Meanwhile, it will help the other two agents in reducing their search space.

Cooperation between AAA and BRS with SRA

The SRA prepares the restoration plan once a black-out area is identified. For this restoration plan it is important to know elements damaged and permanently faulty in order not to include them within the plan. The AAA and BRS are the agents more capable of identifying them, because failed operations are registered as alarms. These agents have to decide - at their Archon Layers - whether to diagnose further disturbances or to perform this support operation.

The advantage of this cooperation is that the SRA is free to analyse alarms, and can concentrate in creating the plan. In the worst case the plan will need to be amended, but the new one will be ready earlier than if this mechanism were not implemented.

Cooperation between BAI and SRA

The BAI initially sends the black-out area to the SRA so it can create the plan. It will also periodically update the black-out area and send it to the SRA. In case this agent feels some of the elements base of the plan are specially critical - i.e., a transformer that provides more of the energy to the area to be restored - it will ask the BAI to watch that this element does not get out of service. Again, this activity lets the SRA concentrate on the most important activity for the application.

Cooperation between the HCI and the SRA

The HCI is designed to introduce the user as an additional agent in the community. This agent will mostly gather results from the rest of the agents, but can also take an

114 THE APPLICATION DEMONSTRATORS [Ch. 8

active role, by suggesting alternatives to the restoration plan to the SRA, using a pre-defined language. A "negotiation" will take place between these two agents, interchanging information of different degrees of abstraction - from facts such as "this element is out of service" to guidelines such as "give more importance to blind power balance". At the end an agreement must be achieved and a commonly accepted plan produced.

Additional schemes

Archon provides three important features valuable to the application: priority handling, default reasoning and task sharing. The first one is critical when several disturbances take place: a compromise must be taken between analysing next disturbances - the AAA, BRS and BAI will have to concentrate on that- or prepare a restoration plan -which is always global, general to all disturbances. Negotiation will take place between the agents to concentrate on one issue or another, based on the urgency each agent evaluates.

The second issue is also important: due to the semi-autonomy nature of the agents, the interactions are not fixed and an agent should not be blocked by other not providing an answer at the right time; in case the BAI is not ready with the area isolated initially, the AAA and BRS can estimate from the BAI model and status what the delay will be, and decide to pass to the next phase. However some information interchanges are essential: i.e., the black-out area provided by the BAI, which is required by the SRA to prepare a restoration plan [Arlabosse 90].

The third issue allows dynamic task allocation. As an example, both the AAA and the CSI can detect if alarms arriving correspond to a disturbance. The AAA will ask the CSI to perform this task if it is concentrated on some phase of the diagnostic.

8.4 CIDIM - THE EA TECHNOLOGY APPLICATION

8.4.1 Information used by the CIDIM Application

The following types of information will be available as input to the CIDIM system:

Telemetry:　　　　　　　　　　　Here the term is used to cover all messages received from the network. These messages tell of the operation of circuit breakers, failure of transformers and can indicate when telemetry is lost from one substation.

Telephone Calls:　　　　　　　　The low voltage network has less telemetry than the high voltage so here use can be made of telephone calls from customers reporting loss of supply. By asking customers the time of power loss - this may only be known approximately - and their postcode it is possible to diagnose faults on the low voltage network.

Lightning Information:　　　　　Overhead power lines can be damaged by lightning. A knowledge of the location of lightning strikes can help the Control Engineer direct the search for the location of the damage when a fault occurs. This will help in reducing the time required before restoration of power is achieved.

Voltage Indications: Indications of the voltage at strategic points of the network are already available in the Control Room. If this information can be made available to CIDIM then it can be used to perform load analysis can also may help in resolving conflicts about the state of switches in the network.

User Volunteered Information: Since some of the circuit breakers in the network may not be telemetered there is a need for the user to volunteer information. The user will be able to find out this information by contacting field staff or other centres of control.

8.4.2 Generic Tasks in CIDIM

The major tasks in CIDIM are shown below in Table 2:

TASK	Network Representation	AI/ Conventional	Numerical	Input Information	Time Response
1) Diagnose HV Faults	YES	AI	NO	Telemetry	1-2 m elapsed
2) Diagnose LV Faults	YES	AI	NO	Telemetry Lightning Telephone	1-20 m elapsed
3) Answer Queries on lightning	NO	CONV	NO	Lightning	< 3 s
4) Security Analysis	YES	CONV	YES	Voltage	1- 2 m
5) Switch Planning	YES	AI	NO	User Input	20 m elapsed
6) Switch Checking	YES	AI	NO	User Input	> 5 s
7) Schedule recheck	YES	AI	NO	Output of 5	1 min
8) Indentifying Network Insecurities	NO	AI	NO	Fault Reports Output of 5 Telemetry	< 5s
9) Provide Network Data	YES	CONV	NO	Network Data	2 s - 5 m
10) User Interface	YES	AI CONV	NO	Output of 1-9	< 5 s

Table 2

8.4.3 Agents in CIDIM

First considerations with tasks and Agents

One of the main factors which decided the number and type of agents within the CIDIM application was the existence of pre-existing software. The HVDA [Cockburn 91, Bramer 88], WWA and SPA [Brailsford 87] were all existing programs which were not written in LISP (the Archon standard language) and were built as stand-alone systems. This means that for the HVDA and SPA a network representation and storage facility were already provided. The method of representation used was not the same in each case. This was acceptable for prototype systems but if many systems use the same type of information e.g. network data, then it causes less consistency problems to have one master copy which all agents can use. Thus the Information Agent was introduced as an intelligent front end to a network database. The HVDA already had some telemetry handling capabilities but these were quite separate from its fault diagnosis capabilities. Since the LVDA and other agents require telemetry as input it made sense to have one agent dealing solely with telemetry. High and Low Voltage diagnosis are done by separate systems since the information used to diagnose faults is different. Thus agents were planned based on existing systems or because of the need to provide services to more than one agent.

Agent Descriptions

There will be ten agents within the CIDIM application as shown in Figure 8.3 below. These agents are:

TA (Telemetry Agent) Receives telemetry from the outside world and reformats it. This is necessary because different electricity companies within the U.K. have different telemetry formats. Telemetry is filtered and sent on to interested agents. Filtering the telemetry involves removing that from outside the area of network stored in the Information Agent and telemetry which is not of interest to the application. The TA also keeps track of the state of all switches in the network. This is done here since the telemetry received by the TA tells of changes in switch state. For untelemetered switches it is necessary that user reports of switch state changes are directed to the TA.

IA (Information Agent) Has all the static information about the network such as connectivity of pieces of plant. This information is made available to other agents on request.

WWA (Weather Watch Agent) Receives data about lightning strikes. The WWA can display these on a map and can also answer queries so that it is possible to find out if there were any lightning strikes near a fault at a given time.

SA (Security Agent) If the voltage indications mentioned above are accessible to the SA then this program will be able to determine which lines are overloaded. As well as for the current situation the program does the calculations proposing what would happen if there was another fault on the network. Since it performs these "what-if" calculations assuming a fault on each line in the network in turn (only assuming one fault at a time not an accumulation of faults) the program can take some time to run. Part of the use of the rest of CIDIM to the SA will be in helping to decide when it is necessary to rerun the computationally expensive part of the program again.

HVDA (High Voltage Diagnosis Agent) Using telemetry from the TA the HVDA will diagnose the location, time and type (permanent or transient) of faults on the network. It can also identify where there is no power - deadzones- whether these are caused by faults or by work on the network.

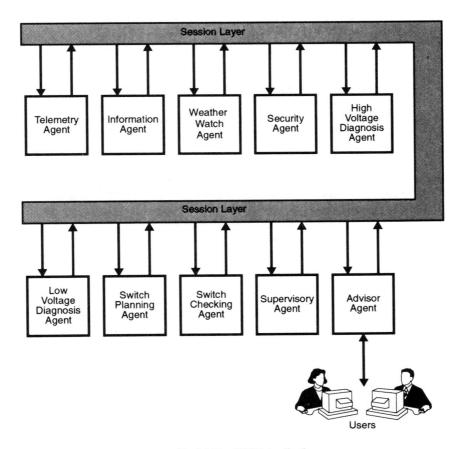

Fig. 8.3 The CIDIM Application

LVDA (Low Voltage Diagnosis Agent) Since there is less telemetry on the low voltage network the LVDA uses telephone calls from customers and lightning information as well as telemetry. In order to determine where customers are connected to the network the LVDA will use customers post codes. This is necessary since the full connectivity of customers to the network is not recorded but an estimation relating customer post code to post codes fed from a transformer can be done. Since there is a large amount of Low Voltage network the LVDA will load network data from the IA as it is required.

SPA (Switch Planning Agent) After a fault occurs the control engineer needs to locate it so that repair can be carried out. This is done in conjunction with Field Staff and CIDIM does not play an active role in this activity except that the Control Engineer may use CIDIM as an information source for network or lightning data. After locating a fault a Switching Plan needs to be created in order to ensure that the area of network around the fault is fully isolated and safe to work on. The SPA does not create these plans automatically but is user driven. What it does is to make it easier for the Control Engineer to create such plans and it performs safety checks on the steps of such plans.

SCA (Switch Checking Agent) Rather than make a full switching plan the Control Engineer may want to just check that it is safe to operate one switch. This may be because the switch is being operated to restore power to an area by providing an alternative route. As well as these safety checks the SCA will be able to recheck a Switching Plan nearer the time it is carried out.

SVA (Supervisory Agent) The Supervisory Agent will receive fault reports from both the HVDA and LVDA and Switching plans from the SPA. It will allow queries on this data so that a subset can be accesses e.g. to be displayed by the Advisor Agent to the user. The SVA will also look for relations between the information it receives such as when a fault occurs in an area where work is soon to take place. In this case a warning to the user may help re-plan the work rather than find out it is not possible.

AVA (Advisor Agent) The AVA is the user interface agent to the CIDIM application. It will display events to the user and accept user input.

8.4.4 Cooperation Overview of the CIDIM Application

The agents will at times cooperate in order to perform tasks or to exchange useful information. Although the two demonstrators have not yet been built some examples of the types of cooperation expected have been identified and are given below.

Cooperative Situations In EA Technology Application (CIDIM)
More detailed and extensive descriptions of cooperative situations for this application can be found in the appendix.

Cooperation between HVDA and LVDA

If the HVDA informs the LVDA of HV faults and the LVDA can recognise those which cause loss of supply to the LV network then the LVDA can save time by attributing some loss-of-supply calls to HV faults rather than trying to diagnose LV faults. This will also stop the LVDA producing incorrect diagnoses - i.e. attributing the cause as an LV fault when it is fact an HV fault.

Cooperation between HVDA and SVA

The HVDA has the necessary information to produce partial high level restoration plans for each deadzone. The SVA will use additional knowledge to expand these partial plans on request to make full high level restoration plans.

Cooperation between TA and LVDA

The LVDA and TA both have the ability to estimate if LV faults are transient or permanent. The choice of which agent to use could be determined by activity level. This knowledge can alter the scheduling for the LVDA IS.

Cooperation between TA, LVDA and HVDA

Telemetry messages can be lost from either a single circuit breaker or from a whole substation. In the latter case there is an indication that telemetry has been lost; in the former case there is no such indication. When telemetry is missing the agents can help each other, for example the HVDA might be able to infer the state of a HV circuit breaker because of the known presence of an LV fault. The LVDA would have diagnosed this fault just using customer telephone call complaints.

Cooperation between SVA and HVDA

Two Agents performing the same task but at a different level of thoroughness. When one is busy it can suspend the task as long as the other continues to perform it. The quality of the result depends on which agent is performing the task; the best result is when both the HVDA and SVA are involved.

Cooperation between WWA and IA

The WWA needs the help of the IA to answer queries. If the IA is busy the WWA can change the order in which the query is structured so that on average less requests are made of the IA. If the IA is not working at all the WWA can give its best answer which could either confirm that no lightning is present or be "don't know"; by itself it cannot answer definitely whether there was lightning at a given 'geographic location' at a given 'time'.

Cooperation between HVDA, TA, LVDA and AVA

The knowledge about the state of switches in the network is provided by the TA but other agents may have conflicting information, such as customer telephone calls or knowledge of how protection operates, which may suggest that the network is in fact in a different state. In some cases it is known that the telemetry is not functioning properly so then it may be best to make these other agents views of the network state known globally throughout the CIDIM system.

8.5 CONCLUSIONS

The experience achieved so far on the applications is quite promising. An important aspect of the project so far has been developer's requirements. The facilities for developing and integrating distributed systems are identified but are not yet available for experimentation due to the time scale of the related tasks in the project. One of them is the set of tools required to facilitate the introduction of the self and acquaintances models and to preserve cross coherence among the agents, i.e. tasks, interests, capabilities. Also the introduction of domain information and knowledge into the Archon Layer is critical: this knowledge controls the scheduling within the agent, and fine tuning is likely to be required for an efficient application. Dry-run facilities with logging of results are also important.

The requirements analysis undertaken by the application partners, which included expanded versions of the cooperative situations from the above sections as well as a list of application requirements of the Archon Layer, has contributed to the specifications of the various modules of the Archon Layer. This means that many of the functionalities required to implement the cooperative situations described in this chapter are planned for the Archon Layer e.g. Intelligent Message Handling [Arlabosse 90], Conditional Task Initiation. Additional cooperation capabilities, not yet used in the applications, appear to be quite interesting for both demonstrators. Some are standard in the project and others are tentative. Information Translation between agents will ease the integration of agents, i.e. some agents have different representations of the network: in Iberdrola the network of the restoration agent is obtained from the "applications files" within the control computer, while the network of the disturbance diagnosis agents is generated from the "SCADA files". Dead lock detection and avoidance mechanisms are also required. Finally, the use of "contexts" at the Archon Layer level is convenient: some facts are true in one context (e.g. disturbance), while false in other. Code could then be executed in parallel with different facts, and for the same performance development simplified. The generality of Archon mechanisms allows applications of very different nature to be implemented in a distributed fashion, being capable of incorporating different types of agents: Expert Systems, Databases, existing systems with minor modification, etc. It makes control and interaction knowledge explicit rather than enveloped in the application subsystems.

8.5.1 Related work

A valid example of this applicability are tutoring systems. Iberdrola is involved in ESPRIT project ITSIE, dealing with intelligent training systems in industrial environments. The demonstrator, an Intelligent Tutoring System (ITS) for fossil fuel power plants, is composed of several subsystems showing "intelligent" interaction with similar requirements to "Archon-type" applications. These subsystems are:

o   Two databases, one containing domain knowledge and other containing the trainee profile.
o   One qualitative and one quantitative simulator of the power plant.
o   The Monitor of the trainee's actions during the practical exercises.
o   The Executable Expertise Subsystem, which performs simulated procedures and analysis.
o   The Pedagogue subsystem, which simulates the human instructor.

o   The Human Computer Interface.

Interactions are conditioned by the functionality desired for training: expert simulation of exercises and the trainee's practical performance of exercises. The first case implies a strong interaction between the last three subsystems, while the second one implies major cooperation between the Monitor, the Pedagogue and the HCI.

In a similar vein to this application many others are envisaged. The experience so far within the project shows that the availability of Archon - and other similar environments - will assist in the development of complex software applications at a reasonable cost/performance ratio.

9
Glossary of Terms

Acquaintance Model (AAM)
    "Acquaintance models provide a mechanism by which agents can explicitly represent information about other "interesting" agents [...] known in the community. [...] agents will not necessarily model all community members, only those with which they may interact." [Abraham82, Agha86, Agha85, Bond88, Cammarata83, Decker87, Durfee87, Gasser87, Kornfield81, Lesser81, Lesser80, Wesson81, Zhang88]

Agent (ARCHON Agent)
    An Archon Agent consists of a (possibly pre-existing) *Intelligent System* and the *Archon Layer*, which provides the additional means for cooperation. See Chapter 1.4.

Agent Information Management Module
    see Chapter 5.1.2.

Archon Layer (AL)
    The Archon Layer is the component of an agent which "provides services useful across all the applications to allow cooperation between agents". The Archon Layer in a way acts like a bridge between the Application system plane and the Archon plane. See Chapter 2.3.1.

Contract Net
    "In the contract net approach to negotiation, a contract is an explicit agreement between a node that generates a task (the manager) and a node willing to execute the task (the contractor). [...] Individual nodes are not designated a priori as manager or contractor; these are only roles, and any node can take on either role dynamically during the course of problem solving. Nodes are therefore not statically tied to a control hierarchy." [Smith/Davis81]

Cooperation
    [Intelligent systems] "cooperate in the sense that no one of them has sufficient information to solve the entire problem; mutual sharing of information is necessary to allow the group as a whole to produce the answer." [Smith/Davis81]

Distributed Problem Solving (DPS)
DPS considers how the work of solving a particular problem can be divided up between a number of agents that cooperate at the level of dividing and sharing knowledge about the problem and about developing the solution.

Granularity
Describes the "level of decomposition. DPS refers to coarse-grain (task-level) decomposition, as opposed to fine-grain (statement-level) decomposition. Decomposing a problem at a coarse level is often more cognitively oriented than a fine-grain efficiency-oriented approach." [Decker87]

Heterogeneous System
Computer systems that differ in at least one of the following characteristics: run-time environment (hardware); programming language; philosophy (e.g. data bases, Expert Systems); architecture (frames, blackboards,...); semantics capabilities; parameters the systems are evaluating.

High Level Communication Module
All message passing between agents is done through the HLCM. It is thus each agent's connection to any other agent. It may be subdivided into two sub-modules: IN-HLCM managing in-coming messages, OUT-HLCM constructing and delivering outgoing messages. The main functions of the IN-HLCM are: scheduling and filtering of messages. The main functions of the OUT-HLCM are: format out-going messages, identify destinations, filtering. See Chapter 4.2.2.

Intelligent System (IS)
An existing or to be developed executable computer program that can carry out tasks (AI-type tasks as well as conventional numeric or database tasks) relevant to a specific application domain.

KADS
The name of a methodology for the development of KBSs. It was developed under two projects carried out in the ESPRIT.

Loosely-coupled
"means that individual KSs spend the great percentage of their time in computation rather than communication." [Smith/Davis81]

Low Level Behaviour
See Chapter 3.1

Monitor
The Monitor is the control instance of each agent. It represents the only connection between the Archon Layer and the control of the I.S. See chapter 3.3.1 and 3.3.2.

Multi-Agent System (MAS)
MAS research is concerned with coordinating intelligent behaviour among a collection of (possibly pre-existing) autonomous intelligent agents, how they can coordinate their knowledge, goals, skills, and plans jointly to take actions or solve problems. [Bond88]

Normative Model
The normative model serves to define components necessary to effectuate a certain problem solving behaviour. The type of problem solving tasks to be incorporated in the normative model all lie within the domain of industrial process control. The *Normative model* has two components: diagrams for application design, design methodologies for cooperation. The diagrams for application design are schemas which generally describe a problem type. Problem types can either be BASIC problem types (diagnosis, planning, control, etc.) or COMPOUND problem types. The methodologies for cooperation are theories that describe different aspects of cooperation, e.g. problem decomposition and organisational theory.

Open System Interconnection (OSI)
A reference model for networks developed by the International Standardisation Organisation (ISO).

Planning and Coordination Module
See Chapter 3.3.1 and 3.3.2.

Partial Global Plans (PGP)
"The representation of how several nodes are working toward a larger goal. Contains information about the larger goal, the major plan steps that are occurring concurrently, and how the partial solutions formed by the nodes should be integrated together." [Durfee/Lesser87]

Reactivity
See Chapter 3.1.

Reconceptualization
See Chapter 3.1.1.

Result Sharing
The type of interaction between agents so that the agents assist one another by the exchange of partial results based on somewhat different perspectives on the overall problem. [Smith/Davis 1981]

Self Model (SM)
The agent's self-model is "the agent's representation of its own capabilities and needs.

Semi-Autonomous
Autonomy is defined by looking at the activities an agent can accomplish between waiting times [waiting time = time spent by an agent waiting for some event con-

trolled by another agent to happen]. If this activity can be seen as "complete" (e.g. it solves a subgoal), then the agent is autonomous. Whilst the coupling level measures the "quantity" of activity an agent is able to perform independently from its acquaintances, the autonomy level describes the "quality" of this activity. "Agents are semi-autonomous in that each subgoal can usually be performed by a single agent" [Lesser81]. "... an agent is autonomous if it is capable of acting intelligently and rationally, ... or if it is adaptive to global conditions" [Sridharan87]. "An autonomous agent has its own existence, which is not justified by the existence of other agents" [Demazeau90]. See also [Muller88].

In Archon, the term 'semi-autonomous' refers to the dependency between those systems: It can generally be of three kinds: "information dependency", "control dependency", "resource dependency". What we mean by semi-autonomous is that no control dependency exists between subsystems. At the functional level this means that no agent can inject items in the agenda of its acquaintances, each agent controls its own agenda. Agent self determination is the assumption which mainly effects cooperation and, as a consequence, communication. Each agent is the only one capable of determining its own actions. Other agents may only influence its decision by sending appropriate messages.

Task Sharing

The type of interaction between agents so the agents assist one another by sharing the computational load for the execution of subtasks of the overall problem. [Smith/Davis 1981]

Abbreviations:

AAM	Agent Acquaintance Model
AIM	Agent Information Management
AL	Archon Layer
ARCHON	Architecture for Cooperative Heterogeneous ON-line systems
CAD	Computer-Aided Design
CF	Certainty factor
DAI	Distributed Artificial Intelligence
DPS	Distributed Problem Solving
HCI	Human Computer Interface
HLCM	High-Level Communication Module
IS	Intelligent System
ISA	Information Sharing Architecture
KBS	Knowledge-Based System
KS	Knowledge Source
MAS	Multi Agent System
PCM	Planning and Coordination Module
PGP	Partial Global Plans
SM	Self Model
3DIS	3 Dimensional Information Space
UIA	User Interface Agent

10
References

Abraham M.F., 'Modern Sociology Theory'. Oxford University Press, 1982

Afsarmanesh H., McLeod D., 'The 3DIS: An Extensible Object-Oriented Information Management Environment', ACM Transactions on Information Systems Vol. 7(4) pp. 339-377, 1989

Afsarmanesh H., Brotoatmodjo E., Byeon E., and Parker A., 'The EVE VLSI Management Environment,' in Proceedings of the IEEE International Conference on Computer-Aided Design, 1989b

Agha G., Hewitt C.E., 'Concurrent programming using ACTORS: Exploiting large scale parallelism'. AI memo 865, MIT, 1985

Agha G., 'ACTORS: A Model of Concurrent Computation in Distributed Systems'. MIT Press, 1986

Arlabosse F., Biermann J., Gaussens E., Wittig T., 'Industrial Control: A Challenge for the Applications of AI', Proceedings of the ESPRIT Conference 1987, North-Holland, 1987

Arlabosse F., Gaussens E., Gureghian D., Longtier J.M., Becker S., Wittig T., 'Requirement Analysis for Agent and Message Scheduling', ARCHON Technical Report TR 5/5-90

Avouris N.M., Liedekerke M.H.V., Sommaruga, L., 'Evaluating the CooperA Experiment', in proc. of 9th DAI Workshop, pp 351-366, 1989

Avouris, N.M., Lekkas G., 'Cooperating Expert Systems: experience and perspectives', in proceedings of 3rd Panhellenic Conference in Informatics, Athens, (in Greek), May 1991

Berry D.C., Broadbent D.E.,'Expert Systems and the Man-Machine Interface: Part II The User Interface, Expert Systems, 4, 1987

Bond A.H., Gasser L., 'Reading in Distributed Artificial Intelligence'. Morgan Kaufmann, 1988

Brailsford J.R., Cross A.D., Raven P.F., 'The Switching Schedule Production Assistant - a knowledge based system for the electrical power distribution engineer', IEE Digest 1987/83.

Bramer M.A., Muirden D., Pierce J., Platts J.C., Vipond D.L., 'Faust - An expert system for diagnosing faults in an electricity supply system', In 'Research & Development in Expert Systems 5', Kelly B., Rector A. (eds) Cambridge University Press, 1988

Brandau R., Weihmayer R., 'Heterogeneous Multi-Agent Cooperative Problem Solving in a Telecommunication Network Management Domain', in proc. DAI workshop, pp 41-57, 1989

Cammarata S., McArthur D., Steeb R., 'Strategies of cooperation in distributed problem solving'. Proc. 8th IJCAI, pp. 767 - 770, Aug. 1983

Cockburn, D, McDonald, J R, Burt, G, Brailsford, J R, Beaton, J, & Lo, K L., 'Expert Systems for On-line Fault Diagnosis in Electrical Power Networks', In 11th International Conference on Electricity Distribution 1991, Volume 1 Session 4, 1991

Corera J.M., Echavarri J., Laresgoiti I., Perez J., 'Description of the Iberdrola Demonstrator', ARCHON Technical Report 16/11-91, 1991

Corkill D., Gallagher K., 'Tuning A Blackboard-based Application: A case study using GBB', Proc. AAAI-88, 1988

Davis R., Smith R.G., 'Negotiation as a Metaphor for Distributed Problem Solving', Artificial Intelligence 20, 1983

Demazeau Y., Muller J.-P., 'Decentralized Artificial Intelligence', Elsevier Science Publishers B.V. (North-Holland), 1990

Decker K.S.,' Distributed problem solving techniques: a survey', IEEE trans. s.m.c. Vol. SMC-17 No.5, pp. 729-740, Sept/Oct 1987

Durfee E.H., Lesser V.R., 'Using Partial Global Plans to Coordinate Distributed Problem Solvers', Proceedings of IJCAI-87, 1987

Durfee E.H., 'A Unified Approach to Dynamic Coordination: Planning Actions and Interactions in a Distributed Problem Solving Network', COINS Technical Report 87-84, Univ. of Massachusetts at Amherst, 1987

Durfee E.H., Lesser V.R., Corkill D.D., 'Cooperation through Communication in a distributed problem solving network'. In Distributed Artificial Intelligence (ed. M.N.Huhns), pp 119-153, Pitman Publishing, 1987

Durfee E.H., Lesser V.R., Corkill D.D., 'Coherent Cooperation Among Communicating Problem Solvers', IEEE Trans. Computers C-36, 1987

Fox,M.S., 'An Organizational View of Distributed Systems', IEEE Trans. on SMC, 11, 1, pp 70-80, 1981

Fuchs J., Skarek P., Varga L.Z., Wildner-Malandain E.,'Distributed Cooperative Architecture for Accelerator Operation', 2nd International Workshop on Software Engineering, Artificial Intelligence and Expert Systems for High Energy and Nuclear Physics, L'Agelonde, 1992

Gasser L., Braganza C., Herman N., 'MACE: a flexible testbed for distributed AI research'. In Distributed Artificial Intelligence (ed. M.N.Huhns), pp 119-153 Pitman Publishing, 1987

Gasser,L., Braganza,C. and Herman,N., 'Implementing Distributed AI systems using MACE', in Readings in Distributed Artificial Intelligence (eds A.H.Bond & L.Gasser), pp 445-451, Morgan-Kaufmann, 1988

Georgeff,M., 'A Theory of Action for Multi-Agent Planning', in Proc. of AAAI 1984, pp 121-125, 1984

Ginsberg M.L., 'Knowledge Interchange Format: The KIF of Death', AI Magazine, Vol 12 No 3, 1991

de Greef P., Breuker J., de Jong T., 'Modality : an analysis of functions, user control and communication in knowledge based systems,' University of Amsterdam, 1988

Hall L.E., Avouris N.M., Cross A.D., 'Interface design issues for Cooperating Expert Systems', Proceedings of Avignon90, 10th Int Conference in Expert Systems, pp 455- 469 Avignon, May 1990

Hartson H.R., Hix D., 'Human-Computer Interface Development: Concepts and Systems for its Management', ACM Comp. Surveys, Vol 21, No 1, pp 5-92, March 1989

Hayes-Roth B., 'A Blackboard Architecture for Control' Artificial Intelligence No 26, 1987

Hayes-Roth B., Washington R., Seiver A., 'Intelligent Monitoring and Control', Proc. IJCAI-89, Detroit, 1989

Hayes-Roth F., Erman L.D., Fouse S., Lark J.S., Davidson J., 'ABE: A cooperative Operating System and Development Environment', in AI Tools and Techniques', M. Richer (ed) Ablex Publishing, Norwood, NJ, 1988

Heimbinger D., McLeod D., 'A Federated Architecture for Information Management,' ACM Transactions on Office Information Systems Vol. 3(3) pp. 253-278, 1985

Hickman F.R., Killin J.L., Land L., Mulhall T., Porter D., Taylor R.M., 'Analysis for Knowledge-based Systems', Ellis Horwood, 1988

Hollnagel E., GRADIENT Technical Overview, CRI Report, Esprit Project 857, Copenhagen, 1991

Howey K.R., Wilson M.R., Hannigan S., 'Developing a User Requirements Specification for IKBS Design', People and Computers V by A. Sutcliffe & L. Macauley, Cambridge University Press, Cambridge 1989.

Kass R., Finin T., 'The Role of User Models in Cooperative Interactive Systems', International Journal of Intelligent Systems, 4, 1989

King R.E., 'Fuzzy logic control of a cement kiln precalciner flash furnace'. Proc IEEE Conf on Appl of Adaptive & Multivariable Systems, Hull, England, pp 56-59, Sep 1982

King R.E., Karonis F.C., 'Multi-level expert control of a large scale industrial process'. In: 'Fuzzy Computing', Eds: Gupta M.M., Yamakawa T., North Holland Publ Co, 1988

Kornfield W.A., Hewitt C.E., 'The scientific community metaphor'. IEEE trans. s.m.c. Vol. SMC-11 pp. 24 - 33 Jan. 1981

Laresgoiti I., Perez J., Amantegi J., Echavarri J., 'Development of an Expert System for Disturbance Analysis in an electric al Network', Symposium on Expert Systems Application to Power Systems, Stockholm, Helsinki, 1990

Lenat D.B., 'Beings: Knowledge as Interacting Experts', in Proceedings of the 1975 International Joint Conference on Artificial Intelligence, pp 126- 133, 1975

Lesser V.R., Erman L.D., 'Distributed Interpretation: a Model and Experiment'. IEEE Trans. Comput., Vol. C- 29(12), pp.1144-1163, Dec. 1980

Lesser V.R., Corkill D.D., 'Functionally Accurate, Cooperative Distributed Systems'. IEEE Transaction on Systems, Man, and Cybernetics, SMC-11, No. 1, January 1981.

Lesser V.R., Corkill D.D., 'The distributed Vehicle Monitoring Testbed: A Tool for investigating problem solving networks' AI Magazine No 4, 1983

Lesser V.R., Corkill D.D., 'Distributed Problem Solving', In: Encyclopaedia of Artificial Intelligence, pp245-251, 1987

Lesser,V.R., Pavlin,J. and Durfee,E.H., 'Approximate Processing in Real-Time Problem Solving', AI Magazine, Spring 1988, pp 49-61, 1988

Lesser V.R., Corkill D.D., Whitehair R.C., Hernandez J.A., 'Focus of Control Through Goal Relationships', Proc. IJCAI-89, Detroit, 1989

Loingtier, J.M., 'ALAN: An Agent Language for Cooperation'. In: IJCAI Workshop on Objects and AI, Sidney, 1991

Macaulay L., Fowler C., Kirby M., Hutt A., 'USTM: A new approach to requirements specification', in Interacting with Computers, vol 2, No 1, pp92-118, April 1990

Malandain E., Skarek P., 'An Expert System for Accelerator Fault Diagnosis', IEEE Particle Accelerator Conf., Washington DC, Vol. I, p. 559, 1987

Meyer W., 'Expert Systems in Factory Management - Knowledge-Based CIM'. Ellis Horwood, 1990

Muller J.-P., Demazeau Y., 'Decentralized Artificial Intelligence'. Proceedings of First European Workshop on Modelling an Autonomous Agent in a Multi- Agent World, Elsevier Science Publishers B.V. (North-Holland), 1990

Oliveira E., Qiegang L., Camacho R., 'Controlling Cooperative Experts in a Real-Time System', submitted to the Third International Conference on Software Engineering for Real Time Systems, U.K., 1991

Oliveira E., Qiegang L., 'Towards A Generic Monitor For Cooperation', AAAI-91 Blackboard Workshop, U.S.A, 1991

Oliveira E., Camacho R., 'A Shell for Cooperating Expert Systems' Expert Systems Int. Journal of Knowledge Engineering, May 1991, Learned Information, Oxford, 1991

Oliveira E., Camacho R., Ramos C., 'A Multi-Agent Environment in Robotics' in Robotica Int. Journal of I.E. Research in Robotics and Artificial Intelligence, Vol 4 Part 9, Cambridge University Press, Oct. 1991

O'Reilly,C.A. and Cromarty,A.S, 'Fast is not 'Real Time': Designing Effective Real Time AI Systems', in Applications of AI (ed J.F.Gilmore), 1985

Rich, Elain, 'User Modeling via Stereotypes', Cognitive Science 3, 329-354, 1979

Rosenshein J.S., 'Synchronisation of Multi-Agent Plans', Proc. of the AAAI, pp115-119, 1982

Sathi A., Fox M.S., 'Constraint directed negotiation of resource allocations', In: Gasser, Huhns, DAI vol.2, 1989

Shneiderman B., 'Designing the User Interface: Strategies for Effective Human-Computer Interaction', Addison Wesley Publ., 1987

Simon,H.A., 'Models of Man', John Wiley and Sons, 1957

Sleeman, D.H., 'UMFE: A User Modelling Front End Subsystem', Int. Journal Man-Machine Communication, 1986

REFERENCES

Smith R.G., Davis R., 'Framework for Cooperation in Distributed problem Solving'. IEEE on Systems, Man, and Cub., Vol. SMC-11, No. 1, pp 61-70, Jan 1981

Smith D., Broadwell M., 'The Pilot's Associate: An overview', in SAE Aerotech Conference, Los Angeles, CA, May 1988

Sommaruga L., Avouris N.M., Van Liedekerke M.H.: 'Studies in Distributed A.I.: Development of the testbed environment CooperA', JRC Technical Note I.89.63, CITE, JRC Ispra, May 1989.

Sridharan N.S., '1986 Workshop on distributed AI'. AI Magazine Fall 1987 pp. 75-85

Stankovic,J.A., 'Misconceptions About Real Time Computing', IEEE Computer, pp 10-18, 1988

Sutcliffe A., 'Human-Computer Interface Design', MacMillan Education, London, 1988

Tanenbaum,A.S., 'Computer Networks', Second Edition, Prentice Hall, 1989

Wahlster W., Kobsa A., 'Dialogue-Based User Models', Proceedings of the IEEE, Vol. 74, No. 7, July 1986

Wesson R., Hayes-Roth F., Burge J.W., Stasz C., Sunshine C., 'Network structure for distributed situation assessment'. IEEE trans. Vol. SMC-11, pp. 5 - 23, Jan 1981

Wittig T., 'Power Systems fall under KRITIC's Eye',In: Modern Power Systems, London, 1986

Wittig T., 'Cooperating Expert Systems', In: Universidad Internacional Menendez Pelayo, Summer-School on Expert Systems, Santander-91, 1992

Zhang C., Bell D.A., 'HECODES: a Framework for Heterogeneous Cooperative Distributed Expert System'. Dept. of Information Systems, University of Ulster at Jordans town, N.Ireland, U.K., 1988

TECHNICAL REPORTS PRODUCED BY ARCHON

The following list contains all Technical Reports produced by ARCHON so far. These reports are public and available from Atlas Elektronik GmbH, ARCHON Management Dept. TEF3, Sebaldsbrücker Heerstr. 235, D-2800 Bremen, Germany.

TR 1 - *ARCHON - An Architecture for Cooperative Heterogeneous On-line Systems*
  Wittig T.
  In: Brauer, Freksa (eds): Wissensbasierte Systeme, 3. International Congress, Munich 1989. Informatik Fachberichte 227, Springer Verlag, Heidelberg, 1989

TR 2 - *ARCHON - An Architecture for Cooperative Heterogeneous On-line Systems*
  Mamdani E.H., Wittig T.
  Status Report for the ESPRIT Conference 1989

TR 3 - *Cooperation in a Multi-Agent Environment*
  Jennings N.R., Roda C., Mamdani E.H., 1990

TR 4 - *Communication between Cooperating Agents*
  Roda C., Jennings N.R., Mamdani E.H., 1990

TR 5 - *Requirement Analysis for Agent and Message Scheduling*
  Arlabosse F., Gaussens E., Gureghian D., Longtier J.M, Becker S., Wittig T., 1990

TR 6 - *Interface Design Issues for Cooperating Expert Systems*
  Hall L.E., Avouris N.M., Cross A.D.
  In: Proceedings of Avignon90, 10th International Conference in Expert Systems, pp 455-469, Avignon, May 1990

TR 7 - *A Hybrid Framework for Representing Uncertain Knowledge*
  Saffiotti, A.
  AAAI-90 Workshop on Uncertainty, 1990

TR 8 - *Using Dempster-Shafer Theory in Knowledge Representation*
  Saffiotti A.
  6th Conference on Uncertainty in AI, Boston, 1990

TR 9 - *ARCHON - Architecture for Cooperating Heterogeneous On- Line Systems -Status Report*
  Becker S., Ehlers J.
  Status Report for the ESPRIT Conference Week 1990

TR 10 - *A Multi-Agent Environment in Robotics*
  Oliveira E., Camacho R., Ramos C.
  In: Robotica International Journal of E.I. and Research on Artificial Intelligence and Robotics, Cambridge University Press, Vol 9, No 4, October 1991

TR 11 - *The Cooperation Framework of ARCHON*
Roda C., Mamdani E.H., Stassinopoulos G., Tsatsaros T., Spyropoulou M.
Proceedings of the 1990 TMN Workshop

TR 12 - *Choosing among Uncertainty Management Techniques: A Case Study*
Saffiotti A., Umkehrer E., 1991

TR 13 - *Examples of Cooperative Situations and their Implementation*
Corera, Jennings, et. al.
In preparation

TR 14 - *Monitoring Cooperation in Distributed Problem Solving*
Oliveira E., Qiegang L.
In: AAAI Workshop on Blackboard Systems, 1991, Anaheim, Los Angeles, USA

TR 15 - *A Shell for Cooperating Expert Systems*
Oliveira E., Camacho R.
In: Expert Systems, International Journal of Knowledge Engineering, Learned Information, Oxford, Vol 8 No 2, May 1991

TR 16 - *Description of the Iberdrola Demonstrator*
Corera J.M., Echavarri J., Laresgoiti I., Perez J.
In Preparation

TR 17 - *Intelligent Communication Support for Co-operating Expert Systems*
Tsatsaros T., Spyropoulou M., Zarkadakis G., Stassinopoulos G.
In Preparation

TR 18 - *Development of two Large Industrial Applications within a Distributed Artificial Intelligence Framework*
Corera J.M., Echavarri J., Cross A., Cockburn D., Laresgoiti I., Perez, J., 1991

TR 19 - *ALAN: An Agent Language for Cooperation*
Loingtier, J.M.
In: IJCAI Workshop on Objects and AI, 1991, Sidney

TR 20 - *Diagnosing Faults in Electrical Networks*
Barandiaran J., Laresgoiti I., Perez J., Corera J., Echavarri I.
In: EXPERSYS-91 Conference, 1991, Paris, France

TR 21 - *Solving Complex Problems using Diverse Viewpoints (In Spanish with English Abstract)*
Barandiaran J., Laresgoiti I., Perez J., Corera J., Echavarri J.
In: AEPIA 91 Conference, 1991, Madrid, Spain

TR 22 - *Modeling of Agent Scheduling and Distribution*
Afsarmenesh H., Tuijman F., van Albada G.D., Hertzberger L.O., 1991

TR 23 - *ISA: An Architecture to support Sharing and Exchange of Information among Archon Agents*
Afsarmanesh H., Tuijnman F.
In Preparation

TR 24 - *The Impact of Heterogeneity on Cooperating Agents*
Roda C., Jennings N.R., Mamdani E.H.
In: AAAI Workshop on Cooperation among Heterogeneous Intelligent Systems, 1991, Anaheim, Los Angeles, USA

TR 25 - *Cooperation in Industrial Systems*
Jennings N.R.
In: Proceedings of the ESPRIT Conference 1991, p253

TR 26 - *Distributed Cooperative Architecture for Accelerator Operation*
Fuchs J., Skarek P., Varga L.Z., Wildner-Malandain E.
In: 2nd International Workshop on Software Engineering, Artificial Intelligence and Expert Systems for High Energy and Nuclear Physics, 13.-18.1.1992, L'Agelonde

KIP™ is a registered Trademark by the ARCHON partners.